BEST FRIENDS, SECRET LOVERS

JESSICA LEMMON

THE SECRET TWIN

CATHERINE MANN

MILLS & BOON

First Published in Great Britain 2019
by Mills & Boon, an imprint of HarperCollinsPublishers,
1 London Bridge Street, London, SE1 9GF

Best Friends, Secret Lovers © 2019 Jessica Lemmon
The Secret Twin © 2019 Catherine Mann

ISBN: 978-0-263-27171-3

0219

MIX
Paper from
responsible sources
FSC® C007454

This book is produced from independently certified FSC™ paper to ensure responsible forest management.

For more information visit: www.harpercollins.co.uk/green

Printed and bound in Spain
by CPI, Barcelona

BEST FRIENDS, SECRET LOVERS

JESSICA LEMMON

For Jules. I'm so blessed to call you a friend.

Prologue

"Twenty minutes *minimum*, or else she'll tell everyone you're horrendous in bed."

"If you're down there for longer than seven minutes, you dumb Brit, you have no idea what you're doing."

"Spoken like a guy who has no idea what he's doing."

Flynn Parker leaned back in his chair, his broken leg propped on the ottoman, and listened to his two friends argue about sex. Pleasing women in particular.

"If either of you knew what you were doing, you wouldn't be single," he informed his buddies.

Gage Fleming and Reid Singleton blinked over at Flynn as if they'd forgotten he was sitting there. Drunk as they were, they might have. Gage grabbed the nearly empty whiskey bottle resting on Flynn's footstool and splashed another inch into Reid's glass and his own.

But not Flynn's. Thanks to the pain medication he was on, the only buzz he would be enjoying was courtesy of Percocet.

"You're one to talk," Reid said, his British accent

slurred from the drink. "Your ring finger is currently un-inhabited."

"The reason for this trip." Gage clanked his glass with Reid's, then with Flynn's water bottle.

Flynn would drink to that. His recent split from Veronica was what drove them all up here, to the mountains in Colorado to go skiing. The last time they were in Flynn's father's cabin had been their sophomore year in college. The damn place must be a time machine because they'd devolved into kids just by being here.

Gage and Reid had been nonstop swapping stories, bragging about their alleged prowess, and Flynn had been foolish enough to try the challenging slope…again. His lack of practice led to his taking a snowy tumble down the hill. Just like the last time, he'd ended up in the hospital. *Unlike* the last time, he'd broken a bone.

Skiing wasn't his forte.

So. Veronica.

The ex-wife who had recently ruined his life and his outlook. His buddies had come here under the guise of pulling him out of his funk, but he knew they were mostly here because they hadn't left each other's sides since they were in college. Sure, Reid had fled back home to London for a short time, but he'd come back. They'd all known he would.

Before he boarded the plane for this vacation, Flynn had learned two things: One, that his father's diagnosis of "pneumonia" was terminal cancer and Emmons Parker would likely die soon, making fifty-three the age to beat for Flynn; and two, that when he returned home he'd be sitting in his father's office with the title of president behind his name.

Running Monarch was all Flynn had ever wanted.

Was.

Despite years of showing an interest and trying to please

his father, Emmons Parker had shooed Flynn away rather than pulled him in. Now the empire was on Flynn's shoulders, and his alone.

Reid howled with laughter at something Gage said and Flynn blinked his friends into focus. No, he wasn't alone. He had Reid, and Gage, and the best friend who'd been a part of his life longer than those two, Sabrina Douglas. His best friends worked at Monarch with him, and with them in his corner, Flynn knew he could get through this.

The senior employees were going to freak out when they found out Flynn was going to be president. He'd been accused of "coasting" before and would be in charge of all of their well-beings, which Flynn took as seriously as his next line of thought—the pact he'd been ruminating about since before his leg snapped in two on that slope.

"Remember that pact we made in college? The one where we swore never to get married."

Reid let out a hearty "Ha!" UK-born Reid Singleton was planning on staying as unattached as his last name implied. "Right here in this room, I believe."

Gage pursed his lips, his brows closing in the slightest bit over his nose. "We were hammered on Jägerbombs that night. God knows what else we said."

"I didn't adhere to it. I should have." Flynn had been swept up by love and life. He hadn't taken that pact seriously. A mistake.

Gage frowned. "It's understandable why you'd say that now. You've been through the wringer. Back then no one expected to find permanence."

"None of us *wanted* to," Reid corrected.

Flynn pointed at Gage with his water bottle. "You and this new girl have been dating, what, a month?"

"Something like that."

"Get out now." Reid offered a hearty belch. He lifted his eyebrows and downed his portion of whiskey, cheeks filling

before he swallowed it down. "You and I, Gage, we stuck
to the pact." He smiled, then added, "If you were Flynn,
you'd have married her by now."

Reid wasn't exaggerating. Flynn and Veronica had been
married on their thirty-day dating anniversary. Insanity.
That they'd lasted three years was more a testament to Flynn's stubbornness than their meant-to-be-ness.

The final straw had been Veronica screwing his brother.
Whatever, he thought, as the sting of betrayal shocked
his system afresh. He'd never liked Julian much anyway.

"He's doing the thing," Reid muttered *not* quietly, given
his state of inebriation. His gaze met Flynn's, but he spoke
to Gage. "Where he's thinking of her."

"I can hear you, *wanker*." Flynn lost his marriage, not
his hearing. Though "lost" would imply he'd misplaced it.
It hadn't been misplaced, it'd been disassembled. Piece by
piece until the felling blow was Veronica's head turning
for none other than his older, more artsy brother. She was
the free spirit, and Flynn was the numbers guy. The boring guy. The emotionally constipated guy.

Her words.

"Hey." Gage snapped his fingers. "Knock it off, Flynn.
We're here to celebrate your divorce, not have you traipse
down depression trail."

But Flynn wasn't budging on this. He'd given it a lot of
thought since he'd tumbled down that hill. It was like life
had to literally knock him on his ass to get him to wake up.

"I'm reinstating the pact," Flynn said, his tone grave.
Even Reid stopped smiling. "No marriage. Not ever. It's
not worth the heartache, or the broken leg, or hanging out
with the two worst comrades in this solar system."

At that Reid looked wounded, Gage affronted.

"Piss off, Parker."

"Yeah," Gage agreed. "What Reid said."

With effort, Flynn sat up, carefully moving every other limb save his broken leg so he could lean forward. "I don't want either of you to go through this. Not ever."

"You're serious," Gage said after a prolonged silence.

Flynn remained silent.

Gage watched him a moment, a flash of sobriety in the depths of his brown eyes. "Okay. What'd we say?"

"We promised never to get married," Reid said. "And then we swore on our tallywackers."

Gage chuckled at Reid's choice of phrasing.

"Which means yours should have fallen off by now." Reid's face contorted as he studied Flynn. "It didn't, did it?"

"No." Flynn gave him an impatient look. "It didn't."

Reid swiped his hand over his brow in mock relief.

"Come on, Parker, you're high on drugs," Gage said with a head shake. "We made that pact because your mom was sick and your dad was miserable, and because Natalie had just dumped me. We were all heartbroken then." He considered Reid. "Except for Reid. I'm not sure why he did it."

"Never getting married anyway." Reid shrugged. "All for one."

"So? Swear again," Flynn repeated. "On your *tallywackers*." That earned a smile from Reid. "Big or small, they count."

The first time they'd made the pact none of them truly knew heartache. Breakups were hard, but the decimation of a marriage following the ultimate betrayal? Much worse. Reid and Gage didn't know how bad things could get and Flynn would like to keep it that way. He didn't want either of them to feel as eviscerated as he did right now—as he had for the last three months. All pain he could have avoided if he'd taken that pact seriously.

His buddies might never find themselves dating women who slept with their family members, but it wouldn't matter how the divorce happened, only that it did. He'd heard the statistics. That 50 percent of marriages ending in divorce was up to around 75 nowadays.

He'd heard some people say they didn't harbor regret because if they'd never married, and divorced, they wouldn't have learned life's lessons. Blah, blah, blah.

Bullshit.

Flynn regretted saying "I do" to Veronica all the way down to his churning stomach. The heartbreak over her choosing his brother would have been more bearable if she'd told him up front rather than three years into an insufferable marriage.

"I swear," Reid said, almost too serious as he crashed his glass into Flynn's water bottle, then looked at Gage expectantly.

"Fine. This is stupid, but fine." Gage lifted his glass.

"Say it," Flynn said, not cracking the slightest smile. "Or it doesn't count."

"I promise," Gage said. "I won't get married."

"Say *never*, and we all drink," Flynn said.

"Wait." Reid held up a finger. "What if one of us caves again? Like hearts-and-flowers Gage over here."

"Shut up, Reid."

"One of your monthlong girlfriends could turn into the real thing if you're not careful."

"I'm careful," Gage growled.

"You'd better be." Flynn stared down his friends. The enormity of the situation settled around them, the only sound in the room the fire crackling in the background. "The lie of forever isn't worth it in the end."

Reid eyed Flynn's broken leg, a reminder of what Flynn's stupidity had cost him, and then exchanged glances with Gage. These men were more like Flynn's brothers than his own flesh and blood. They'd do anything for him—including vowing to remain single forever.

"Never," Gage agreed, holding up his own glass.

Reid and Flynn nodded in unison, and then they drank on it.

One

Flynn Parker, his stomach in a double knot, attempted to do the same to his tie. His hands were shaking from too much coffee and not enough sleep. It wasn't helping that the tiny room in the back of the funeral home was nearing eighty degrees.

Sweat beaded on his forehead and slicked his palms. He closed his eyes, shutting out his haggard reflection, and blew out a long, slow breath.

The service for his father was over, and when Flynn had left the sweltering room, the first thing he'd done was yank at his tie. Bad move. He'd never return it to its previous state.

God help him, he didn't know if he could watch his father being lowered into the dirt. They'd had their differences—about a million of them at last count. Death was final, but burial even more so.

"There you are." Sabrina Douglas, his best friend since college, stepped into view in the tall mirror at the back of the funeral home. "Need help?"

"Why is it so hot in here?" he barked rather than answer her.

She clucked her tongue at his overreaction. Much like this moment, she'd come in and out of focus over the years, but she'd always been a constant in his life. She'd been at his side at work, diligently ushering in the new age as he acclimated as president of the management consulting firm he now owned. She'd been with him for every personal moment from his and Veronica's wedding to his thirtieth birthday—*their* thirtieth birthday, he mentally corrected. Sabrina was born four minutes ahead of him on the same damn day. She'd jokingly called them "twins" when they first met in psych class at the University of Washington, but that nickname quickly fizzled when they realized they were nothing alike.

Nothing alike, but unable to shake each other.

Her brow crinkled over a black-framed pair of glasses as she reached for the length of silk around his neck and attempted to retie it.

"I do it every morning," he muttered, Sabrina's sweet floral perfume tickling his nose. She always smelled good, but he hadn't noticed in a while.

A long while.

His frown deepened. They hadn't been as close in the years he was married to Veronica. His hanging out with Reid and Gage hadn't changed, but it was as if Veronica and Sabrina had an unspoken agreement that Sabrina wasn't welcome into the inner circle. As a result, Flynn mostly saw her at work rather than outside it. The thought bothered him.

"I don't know what's wrong with me." He was speaking of his own reverie as much as his lack of ability to tie his necktie.

"Flynn…"

He put his hands on hers to stop whatever apology-slash-life-lesson he suspected was percolating. As gently as he could muster, he said, "Don't."

Sabrina leveled him with a wide-eyed hazel stare. Her eyes were beautiful. Piercing green-gold, and behind her glasses they appeared twice as large. She'd been with him through the divorce from Veronica, through his father's illness and subsequent death. The last couple of months for Flynn had started to resemble the life of Job from the Bible. He hadn't contracted a case of boils as the Monarch offices collapsed in on themselves, *yet*. He wasn't going to tempt fate by stating he was out of the woods.

Emmons Parker knew what his sons had been through, so when he'd had his lawyer schedule the meetings to read the will, he'd made sure they happened on separate days.

Flynn on a Sunday. Julian on a Monday.

Unfortunately, Flynn knew Veronica had gone to the reading with Julian, even though he'd rather not know a thing about either of them. Goddamn Facebook.

Julian inherited their father's beloved antique car collection and the regal Colonial with the cherry tree in the front yard where they'd grown up. Flynn inherited the cabin in Colorado as well as the business and his father's penthouse apartment downtown. Julian was "starting a family," or so the lawyer had read from the will, so that was why Emmons had bequeathed their mother's beloved home with the evenly spaced shutters to his oldest, and least trustworthy, son.

The son who was starting a family with Flynn's former wife.

Today Flynn had accepted hugs and handshakes from family and friends but had successfully avoided Julian and Veronica. His ex-wife kept a close eye on Flynn, but he refused to approach her. Her guilt was too little and way too late.

"I don't know what to do." Sabrina spoke around what

sounded like a lump clogging her throat. She was hurting for him. The way she'd hurt for him when Veronica left him. Her pink lips pressed together and her chin shook. "Sorry."

Abandoning the tie, she swiped the hollows of her eyes under her glasses, careful of the eye makeup that had been applied boldly yet carefully as per her style.

He didn't hesitate to pull her close, shushing her as she sniffed. The warmth of that embrace—of holding on to someone who cared for him so deeply and knew him so well—was enough to make a lump form in his own throat. She held on to him like she might shatter, and so he concentrated on rubbing her back and telling her the truth. "You're doing exactly what you need to do, Sabrina. Just your being here is enough."

She let go of him and snagged a tissue from a nearby box. She lifted her glasses and dabbed her eyes, leaning in and checking her reflection. "I'm not helping."

"You're helping." She was gloriously sensitive. Attuned. Empathetic. Some days he hated that for her—it made her more at risk of being hurt. He watched her reflection, wondering if she saw herself as he did. A tall, strong, beautiful woman, her sleek brown hair framing smooth skin and glasses that made her appear approachable and smart at the same time. She wore a black dress and stockings, her heeled shoes tall enough that when she'd held him a moment ago she didn't have to stretch onto her toes to wrap her arms around his neck.

"Okay. I'm okay. I'm sorry." She nodded, the tissue wadded in one hand. Evidently this okay/sorry combo marked the end of her cry and the beginning of her being his support system. "If there's anything you need—"

"Let's skip it," he blurted. The moment the words were out of his mouth, he knew it was the right thing to do.

"Skip...the rest of the funeral?" Her face pinched with indecision.

"Why not?" He'd seen everyone. He'd listened as the priest spoke of Emmons as if he was a saint. Frankly, Flynn had heard enough false praise for his old man to last a lifetime.

Her mouth opened, probably to argue, but he didn't let her continue.

"I can do it. I just don't want to." He shook his head as he tried to think of another cohesive sentence to add to the protest, but none came. So he added, "At all," and hoped that it punctuated his point.

She jerked her head into a nod. "Okay. Let's skip it."

Relief was like a third person in the room.

"Chaz's?" she offered. "I'm *dying* for fish and chips." Her eyes rounded as her hand covered her mouth. "Oh. That was...really inappropriate phrasing for a funeral."

He had to smile. Recently he'd noticed how absent from his life she'd been. It'd be good to go out with her to somewhere that wasn't work. "Let's get outta here."

"Are you kidding me?" His brother, Julian, appeared in the doorway, his lip curled in disgust. "You're walking out on our father's funeral?"

Like he had any room to call Flynn's ethics into question.

Veronica's blonde head peeked around Julian's shoulder. Her gaze flitted to Flynn and then Sabrina, and Flynn's limbs went corpse-cold.

"Honey," she whispered to Julian. "Let's not do this here."

Honey. God, what a mess.

Sabrina took a step closer to Flynn in support. His best friend at his side. He didn't need her to defend him, but he appreciated the gesture more than she knew.

Julian shrugged off Veronica's hand from his suit jacket and glared at his brother. It was one of Dad's suits—too wide in the shoulders. A little short in the torso.

Julian didn't own a suit. He painted for a living and his

creativity was why Veronica said he'd won her heart. Evidently, she found Flynn incapable of being "spontaneous," or "thoughtful," or "monogamous."

No, wait. That last one was *her*.

"You're not going to stand over your own father's grave?" Julian spat. Veronica murmured another "honey," but he ignored it.

"You've made it clear that it's none of my business what you do or don't do." Flynn tore his gaze from Julian to spear Veronica with a glare. "Both of you. Same goes for me."

Her blue eyes rounded. He used to think she was gorgeous—with her full, blond hair and designer clothes. The way her nails were always done and her makeup perfectly painted on. Now he'd seen what was under the mask.

Selfishness. Betrayal. Lies.

So many lies.

"Don't judge me, Flynn," she snapped.

"You used to be more attractive." The sound of his own voice startled him. He hadn't meant to say that out loud.

"Son of a bitch!" Julian lunged, came at him with a sloppy swing that Flynn easily dodged. He'd learned how to fistfight from Gage and Reid, and Julian only dragged a paint-filled brush down a canvas.

Flynn ducked to avoid a left, weaved when Julian attempted a right, cracked his fist into his older brother's nose. Julian staggered, lost his balance and fell onto his ass on the ground. Sabrina gasped, and Veronica shrieked. Julian puffed out a curse word as blood streamed from his nose.

"Honey. *Honey.* Talk to me." Veronica was on her knees over Julian's groaning form and Flynn didn't know what sickened him more. That his ex-wife cared about his brother's well-being more than the man she'd vowed to love forever, or that Flynn had lost his temper with Julian and hit him.

Both made his stomach toss.

"Are you okay?" Sabrina came into focus, her eyebrows tenderly bowed as she watched him with concern. He hated her seeing him like this—broken, weak—like he'd felt for the last several months.

"I'm *perfect.*" He took her hand and led her from the small room and they encountered Reid and Gage advancing at a fast walk down the hallway.

"We heard a scream." Reid's sharply angled jaw was set, his fists balled at his sides. Gage looked similar, minus the fists. His mouth wore a scowl, his gaze sweeping the area around them for looming danger.

"You okay?" Gage asked Sabrina.

"I didn't scream. That was Veronica."

"We're fine," Flynn said before amending, "Julian's nose is broken."

"Broken?" A fraction of a second passed before Reid's face split into an impressed smile. He clapped Flynn on the shoulder.

"Do *not* encourage him," Sabrina warned.

"So what now?" Gage asked at the same time more of Julian's groaning and Veronica's soothing echoed from the adjacent room.

"We're skipping the rest of the funeral," Flynn announced. "Who wants to go to Chaz's for fish and chips?"

"I do," Reid said, his British accent thickening. The man loved his fish and chips.

Gage, ever the cautious, practical friend, watched Flynn carefully. "You're sure this is what you want to do?"

Flynn thought of his father, angry, yelling. His gutting words about how if he wanted to become as great a man as his father, Flynn would have to first grow a pair. He thought of Emmons's bitter solitude after Mom had succumbed to cancer fifteen years ago. Emmons had suffered that same fate, only unlike Mom, he'd never woken up to what was really important. He'd taken his bitterness with him to the grave. Maybe that's why Flynn couldn't bear seeing his old man lowered into it.

Sabrina wrapped her hand around Flynn's and squeezed his fingers. "Whatever you need. We're here."

Reid and Gage nodded, concurring.

"I'm sure."

That was all it took.

They skirted the crowd patiently waiting for him to take his place as pallbearer. Moved past nameless relatives who had crawled out of the woodwork, and past one of Veronica's friends who asked him if he knew where she or Julian were.

"They're inside," he told her.

Never slowing his walk or letting go of Sabrina's hand, he opened the passenger side door for her while Gage and Reid climbed into the back. Then Flynn reversed out of the church's parking lot and drove straight to Chaz's.

Two

Six months later

At Monarch Consulting, Flynn brewed himself an espresso from the high-end machine, yet another perk—pun intended—of being in charge.

The break room had been his father's private retreat when he was alive and well, and he'd rarely shared the room. Not the case for Flynn. He'd opened up the executive break room to his closest friends, who shared the top floor his father had formerly hogged for himself.

Flynn didn't care who thought he was playing favorites. When he'd returned home from vacation and become president, he'd outfitted the upper floor with three new offices and placed his friends at his sides. They were a good visual reminder that Flynn wasn't running Monarch in a vacuum—or worse, a void.

It was his company now. He could do what he wanted. God knew Emmons had been doing it his way for years.

Monarch Consulting was a management consulting firm,

which was a fancy way of saying they helped other businesses improve their performance and grow. Monarch was dedicated to helping companies find new and better ways of doing things—an irony since Emmons had done things the same way for decades.

Gage Fleming's official title at Monarch was senior sales executive. He was in charge of the entire sales department, which was a perfect fit for his charm and likability. Reid was the IT guy, though they fancied up his nameplate to read Digital Marketing Analyst. Sabrina, with her fun-loving attitude and knack for being a social lubricant, was promoted to brand manager, where she oversaw social media factions as well as design work and rebranding.

Flynn stirred a packet of organic cane sugar into his espresso and thought about his best friends' support of his climb to the very top. They were the glue that kept him together.

"What's up, brother?" announced one of those best friends now. Flynn turned to find Gage strolling into the room. Gage wasn't his biological brother, but was worthy of the title nonetheless.

Oh, that I could choose.

Gage's hair had grown some since Flynn's father's funeral. Now that it was longer, the ends were curling and added a boyish charm to the *mountain* of charm Gage already possessed. Flynn didn't know anyone Gage didn't get along with, and vice versa. It made him an asset at work, and he provided a softer edge for Flynn whenever he needed it—which, lately, was often.

"Surprised you're still upright after the long weekend." Gage slapped Flynn's back.

The long weekend was to celebrate the finalization of Flynn and Veronica's divorce. It couldn't have come soon enough, but Flynn hadn't felt like celebrating. His divorce marked an epic failure that piled onto the other failures he'd been intimately acquainted with lately. In no way would Gage and Reid have let the momentous occasion pass by without acknowledgment.

Acknowledgment in this case meant going out and getting well and truly "pissed," as Reid had put it. And honestly, Flynn had had fun letting go and living in the moment, at least for a weekend.

"I always land on my feet," Flynn grumbled, still tired and, yeah, probably a little hungover from last night. He should've stopped drinking before midnight.

"Good morning, Fleming." Reid sauntered in next. "Morning, Parker." Reid had refused to leave his accent in London. He kept it fine-tuned for one essential reason: women loved it.

Where Flynn was mostly an insensitive, shortsighted, hard-to-love suit, Gage was friendly and well liked, and Reid...well, his other friend was a split between the two of them. Reid had charm in spades but also had a rough edge from a past he'd always been tight-lipped about.

Flynn figured he'd tell them when he was ready. At this rate probably when one of them was on his deathbed.

"Well, well, well, what have we here? Three of Seattle's saddest rich boys."

Sabrina strolled in with her signature walk, somehow expressing both childlike wonder and sophisticated capability. Her slim-fitting skirt, blouse and high-heeled shoes proved she was 100 percent woman. Sabrina had a fun-loving attitude but liked everything in its place. She was the only one who'd balked at the promotion that Flynn had had to talk her into. She put others ahead of herself often, which was so converse to who Veronica was it wasn't even funny.

Sabrina saw the world as a sunshiny bouquet of happiness even though Flynn had cold hard proof that it was a cesspool.

"Whoa." Sab's whiskey-smooth voice dipped as she took in Flynn. "You look like last night handed you your own backside." Her eyebrows met the frame of her glasses as she studied Gage and Reid. "You guys don't look that great either. Were you… Oh my gosh. It's final, isn't it? It's done?"

"He's single with a capital *S*," Reid confirmed.

Her smile was short-lived as she approached Flynn. "Are you okay?"

"I'm fine."

"Are you sure?"

That question right there was why he hadn't told her about the finalization of the divorce. He wanted to drink away his feelings on the topic, not discuss them.

Flynn sent a glance over her head to Reid and Gage.

Little help, guys?

"You wouldn't have wanted to accompany us even if we invited you," Gage said.

"What's that supposed to mean?" Her frown returned, but she aimed it at affable Gage, which was fun to watch. He finished stirring his own coffee and sent her a grim head shake.

"Darling." Reid looped an arm around her shoulders. "Don't make us say it."

"Ugh. Did you all pick up girls?" She asked everyone but her eyes tracked to Flynn and stayed there. "And why wasn't I invited? I'm an excellent wingwoman."

Flynn felt a zip of discomfort at the idea of Sabrina fixing him up with a woman—or being there while he trotted out his A game to impress one. He'd suffered a few crash-and-burns last night and was glad she wasn't there to witness them.

Sabrina pursed her lips in consideration. "Did the evening have anything to do with you three reaffirming your dumb pact?"

"It's not dumb," Flynn was the first to say. Family and marriage and happily ever after were ideas that he used to hold sacred. He'd seen the flip side of that coin. Broken promises and regret.

Divorce had changed him.

"You're single with us, love. Did you want in on the pact?" Reid smiled as he refilled his paper Starbucks cup.

"No, I do not. And I'm single by choice. You're single—" she poked Reid in the chest "—because you're a lemming."

"I'm to believe you're single by choice," Reid stated flatly. She wisely ignored the barb.

"A pact to not fall in love is juvenile and shortsighted."

"We can fall in love," Gage argued. "We agreed not to marry."

"Pathetic." She rolled her eyes and Flynn lost his patience.

"Sabrina." He dipped his voice to its most authoritative tone. "It's not a joke."

She craned her chin to take in all six feet of him and gave him a withering glare that would've shrunk a lesser man's balls.

"I *know* it's not a joke. But it's still pathetic."

She turned for the coffeemaker and Reid chuckled. "You have no effect on her, mate."

"Yeah, well, vice versa," Flynn said, but felt the untruth hiding behind his statement. Sabrina had enough of an effect on him that he treated her differently than he did Reid and Gage. As present as she was in his life, it'd always been impossible to slot her in as one of the "guys." And in a weird way he'd protected her when he'd excluded her from last night's shenanigans as well as the skiing weekend. Flynn was jaded to the nth degree. Sabrina wasn't. He needed her to stay positive and sunshiny. He needed her to be okay. For her own sake, sure, but also for his.

"Heartbreak isn't a myth," Reid called out to her as she walked for the door. "You'll see that someday."

"Morons." She strolled out but did so with a twitch in her walk and a smile on her face. Immune to all of them, evidently.

Three

Sabrina had lectured Flynn as much as she dared. She'd pushed him to the point of real anger—not the showy all-bark/no-bite thing he'd just done in "the Suit Café" as she liked to call their private break room, but real, shaking, red-faced anger. Which was why she recognized the sound of that booming timbre when she passed by a closed conference room door later the same afternoon.

Definitely, that was Flynn shouting a few choice words, and definitely, that was the voice of Mac Langley, a senior executive who had been hired on at the beginning by Emmons Parker himself.

She bristled as more swearing pierced the air. She'd seen a glimpse of the old Flynn when the four of them had fled the funeral to go to Chaz's for fish and chips and ice-cold beers. In that moment she'd realized how much she missed hanging out with him, and how his marriage to Veronica had been the beginning of her new, more distant BFF. In college Sabrina used to bake him cookies, do his laundry, make sure he was eating while studying.

She felt that instinct to take care of him anew. Maybe because Veronica was so classless, having tossed aside what she and Flynn had, or simply because Sabrina wanted Flynn to be happy again and their college years were when she remembered his being happiest.

Flynn loudly insulted Mac again and Sabrina winced. There'd be no putting that horse back into the barn. No man could call another man that and not pay the price. It'd take time to smooth over, and some distance. And with a man like Mac, the distance would have to be Tokyo to London.

The heavy wooden door did little to mute the noise, and as a result a few employees had gathered outside it—staring in slack-jawed bewilderment.

When the shouts ceased, a charge of electricity lingered like the stench from a burnt grilled cheese sandwich—like the tension couldn't be contained by the room and had crept out under the door.

She pasted a smile on her face and turned toward the gathering crowd—two gawping interns and Gage.

"Yikes." Gage smirked, sipped his coffee and eyed the interns. "Unless you want to be on the receiving end of more of that," he leaned in to say, "you might want to clear the corridor before they come out."

He kept his tone light and playful, adding a wink for the benefit of the two younger girls, and when he smiled they tittered and scooted off, their tones hushed.

"Do you have to charm everyone you come in contact with?"

"I wasn't charming them. I was being myself." He grinned. Gage was both boyish and likable. The thing was he wasn't lying. He *hadn't* been trying to charm them. Flirting came as naturally to him as breathing. Still, she doubted the wink-and-smile routine would silence the girls permanently. They would tell a friend or two or be overheard dishing in the employee lounge and then the entire company would know about Flynn's outburst. Damage control would take a miracle.

She didn't want anyone to think poorly of him, even though he'd been an ogre since he'd taken over the company. But couldn't they see he was hurting? He needed support, not criticism.

Gage came to stand next to her where he, too, watched the door. "Who's in there with him?"

"Mac. And, judging by the voices, a few other executives. I don't hear Reid."

He shook his head. "I passed by him in his office before doing a lap to check on the sales team."

A meeting where none of them had been included. Hmm. She wondered who had called it.

"Did something happen this weekend?" she asked as they faced the door. Maybe the bar night where many drinks were consumed prompted Flynn to admit his feelings...though, she doubted it.

"Drinks. More drinks. Reaffirmation that the pact was the right thing to do." Gage shrugged.

"Seriously how can you continue with that cockamamie idea?"

"You know no one says *cockamamie* any more, right?"

"Veronica is a hot mess, but you can't celebrate the end of her and Flynn's marriage like a...a..."

"Bachelor party?"

"Yes." She pointed at him in confirmation. "Like a bachelor party. Especially when you are celebrating being bachelors forever and ever, amen."

"Sabrina. If you want in on the pact, just yell."

"Pass." She rolled her eyes. Why did everyone keep offering her an "in" like she wanted to be a part of that? "I've never been married, but I've watched friends go through it. Divorce is devastating. And after losing his father, it'll be like another death he'll have to grieve. A weekend of shots isn't going to remedy it."

Over the last six months, she'd watched Flynn deal with his father's death. The grief had hovered in the anger stage for a while, before he'd seemed to lighten up. The day they did a champagne toast to their new offices, Flynn was all smiles. He stated how Monarch was going through a rebirth. There was a sincere speech during which Flynn thanked them for sticking with him, which simultaneously broke her heart and mended it at the same time. Now the optimistic Flynn was nowhere to be found. He'd looped around to the anger stage again and was stuck in the rut worn of his own making.

"He's busy." Gage palmed her shoulder supportively. "Running this place is stressful and he doesn't have the respect he deserves. Don't worry about his emotional state, Sab. He's doing what needs to be done. That's all."

But that wasn't "all" no matter how much denial Reid and Gage were in. She *knew* Flynn. Knew his moods and knew his values. Sure, they'd suffered a bit of distance since his marriage to Veronica, but Sabrina had still seen him day in and out at work. She'd shared countless meetings and lunches with him.

He used to be lighthearted and open and gentle. He used to be happy. Who he was now wasn't in the same stratosphere as happy. Though if she thought about it for longer than three seconds, she might admit that he hadn't been truly happy in years. Veronica, even when she hadn't been cheating on Flynn with his brother, wasn't an easygoing person. She had a way of sucking the oxygen from the room. As much as Flynn had scrambled to appease her, it was rare that she was contented.

Sabrina shook her head, as sickened now as she was then. Flynn deserved better.

"It's more than that," she told Gage.

"He's fine. Probably needs to get laid."

Sabrina recoiled, but not at Gage's choice of phrasing. Gage and Reid, along with Flynn, had been close friends since college. She was comfortable around them in and outside of work. No, what had her feeling *uncomfortable* was the idea of Flynn sleeping with someone else. She'd grown accustomed to his belonging to Veronica, but the thought of him with someone else...

"Gross."

He shrugged and then turned in the direction of the elevator.

What a pile of crap-male logic.

Flynn needed time and space to acclimate—time to *heal*—and the last thing he needed was to spend time with a nameless, faceless woman.

He'd spent years with a woman who had both a face and a name. Sabrina felt possessive of him at first, but quickly determined that wasn't fair. She'd never had a claim on him. As his best friend, sure, and that meant she supported him no matter what—that hadn't changed. She'd tell him exactly what she thought if he started entertaining the idea of taking home a random...*floozy* in the hopes of improving his mood.

As she was contemplating whether anyone still used the word *floozy*, the door opened. A swarm of suits filed out of the room. Most of them were the senior members of the staff, the men and women who had helped build Monarch back when Emmons had started the company with nothing more than a legal pad and a number two pencil. It was admirable that Emmons Parker had built a consulting business from scratch, and even more so that it'd become the top management consulting firm for not only Seattle but also for a great deal of the Pacific Northwest.

He'd demanded excellence from all of them, in particular Flynn, who had been strong-armed into the executive level within the firm. When Flynn graduated college, he'd landed Gage and Sabrina internships. Reid started a few years later, after an unsuccessful trip back home to London resulted in his admitting that he preferred living in America. Sabrina wasn't surprised. Reid was much more suited to Seattle than London. And the weather was similar.

She stepped out of the way of Mac, who was marching past her, propelled by the steam coming out of his ears. He wore an unstylish brown suit and his jowls hung over the tightly buttoned collar at his neck. His tie was tight and short, his arms ramrod stiff at his sides, and his hands were balled into ham-sized fists.

The rest of the executives who ran various departments of Monarch paraded out next, but no one appeared as incensed as Mac.

She offered a paper-thin smile at Belinda, Monarch's legal counsel. Belinda was smart and tough, but also a human being who cared, which made her one of Sabrina's favorite people.

"What's going on?" Sabrina whispered, following Belinda's lead away from the pack.

Belinda stopped and watched the rest of the crew wander off in various directions of the office before leveling with Sabrina in her honest, curt way. "You need to get Flynn out of here, Sabrina, or they're going to revolt."

"Oh-kay. I can…take him to lunch or something."

"Not for an hour. For a few weeks. A month. Long enough for him to remember what is important or they're going to abandon ship. Son of Emmons Parker or not, he doesn't have their support."

"I've never had their support," Flynn boomed from behind Belinda. To her credit, she didn't wilt or jerk in surprise. She simply turned and shook her head.

"You heard my suggestion," she told him with a pointed glance before leaving Flynn and Sabrina alone.

"What happened in there? You guys brought down the house."

"What *happened* is that they're blaming me for stock prices taking a dive. Like it's my fault Emmons died and made our investors twitchy."

He dragged a hand over his short, stylish brown hair and closed his eyes. Long lashes shadowed chiseled cheeks and a firm, angled jaw. If there was only one attribute Flynn had inherited from his father it was his staggering good looks. Emmons, even for an older guy, had been handsome...until he opened his mouth. Flynn wielded those strong Parker genes like a champ, wearing jeans and Ts or suits and ties and looking at home in either. He wore the latter now, a dark suit and smart pale blue shirt with a deeper blue tie. A line marred his brow—that was a more recent feature. He'd had it since he'd taken over Monarch and inherited the problems that came with it.

"They have to know that the company was declining as soon as the *Seattle Times* ran the article that announced your father was ailing," she told him. "That has nothing to do with you."

"They don't care, Sab." He turned on his heel and marched to the elevator. She followed since her office was on the same floor as his. He held the door for her when he saw her coming and she stepped in next to him as the elevator traveled up the three floors she had intended to walk so she could count them on her fitness tracker.

"Belinda said—"

"Mac is a horse's ass. He's been pissed off since I pulled my friends into the inner sanctum instead of him, and this quarter's numbers are the perfect excuse to summon the townsfolk to bring their pitchforks. Belinda wants me to run from him like a scared rabbit." He glowered at Sabrina. "Do I look like a rabbit to you?"

"No. You don't." She gripped his arm in an attempt to

connect with him, to break through the wall of anger he was behind. His features softened as his mouth went flat and a strange sort of awareness crackled in the air between them. An electric current ran the length of her arm and skimmed her form like a caress. Even her toes tingled inside her Christian Louboutin pumps.

She yanked her hand away, alarmed at the reaction. This was Flynn, *her best friend*. Whatever rogue reaction her body was having to him was…well, crazy.

She shook out her hand as if to clear the buzz of awareness from her body. "You'll have to tell me what's going on sooner or later."

He watched her carefully, his blue eyes revealing nothing. They were more gray today thanks to the color of his suit jacket. Handsome even when he was angry.

Veronica was an idiot.

A surge of anger replaced the tingles. Whenever she thought of his ex-wife's betrayal, Sabrina wanted to scream. He was too amazing a person to settle for someone who would discard him so carelessly.

"Flynn."

He sighed, which meant she'd won, and she had to fight not to smile. The elevator doors swept aside and he gestured for her to go ahead of him. "My office."

She led the way, walking into the glass-walled room and waiting for him to follow before she shut the door.

His assistant, Yasmine, was out sick today so Sabrina didn't bother shutting the blinds. The only other two people on this floor wouldn't heed a closed blind any more than she would. Like her, Gage and Reid had an all-access pass to everything Monarch and everything Flynn. Their loyalty to him ran as deeply and broadly as her own, which was why she pegged him with an honest question the moment he propped his hands on his waist and glared down at her.

"What is going on with you?"

Admittedly, her intervention was about six weeks too late. She'd assumed he'd bounce back any moment. A possibility that grew further and further away as the days passed.

"Meaning?"

Short of grabbing him by the shoulders and giving him a good shake, she didn't know how to reach him except to ask point-blank. "Meaning, what was the screaming about downstairs? What was it *really* about? I don't want some generic comment about how you and Mac don't see eye to eye."

"Nothing." His face pleated.

Deciding to wait him out, she straightened her back and folded her arms over her chest. She wasn't going to let him throw up a smokescreen and keep her out of this any longer.

"No one here believes I can do this job," he said.

"They're wrong."

"They want my father back. They want a ruthless, impersonal asshole to sit in this office and deliver their bonuses." Flynn sat down in his chair and spread his arms. "I'm filling the ruthless, impersonal asshole part of the request and they're not appeased. They're like…like an active volcano that needs a virgin sacrifice."

She lifted an eyebrow at the metaphor.

"Know anyone?" His lips twitched at his own joke.

She smiled and the tension in the room eased. "I'm sorry to say that my V-card was awarded to Bennie Todd our freshman year in college."

"Your first clue that was a mistake was that his name was *Bennie*."

"Yuck. We're not talking about him."

His eyes flickered playfully. The Flynn she knew and loved was still inside the corporate mannequin she was currently addressing. Thank God.

He'd always sworn he'd never turn into his father. And yet after his father's illness and subsequent death, after finding out Veronica had screwed him over, Flynn had de-volved into a close simulation of Emmons Parker.

His face drawn, he stood and gestured for her to take his chair. "Have a seat. I want to show you something."

She sat in his plush, ergonomic chair and he leaned over her, the musky smell of him familiar and not at the same time. He'd been this close to her a million times, but this was the first time she noticed her heart rate ratcheting up while he casually tapped in the password on his laptop. What was with her today? Had it really been that long since she had male attention?

Yes, she thought glumly.

"Read this." He opened an email addressed from Mac and backed away, taking his manly scent—and her bizarre reaction to it—with him.

"They're threatening to leave," he said.

She read the subject of the email aloud. "Tender of res-ignation?"

"Yes. From our CFO, director of human resources and vice president. They're going to start a new company and take most of our office with them. Or at least that's the threat. If I agree to Belinda's suggestion and take an ex-tended break, they'll stick around and give me a second chance."

"It's mutiny." She could hardly believe this many big-wigs at Monarch would agree to such an insane plan.

"To say the least. If we were to attempt to keep Monarch afloat after they left, I doubt we'd be able to stay open while we trained a new…everyone." He gestured his frustration with a sweep of his arm.

He was right. Hiring that many new executives would take months. Monarch would fold like a pizza box.

"I'm not backing down."

"What do they believe will change if you take an ex-tended break?"

"They think I'm burned out and need to take some time to *reflect*." He said it like it was a swear word.

"Well…"

How to agree and not side against Flynn? That was the question…

"Is reflecting so bad? You didn't take bereavement after your father passed."

His face hardened. Even twenty-three years younger than his late father, Flynn was a picture-perfect match for dear old Dad.

The execs were used to the way things were, and when Flynn implemented new things—*good* things that the company needed—the change hadn't gone over well. Flynn was the future of Monarch and had always been more forward thinking than his father.

"It's a bluff," he said.

She wasn't so sure. Mac was powerful. Both in position and in his ability to convince his colleagues to go along with his scheme.

"Would a monthlong sabbatical be that bad?" She turned in her chair and met his gaze, which burned through her. Eyes she'd looked into on many occasions, and never failed to make her feel stable and like she mattered.

"If I leave for a month, God knows what those dinosaurs would do to the place." Flynn would never voluntarily abandon ship—even if it was for a break he was in desperate need of taking.

"Reid's here. Gage is here. They wouldn't let Mac ruin your company." And neither would she… But she wouldn't be here once she convinced Flynn to take a hiatus. Belinda had plainly told Sabrina to "get him out of here" and Sabrina wouldn't leave him to his own devices. Without work distracting him, she knew he'd be unpacking some hefty emotional baggage.

She refused to let him go through that alone.

Four

"So? Advice?" Sabrina raised her eyebrows at her younger brother, who lifted his frosted beer mug and shrugged one shoulder.

Luke had thick, dark hair like hers but was blessed with their mother's electric-green eyes. The jerk. The best Sabrina could hope for in that department was "greenish."

"Leave him alone?" He smirked. Two years her junior, Luke's twenty-eight was balanced by an even-keeled sense of humor and a huge brain. He was gifted and had embarrassed her a million times in the past by challenging some poor, hapless soul to a math contest he'd always win.

"Kidding." Luke gave her hand a playful tap. "He's been through hell, I'll give him that."

"He has. And that pact is ridiculous."

"Eh, I can't fault him for that."

Of course he couldn't. Luke was male and therefore incapable of being reasonable. "You're saying that because of Dawn."

Luke's eyes darted to one side and his jaw went taut

at the mention of his ex's name. "You're one to talk, Sab. Name the last guy you've been over the moon for besides your precious Flynn."

"I'm not in love with Flynn, moron. You've been trotting out that argument for over a decade now. We're friends and it works, and stop changing the subject."

In spite of the fact she kept noticing Flynn's looks, his smell and his overall presence at work. That was just… That was just… Well, okay, she didn't know what it was. But it would pass. It had to.

Remarkably, Luke let the argument go. With a sigh, he settled his beer mug—now empty—on the table between them and signaled the bartender that he'd like another. He waited until it was delivered to say what he had to say.

"Dawn's getting married."

"What? You guys broke up like three minutes ago!"

He shrugged.

"I'm sorry."

"I'm just saying Flynn's idea isn't a bad one. After Dawn, I barely want to date. I don't think at this rate we'll ever give Mom the grandchildren she's been crowing about."

Their mother, Sarah, was infamous for bringing up significant others and babies and how many of her close friends were becoming grandparents. Luke wasn't the only one banging the "Sabrina loves Flynn" drum. Sab had argued with her mother on several occasions—some of them in front of Flynn. Then he was married and her mother's pushing, thankfully, came to a halt.

"Now that his divorce is final, Mom's going to start up again." Sabrina rolled her eyes. Just what she needed. Someone stoking the flames of Flynn Awareness that had flickered to life.

"Better armor up. Or get pregnant." The comment earned her brother a slug in the biceps that hurt her hand more than it hurt his rock-hard arms. She shook out her fingers.

"Yikes. Are you lifting again?"

"Yes." He rolled up a T-shirt sleeve and showed off his guns. She couldn't resist a squeeze.

"Unbelievable."

"Come to the gym with me. First session's free." For all his brainpower, Luke had opted to become a fitness trainer, blowing the idea of "dumb jock" out of the water. It was pretty simple math. Women found him irresistible and booked countless sessions with him. He made a great living giving them his full attention.

"No thanks. I'll stick to my yoga and meditation." Her cell phone buzzed and she dug it from the bottom of her purse.

A text from Flynn read: Busy?

She keyed in a reply of: No. What's up?

Need you.

She stared at those two words, a dozen thoughts pinging through her head as her heart pattered out an SOS. She reminded herself not to be weird and typed in a reply.

Where are you?

Then her phone vanished from her hand.

"Hey!" she squawked as Luke held it out of reach.

"I knew it." He smirked. "This is a booty call, Sab."

"It is not." She swiped at the phone but he kept it away from her. Until she grabbed his ear and yanked.

"Ow! Are you serious?" Her brother rubbed his ear, affronted. "We're not ten years old any longer."

"Could've fooled me." She glared at him before reading Flynn's one-word reply. Home.

Not his old home, but the new one. Julian had been awarded the family estate and Flynn had been given Emmons Parker's Seattle penthouse. Forty-five hundred square feet of steel beams and glass, charcoal-gray floors and dark cabinetry built by the finest designers.

She pecked in her response—that she'd be there in ten minutes—bottomed out her sparkling water and stood, blowing her brother a kiss. "Later, Einstein."

"Booty call," he replied.

"Shut up."

"Be safe!" he called behind her, his laughter chasing her out the door.

At Flynn's building, she pulled into the private parking area where she used the code he'd given her and tucked her compact into the spare space next to his car. Inside, she took the elevator to the penthouse, again using a passcode to zoom to the uppermost floor. The building felt far too serious for him.

Or for who Flynn used to be, anyway. He was pretty serious nowadays.

His seriousness had tripled when he and Veronica were married. Sabrina didn't want to be unfair, but credit was due where it was due. He'd been a committed husband and now that Sabrina didn't have to play nice any longer, she'd admit that Veronica had kept Flynn running in circles. His ex-wife had wanted to be pleased at every turn. With jewelry, more money and bigger, better everything. The house they'd lived in on Main and Eastwood was a friggin' mansion and *still* Veronica had whined about it.

With that unsavory thought simmering in her veins, she stepped from the elevator and into his foyer, announcing herself as she walked in. Expectedly, her voice bounced off the high beams and rang from the glass windows. She opened her mouth to sing a song from *The Sound of Music* when she spotted Flynn walking down the slatted stairs.

"Don't you dare," he warned.

"Spoilsport." She blew out a breath without belting out a single note and then relinquished her purse and coat to the dining room table. A white block with white chairs and in the center, oh, look, a white bowl with some weird porcelain white orbs in it. She palmed one and tested its weight. "Your decorator has no personality."

"I didn't hire the decorator for her personality." Flynn glanced up from the iPad in his hand. "I hired the decorator to remove my father's personality."

She glanced around at the square black sofa and gray coffee tables. The gray rug. The white mantel over which hung a framed painting of a black smudge on a white background.

"Success," she agreed with a placid smile. "What'd you need me for? I was under the impression you were sad or drunk or having some sort of belated episode because of the divorce."

"What I am about to have is enough Chinese food to feed an army."

"What about Gage and Reid?"

"What about them?"

"Um." What she couldn't say was that she felt the out-of-place need for a buffer or two. "Wouldn't they suffice in helping you rid yourself of excess takeout?"

Setting aside the iPad, he looked down at her, his handsome smile dazzling. "I'd rather hang with you. I've felt lately like you've been on the outside for too long."

"The outside?"

"In the background." His mouth pulled down at the edges. "The four of us used to hang out more. Outside of work. And then...we didn't."

Sabrina's heart swelled. She'd missed him over the last

three years he'd been married, but accepted that marriage required attention. Still, it was nice to know that she mattered and that he'd missed her.

"Aw." She beamed at the compliment and patted his cheek, not thinking a thing of it. Until she became acutely aware of the warmth from his skin and the rough scrape of his facial hair as she swept her fingers away. She cleared her throat and reminded herself that Flynn was her friend and nothing more. "There, was that so hard?"

His smile returned. "Begging is unattractive."

An hour later, they sat at the dining room table, food containers, an iPad, laptop and a manila folder stuffed with reports between them. They'd eaten a little of everything before cracking open a few beers, and that's when Flynn brought out the work accoutrements.

Tonight reminded her of late-night study sessions when they were in college. She'd been reflecting on those days more often than before lately and on how simple life had been back then.

"It'll work," he concluded.

Chin resting on her hand, elbow on the table, she yawned. "I think you're cruel and should offer me a refill for making me work late on a Friday."

"I fed you." He frowned. "Do you want another drink?"

"Do you have Perrier?"

"Perrier is not a drink." But he turned for the fridge and came back with a bottle of sparkling water for her. He even went to the trouble of spinning off the top and then proffering a highball glass. "I'd appreciate your thoughts."

His hands landed on her shoulders, kneading the tired muscles. She was torn between moaning in pleasure and freezing in place. Luke really had gotten into her head with that "booty call" comment.

Flynn's hands left her shoulders and she shakily filled

her glass and took her time sipping the sparkling water before she told him what she thought—about his idea. "It won't work."

Even his frown was frowning.

"If there were ten of you working eighty hours a week, *maybe* you could make up for losing half your staff. As it stands, even if Gage and Reid and I double our workloads along with you, I don't see how Monarch would survive everyone walking out."

"So I should let them force *me* into walking out?"

"It's a *vacation*," she reminded him on a soft laugh. "You've heard of them, right? You take a few days or weeks to relax and do something that's not work."

"My father built this business from scratch. I don't see why I can't put my head down and plow forward and end up in a better position."

"The staff is resisting change. Maybe when you're not there—but your changes are still implemented—they'll come to see you're right. If they need to flex their muscles and try to put you in your place, it's not like they'll succeed. It's for show. You're still in charge."

"My father would have died before letting anyone tell him how to run his business. Including me."

"He *did* die, Flynn." She reached across the table to palm his forearm. She understood why Flynn was angry with Emmons. Flynn had tried to impart his ideas at Monarch but had always been shut down by his father. Now was Flynn's chance to shine and he was being shut down by his father's ilk. It was insulting.

Flynn had lost the jacket, loosened the tie, but left on the starched shirt. There was a time he'd have his sleeves rolled up and would've laughed and lounged through both the meal and the beer. They'd had plenty of after-hours staff meetings, just Sabrina, Flynn and the guys, and Flynn was usually a hum of excitement. Now, that hum was gone.

There wasn't any excitement, just rote habits. He was as cold as his current environment.

"You're *not* him, and you don't have to become him," she said. "Not for Mac or Belinda or anyone else who believes that Monarch can only be run the way Emmons ran it."

Flynn's mouth compressed into a silent line.

"I hate seeing you like this. I know you're sick to death of me lecturing you, but if you don't loosen your hold, you're going to have a breakdown. Or a heart attack. Or—"

"Get cancer?" he finished for her. "I'm thirty years old, Sabrina. Hardly in the market for the thing that's going to kill me."

She flinched. Imagining Flynn dead was a fast track to revisiting her dinner. She tried again with even more honesty.

"*I miss you.* The old you. The *you* that knew where work stopped and fun started. Now you're like…" She waved in his general direction. "…a robot."

His features didn't soften in the slightest.

"Remember when we used to stumble out of college parties or go to the pub for Saint Patrick's Day? Remember playing poker until all hours of the night?"

"I remember you losing and refusing to pay up."

"It was strip poker and I was the only girl there!"

"Reid's idea." He let loose another smile and it resembled one that was carefree. "I don't know why you balked. I'd seen you in your underwear before."

"Yes, but not…not them." Her cheeks warmed. Yes, Flynn had seen her in her underwear. In her dorm room when he'd come to wake her up, or when she was changing to go out to a party. But that was different somehow.

She palmed her cheek to hide her hectic coloring. "I miss those days. What happened to us?"

"We grew up. We started working." He reached for her

hand, his thumb skimming over hers as he watched her closely. "I'm sorry if you've felt shut out lately."

A lump of emotion tightened her throat and she nodded, blinking to keep from crying. She had felt left out, and had made peace with seeing him at work and the occasional after-work dinner, but that wasn't enough.

"We used to be inseparable."

"I remember." His secret smile was all for her and she reveled in it. No one was here to intrude or put him on the clock or demand he stop being himself.

"When's the last time you took the time to do something you love?"

"A while," he admitted.

"Same. I've been wanting to paint again and I haven't had the time." Her eyes went to the mantel and that sorry excuse for art he had hanging over it. "I'd like to replace that lifeless painting with a Sabrina Douglas original."

"Clown on a bicycle? Elephant balancing on a waffle cone?"

"That was my circus era and I'm over it. You certainly have enough space in this vault for me to spread out a canvas or two." She moved to tug her hand away but he held fast. His blue eyes were locked on hers when he squeezed her fingers.

"I'll think about it."

"That's all I ask."

For now.

Five

Flynn thought long and hard about what Sabrina said while he lay staring at the glass ceiling in his living room. The stars were bright, the sky a navy blue canvas. A canvas like Sabrina wanted to paint and hang over his fireplace.

From his position on the sofa, he turned his head and looked at the black-and-white painting that was as bland as Sabrina had hinted. His life—his entire life—could use some color. A color other than monotone neutrals or angry reds. A color like Sabrina. Splashy yellow or citrusy orange, he thought with a smile.

Tonight might have been the first time in months he'd stopped to evaluate any part of his existence. If he hadn't been gathering information for his lawyer for the divorce, he'd been making funeral arrangements for his father, or relocating to this apartment after first removing every single trace of Emmons Parker. Fat lot of good it did him to erase his father from the apartment when Flynn himself was morphing into a younger version of his old man.

He couldn't let it happen. *Wouldn't* let it happen. Sabrina was right. He used to make time to do the things he loved, rather than serve at the pleasure of a sixty-plus-hour week.

The last year had been a blur of takeout, reports and meetings. He pulled a hand over his stomach, and while he hadn't developed a gut in the slightest, his abs weren't as chiseled as they could've been. At last glance in the mirror, his eyes weren't as bright either. The dark circles were a result of restless sleep, and the shadow of scruff on his jaw was unkempt enough that he looked more homeless than stylish.

Sabrina's being here had been reminder enough of what he'd been missing—her presence. And now she was offering to take a hiatus with him to help him out.

After years of her doing things for him, the least he could do was listen to her. His plan to work around his execs' bailing wasn't foolproof. Somewhere in the back of his stubborn mind he'd known that all along. Sabrina was unflinchingly honest when she'd told him she missed him and who he used to be. Which meant he was on the fast track to turning into a bitter, iron-hard man like his father.

That glaring truth made deciding easier.

First thing Monday morning, Flynn would call a meeting with his three best friends. A strategy meeting. He could walk away if he knew the place wasn't eroding in his absence. And if he armed Gage and Reid with what they needed to keep Mac from overriding every implementation he'd put in place, then Flynn could actually relax.

The shiver of relief was foreign, but welcome. He'd tried running the company his father's way. It was time to try a different strategy—Sabrina's strategy. Flynn had lost sight of what was important.

It was time to get it back.

Monday morning at Monarch looked the same as it had last week. Flynn was pouring himself a cup of coffee when Gage walked in.

"Morning. Get yourself fired yet?"

"Not yet." Flynn leaned against the counter.

Reid sauntered in next. "Morning, gentlemen."

"Singleton." Flynn dipped his chin. Gage saluted.

"Do you ever have one of those really good dreams," Reid said as he rinsed his travel mug and set it in the drainer to drip dry, "where you're with a woman and you're so in tune with her that even the sunlight doesn't snap you out of it?" He moved to the espresso machine and started the process of creating his next cup while Flynn blinked at him in disbelief.

His best friend had read his mind.

"Just this morning," Flynn answered. "Except I woke up before I saw who it was."

"Perfect." Reid nodded in approval. "Bloody perfect. When you can't see who it is, all the better."

Flynn had spent the weekend sleeping on the sofa despite a brand-new $8,000 bed in the master bedroom. The vestiges of a vividly erotic dream loosened its hold the moment the sun crept over the horizon. He'd made a futile attempt to hang on with both hands, long enough to figure out who belonged to that husky voice murmuring not-so-sweet nothings into his ear.

"How far'd you get?" Reid asked. At Flynn's questioning glance, he added, "Were you actually laid in your dream or are you still blue-balled from it?"

"Not far enough," he mumbled. It cut off before the good part.

"Mate." Reid shook his head. "We need to get you a girl."

"He's right." Gage moved Reid's espresso aside to make his own. "You can't handle this much stress and not have sex. Stephenie has a friend, by the way."

"I thought you'd stopped seeing Stephenie." Reid leaned a hip on the counter, settling in next to Flynn.

"I did." Gage poured milk into the steel carafe for steaming. "She'd let me set up Flynn with her sister. Steph and I didn't end badly. We just ended."

"You ended it," Flynn guessed.

"I don't need *serious* to have a good time. And you, my friend—" Gage dipped his chin at Flynn "—are way too serious lately."

"So I'm told."

The room filled with the sound of the steamer frothing milk to a perfect foamy consistency. If Flynn needed a second to Sabrina's "serious" motion, he'd just heard it.

A hazy, golden image filtered through his memory, the sun at the mystery woman's back, a shadow blotting out her face. He closed his eyes and tried to see the woman with the sultry voice, but she faded much like early this morning. Odd. He'd never had such a lucid dream. God help him if that face belonged to Veronica. He didn't have that much time to dedicate to therapy.

"We're here for the meeting you called, Parker. Where are we doing it?" Gage asked him.

"Yeah." Reid straightened from his lean, a delicate espresso cup dwarfed in one hand. "And what's it about? Are you retiring to live off your millions?"

"Dad's millions were wrapped up in assets, not lying around in the bank."

"Bummer." Gage shook his head.

"You wouldn't quit if you had millions, would you?" Reid asked.

"I would." Gage shrugged. "I can find something else to do with my time."

"Like what?" Sabrina strolled in, her phone in hand. "Which one of you fine baristas is whipping me up a cappuccino?"

"Gage," Reid answered.

Gage retorted and Reid argued something back that

Flynn missed. Reason being was that he was staring in shock as the face from his dream crystallized.

The golden light receded as she leaned forward over him. He swept her mussed dark hair from her face with his fingers as her mouth dropped open in a cry of pleasure.

"What the *hell*?"

The coffee banter stopped abruptly and they all turned their attention on him.

"What the hell...what?" Sabrina tipped her head and sent her long hair—the same long, dark hair from his dream—sliding over one shoulder. Desire walloped Flynn like a two-by-four to the gut.

No.

No, no, no, he mentally reprimanded himself, but the rest of his body parts had other ideas.

His eyes took in her jewel-toned red dress and then fastened on the delicate gold chain sitting at the base of her throat. His ears delighted at her kittenish laugh in response to something Reid said. And the one part of him that absolutely should *not* be reacting to her stirred in interest as if waking from a deep, deep sleep.

"Aren't you jealous?" Reid asked. And because his arm was slung around Sabrina's neck, it took Flynn a second to clear the fuzz from his head. "Of our fancy coffees."

"Flynn should make my cappuccino, and then he can make himself one, too." Sabrina sashayed over to him, her skirt moving with her long legs, ending in a pair of pointy-toed black high heels. She took his mug from him and he stiffened. And he did mean *all* of him.

"What do you have in there?" The husk in her voice caused his mind to nosedive into the gutter. But she wasn't talking about what was going on in his pants, she was referring to his coffee mug. She sipped and then wrinkled her cute nose.

"Plain old drip. *Boh*-ring. Cappuccinos for everyone and

then we'll get started. Oh! We could have the meeting in here!" She carried the mug to the sink and dumped it. "I'd much rather sit over there than in that conference room."

"Over there" was a grouping of leather sofas and chairs. Flynn focused on the furniture, desperate to reroute his thoughts from the insane idea that Sabrina was anything other than his best friend. He'd already done her a disservice by benching her. She didn't need him sexualizing her on top of it.

But thinking of the words *on top* only served as a reminder of where she was in his dream. On top of *him*.

"Must've been the pizza." He said that aloud and earned some raised eyebrows from his two male friends. He forced a shaky smile and went to the espresso machine, hoping to busy his hands for a bit, too. "Cappuccinos all around."

Mugs empty, they lounged in the executive break room. Reid, leg crossed ankle-to-knee in one of the leather chairs, propped his grotesquely handsome head up with one hand, eyes narrowed in thought as Flynn continued listing the details that would need handling when—eventually—he extracted himself from Monarch as Sabrina had suggested. Gage sat across from him in the matching chair, his cell phone in hand as he typed notes into it. Sabrina had chosen the couch across from Flynn. She'd been scribbling notes in a fancy spiral-bound notebook she'd run to her office to fetch before they started.

Flynn had been glad for the break. Her leaving the room had given him a chance to settle his formerly unsettled self. By the time she'd returned, he was back to looking at her like a coworker and friend and not like a man who apparently needed to get laid more than he needed a third cappuccino.

"Understanding that spring is a busy season for us…" His mouth continued on autopilot, but his brain took a sharp left turn when Sabrina set aside her notebook and pen to slip off one shoe. She set the spiked heel on the ground and crossed her leg, massaging one arch with insistent fingers. He watched the movement, his eyes fastened on red fingernails, not too long, not too short. His own voice was an echo, and he hoped to God Reid and Gage weren't staring at him while he stared at Sabrina. Not that it mattered. Flynn wasn't capable of stopping.

She bent to slip her shoe on and the neck of her dress gapped, giving him an eyeful of the shadow between her breasts. The lost dream cannonballed back into his subconscious so hard he sucked in a breath midsentence and didn't recover right away.

Sabrina over him.

Sabrina's red mouth parted to say his name.

Sabrina's long hair covering her nipples and hiding them from view.

Were they pink? Peach? Dusky tan? Or—

"As soon as what?" Reid asked, leaning forward, his elbows on his knees and his attention on Flynn.

Flynn snapped his head around to face Reid, who thankfully wasn't wearing an *I Know What You Did Last Summer* smirk.

"Sorry. Where was I?"

"You said you figured you could take time off as soon as…"

As soon as I pull my head from my ass. Or, more accurately, Sabrina's cleavage.

"May. I can take off in May." What the hell was wrong with him? Maybe he was heading for a breakdown.

"May!" Sabrina yipped, her voice a high-pitched complaint rather than the soothing alto of his dream. "I'm not letting you wait until May. Hiatus starts *now*."

Her stern exclamation glanced off him like a butterfly's wing. He'd known her for a hundred years and had never wondered what color her nipples were. Did he notice she had boobs? Sure. Had he guessed what cup size she wore? Absolutely. Did he notice when other guys looked at her while she wore a bikini at the beach? You bet. But other than unwitting glimpses that were more male programming than intentional ogling, he'd never mentally stripped her down for his own pleasure.

She was his best friend. It'd never occurred to him to imagine the color of her nipples any more than he would imagine the color of Gage's.

Flynn had no earthly clue how he'd made the leap from sharing Chinese food with her on Friday to waking Monday with morning wood from a dream where she was stark naked and moaning his name.

Unless she'd been right about his not dealing with the emotional toll the last year had taken. His entire life had been in upheaval when he'd been handed the company. He'd been acting president, but there was a safety net in place—his father. After Emmons had passed, Flynn was on his own. He'd lost his mother at fifteen, his brother to betrayal and his father right around the same time. He had no one, save the three people in this room.

He couldn't let them down. Taking his mind and hands off the controls would have to come with some sort of re-assurance—the reason for this meeting, or else Monarch Consulting would sink like the *Titanic*.

Flynn wiped his sweaty brow and attempted to regroup. Not a simple task since Sabrina spoke next, forcing him to look directly at her.

Six

"Are you insane?"

Even as she asked the question, she thought to herself that while Flynn wasn't insane, he certainly did look a little…unhinged. His gaze wouldn't settle in one place, bouncing from her face to Gage to Reid to his lap before going around again. Maybe he'd had too much coffee.

"May is two months away," Gage said. Sabrina was glad she wasn't the only one who'd noticed that.

"So?"

"*So*, it's not going to take *two months* for you to hand over our assignments." Gage set his phone aside and sat on the edge of the chair. "We're capable of doing what needs to be done."

"I emailed Rose my vacation hours this morning," Sabrina said of the HR manager. "We're taking off starting Monday."

"We?" Reid turned toward her. "Where are you going? And why are you at this meeting if you're not going to be here helping us battle the powers of evil?"

"I oversee design and social media and my teams are perfectly capable of handling my being away from the office. Plus, I already told them they can reach out if there's an emergency."

"You said you wanted to paint," Flynn said, his voice gruff.

"I do. I will."

"You lectured me nonstop Friday night about taking time away and doing something other than working and now you're promising your team you're available for an emergency? You said you'd paint me something for the mantel."

"You two went out on Friday? I wasn't invited." Reid frowned.

"Fine. I'll ignore my phone and email, too," she told Flynn before turning to the other two. "We ate Chinese in Flynn's personality-free apartment—"

"Penthouse," Flynn corrected.

"Sorry. His personality-free *penthouse*." She flashed him a smile. "Where I tried to explain to him that vacation is different from retirement."

"I still don't understand why we weren't invited." Reid tipped his chin at Gage. "Where were you on Friday, Fleming?"

"My sister's boyfriend dumped her so I was on ice cream duty. I couldn't have showed up anyway."

"Well, I could've." Reid folded his arms over his thick chest. His dark hair was slightly wavy, his jaw angled and stubborn. His mouth was full and his eyes were piercing blue. If he wasn't acting like a ten-year-old right now, she might admit he was stupidly attractive.

"This isn't about you, Reid." She sighed. "It's about Flynn and how he's different than he used to be. Admit it, he's not the guy you became best friends with. If you were married to him, you'd be in counseling right now."

"If I was married at all I'd be in counseling right now," Reid quipped.

Gage laughed, but sobered when Sabrina communicated via a patient expression that she could use backup. Thankfully he showed up for her.

"Sabrina has a point," Gage said. Flynn shot him a glare that plainly said he did *not* want to talk about it. "Hear me out. Since Veronica…uh, *left*…you haven't been yourself. I understand that she and Julian simultaneously stabbed you in the back and kicked you in the balls. I've tried to be here for you, buddy. And your dad dying was another blow. I know you believe you don't have to mourn him as long since you two never got along, but you do."

"Agreed," Reid interjected. "I hate to admit it, but Sab is right." He winked at her to let her know he was teasing. "Since the funeral, you've been behaving like Emmons back from the dead. Frankly, none of us want to work with the next generation of wanker."

"You want to try running this place?" Flynn practically yelled.

"Yes." Reid didn't so much as flinch. "While you, and evidently Sabrina, paint and ride horses bareback or live in a yurt or whatever she has planned for you."

"Things to Do When You're Twenty-Two," Sabrina announced proudly. Every pair of eyes swiveled to her in question. "That's what Flynn and I are doing. We're going to live like we did in college."

"In a cramped dorm that smells of old gym socks?" Gage asked. She ignored him.

"I'm going to help Flynn remember what life was like before we were given the keys to the city. Before there was a Veronica. Before any of us knew we'd be running the biggest consulting firm in the Pacific Northwest. Before I could afford a six-hundred-dollar pair of shoes." Flynn's gaze lingered on her shoes for a moment before it met her eyes. "When we used to share a car because we couldn't be bothered to own one separately.

"Back when Bennie took my virginity and Gage was engaged." She sent him a glance and he paled slightly at the mention. She focused on Reid. "Back when you were sleeping your way through half of campus."

"It was a service I provided. Girls back then didn't know what good sex was until they met me." He offered a cocky smile.

"You two were twin disasters back then, but Flynn and I… We were good." She smiled at her best friend and his features softened. "We were better than we are now with our expensive sports cars and our gourmet coffees and our bespoke clothing. We were better than the corporate drones we're turning into."

"I'm not a drone," Gage argued.

"Me neither. We take umbrage to that accusation." Reid straightened his shirtsleeve. "Though I do enjoy nice cuff links."

"I wouldn't go back to being engaged. That was a mistake." Gage's tone suggested he needed to state that for the record.

"Hear, hear," Reid agreed. "I had a lot of fun in college, but I have no interest in reliving my past."

"That's why you're not invited to our hiatus," Sabrina said, her tone implying the "duh" she didn't say. "You may be fine balancing work and play, but I, for one, am terrible at it. And so is Flynn. I need to paint and he needs to focus on something other than Monarch's well-being."

Stress showed in the lines on the sides of Flynn's eyes and the downturn of his mouth. Two more months of not dealing with his feelings and she feared she'd lose her momentum. He was saying yes to the hiatus, which was huge. It'd take only a nudge for him to agree to starting it on Monday.

"Flynn. You can trust Reid and Gage. Monarch won't implode if you walk away. You can start your hiatus on Monday. With me." She reached over and palmed his knee, noting that his nostrils flared when she did. The way he looked at her wasn't impatient or upset, but more...*aware*. It reminded her of the way she'd looked at him on Friday evening.

"I'll put it in my calendar." Gage lifted his phone, typing as he slowly spoke the words, "Flynn and Sabrina's sabba...ti...cal. There. Done." He showed them the screen. "Monday's Valentine's Day by the way."

"I know." Sabrina grinned. "Flynn and I are going out."

"On Valentine's Day?" Reid's voice was comically high. "That day should be treated tenderly. Every single man knows that occasion is a minefield. What are you going to do, love? Take him to a fancy couples' dinner and shag him afterward?"

Sabrina let out an uncomfortable laugh, looking to Flynn to laugh with her, but he looked as if a grenade had gone off in his general vicinity. His shoulders were hunched and his face was a mask of horror. So...possibly she misread his expression a moment ago.

"Thanks a lot." She let out a grunt. "I wouldn't be *that* bad to sleep with!"

Flynn rubbed his eyes with the heels of his hands.

"I'd happily sleep with you, Sab. I've been offering for years."

"No way." She rolled her eyes at Reid's offer. She couldn't imagine sleeping with, kissing or being romantically involved with Gage or Reid. She winked over at Gage, who smiled affably. They were like brothers.

Her gaze locked with Flynn's next and they had a brief staring contest. His slightly crazed expression was gone and now he simply watched her.

Flynn was...not like a brother.

But there was a deeper camaraderie between them that was worth resurrecting. And it'd be fun to go out on Valentine's Day with him. They could make new memories since neither of them had ever been single at the same time as the other.

She blinked as that thought took hold.

Until now.

"So now you're dating Flynn and we're still not calling it dating?"

Her brother, Luke, delivered doughnuts to her place on Saturday morning. One of which was a cruller that she tore in half and dunked into her coffee.

Mmm. Coffee and crullers.

"Hello?" Luke snapped his fingers in her face. "You and that doughnut are having a moment that's making me uncomfortable."

"You'll live." She tore off another bite and stuffed it into her mouth.

Her apartment was in the city not far from Flynn's, but the two residences were worlds apart. His, a penthouse and shrine to all things soulless, and hers an artsy loft filled with cozy accents. A red faux leather sofa sat on a patterned gold-and-red rug, a plaid blanket tossed over one arm. Framed art hung on the wall, one of them Sabrina's own: a whimsical painting of an owl sitting on a cat's head that always made her smile. Butter-yellow '50s-style chairs she'd reupholstered after salvaging them from a trash heap circled a scarred round kitchen table that she and Luke sat at now.

"Flynn lives in a barren wasteland of a penthouse, but the view is a million times better," she said, scowling out at the view of a nearby brick wall.

When she'd first rented her place, she'd fallen in love with the C-shape of the building and the ivy climbing the rust-red-and-brown bricked facade. Now, though, she'd like a view of the sunset. Or a sunrise. As it was, very little vitamin D streamed through her kitchen windows, and only for a few choice hours a day.

"That's most rich guys, isn't it?" Luke smirked.

"Oh, like you don't have aspirations to make millions."

"I do. Off my Instagram account. Eventually." He religiously posted at-the-gym selfies. Luke had rippling abs and a great smile and if she were to ask any female her opinion of him, she could guess the answer. Her girlfriends in college had labeled him "hot" even when he was younger, and his loyal league of followers contended that he was gorgeous.

"And when you make your millions, will you live on a top floor and invite me over for doughnuts?"

"No. I'll live on a few hundred acres and buy a llama."

"A llama." She hoisted one eyebrow.

He grinned. She shook her head. He was still *just Luke* to her, no matter what thousands of random women thought of him.

"Tell me about your Valentine's Day date with Flynn." He chose an éclair from the white cardboard box. She wiggled her fingers over a bear claw and then a powdered jelly before grabbing another cruller. She was a purist. Sue her.

"It's not a date. I mean, it is but it'd be the same as if I went out on V-day date with a girlfriend. Like Cammie."

"Mmm, Cammie." A quick lift of Luke's eyebrows paired with a devilish smile.

"*No.* We've been through this. You're not allowed to date my friends because it'd be weird and awkward and…no." Plus, Cammie moved to Chicago last year. Sabrina missed having a girlfriend close by.

"Flynn is dating you and he's my friend."

"We're *not* dating," she reiterated. "And he's not your friend. You know him. There's a difference."

Affronted, Luke pouted before taking a giant bite of the éclair.

"And we're not going to a cliché superfancy, elegant dinner. We're going to Pike Place Market and having breakfast, then hearing a cheesemonger speak about artisan cheeses, and then—"

"Did you just use the word *cheesemonger*?"

"—*and then* we're going to finish up with a trapeze show." The part she was most excited about.

Luke made a face.

"It'll be fun."

"It sounds lame."

She punched him in the arm but he was asking for it, delivered doughnuts or no.

"I thought you were supposed to be reliving your college years. The Market was built, what, a few years ago?"

"We're reliving the *spirit* of our college years."

"I'll give you this, Sabs." He stood to grab the coffeepot and refilled both their mugs. "Your date sounds positively *unromantic*. Fifty points to you. I guess Flynn is only a friend."

That rankled her, especially after she and Flynn had been exchanging some eye-locks and subtle touches that had felt, while not romantic, at least *sensual*. Rather than clue her brother in, or entertain the words *sensual* and *Flynn* in the same thought, she mumbled, "Right."

Seven

The rain fell on a cool fifty-degree day that the weatherman said felt more like thirty-seven degrees. No matter. Sabrina had convinced Flynn to start his hiatus Monday—today—and she was determined to both pry her best friend out of his shell and enjoy herself.

They started with breakfast, tucking into a small table for two near the window where they could watch the foot traffic pass by. She ordered a cappuccino and orange juice and a glass of water.

"Like you, I usually drink my breakfast," Flynn said after ordering coffee for himself. He could give her all the hell she wanted so long as he was here with her.

When their drinks arrived, she resumed her sermon from the ride over about how he needed time off. "It'll take you a while to get used to relaxing."

"I'm relaxed." His mouth pulled to the side in frustration and he lifted his steaming coffee mug to his lips.

"Yes. With your shoulders clinging to your earlobes and

that Grouchy Smurf expression on your face, you're very convincing."

He forcefully dropped his shoulders and eased his eyebrows from their home at the center of his forehead.

"It's okay to admit you have emotions to deal with. It's okay to talk about your father. Or Veronica and Julian—or either of them apart from the other."

"How can I talk about them apart from the other if they're never apart?"

Sabrina stirred her cappuccino before taking a warm, frothy sip. As carefully as if she were disarming a bomb, she asked a question that pained her to the core.

"Do you miss her?"

He took a breath and leaned on the table, his arms folded. Huddled close over the small table for two, he pegged her with honest blue eyes. "No. I don't."

That pause had made her nervous for a second. Her chest expanded as she took a deep breath of her own. Then she pulled her own shoulders out from under her ears. Sabrina was there for Flynn's engagement and the wedding and the aftermath. She knew what Flynn was like dating Veronica, being betrothed to Veronica and then married to her. Sabrina had watched the evolution—the *de*volution—of him throughout the process. It broke her heart to watch him be used up and discarded.

"I don't miss her either."

He returned her smirk with a soft smile of his own.

"She never liked me."

"She did so." His low baritone skittered along her nerve endings, that inconvenient awareness kicking up like dust in a windstorm.

"You don't have to lie to me now. It's not like she's sitting here. She tolerated me because you and I were friends and we share a birthday and because I'm too loyal to leave you."

"I wouldn't sweat it. She's clearly not stable since she's with Julian." He let out a small breath of a laugh and she clung to it. She'd love to hear Flynn laugh like he used to, big and bold. Watch how it crinkled his eyes. She loved so many aspects about him, but his laugh was at the top of her list.

"It's fitting to be out with you on Valentine's Day," she told him. "You might be the only guy in my life aside from Luke who I've cared about consistently."

"Never ruin a friendship with dating, right?"

"Right." She smiled but then it faded. "We were never tempted to date, were we?"

Mug lifted, he sent her a Reid-worthy wink. "Not until today."

"It recently occurred to me that we were always dating someone other than each other. Do you think that was why we never dated, or were we just too smart to get involved?"

"We weren't always dating other people. I had long stints of being single."

"Yes, but they never coincided with my stints of being single." She was right about this. She knew it. "Go through your list."

"My *list?*"

"The list of girls you dated from your college freshman year through now."

"How am I supposed to remember that?" He swiped his jaw, and his stubble made a scratchy sound on his palm, reminding her of when she touched his face last week. She shifted in her seat and shut out the strange observation.

"I need corroborated evidence."

"Who the hell's going to corroborate?"

"Me. I remember who we dated in college."

"Everyone?"

"Everyone."

"That is a useless amount of information to store in your noggin, Sab."

"Nevertheless it's there. Go. You can start with Anna Kelly."

"Anna Kelly does not count."

"You and I had first met. You were dating her and I was seeing Louis Watson."

"Good ole Louie."

"We went on that—"

"Disastrous double date," he filled in for her. "Louis didn't know better than to talk politics."

"She baited him! Anyway, so there was that. Then I broke up with Louis and started seeing Phillip."

"Cock."

"Cox."

"He was an idiot. Okay, let's see…that was when I was with Martha Bryant. For a few weeks and then another M. Melissa…something?"

"Murphy. Don't act like you don't remember her just because she was crazy."

"God, she so was."

"And you stayed with her for like, ever."

"Only for a few months. I had a weakness for crazy back then. And then I dated Janet Martinez."

Her name rolled off his tongue in a way that made Sabrina seasick. "She was gorgeous. What happened to her? Did she ever become a swimsuit model?"

"Yes."

"Lie!"

"Truth. She didn't land *Sports Illustrated*, but she was on the covers of a few health mags. She lives in Los Angeles. Or did the last time I saw her."

"When did you see her? You didn't tell me that." A misplaced pang of jealousy shot through her.

"She was in town randomly a few years ago and was considering hiring Monarch."

"For what?"

"She owns a company that makes surfboards."

"Wow. I didn't date anyone that interesting ever. Unless... Ray Bell."

"Puke. He was *not* interesting."

"He was!"

"You were too good for him."

"As were you for Janet," she shot back.

"Which was why I started dating Teresa."

"And after Ray dumped me, I dated Mark Walker for a long while."

"I thought he was the one."

"I thought Teresa was the one for you. She was smart, funny."

"And only dating me to get close to Reid."

"To his credit, he didn't take her up on it," Sabrina pointed out. "That's what friends should do. Reid's a good friend."

"He is." Flynn examined his coffee. "Wish I'd have seen Veronica coming. She blindsided me."

"True story." Sabrina had witnessed it firsthand. Flynn was fresh off a breakup with Teresa and smarting over it. Gage's engagement had ended so he was as sad a sack as Flynn. Reid was in charge of keeping them from moping and so he dragged them to a party one random Friday night and that's where Flynn met Veronica. She'd swept in and convinced him—and the rest of his friends—that she was the woman Flynn needed.

"I guess Julian didn't abide by the friend code."

"I guess not," she concurred sadly. Because it *was* sad. Devastatingly upsetting, actually. How could Veronica leave Flynn when her job was to love him more than she loved herself?

"I really hate her sometimes." Sabrina pressed her lips together, wanting to swallow the words she shouldn't have said.

They were true, though. She didn't hate Veronica only because of the cheating and leaving. Sabrina had felt that surge of bitterness toward the woman throughout Flynn's marriage for one simple reason: Veronica was selfish. As had now been proved.

"I'm sorry I said that."

"Don't be," Flynn said.

They were interrupted by the delivery of waffles and a refill of coffee for Flynn. A plate of bacon appeared, smoky and inviting, and he moved it to the center of the table like he always had. Sabrina never ordered bacon because it was unhealthy and, frankly, she felt sort of bad for the pigs. He suffered no such guilt and knew she would cave and have a bite or two. He always shared.

"Hate whomever you want." He pointed at her with a strip of bacon before taking a bite and blessedly changed the subject. "After all, I hated Craig."

"Craig Ross."

A minor blip to get her over Ray. It worked on the short term and then she realized he was a complete narcissist. She dumped him shortly after they started seeing each other.

"And there you have it," she stated. "I've been single most of the time you and Veronica were married. But this is the first time you have been single at the same time as me."

"But you've dated."

"Nothing serious."

"Meaning?" He paused, fork holding a bite of waffle midair, syrup drizzling onto the plate.

"Meaning...nothing serious."

"No permanent plans, you mean."

"No...other things, too." She dived into her own waffle.

"No sex?"

Okay, that was a little loud.

"Shh!" She and Flynn had talked about sex and dating plenty but now that his physical presence was *more* present than ever, she felt strangely shy about the topic.

He chuckled and ate his waffle, shaking his head as he cut another piece precisely along the squares.

"It's not funny. It was a choice."

"Aren't you going mad?"

"Are you?"

His pleasant smile faded and there was a brief, poignant moment where their eyes met and the rest of the dining room faded into the background. She counted her heartbeats—one, two, three—and then Flynn blinked and the moment was over.

"I'm failing at cheering you up," she said.

"No. I started it. I have no right to judge you for your choices, Douglas."

"Well. Thanks. I just…didn't want to be attached to the wrong guy again. Sex makes everything blurry."

"God. Dating." He made a face. "I'm not in the market—"

"Actually, you are *at* the Market."

His smile was a victory in itself.

"I'm not in the market," he repeated, "for a relationship or a date. Gage and Reid think sex is going to magically fix everything. But you're right. It won't."

That was a relief. She didn't want him to go find someone else either. It was too soon.

"Sex has a way of uncovering feelings you've been ignoring."

His blue eyes grew dark as he studied her.

"What do you mean?" he asked after a pregnant pause.

"In the same way alcohol acts as truth serum, sex makes you face facts. Like if the attraction wasn't actually there, and when you have sex it's dull. Or, on the flip side of that same coin, if there is a spark, sex heightens every sensation and it's incredible."

Flynn's cheeks went a ruddy, pinkish color. "Incredible?"

"Sometimes." She swallowed thickly. "Unless it's just me."

"It might be you," he muttered cryptically before grabbing another slice of bacon. "Help me eat this."

Sabrina's statement at breakfast followed Flynn around like a bad omen.

"Sex has a way of uncovering feelings you've been ignoring."

He'd like to believe that wasn't true, but it *felt* true. Right about now, watching her with an itchy, foreign sort of *need*, it felt really, really true.

"Stop grimacing," she whispered as the cheese tour continued.

Their group of eight dairy-delighted couples were eating their way through various artisanal cheeses and the tour wasn't half over yet. Their guide, head cheesemonger Cathy Bates—yes, that was her real name—had just served samples of blueberry-covered goat cheese. Sabrina must've assumed that was what turned his mood.

"Who can eat this much cheese? No one," he growled under his breath.

Sabrina shot him a feisty smile that was like a kick in the teeth. It rattled his brains around in his skull and his entire being gravitated closer to her. Until this morning, he'd never laid out their timelines and dating habits side by side. They'd never talked about how they were always overlapping each other with other people.

It was an odd thing to notice.

Why had Sabrina noticed?

He watched her as cheese samples were passed around but he couldn't detect by looking if she'd had the same sort of semierotic dream about him as he'd had about her, or if she was thinking of him in any way other than as her pal Flynn.

He'd never looked at her any differently until that dream. Sabrina Douglas was his best girl friend. Girl *space* friend. Not a woman he'd pursue sexually.

She hummed her pleasure and wiggled her hips while she ate a graham cracker topped with goat cheese, and Flynn felt a definite stir in his gut. For the first time in his life, sex wasn't off the table for him and Sabrina.

Which meant he needed his head examined.

Pairing with the confusing thoughts was a palpable relief that down south he was operating as usual. He'd worried after the one-two punch of losing his wife to his brother and his father to cancer he'd never be back to normal.

Now that he reconsidered, who cared that a mental wire had crossed and put Sab's face in his fantasies? He'd had weird dreams before and they hadn't changed the course of his life.

After the tasting, Sabrina chattered about her favorite cheeses and how she couldn't believe they didn't serve wine at the tour.

"What kind of establishment doesn't offer you wine with cheese?" she exclaimed as they strolled down the board-walk. She was a few feet ahead of him yelling at the wind, her jeans and Converse sneakers paired with an army-green jacket that stopped at her waist. Which gave him a great view of her ass—another part of her he'd noticed before but not like he was noticing now.

Not helping matters was the fact that he didn't have to wonder what kind of underwear she wore beneath that tight denim. He *knew*.

No amount of trying to forget would erase the image of her wearing a black thong that perfectly split those cheeks into two bitable orbs.

"What do you think?" She spun and faced him, the wind kicking her hair forward, a few strands sticking to her lip gloss. He was walking forward when she stopped so he reached her in two steps. Before he thought it through, he swept those strands away from her sticky lip stuff, ran his fingers along her cheek and tipped her chin, his head a riot of bad ideas.

With a deep swallow, he called up ironclad Parker willpower and stopped touching his best friend. "I think you're right."

His voice was as rough as gravel.

"You're distracted. Are you thinking about work?"

"Yes," he lied through his teeth.

"You're going to have to let it go at some point. Give in to the urge." She drew out the word *urge*, perfectly pursing her lips and leaning forward with a playful twinkle in her eyes that would tempt any mortal man to sin.

And since Flynn was nothing less than mortal, he palmed the back of her head and pressed his mouth to hers.

Eight

What. Was. Happening?

A useless question since the answer was as plain as the tip of Flynn's nose on her face, because *Flynn Parker was kissing her.*

Her eyes were open in shock and she was using every one of her senses to rationalize this moment. But she couldn't. There was absolutely no way to sort out why his lips were on hers.

Time *slowed*.

She'd never imagined what his mouth would taste like, but now she knew. It was firm and sure with a hint of sweetness from the blueberry cheese they'd sampled. His kiss was delicious and confident. He held her as her knees softened and her eyelids slid shut. Sight lost, her body was a mangle of sensations as she became aware of every part of her touching every part of him.

His hand in her hair. His other hand on her hip beneath her coat, squeezing as he pulled her in tighter. The feel of his always-there scruff scraping her jaw. The low groan in his throat that reverberated in her belly and lower still…

She jerked her head back to separate their mouths, her eyes flying open. His mouth was still pursed, his lips shimmering a little from the gloss she'd transferred to them. She witnessed his every microexpression as it happened. His eyebrows ticked in the center, his mouth relaxed, and his eyes followed the hand that slid down her hair as he played with the strands between his fingers.

She opened her mouth to say something—to say anything—but no words came. Just an ineffectual breath of surprise. Unable to speak, or reason, or tame her now-overexcited female hormones, she waited for him to speak.

When he did she was more confused than ever.

"I don't want to go to the trapeze thing," he said.

"Oh-kay."

"What was between cheese and the trapeze?"

A slightly hysterical giggle burst from her. A release valve—not only was "cheese" and "trapeze" funny in the same sentence but Flynn grabbing her up and kissing the sense out of her was ridiculous.

Omigosh. I kissed Flynn Parker.

She touched her lips, reliving what seconds ago had her rising to her tiptoes—the kiss. A really great kiss.

"Shopping," she croaked when she was finally able to utter a coherent word.

"For what?"

"For…whatever." She shrugged, feeling awkward that they weren't talking about The Kiss. Feeling more awkward about standing here not bringing it up. "Um, Flynn?"

"I know." He pinched the bridge of his nose and while he collected himself she used the moment to check him out. Brown leather jacket, worn jeans, brown lace-up boots. He looked sturdy and capable and…now that she thought about it, pretty damn kissable, too. It was as if every subtle nuance she'd noticed about him over the last week had come into sharp focus. Flynn was still her best friend, but he was also freaking *hot*.

"What…was that?" she ventured, feeling like she should ask and that she shouldn't at the same time.

He raised an arm and dropped it helplessly, but no explanation came.

Tentatively, she touched his chest. This time when their eyes met a sizzle electrocuted the scant bit of air separating them.

"Let me guess. You're going to suggest we don't do that again," he murmured.

She became vaguely aware of the couples walking by, but since it was Valentine's Day none of them stopped to gawk at a man and woman standing in the center of the pier kissing.

"Why? Was it bad?" Her voice was accidentally sultry and airy. She wasn't *trying* to impress or woo him. It just sort of…happened. Maybe it was nerves.

"It wasn't bad for me." A muscle in his jaw twitched as he watched her mouth. Those blue eyes froze her in place when he demanded, "Why'd you ask? Was it bad for you?"

"It was different." That wasn't the best word for it, but it was the safest. "Not bad."

"Not bad. Okay." He raised his eyebrows and with them his voice. "Where do you want to shop?"

"We're just going to…"

"Shop. And since we're skipping the trapeze show, do something else."

"Like what?"

Like more kissing? a wanton part of her shouted with an exuberant round of applause.

"Whatever."

"Well, the show included dinner. I'm not sure where

we'll find reservations this late." She gave him a light shove when he didn't respond. "I've been wanting to see it."

"I've been wanting to check my work email. We can't always have what we want."

"You can't kiss me and then tell me I can't have nice things!" she said, unable to bank her smile.

His mouth spread into a slow grin. One filled with promise and wicked intentions, and one grin in particular she'd never, *ever* had aimed in her direction.

He was so attractive her brain skipped like a vinyl record.

"Fine. You win. You can have your show." He put his hand on her back and they walked to the nearest store side by side. His hand naturally fell away and she was left wondering if she could barter—no trapeze show in exchange for more kisses.

That'd be wrong, she quickly amended.

Right? she asked internally, but at the moment the rest of her had nothing to say.

"Sabrina *Douglas*?" Gage asked after Flynn told him what had happened last weekend.

"Do you know any other Sabrinas?" Flynn raised his beer glass and swallowed down some of the brew. Gage and Reid had wanted to go out, so here they were. *Out.* Chaz's, on the edge of downtown where they'd come on a zillion occasions, including when Flynn ditched his father's funeral. He shoved the memory aside. He had enough on his mind. Like making out with his best friend, who'd determined the kiss wasn't bad.

"*Our* Sabrina?" Reid asked, but he looked far less alarmed than Gage.

"Yes." Flynn set his glass down and stared into it.

The memory of pulling her to him and lighting her up with a kiss hadn't faded over the week. It was as crystal clear as if it'd happened seven seconds ago instead of seven days. He could still feel her mouth on his, her hip under his palm, the soft sigh of her breath tickling his lips. Her wide-eyed, startled expression was etched into his mind like the Ten Commandments into a stone tablet.

"Then what happened?" That was Gage, still sorting it out.

"Then we went shopping and watched a trapeze act. Then I dropped her off at home."

"And then you shagged," Reid filled in matter-of-factly.

"No. I dropped her off at home."

"And you made out in the doorway, tearing at each other's clothes regardless of passersby," Reid tried again.

"The kiss was a mistake," Flynn said patiently. "I knew it. She knew it. She stepped out of my car and walked to her building—"

"And then turned and begged you for one final kiss goodbye before she went up?" Reid appeared genuinely perplexed.

"Dude." Gage recoiled. "This isn't a choose-your-own adventure."

"It makes no sense, is all." Reid was still frowning in contemplation.

"Again, nothing happened," Flynn told them.

"You're truly incapable of enjoying yourself, do you realize that?" Reid leaned to one side to mutter to Gage, "It's worse than we thought."

"It sounds pretty bad already." Gage looked at Flynn. "What do you do now?"

"I haven't seen her since Valentine's Day, but we've been texting."

"You mean sexting," Reid corrected.

"What is the matter with you?" Flynn grumbled.

"You want the list in alphabetical order or in order of importance?" Gage chuckled.

Reid let the comment slide. "If you're not going to shag, then you need to fix it. Before something awful happens like she quits and we have to replace her. Sabrina isn't only your friend, you know. We all need her."

"She's not quitting. We're fine. It happened. I just didn't want there to be any awkwardness when we're inevitably in the office together again. So now you know. Don't make a big deal about it."

Reid snorted.

"I'm serious."

"You're the one who brought it up." Reid smiled at a passing waitress and she almost tripped over her own feet. He turned back to Flynn. "You tried to log in to your work email."

"How do you know that?" So, yeah, he'd attempted to check his work email three times. On the third try he was locked out for having the wrong password. A lightbulb glowed to life over his head. "You changed my password."

"You don't let me run your IT department for nothing." Good-looking and ridiculously smart shouldn't have been a combo that God allowed.

"I didn't agree to be shut out entirely."

"That was implied," Gage chimed in, the traitor.

"You're in sales. What do you know?"

"Sales brings in the money. I'm a direct link to Monarch's success. Don't be angry with me because you don't know how to relax."

"Refills?" the waitress who'd nearly stumbled stopped to ask, her eyes on Reid.

"Please, love," he responded, all British charm.

"And a round of tequila," Gage told her. She tore her eyes off Reid but her gaze lingered on Gage long enough that Flynn assessed a passing admiration. Then she turned to ask Flynn if he also needed a refill.

"I'm good," Flynn told her. "Word of advice, stay away

from him." He pointed to Reid, who promptly lost his smile, and then gestured to Gage. "And him."

Propping a hand on her hip, she faced Flynn, pushing out her chest. Her breasts threatened to overflow from her tight, V-neck shirt. Her blond hair was pinned into a sloppy bun, her figure curvy and attractive.

"So your friends would recommend I go out with you?"

"Incorrect, love," Reid piped up. "My pal Flynn is not the one for you."

"No? Why not?" she asked, flirting.

"He's far too serious for a girl like you. You look like someone who knows how to have fun."

"I do." She tipped her head toward Reid, mischief in her dark brown eyes.

"As do I."

"Hmm. I don't know." She turned back to Flynn. "I like serious sometimes. I'm Reba." She offered a hand and Flynn shook it. "Would you like to have a drink with me tonight, Serious Flynn? I'm off at eleven and I don't work until noon tomorrow. That gives me a space of thirteen open hours if you'd like to fill them."

She swiped her tongue along her lips and it took a count of ten while staring up at her, her hand in his grip, for Flynn to realize what Reba was offering. To sleep with him tonight after her shift and then to sleep in with him tomorrow.

"Sorry. I have plans." He dropped her hand and her smile fell. With a slightly embarrassed expression, she promised to return with their beers. Gage and Reid glared at him like they'd been personally offended.

"What gives?" Reid shook his head in disbelief. "She tied a bow on that offer."

"Nothing *gives*. I'm not interested."

"In her," Gage supplied.

"In anyone," Flynn growled.

"Except for Sabrina." Now Gage was smiling. He and

Reid exchanged glances and, as if the universe intuited that he needed another challenge, Flynn's cell phone picked that instant to buzz in his pocket. He studied the screen and the words on it before standing from his chair. "Thanks for the beer."

"What about your shot?" Reid asked.

"Give it to Reba."

"Who was the text from?" Gage asked, but he knew. And Reid had figured it out, too, if his shit-eating grin was anything to go by.

"It's Sabrina," Reid guessed. Correctly.

"Change my password back," Flynn told him.

"Not for another month."

"I mean it."

"What are you going to do, fire me?" he called after him.

"Tell Sabrina we said hi!" That was Gage.

Assholes.

Nine

Luke was out of town and her landlord was ignoring her calls. Sabrina had spent the last two days without clean water, even though various other units on her floor had plenty. She knew—she'd knocked on doors and asked. She'd been brushing her teeth and washing her face and other body parts at the sink using jugs of distilled water and washcloths, but this was getting ridiculous.

Desperate, she'd texted Flynn a mile-long message detailing how she really wanted to take a shower and cook something and how Luke was gone and her landlord was a neglectful jerk, and could she please, *please* come over for an hour. Just long enough to return to feeling human again.

Then she stared at the screen waiting for his response. According to the time on her phone she'd sent the text eight minutes ago.

Things had been fairly normal between them since Valentine's Day, she supposed. She'd checked in on him to make sure he wasn't working every day and then went about enjoying her vacation...sort of.

A stack of canvases leaned against an easel and her paints were lined up on the kitchen table like colorful little soldiers. But the canvases were as dry as her shower floor. Inspiration hadn't arrived with the downtime like it was supposed to, so instead of creating art, she'd been reading novels and cleaning her apartment. The place was sparkling, not a speck of dust to be found anywhere, and her to-be-read pile was in a reusable tote to be returned to Mrs. Abernathy across the hall. That woman loved her romance novels and had lent Sabrina a stack of them a while back. Until now, she hadn't taken time to read them.

She also learned that reading romance novels after a confusing kiss from her best friend meant her mind would slot *him* into the hero role in every book. So far Flynn had starred as the rakish Scot who fell for a married, time-traveling lass, a widower artist pining for his deceased wife's best friend and a ridiculously cocky NFL player who won over a type-A journalist.

No matter how the author portrayed the hero, dark hair, red hair, brown eyes or green, Sabrina gave every hero Flynn's full, firm lips and warm, broad hands. Each of them had his expressive blue eyes and permanent scruff and angled jaw. And when she arrived at the sex scenes— *hoo boy!* She knew what Flynn looked like with his shirt off, and wearing nothing but board shorts, but she'd never seen him *naked*.

Mercy, the authors were descriptive about *that part* of the hero. She'd allowed herself the luxury of attaching that talented member to the Flynn in her head. As a result, she'd had a week's worth of reading that had proved to be more sexually frustrating than relaxing. She needed to have sex with someone other than herself and soon. She didn't know what the equivalent of female blue balls was, but she had them.

Was it any wonder she'd reached out to Flynn after all she'd done was imagine him in every scenario?

It might be wrong, but it felt right.

Just like texting him had been right but felt *wrong*. She wished there was a way to retract the text, but there it sat. Unanswered. Maybe she could borrow Mrs. Abernathy's shower instead. That might be safer.

At the fifteen-minute mark without a response, she decided to let him off the hook. She was keying in the words *Never mind* when her phone rang in her hand. The photo on the screen was one of Flynn sitting at his desk, *GQ* posed as he leaned back in the leather chair. It was the day he'd moved to the office upstairs after his father left Monarch and announced that he was ill.

Flynn looked unhappy even lampooning for the camera like she'd asked. She'd hoped asking him to be silly with her for a second would improve his mood, but cheering him up had been an uphill climb ever since.

"Hi," she answered, and began to pace the room.

"I'm coming over. Pack what you need for the weekend. I'm going to have a chat with your landlord, but in the meantime, you're staying with me."

"Uh…" *What?* "No, that's okay. I just need a quick shower."

"Sabrina, I'm already pissed this has been going on so long and you haven't told me."

"I didn't want to bother you." Plus, she didn't know how to behave after he'd kissed her and then acted like he hadn't for the last week.

"See you in a few minutes." He disconnected and she quirked her mouth indecisively before turning for her dresser and pulling open the top drawer.

"No big deal," she reassured herself as she riffled through her undergarments, but when her fingertips encountered clingy satin and soft lace thongs, she bit down on her bottom lip. A surge of warmth slid through her like honey as a mashup of love scenes from the novels she'd read this week flickered in the forefront of her mind like a dirty movie. One that starred Flynn. She held up the silky red underwear.

Definitely this was a bad idea.

She dug deeper in the drawer and pulled out her sensible cotton bikini briefs. They came in a package of four: two navy blue, one red and one white. There. Harmless. She threw them on the bed and then bypassed the sexy bra, choosing the nude one instead. It was designed to be worn under T-shirts and not reveal her nipples, and if that wasn't the perfect choice for a platonic night or two spent at Flynn's she didn't know what was.

From there she chucked a few pairs of jeans, a dress and T-shirts as well as a nice blouse onto the bed. Shoes were last. Since she was wearing her trusty Converses, a pair of flats would do nicely with the dress or jeans. Plus, she wasn't going to be at Flynn's for long. A night or two, tops. She was sure her landlord would have the plumbing issue fixed soon, she thought with a spear of doubt.

She could admit that it wasn't the worst idea for her and Flynn to be around each other in person. They could tackle the issue of The Kiss head-on. It was totally possible he'd been caught up in the spirit of Valentine's Day at the Market. Maybe she had, as well. Maybe they'd both been swamped by a rogue wave of pheromones from the other happy couples walking the pier that day. That could've been what made him—

"Kiss me until I couldn't remember my own name." She shook her head and sighed. She sounded like one of Mrs. Abernathy's romance novels.

A sharp rap at her front door startled her and she let out a pathetic yelp.

Shaking off her tender nerves, she drew a breath before

facing Flynn for the first time since last Monday. He stood in her doorway, sexy as hell, and her gaze took it upon itself to hungrily rove over his jeans and sweater.

He looked like the same old Flynn, but different.

Because you know what he tastes like.

His blue eyes flashed with either an answering awareness or leftover angst about her plumbing situation. She couldn't tell which. She noticed he took a brief inventory of her jeans and long-sleeved shirt before ending at her sock-covered feet. From there he snapped his gaze to the bed covered in her clothes.

"I didn't know what to pack…" She didn't bother finishing that sentence, gesturing for him to come in while she dug a suitcase from the back of her closet. She started piling clothes into it while Flynn wandered around her studio, taking in the blank canvases on the floor.

"Not inspired?" His deep voice tickled down her spine like it had over the phone. Flynn had a deep baritone that was gruff and gentle at the same time.

Just like his mouth.

She was inspired all right, but not to paint.

"This is a bad idea," she blurted out, halfway into her packing. "You don't want me living with you even on the temporary. I'm messy and chatty and wake up in the middle of the night to eat ice cream."

"I have ice cream. I also have just shy of five thousand square feet going to waste. And plenty of clean water."

"But—"

"I didn't ask. Pack." He surveyed her art supplies. "You can bring this stuff, too. I think the easel will fit in the backseat."

"Don't be silly! It's only for a few days."

"Sab, you live in a building that was erected sometime around the fall of Rome. The plumbing issue could be bigger and deeper than you think."

The words *erected* and *bigger* and *deeper* paraded through her head like characters in a pornographic movie. He didn't mean any of them the way she was envisioning them, but she still had trouble meeting his stern gaze.

"Pack extra clothes in case. If you need more, you can pick them up later."

"Moving me in wasn't what you had in mind when you took a hiatus, I bet." She shoved more clothes into the suitcase.

"I didn't have a hiatus in mind. You're the one who made me do it." He bent and lifted the canvases.

"I haven't been able to paint, so don't bother with those."

"I haven't been able to relax, and watching you paint is relaxing. Will you at least try for the sake of my sanity?" His mouth quirked and again she had the irrational notion that she'd like to kiss that quirk right off his face.

"I'll try," she said, simultaneously talking about painting and not attacking him like a feral female predator.

"I'll run these to the car. Oh, and Sab?"

"Yes?"

"Remember those cookies you used to make? The ones with the M&M's?"

"Yes…"

"If you have the stuff to make those, bring it."

She smiled, remembering making him M&M cookies years ago. He'd devour at least a half a dozen the moment they came out of the oven. "I have the stuff."

"Good." With a final nod and not another word, he made the first trip down to his car with the canvases.

Sabrina resumed her packing, reminding herself that being tempted by Flynn and giving in to temptation didn't have to coincide.

"You've got this," she said aloud, but she wasn't sure she believed it.

Ten

Flynn set Sabrina up in a spare bedroom, one furnished with a dresser, night tables and a bedside lamp. The bed in there was new, like every bed in the penthouse. He'd be damned if he would sleep one more night in a bed he used to share with his cheating ex-wife.

After Veronica had confessed she'd been "seeing" Julian, which was a nice way to say "screwing" him, she'd stayed in the three-story behemoth that she and Flynn had bought together. Fine by him, since he'd never wanted to live there in the first place. At the time, he'd rented a small apartment downtown.

He felt as if he didn't belong anywhere. Not in his marital house overlooking a pond, not in this glass-and-steel shrine that reminded him of his father's cold presence, and though he'd loved his mother and the estate reminded him of her, he didn't feel as if he belonged there either. Just as well since the rose gardens had fallen to ruin when she died. How fitting that the place had been left to Julian.

It didn't surprise Flynn that Veronica had moved in immediately. She'd always crowed about how she wanted more space inside and out, and the estate, with its orchards and acreage and maid's quarters, would definitely tick both boxes.

And now he was moving Sabrina into his place without thinking about it for longer than thirty seconds.

Reason being he shouldn't *have to* think about it for longer than thirty seconds. She was his best friend and had been for years, and she needed a place to stay. The fact that he'd kissed her last week shouldn't matter.

It shouldn't, but it did.

He was determined to push past the bizarre urge to kiss her again, confident that once she was in his space, painting or baking M&M cookies, they'd snap back to the old *them*—the *them* that didn't look at each other like they wondered what the other looked like naked.

He pictured her naked and groaned. It was a stretch, but he clung to the idea that he could unring that bell. It wasn't looking good since the buzz reverberated off his balls every time he thought about her.

He dragged in the easel, Sabrina's suitcase and the last of the canvases tucked under one arm. She was unpacking the makings of cookies onto his countertop and clucked her tongue to reprimand him.

"I told you I'd help." She moved to take the canvases and he let her, then he leaned the easel against the wall.

"This is the last of it. Besides, you've helped plenty."

In the bedroom he rested her suitcase against two smaller totes. The suitcase was bright pink, one tote neon green, the other white with bright flowers, adding energy to the apartment's palette of neutrals. If Sabrina being here infused him with a similar energy, he wouldn't complain. He'd been living in black and white for far too long.

Until Valentine's Day, when she'd taken him to breakfast, on a cheese tour, and made him sit through a trapeze act he'd found fascinating rather than emasculating, he hadn't noticed just how long it'd been since he felt... well, *alive*.

His life had been a blur of Mondays, and he'd been working every day until he dropped. He'd been under the mistaken notion that if he kept moving forward he'd never have to think about Veronica or Julian or Emmons ever again.

"Bastards."

"Yikes. Are you talking to the luggage?" Sabrina asked from the doorway.

She'd tied on her Converses and slipped a denim jacket over her T-shirt. Her hair was pulled off her face partway, the length of the back draping over her shoulders. She was gorgeous. So stupidly, insanely gorgeous he wondered how he'd kept his hands off her for this long.

"I'm here if you need to talk." Her dark eyes studied him carefully.

"I don't need to talk." What he wanted was to not talk, preferably while her mouth occupied his.

"Okay." She patted him on the arm.

It was the first time she'd touched him since Monday and he wanted it to feel as pedestrian as any pat from any hand belonging to any random person. A certain member of his anatomy below his belt buckle had other ideas, kicking into third gear like it was trying to break free of his zipper to get to her.

"Are you too tired to bake cookies?" he asked, desperate for a subject change.

"Are you too tired to help?" She hoisted an eyebrow.

"Can I drink a beer while helping?"

"Hmm." She tapped her finger on lips he wanted on his more than a damn cookie. "I'll allow it."

With a wink that had him swallowing another groan, she led the way to the kitchen.

* * *

Sabrina dusted her hands on her jeans and set the last tray of M&M cookies on top of the stove. Flynn came jogging into the kitchen from the adjacent TV room to snag one.

"Those are piping—"

"Hot!" He blew out a steaming breath, a bite of cookie hovering on his tongue, and then needlessly repeated, "Hot."

"Yeah, I know."

He took another bite, his eyes closing as he chewed. He moaned almost sensually. She tried not to notice as she slid the spatula beneath each cookie and transferred them to the cooling rack—also brought from her apartment.

She hadn't baked him cookies for years and yet nothing about the scenario had changed.

She'd pull them out of the oven and he'd run in, eating one while simultaneously complaining they were "hot." Then he'd blow on the remaining half of the cookie in his hand before dropping it into his mouth with a moan of pleasure.

"Amazing." Over her shoulder, he reached for another. "So good."

The words were muttered into her ear and answering shivers tracked down her spine. Nothing had changed, and yet *everything* had changed.

She turned to warn him that the cookies were still as hot as before, and came nearly nose to nose with him.

It was like they were magnetized.

Cookie in hand, he didn't move when her breast brushed his shirt. She didn't back away and neither did he.

Someone should...

"Want a bite?" His nostrils flared as he took a slow perusal of her face.

"No thanks," she said quickly. "They're too…hot." That last word came out on a strangled whisper.

He backed up a step, broke the cookie in two and carefully blew on the halves. She watched his mouth, mesmerized by the sudden hold he had over her. The powerful, almost animal reaction she had to him. She wondered if it'd always been inevitable, but ignored. And if it had always been there, how had she ignored something so *explosive*? It was the difference between a warm burner on a stove versus a roaring bonfire throwing sparks into the air.

In this case, Flynn was the fire, and she was the wood, unable to keep from catching aflame whenever he touched her.

He offered half a cookie and she took it, brushing her fingers against his. They ate their halves, he in one big bite and she in three little ones. She jerked her gaze to the stove and back to him again.

"We should talk," he said.

"I agree."

"You first."

"Chicken."

"I'm not scared. I'm smart. Go."

She would've laughed if she didn't want him so damn much.

"When you kissed me on Valentine's Day, you opened Pandora's box. When I'm around you, it's all I think about."

Well, not *all*. She'd thought about a hell of a lot more than kissing him, but she wasn't going to reveal *that*.

"Agreed," he said. "And you have a suggestion?"

"I do."

"You're not going back to your apartment. That's final. Not until you have running water that's not the color of rust-stained pipes."

"I wasn't going to suggest that."

His head jerked as he studied her curiously.

She licked her lips, willing herself to say what she was thinking. There was a very big chance Flynn would refuse her, which would be bad for both her ego and their friendship.

If he agreed it could *also* be bad for their friendship.

Which was why she started with, "Promise me we'll always be friends because we've always been friends. It's not worth throwing away because of a weird wrinkle in the universe where we explored a possibly brief attraction for each other."

"Never," he agreed without hesitation. "I'd never let you go, Sab. You know that." His eyebrows were a pair of angry slashes.

"I know. I wanted to say it before I made a suggestion."

"Which is?"

"I think you should kiss me again."

He didn't react like she thought. He didn't recoil, nor did he lean forward. He stood motionless, watching her as carefully as a hunter approaching a skittish deer.

"I'm pretty sure that moment on the pier was a fluke," she continued. "And since we never *really* talked about it, and I was caught off guard, I thought if we tried it again we could finally put it behind us. Especially if this time there aren't any sparks."

"You felt sparks?" His question was an interested murmur as he closed the gap between them.

Yes.

"I...it's an expression." She pressed her lips together.

"And you think we should try again to make sure there are no...sparks." Seeming more comfortable with the idea than she was, he lifted a hand and slid his fingers into her hair. When those fingertips touched the back of her scalp, a shot of desire blasted through her limbs.

She swallowed thickly. "Then we can go back to...to... the way things were before."

"Friends without kissing."

"Friends without kissing."

His other hand moved to her hip, and his fingers were in her hair. She'd seen Flynn kiss other women before, but she'd never paid close attention. Now she couldn't *not* pay attention.

It was as if the world had tipped violently on its axis, putting her squarely in his personal space and sharpening her awareness to a fine point.

She heard his breathing speed up, felt his heart thudding under her hand when she placed her palm on his chest. His eyelids drew down as he tilted her head gently and moved his mouth closer to hers.

Instinctively, she did the same.

When their mouths met, it wasn't surprising or awkward. The kiss was tender and curious as he stroked her jaw with his thumb and moved his mouth over hers. He opened, encouraging her to do the same. She complied, accepting his tongue on hers.

And, *Oh, yes, please, God, don't stop.*

It was like someone plugged her into a power source. Her body vibrated with need as her mouth moved eagerly over his. She couldn't get enough of the new, unfamiliar taste. Their tongues kept rhythm without their trying. Stroke, in. Stroke, out. It was mind-numbingly *incredible*.

He moved his hand from her hip to her back and tightened his hold. Her thundering heartbeat echoed between her legs as blood thrummed in her ears.

Then he pulled away, his chest moving up and down beneath her fingers, his eyes a murky, dark ocean blue. His hips tilted forward of their own volition and that's when she felt it. The very determined ridge of his erection pressing into her belly.

Her mouth opened and closed once, then twice, but no

sounds emerged. He'd yet to let go of her and she'd yet to untangle herself from his hold.

There weren't sparks this time around, that was an honest-to-goodness forest fire. An atom bomb. The burning surface of a thousand suns.

She blinked, wanting to *I Dream of Jeannie* herself back into last week before her entire life turned into a friends-to-lovers romance, but her surroundings didn't so much as wiggle.

Which meant this was real.

She was attracted to Flynn. *For real.*

And given his physical reaction and the way he was leaning in for another taste of her lips, it seemed Flynn was just as attracted to her.

Eleven

A breath away from laying his lips on Sabrina's for another taste, the knob turned back and forth on the front door like someone was attempting to barge in.

"I know you're in there!" came a voice from the other side.

"Reid," Sabrina breathed against Flynn's lips.

"I don't hear anything," he murmured, regretting giving Reid the passcode to his penthouse floor.

She flashed him a brief smile, but he detected worry in her eyes. "I should…"

She backed away like he'd caught fire, and damn if he didn't feel like he had. That experimental revisit to the Valentine's Day kiss had proved her theory 100 percent wrong.

They were attracted to each other. Either by proximity or convenience, or Sab's pointing out that they were single for the first time at the same time. Didn't matter why.

Now that he'd had a taste, he wanted more.

"You got a girl in there or something?" Gage shouted through the door as the knob jiggled again.

Sabrina's wide-eyed panic would've been cute if Flynn wasn't so turned on his brain was barely functioning.

"I was out with them tonight. Apparently they didn't like that I left them unsupervised." Thumbing her bottom lip, he sent a final longing look at her mouth before letting her dash out of the kitchen. She checked her hair and face in the mirror in the living room and he had to smile when she wrinkled her nose, worried.

"I look like I've been making out," she whispered.

"Hell yeah, you do." He couldn't hide his pride any more than she could hide those warm, rosy cheeks or the flush on her neck. "Gimme a second. I'll kill them, we'll hide the bodies and then we'll return to what we were doing."

With a wink to Sabrina, Flynn jerked open the door and blocked the crack with his body. "What do you want?"

Reid held up a six-pack of beer with one bottle missing as Gage held up the missing bottle. "We thought you might want company."

"And we want to know what happened with Sab...rin...a..." Reid's voice trailed off as Flynn widened the gap in the doorway to reveal Sabrina standing in the center of his foyer.

"Hey, guys!" she chirped. "I made cookies. Just like the old days!"

Reid swore and Gage ducked his head to hide a laugh.

"Come in. It's just cookies." *And kissing.* But they'd officially shut down that last part.

"Hello, Sabrina," Reid said like he was addressing his arch nemesis. "Beer?"

"No thanks. I'm going to bed. I'm exhausted."

Reid grinned and Sabrina backtracked, making herself appear guiltier in the process.

"I'm staying here. Temporarily. I'm staying in the guest room. My pipes are leaking and I don't have clean water. Plus, I need a shower, so I'll do that. In the guest bathroom, obviously." An uncomfortable giggle. "Not anywhere near Flynn's bedroom. I mean, not that it would matter."

Flynn shook his head and she gave him an apologetic shrug. He was going to catch hell from his best friends the second she fled the room, which she did three seconds after ensuring the oven was off.

Once she was ensconced in her bedroom and the shower cranked on in the attached bath, Flynn grabbed one of Reid's beers and headed for the living room.

"Well, well…" Gage, who'd helped himself to a cookie, swaggered in with Reid on his heels. "Sabrina has leaky pipes and your suggestion was for her to move in with you?"

"What would you have done?" Flynn asked, tipping the bottle.

"Called a plumber?" Reid suggested before having a seat on the sofa.

"I'm going to do that tomorrow. As well as rip her landlord a new one for neglecting her needs."

"Seems like you're in charge of *her needs* now." Reid's eyebrows jumped.

"In the meantime," Flynn continued, ignoring Reid's accusation, "she needed a place to stay. I'd have offered you both the same if the situation were reversed."

"Except you didn't kiss us at the Market on Valentine's Day," Gage supplied.

"And I wouldn't have made you cookies." Reid took in the canvases stacked by the window. "She appears to be staying awhile."

"As long as she needs."

Flynn didn't owe either of them explanations. But a few in his and Sabrina's defense filled his throat. She was also his best friend, she needed him and he wanted her here. Since those sounded like excuses, he said nothing.

"We didn't come over here to bust your balls about Sabrina, believe it or not," Gage said.

"Why are you here?" Flynn asked.

"We have a work conundrum," Reid answered.

"You changed my email password to keep me away from work." Flynn narrowed his eyelids in suspicion. "And now you *want me* to work?"

Did they have any idea how epically off their timing was?

"Right." Reid pursed his lips for a full three seconds before admitting, "We have...an issue. A minor issue, but one that could use your...expertise."

They had Flynn's attention. He tracked to the chair in the living room and sat, elbows on his knees. He leaned in with interest. "Tell me."

She'd heard Reid and Gage leave sometime around 1:00 a.m. She'd fallen into bed right out of the shower, and was asleep seconds after her head hit the pillow. Which explained the crinkled hairdo she was currently trying to tame with a brush and smoothing spray in her private bathroom. Long plagued by insomnia, she'd hoped she was through that phase of her life but it'd started up again around the same time as Flynn and Veronica split.

Which she'd thought was a coincidence until recently.

She'd tossed and turned and watched out the window at the city lights and the insistent moon that wasn't looking to give up its coveted spot in the sky to the sun anytime soon. Finally, she'd given up and climbed out of bed—still in her long-sleeved shirt from earlier, and panties and socks. She'd forgotten to pack pajamas, a situation she would rectify in the morning.

Cracking her bedroom door the slightest bit, she peeked down the silent hallway in one direction and toward the staircase in the other before deciding to risk running downstairs in her underwear for the midnight snack she'd been craving since her eyes popped open.

The moment her toes touched the wood floors of the hallway, the door at the end swung aside and Flynn ambled out shirtless. He was rubbing his eyes and looking as groggy and sleep-deprived as she felt, but by her estimation he looked much better in that state.

Her eyes feasted on the strong column of his neck, the wide set of his chest and trim stomach tapering to a pair of distracting Vs delineating either side of his hips. His boxer briefs were black, snugly fitting thick thighs that led down to sturdy male bare feet. By the time her inventory was complete, he noticed her standing there and paused about a yard away.

"I couldn't sleep," she said.

He scanned her body much in the way she'd done his, pausing at her panties—utilitarian, but he didn't seem to have the slightest aversion to her red cotton bikini briefs.

"I had to sleep in the shirt I wore," she blurted out. "I forgot my pajamas. I'll pick up some tomorrow."

As she bumbled out those three clumsy sentences, he advanced, backing her to the threshold of her guest bedroom. He touched her arm, a soothing stroke while he watched her. "You can borrow one of my T-shirts."

Her throat made a clicking sound as she swallowed past a very dry tongue.

He stole a glance at her mouth before backing away and scrubbing his face with one palm instead of ravishing her where she stood.

Shame.

When he opened his mouth the words "Ice cream?" fell out, sending her brain for a loop.

"Um…"

"Ice cream or I kiss you again. Those are your options."

A nervous laugh tittered out. "Do you…have tea?"

He flashed a devilish smile that made her knees go gooey. "I have tea."

He strode down the stairs and she watched him, trying to decide if it was okay to follow him in only her underwear while she enjoyed the way he looked from behind.

In the end, she opted not to overthink it. The idea of slipping into a pair of skinny jeans when she was this comfortable was as abhorrent as the idea of putting on a bra. They were adults and Flynn was far from a stranger. So, they'd kissed. So what? That didn't mean he was going to shove her gruffly against a wall and feast on her neck and her nipples, while his hand moved insistently between her legs...

"Mercy," she muttered, her hand over her throat as she came to a halt in the middle of the staircase.

"I know. The wide slats throw you off at first," he called from his position behind the counter, reading her reaction incorrectly.

Her hand tightened on the railing as she completed her descent but not because she was afraid of falling. Flynn was a distracting sight, shirtless in his kitchen. She couldn't see his boxers behind the counter, so for all her imagination knew he could be completely nude. And didn't that introduce a fine visual? Especially after she'd felt the evidence of his arousal against her this evening.

They went about dishing out ice cream and preparing tea in a silent dance, both either too weary or too wary to speak. Once she had filled her cup with hot water and he'd topped his scoops off with chocolate chips, peanut butter and sliced almonds, they went to the living room, where they both angled for the same cushion on the sofa.

"Sorry." She felt weirdly shy—something she'd never been around him.

"Ladies first. You're the guest." He pulled a blanket from the trunk that served as a coffee table. "In case you're cold," he explained. "But if you're not, don't cover up on my account."

She playfully rolled her eyes, but there was a nip in the

air of his cavernous apartment. She pulled the blanket over her lap as she sat and folded her legs beneath her.

Cupping her mug in both hands, she inhaled the spicy cinnamon scent of the tea and hummed happily. Regardless of the kiss or them being nearly naked and in close proximity to each other, she was happy here with him. Flynn had a way of making her life brighter and her day better. It was good to have him back in any capacity.

"Gage and Reid came to debrief me," he said.

"They're not allowed to do that! I told them any emergencies were to go to the management team or me."

"They wouldn't take issues to the management team instead of me if their lives depended on it. You know that."

"I know. But I wanted you to have a real break. What's it been, a week?"

"You deserve a real break, too, Sab." His lingering gaze did a better job of warming her than the blanket. "Bethany in accounting is leaving for Washington Business Loans."

"No!" She liked Bethany. "Why?"

"Reid said her fiancé works there and Bethany would like to work with him. Reid and Gage suggested offering her a pay raise and an extra week's vacation not to leave, but they wanted to clear it with me first."

"Oh. I guess that's reasonable. But then why did they come over and ask in person?"

"My guess? They wanted to have beers and dig up dirt on you and me."

The phrase "you and me" made them sound like a *them*. An idea as foreign as everything else that'd happened this week.

"I didn't help," she admitted. "I was obviously nervous. I talked too much. Ran away too quickly."

Flynn palmed her knee and the heat of his touch infused her very being. "It's not your fault, Sab. I told them about the kiss last week. They suspected more than that had happened after you dashed off to the shower. Don't worry, I told them nothing."

"Well. I guess it's silly to pretend we're doing something wrong." That sentence was one she'd been testing out in her head and now that she'd said it out loud, it was sort of silly.

"If anything, what we're doing feels scarily right." He ate a spoonful of ice cream. "I'm not sure what that means, but I'm sure we should stop overanalyzing it."

"Have you been analyzing it?"

"No. But you have. I can see it in your eyes. I'll bet there's a completed pros/cons list in that brain of yours."

"Not true!"

He cocked his head patiently. And dammit if he wasn't right.

"*Fine*. But I call it a plus/minus list, just so you know."

"What's in my plus column?" He asked that like he couldn't think of a single reason why he'd be a plus.

"You're my best friend," she answered rather than recite his yummy physical attributes. "Ironically, that's item number one in your minus column, too."

Twelve

Okay, yes. He would hand it to Sabrina that this situation was a little...odd. Not their usual mode of operation and possibly a bad idea for the reason she'd placed at the top of both lists: they were best friends.

But there was something to say for the impulsiveness of the Valentine's Day kiss on the pier. And there was even more to say about the kiss in his kitchen that was as premeditated as they came.

"You're worrying about...*this* ruining our friendship?"

A strangled sound left her throat like she couldn't believe he'd asked that question. "Aren't you?"

"I'm not worried about anything. I was told to take a hiatus for the specific reason of not worrying about anything. Isn't that right?"

Her posture relaxed some, her legs moving slightly under the blanket. Her bare legs. Her long, smooth, bare legs.

He wanted to touch her, and not in a soothing way. Not in a consoling way.

He wanted to touch her in a sexual, turn-her-on, see-what-sounds-she-makes-when-she's-coming way. If she decided she'd have him, he'd take her upstairs before she could say the words *plus* or *minus*.

"What do you suggest we do, Flynn? Sit here and make out?"

"That's a good start."

Her delicate throat moved when she swallowed, her eyes flaring with desire.

Yeah, she wanted him, too. It was time she stopped denying it. He set his ice cream bowl aside and carefully took her hot tea from her hands.

"I wasn't done with that."

"You're done with that."

When he reached for the blanket, her hand stopped him. They were frozen in that stance, his hand on her blanket-covered thigh, her hand on his hand and their eyes locked in a battle that wasn't going to end with them going to separate bedrooms if he had anything to say about it.

"Do you want this?" He watched her weigh the options, jerking her gaze away from his and opening her mouth ineffectually before closing it again. "It's a simple question, Sabrina. Do you want this?"

"Yes—"

He didn't let her finish that sentence—finishing it for her by sealing his lips on hers in a deep, driving kiss as he tore the blanket from her lap. She caught his face with her palms, but leaned into him, opening her soft mouth and giving him a taste of what he hadn't gotten enough of earlier this evening.

He ran his hand over her knee to her outer thigh and then to her panties. They weren't the thong he'd expected, but he couldn't care less. She wasn't going to be wearing them long.

After gliding her fingertips over his jaw and his neck, she rerouted and grazed the light patch of chest hair over one nipple. He groaned into her mouth. She responded with a kittenish mewl before digging her blunt fingernails into his rib cage in an effort to draw him closer.

It was the encouragement he needed.

Shifting his weight so he wasn't crushing her, he flattened a palm on her back and pulled her to him. She came willingly, both hands on his abs as he switched their positions and reclined on his back.

With her on top, he held her thick hair away from her face and continued kissing her, the position reminding him of the erotic dream he'd had not so long ago. The strands of her hair tickled his cheeks and her breath came in fast little pants when he gave her a chance to catch it.

It felt good to feel good. It had been a long time for him. And according to her, a *really* long time since Sabrina had felt this good. He couldn't think of a single reason not to make love to her right here on this couch.

He wanted to bury the past year in the soft lemon scent of her skin and give in to the attraction that had rattled them both for the last week-plus. Maybe longer, if he was honest.

She sat up abruptly like she might shove him away, but instead she crisscrossed her arms, grabbed the hem of her shirt and whipped it over her head. Flynn had thought her legs were amazing. Sabrina's legs had nothing on her breasts. Her small shoulders lifted and he zeroed in on her nipples—dark peach and too tempting to resist. He stole a quick glance at her and grinned, and when she grinned back it was as good as permission.

Propped on his elbows, he wrapped one hand around her rib cage and took one beautiful breast deep into his mouth. He let go, teasing and tickling her nipple with his tongue. Her cute kittenish mewls from earlier were long gone. He was rewarded with the sultry moans of a woman at the pinnacle of pleasure. He couldn't allow her to reach the pinnacle yet. There was more to do.

Turning her so her back was to the couch, he gave himself more room to maneuver. He slipped his fingers past the edge of her red panties to stroke her folds. She was wet and she was warm and she was also willing to reciprocate.

While he worked over her other breast, his fingers moving at a hastened speed, she cupped his shaft and gave him a stroke. And another, and then one more, until he had to pull his lips from her body to let out a guttural groan.

"Flynn," came her desperate plea. "I need you."

"I need you, too." So bad he could hardly think. Ending the torture of foreplay, he swept her panties down her legs and paused long enough to strip off his briefs. Only then did he hesitate. There was a small matter of birth control to consider before they continued. "Condom. I have one upstairs."

She nodded hastily. "I'll come with you."

"Yeah," he said with a lopsided smile because damn, he was at ease right now. "That'd be best."

He snatched her hand and helped her up, leaving their dishes and scattered clothing where they lay. They darted up the stairs naked, but not before he gave her a playful swat and sent her ahead of him. He had to get a better look at that ass, and since she'd robbed him of the pleasure of a thong, he hadn't had the chance to admire it yet.

Sabrina naked was a beautiful sight.

Her bottom was heart-shaped, leading to a slim waist, strong back and small shoulders. Each and every inch of her was deliciously toned yet soft and touchable. And touching her was exactly what he intended to do.

At the back of the hallway, she entered his bedroom and turned around. His breath snagged. Not only were her dusky nipples perched on the tips of her breasts like gumdrops, but between her legs she was gloriously bare. He'd noticed when he touched her with his fingers, but seeing it nearly brought him to his knees.

She bit her bottom lip, white teeth scraping plump pink flesh and setting him off like a match to a fuse.

When he caught up to her, he wrapped her in his arms and cupped her bare butt with both hands, giving her cheeks a squeeze. They tumbled backward onto his king-size bed framed by a leather headboard.

She looked good on his deep charcoal-gray duvet and crisp white sheets beneath. The contrast of her dark hair spread over the white pillowcase made him glad he didn't have a drop of color in this room. Sabrina added her own. From her pink cheeks to her bright blue toenail polish.

He found a condom in the nightstand drawer and rolled it on, his hands shaking with anticipation. She must have noticed, because next she caught his wrist and smiled. Then she nodded, anxious to get to the next part—almost as anxious as he.

Positioned over her, he thrust his hips and entered her in one long, smooth stroke. She pressed her head into the pillow, lifting her chin and saying a word that would forever echo in the caverns of his mind.

"Yes."

It was damn nice to hear.

She felt like heaven. Holding him from within as reverently as she held him with her arms now. His throat tightened as he shoved away every thought aside of the woman beneath him. Which wasn't hard to do, since the physical act of making love to Sabrina Douglas was a singular experience.

If there was room for any other thoughts, he couldn't find it.

He rocked into her gently as they found their rhythm in the dark. Save the slice of moonlight painting a stripe on the bedding, the room was marked with shadows. He had no trouble making out the slope of her breasts or the luscious curve of her hips.

And when he had to close his eyes—when the gravity of what was happening between them was too much to bear—he still saw her naked form on the screen of his eyelids.

The vision stayed until he gave in to his powerful release, caught his breath and was finally able to open his eyes.

Thirteen

Light filtered in through slits in her eyelids, but that wasn't what woke Sabrina the next morning. It was the tickling sensation against her forearm that beckoned her toward the sun. When that tickling climbed higher up her arm, she shivered and popped her eyes open.

Goose bumps decorated her arm and the tickling sensation was courtesy of the tip of a dry paintbrush. Flynn dragged the brush over her collarbone and down over the top of her breasts. She was only slightly alarmed to find she was still naked.

The man currently painting her with shudders had made her shudder *plenty* last night before they fell asleep side by side in his very big bed. It'd been a long time since she'd had sex. The physical act of making love was amazing. Almost as amazing as the man she'd made love with.

Flynn's stubble shifted as his smile took over his face. He was a glorious sight. His messy hair was bathed in Seattle's morning sun. His blue eyes dipped to follow the path of the paintbrush down and over the crest of her breast.

She smiled, drugged by this stunning new facet of their relationship.

"You're dressed," she croaked, her morning voice in full effect. "No fair."

"I picked up coffee and croissants. Thought I'd wake you before you slept the day away. And before your coffee went cold."

"What time is it?"

"Little after eleven."

"Eleven!" She bolted upright in bed and looked around for a clock. Not finding one, she pressed a button on her phone. 11:14 a.m. "Wow. I never sleep this late."

His grin endured and she narrowed one eye.

"Don't be cocky."

"Hard not to be." He stood and slid the paintbrush into his back pocket. "Come on. Breakfast awaits."

She didn't know where he bought the croissants, but they were the best she'd ever tasted. Especially with strawberry jam and a healthy dollop of butter. The coffee was perfection, and she had the passing thought that this would be a splendid way to spend every morning.

"You seem to have settled into your hiatus okay," she teased.

"You had a lot to do with that." He slathered a croissant with jam and took a huge bite. After he swallowed, he added, "I thought you being here would help me relax, but I didn't expect you to help me relax that much."

An effervescent giggle tickled her throat. The low hum of a warning sounded in the back of her mind but she ignored it. She didn't want to consider what could've changed—what definitely *had* changed—since last night. "I think it's safe to say that neither of us expected that."

"Or expected it to be that great." His eyebrows jumped as he took another bite.

"It *was* great." Her eyebrows closed in as she turned

over that unexpected thought. "This is oddly comfortable. I guess it shouldn't be odd. It's not like we don't know each other. It's just that now we know each other…biblically."

That earned her a rough chuckle, a sound she loved to hear from her best friend no matter the situation. Only now that chuckle sent chills up and down her arms much like the paintbrush this morning. Sex had added a layer to their friendship that she wasn't done exploring.

"I talked to your landlord."

"And?"

"He bitched a lot about how he regretted buying the building, which he affectionately called a 'dump,' and then he mentioned that they've been looking into leaks in the apartments above you and below, but yours is the one they can't isolate."

"Lovely. I was so adamant about having that apartment in particular." She shook her head with a token amount of regret. At the time she hadn't been thinking about the lack of light coming in through the windows or the noise coming from overhead and on both sides of her since she was in the center of the C-shaped brick building. "I was too busy admiring the rough wood flooring and the open layout and the proximity to the elevator to think of much else."

"Doesn't look like you'll be going back to your own apartment anytime soon. I have plenty of space here." He watched her carefully, as if waiting for her to argue.

That alarm buzzed a little louder, warning her that things were changing—*had changed*, she mentally corrected. But how could she say no? She wanted to make Flynn happy, and herself, and sex with him had ticked both boxes with one overlapping checkmark. Her apartment had sprung a leak—so there was no sense in living like she was in a third-world country when she had Flynn's penthouse on loan. Plus, who was to say that they couldn't go back to normal after a sabbatical filled with great sex and plenty of Flynn's deep chuckles?

There. Now that she'd justified that, she felt like she could respond.

"You do have plenty of space." She shrugged. "I can't think of any reason to leave."

"Good. You should stay. We'll see if we can one-up last night." He waggled his eyebrows and a laugh burst from her lips. Who knew the secret to pulling Flynn from his shell was sex? Who knew they'd be so damn good at it?

His phone vibrated on the table next to him. He broke eye contact for a cursory glance at the screen.

"That better not be work," she warned.

"I don't work anymore."

"Very funny." She sipped her coffee. "Is there at least part of you that's enjoying the break? Besides us sharing a bedroom?" she added, figuring he would've added it for her.

"It still chaps my ass that most of Monarch's grand pooh-bahs would rather send me out the door than come into the twenty-first century with me."

"They're in love with the way things were, which is standard for most old companies. Monarch's stockholders were nervous when Emmons died and there wasn't anything you were going to be able to do to prevent that."

She'd vowed to table this conversation until after his hiatus but since he'd opened the discussion she no longer saw the point in holding her tongue.

"You are *not* your father. The changes you made when you took over were made *because* you're different from your father. I didn't like who you were changing into." She ignored his pleated brow and continued. "I wanted my Flynn back."

He watched her for a long beat. In a way Flynn was never hers, and yet he'd always belonged to her in some fashion. She didn't have the romantic part of his heart—even now.

Her smile came easily when she considered what a relief that was. Flynn's place was at her side. They could care about each other, blow each other's minds in bed and escape their entanglement unscathed. She had faith in both of them—and anyway, he'd already promised their friendship wouldn't change.

"I deserve that." His shoulders lifted and dropped in a sigh of surrender. "You've always looked out for me, Sabrina. Always."

He reached across the table and took her hand, gently holding her fingers, his eyes on his empty plate.

"I always will be." Just as she knew he'd be there for her.

Sabrina collected her pajamas and a few more changes of clothing from her apartment. Flynn had invited her to stay and she'd failed at reasoning her way out of it. Not that she should. They had always needed each other and now they needed each other in a different way, a physical way. She was more than happy to reap the rewards for the rest of their sabbatical.

"Rewards like an insanely hot, wealthy best friend who curls your toes in the evening and makes you laugh in the daytime."

Even though she was talking to herself and no one else was there, she hesitated to use the word *boyfriend* or the phrase "guy she was dating" because that wasn't who Flynn was. Not really.

"Then who is he?" she asked herself after collecting her mail. She walked to her bedroom dresser and plucked out a few shirts along with a few pairs of sexy underwear worthy of hot nights in the sack.

He was…

"Flynn."

That was enough explanation for her.

She hesitated packing pajamas before tossing a shorts

set onto the bed. The oft-ignored top shelf of her closet caught her eye, specifically the spines of her journals. It'd been a long time since she sat and sketched an idea for a painting, or wrote an entry.

A vision of her in a T-shirt, stroking the brush down the canvas, filled her with purpose, and when Flynn stepped into the picture and swept her hair aside to kiss her neck, a zing of excitement flitted through her.

She flipped through the journals in search of inspiration, finally settling on the one filled with sketches of birds. If Flynn's mantel needed anything, it was a breath of life. A bird on a perch watching over his lonely penthouse when she wasn't there sounded perfect. It made her sad to think of "the end," but before she could explore that thought further another journal toppled from the uppermost shelf and fell open.

She bent to retrieve it, smiling at her sloppy college handwriting and doodles in the margins. She'd written about places where she and Flynn—and Gage and Reid—had hung out back in their college years. Chaz's, which had been their hangout ever since, and the restaurant that served the best burger in town: Fresh Burger. Before veggie burgers were trending, they'd served up a black-bean and poblano pepper masterpiece that the guys sometimes chose over basic beef. She slapped the book shut, pleased with her finding. She had another idea for what she and Flynn could do together.

"Besides have sex," she reminded herself. Her mission during this hiatus was to guide Flynn back to his former self.

She packed the journals with the rest of her clothes into a bag and carried her things to the door. She'd just pulled out her front door key to lock up when a thick Chicago-accented voice behind her nearly scared her out of her skin.

"Your boyfriend called about the plumbing. You know

you can call me and talk to me directly. You don't have to
send in the heavy." Her landlord had a thick dark mustache,
a receding hairline and a particularly unpleasant demeanor.

"I *did* call you directly, Simon," she told him patiently.
"You didn't return my calls. Also, Flynn is my best friend
not my boyfriend."

He frowned and so did she. Clarifying that for herself
was one thing, but there really wasn't any reason to do it
for her landlord.

"I'm not sure when we're going to have it fixed." His
dark eyes inventoried her tote bag and her person in a way
that made her uncomfortable.

"Well, you have my number. And Flynn's. Flynn and I
actually are dating, I don't know why I said we weren't."

Fortunately, Mrs. Abernathy picked that opportune moment to open her front door and save Sabrina from their
potentially lecherous landlord.

"You and Flynn are dating! I am so excited!" Mrs. Abernathy rushed out of her apartment and into the hallway.
She was wearing classy appliquéd blue jeans and a floral
top. Her jewelry was gold and shiny, and her nails perfectly manicured. "Did the books help? Tell me the books
helped. I believe that romance novels are magical. They
bring people together."

Rightly sensing this wasn't a topic for him, Simon grumbled something about women that was likely sexist before
hustling down the hall to ruin someone else's day.

"I enjoyed the books," Sabrina told Mrs. Abernathy. She
didn't know if they'd helped but they definitely hadn't hurt.

"I knew you two would be good together. Every time you
insisted that you and Flynn were just friends, I doubted it
in my heart of hearts." She put her hand to the gold chain
around her neck, and her fingers closed around the diamond
dangling there. "My Reginald, when he was alive, was the
most romantic man. Tell me your Flynn is romantic."

Sabrina's cheeks warmed when she thought about what they'd done together last night. Surely there was a PG-rated nugget she could share with her romance-loving neighbor.

"Well…he woke me up this morning by tickling me with a paintbrush. And he also went out and bought coffee and croissants for breakfast." She checked the hallway for Simon once more, but he'd already gone. She lowered her voice anyway when she continued. "And he called Simon and demanded he fix my plumbing issue."

"That's *very* romantic." Mrs. Abernathy's smile faded. "Except for the plumbing situation. Is that still going on?" She checked the hallway, too, before whispering, "I don't like that man."

"I don't think *anyone* likes that man." Sabrina wished her neighbor a good day before turning for the elevator.

As the doors swished shut, Mrs. Abernathy called, "Are you staying with Flynn, then?"

In the closing gap between the elevator doors, Sabrina smiled. "Yes. Yes, I am."

Fourteen

Fresh Burger's salsa fries were a thing of beauty.

Sabrina pulled out a hand-cut fry dripping in fresh pico de gallo, melty cheese and sour cream and groaned in ecstasy around a bite.

She swiped a napkin over her mouth. "If I eat another bite, I'll die."

"Back away from the fries, Douglas."

Watching her eat was fun. Watching her do *anything* was fun. Flynn's brain had been a minefield of what he'd do to her and what he'd like her to do to him the second the sun went down. For that, he needed her not to eat herself into a food coma. He swiped her plate out from in front of her and polished off her fries.

They left Fresh Burger and stepped into cold, spitting rain that was turning to snow—a typical February day in Seattle. Sabrina wrapped her arms around her middle and huddled closer. He held her against him while their steps lined up on the sidewalk. Nothing out of the usual for them, but now it felt different to have her in the cradle of his arms.

Protecting her, watching out for her—those ideas were nothing new. But wanting to please her on a carnal, sexual level? Whole new ballgame. Hell, he wasn't sure it was the same sport.

He'd had plenty of girlfriends and one wife, so he knew how relationships went. This one wasn't like those. It was a mashup of his favorite things: a best friend who was on his side plus an exciting new experience between the sheets. The difference in this relationship was that he wasn't trying to get to know Sabrina. He *knew* Sabrina.

He knew she loved peanut butter and hated olives. He knew she'd fallen off the stage in an eighth grade play and earned the nickname "Crash." He knew that as cool as she'd played it, Craig had broken her heart and she'd spent months wondering if she'd ever recover.

Since Flynn already knew those things about her, he could concentrate on learning other things. Like she had sensitive nipples, or that she slept with her mouth slightly open. That she murmured in her sleep and clung to him like a sloth on a tree limb.

"What are you smiling about? Is it funny that I'm cold?" she complained next to him.

"I'm not smiling because you're cold. Do you want to go home? Watch a movie? Paint?"

"I tried painting today. It didn't work."

"Not true. You took out the paint, but you didn't put a single line of color on that canvas. How am I supposed to replace the artwork over the mantel if you won't create one for me?"

"I'm out of practice," she said when they reached his car. He opened the door for her and she slid in. That halted the conversation until he climbed in next to her and started the engine.

Revving it a few times while he adjusted the heat, he said, "You can't put it off forever."

"Says the man who's supposed to be relaxing."

"Relaxing is boring."

"You spent most of the day on the laptop. Doing what? I know not checking your social media."

No, not that. He'd spent most of the day writing a fresh business plan. One that combined his ideas and his father's way of doing things. He wasn't sure how to blend the two approaches yet, but there had to be a way. Sad that their collaboration had to happen on the wrong side of the grave, but Flynn didn't have much choice. Sab had pointed out that he hadn't taken time off for bereavement. He supposed now was as good a time as any to mourn.

"I was writing for my mental health."

"Journaling?" Her lips pursed and her eyebrows went up.

"Kind of. And no, you can't read it."

"Understood. I have journals I wouldn't want you to read either. Even though I read you the one about Fresh Burger." She dug the journal and a pen out of her bag and drew a checkmark next to the entry. "It'd be cool to do some more of these things." She turned a page. "Do you have Jell-O?"

"Why? Are we going to fill an inflatable swimming pool with it and wrestle?" He shot her a grin.

"No! For Jell-O shots."

Ah, well. He tried.

"What about the time we repainted my dorm?" she asked as she flipped forward to another page. "Your place could use some color."

"The only painting you'll be doing is on canvas. You were the one who said you wanted to make art while you were off work."

Like he was open to halting the transformation into his old man and becoming more like his old self—he also wanted Sabrina to find her old self. She used to be confident; certain about what she wanted. Evidence of both her confidence and certainty made an appearance now and then, but not often enough. He'd hoped her going back to doing what she loved, painting, would unlock that door for her.

She was hell-bent on taking care of him, but what she didn't know was that he was returning the favor. He wasn't the only one in need of change in his life.

So was his best-friend-turned-lover.

Halfway into making their second batch of Jell-O shots, Sabrina was feeling darn pleased with herself for convincing Flynn to give it a try.

After their burger-and-coffee date, they stopped at a supermarket to procure what they needed to make strawberry and lime Jell-O shots. Flynn had a liquor cabinet that was well-stocked, though he hesitated slightly before allowing her to put the Cabo Wabo tequila into the lime Jell-O. He insisted it was better enjoyed straight. Good thing she was convincing.

Plastic containers stacked in his fridge to solidify, Flynn excused himself to the bathroom while she wiped down the countertops with damp paper towels. She lifted his phone to move it when it buzzed in her hand. A quick glance at the screen showed a message from Veronica. A second buzz followed—another message from her, as well.

Sabrina caught the words "so sorry" and "mistake" before she placed the phone facedown on the counter and stared at it like it was a live cobra.

It wasn't her fault she'd seen Veronica's name or accidentally read a word or two, but she would be culpable if she flipped the phone over to read the messages in their entirety.

And oh how she wanted to...

But.

She wouldn't.

She finished cleaning the kitchen and Flynn returned,

cracked open a beer and took a long pull. She waited for him to lift his cell phone and check the screen, but he didn't. Not even when she picked up hers.

"It's supposed to be partly sunny tomorrow." She showed him the cartoon sun and cloud on her cell phone's screen.

"Good day for you to paint," he said, taking another sip from his beer bottle.

She checked her personal email next, deleting a few newsletters from clothing stores before coming across an email from her mom. Her mother lived in Sacramento with Sabrina's stepfather and checked in once a week. She was a technical writer and considered any form of communication other than the written one superfluous. Sabrina was keying in a reply when she noticed Flynn finally reaching for his cell phone.

He gave the screen a cursory glance, frowned and then pocketed it.

It was on the tip of her tongue to ask "why the frown?" but she didn't. When he didn't offer any intel either, she returned her attention to her own phone. She finished the email to her mom and clicked Send, more than a little troubled that Flynn hadn't confided in her that Veronica was clearly trying to weasel her way back into his life.

"What do we do while the Jell-O sets?"

"You have to ask?" He plucked the phone from her hand and gripped her hips, pulling her against him. He dipped his head to kiss her and she wrapped her arms around his neck, enjoying the slow slide of their lips and tongues.

She fit against him like she was designed to be there, her breasts against his chest and her hips nestled against his. How had she never noticed that before? He slanted his head to deepen the kiss, and a low male groan vibrated off her rib cage.

Wait. That last vibration was his phone.

She pulled her lips from his when the buzz came from his pocket again. "Do you need to get that?"

"No." He rerouted them from the kitchen to the stairs, climbing with her while kissing her. Their lips pulled apart several times during the clumsy ascent, their laughter quelled by more kisses.

She shouldn't be jealous of Veronica, for goodness' sake. Veronica wasn't in Flynn's bed—Sabrina was.

"Your room or mine?" Her voice was a seductive purr.

"My bed is bigger." He kept walking her backward, his eyes burning hers and his mouth hovering close. "I have a plan for you and it's going to require a lot of room."

"Oh, really?"

"Probably. Are you a squirmer?"

"Why do you ask?"

"I have to taste you, Sabrina. I have to know."

Her mouth dropped open as a spot between her legs fluttered to life.

"Yeah?" He smirked.

Speechless, she nodded.

In his bedroom, he stood over her and the bed and slowly stripped her. The thin sweater and T-shirt she wore underneath went first. Then he thumbed open her jeans and slipped both hands into them, his palms molding her backside.

"Thong," he praised. "That's more like it."

"I packed some this time."

"Why didn't you before?"

"I… I'm not sure. I guess I was trying to stay in my friend role."

"You're still in the friend role, Sab. It's just that now there are added perks."

"Perks, huh?"

"Do you prefer bonuses?"

"No." She laughed with him as he yanked her jeans to

her feet. He helped her with her shoes and socks and then she stepped from the pant legs.

"Ready to feel good?" From his position on his knees, he looked up at her, his expression as sincere as his offer.

The moment she jerked her head up and down in the affirmative, he put a kiss just under her belly button before dragging his tongue along the waistband of her panties.

Pressing her knees together, she wiggled her hips. He was right. She was a squirmer.

He rolled the thong down to her thighs and she rested her hands on his shoulders when he prompted her to step out of them. Then he tossed them over his head and held her calf gingerly with one hand.

"Throw your leg over my shoulder," he instructed. She did, opening herself to him, her heart thundering as he took in her most private place. He did so approvingly before cupping her backside and leaning in for a slow, intentional taste. That's when her other knee buckled.

He held her to him like he was sampling the sweetest fruit and then feasted on her while she fought to hold herself upright and not dissolve.

When he finally took her over, she folded from the power of her orgasm, coming on a cry that could've woken the dead.

The next thing she knew she was on her back in his bed and his talented mouth was sampling her breasts. She held his head and writhed, sensitive from his earlier pampering. Her hips lifted and bumped against his jean-clad leg between her thighs.

"Please, Flynn." She fumbled with the stud on his jeans and cupped his erection. He drove forward into her hand, allowing her to massage him until she was holding several inches of hard steel.

Shoving his chest, she pushed him to his back and lifted his shirt, revealing abs and a happy trail of hair leading south. She reveled in the thought that it was her trail to follow down, *down* until she reached the promised land. She rolled his jeans and boxer briefs to his thighs and his erection sprang to life, very happy to see her indeed.

Before she gave it a second of thought, she lowered her head and licked him from base to tip.

His hips bucked, accompanying a feral growl. She opened wide and took him into her mouth, running her tongue along the ridge of his penis and slicking him again and again.

He guided her with his hand on the back of her head, his fingers twined in her hair. When she dared look up from her work, she saw the most exquisite combination of pleasure-pain on his face. His desperate need for her turned her on more than what he'd done to her earlier. She doubled her efforts, but he stopped her short, gentling her mouth off him and catching his breath.

He was a sight to behold, shirt rucked up over his bare chest, pants no farther down than his thighs. She liked this uncontrolled, unplanned disarray. It wasn't a way she'd ever experienced him. That there were still new ways for them to be together was exciting.

Before she became too smug, Flynn threw her for another loop.

"On your back or on your knees?" He gave her a wicked grin. "We're doing both, but I'll let you pick where we start."

Fifteen

"It never once occurred to you to have sex to scratch an itch?" Flynn asked.

They'd started with Sabrina on her knees, which thrilled him—he'd known she had confidence stocked away for emergencies—and then finished with him on top, her on her back. Her eyes had blazed into his as he'd thrust them into oblivion. They were very, very good at pleasing each other, that was for damn sure.

They were in his bed, sheets pulled haphazardly over their bodies. Between them, his right hand and her left were intertwined, his thumb moving over hers while they talked.

"Why is that so hard to believe?" she turned her head to ask.

He turned his head and shot her a dubious look. "You are a live firecracker and you dare ask me that question? What have you been doing to get by all this time?"

She rolled her eyes, but her smile widened. He'd flattered her. He liked flattering her. Almost as much as he liked having sex with her. Hell, that was a lie. He liked having sex with her more than anything.

"*I managed.* I haven't seen you taking any strangers home since you and Veronica split."

At the mention of his ex-wife, his mouth pulled into an upside-down U. The truth was, he hadn't wanted anyone after he'd found out Veronica was cheating on him. As emasculating as it was to learn she didn't love him anymore, that had compounded when he found out she'd been fucking Julian. He didn't know which one of them to hate more so he settled on hating both of them. The hate had faded, but the anger was still there. She'd texted him several times today in an attempt at the lamest apology on the planet, which had downgraded his anger to disgust. Though, it might've been more of a lateral move.

No doubt she'd grown tired of Julian the Artist. He looked good on paper—or canvas, as it were—but where real responsibility and presence were required, he was a no-show. Julian cared about Julian more than anyone. It probably shouldn't, but it gave Flynn a shot of satisfaction to know that Veronica was likely comparing the two brothers and noticing that even with his money and inheritance, Julian wasn't measuring up.

"She contacted me," he told Sabrina.

"I know."

Guilt shadowed her face. "I was cleaning the countertop and saw her name pop up on your phone. I didn't read the messages, though."

"She's sorry. Which I already knew."

"Didn't we all," Sabrina said, droll.

"I didn't run out and get laid after we split because I was heartsick and wounded." It was the most truth he'd admitted to anyone—himself included. "She was my world before we fell apart. I should've seen it coming—read the signs. I don't know how I missed it. Guess I was preoccupied with Monarch, which is a lame excuse." Veronica had always told him he couldn't focus on work and her at the same time. God knew he'd tried to satisfy her. Where she was concerned, filling her "needs" seemed to be a bottomless pit.

"Lame, but nonetheless true." Sabrina squeezed his fingers before letting go of his hand and rolling to face him. He stole a peek at her breasts, beautiful and plush resting one on top of the other. He had to force himself to look into her eyes while she talked. Something she'd noticed, given her saucy smile.

"Were you in love with her when you found out she'd been unfaithful? Or had you two been growing apart?"

"We'd been growing apart…like, I don't know, two ships drifting in the ocean. Wow, that is a bad metaphor."

"Horrible."

He allowed himself a small laugh. "We used to be in love. So in love we were stupid with it. We didn't eat or sleep, we just…" He bit his tongue rather than finish the sentence. Best friend or no, he doubted Sabrina would appreciate hearing about past *sexcapades* with his ex-wife. "We wanted to be together all the time. You know how it is."

"I don't, actually." Her eyes roamed the room, not landing on one spot in particular while she spoke. "The day we went through our list of exes, I was thinking about how sad my experience has been with relationships. I was enamored with a few, and smitten by one or two, but I never uttered the *L* word."

"Never?" He didn't like hearing that. Everyone should feel loved and love in return—at least once—even if it was misguided.

"No. I didn't think it would change what was between us for the better."

"And none of those guys expected you to be in love with

them? I would've thought Phillip might've been chirping those three words like a smitten lovebird."

"Oh, he did." Her laughter softened the hard knot in his chest that had been there for too long. "He knew I wasn't that into him, I think. Which hurt his feelings." She bit her lip like she was debating what to say next. "When we broke up, he said it was because he couldn't be second place any longer. He thought I was holding out for you. Wouldn't he have the last laugh if he saw us now? Sleeping together and living together."

Now, obviously, Flynn knew he and Sabrina had just had sex. Also, *obviously*, he was planning on having more sex while she, *yes*, lived here. But hearing that she was both sleeping with him and living with him stated in plain language sounded almost…ominous.

What would anyone say if they knew? If Gage and Reid knew the whole truth. If Veronica knew. If Julian knew…

"Yeah. Unbelievable," Flynn murmured, his mind on the fallout. Fallout he hadn't let himself consider before this moment. He'd been too preoccupied with enjoying himself for a change. It was nice not to play the role of Atlas bearing the weight of the world on his back.

After a long pause, he admitted something else he hadn't planned on saying aloud. "You deserve that, Sab. That stupid love. You deserve to feel it at least once."

"Yeah, maybe," she said, sounding contemplative.

Flynn didn't feel so much contemplative as wary. Sabrina *did* deserve to feel that kind of bone-deep love, but she wasn't going to find it with him. He was good for sex. He was a great friend, but the love part he was done with.

He wouldn't risk diving into the deep end again, not after he'd nearly drowned. It was safer on the shore, with her. It was also completely unfair to tie her up with whatever this was between them when he knew she deserved better.

He cared about her too much to let her go, and he cared too much to keep her. That thought darkened his mood and kept his eyes open and on the ceiling for the next hour while she slept in his arms.

It'd been so long since she'd had a paintbrush in her hand, Sabrina almost didn't know where to start. But once she was over the fear of the blank canvas and drew that first line of paint, she'd be fine.

Noise-canceling headphones over her ears, music piping through them, she danced as she painted those first simple strokes onto the canvas. By the time she'd shaded in the shape of the chickadee, a familiar, easy confidence flooded through her. She could do this. She'd done it dozens of times.

She painted the bird's delicate taupe and tan and white feathers and used a razor-thin brush to fill in his tiny pointed beak and delicate, spindly legs. She placed him on a tender branch and added a few spring buds and lush, green leaves, finishing off the painting by adding a pale blue background.

Pulling her headphones off, she stood back from the easel to admire her work. Still wet, and far from perfect, but the painting was all hers. Created from her imagination and brought to life through acrylics. It was exhilarating to think about what she was capable of with a few simple tools.

Once she'd been completely confident in her painting abilities. She'd endeavored to sell them, or show them at an art exhibit. She didn't let go of that dream all at once. It'd faded slowly. She'd put her brushes and acrylics in her closet, and then she'd tucked away her canvases, as well. She'd been distracted by life and friends and family—Flynn and Luke included—and there suddenly wasn't enough time or room for hobbies.

She frowned, wondering how many other loves she'd sidelined over the years.

"What is that? Sparrow?" Flynn jogged down the stairs wearing jeans and a T-shirt, a laundry hamper hooked under his arm.

"It's a chickadee." She smiled, amused by the sight of Flynn in the midst of doing laundry. "I'm assuming you're sending that out somewhere?"

"Yeah. I'm sending it to the washing machine," he said with a displeased frown.

"I did your laundry in college. You always hated it."

"Who the hell likes to do laundry?" He gave her a sideways smile. "You should feel reassured that I don't need you to do my laundry."

That was too close to "I don't need you" for her to feel reassured about anything. Her very identity was wrapped up in being needed by Flynn, and now wanted by Flynn... a thought she definitely wasn't going to explore deeper.

"I'm going to paint him a friend." She tilted her head to study the painting. "He seems lonely."

"Why? Do they mate for life or something?"

"No, actually." She'd researched them when she'd practiced drawing chickadees in her journal. Sadly, her sweet little bird wasn't a one-chick kind of guy. "They're socially monogamous."

"What the hell's that mean?"

"They're only together to procreate."

"Typical guy. Only there for the sex."

Her laugh was weak as that comment settled into her gut like a heavy stone. Sounded like her current situation with Flynn.

"If you have anything to throw in..." He tilted his head to indicate the laundry room before walking in that direction.

Sabrina's mind retreated back to his college dorm room.

To sitting next to him on his bed while he searched through a pile of clothes for a "cleanish" shirt. The memory was vivid and so welcome.

Remembering who they were to each other eased her nerves. She wasn't some convenient girl and he wasn't a random hot guy. This was Flynn. She knew him better than anyone.

She rinsed the paint off her palette and cleaned her brushes, considering something she had never considered before. What if they had real potential beyond best friends with benefits? What if they'd overlooked it for years? They could blame inconvenience since they'd been dating other people until now, or they could blame their friendship. They'd accepted their role as friends so completely, it hadn't occurred to them to take it to the next level.

But now that they had taken it to the next level, now that they had been naked together on more than one occasion—and she was looking forward to it again—was there more to them than just friends or just sex? And if there was a possibility to move into the next realm, was she brave enough to try?

Wide hands gripped her hips and she jumped, dropping her paintbrushes. They clattered into the stainless steel sink where she'd been cleaning them.

"Oh!" She spun to find Flynn looking pretty damn proud of himself. She gave him a playful shove. "I'm not sure I like this version of you."

He lowered his face until his mouth hovered over hers. "I don't believe you. I think you like this version of me just fine."

Unable to argue, she lifted her chin and placed a sweet kiss on his lips. Just a quick one. He didn't let her get away with quick, though, kissing her deeply and wrapping his arms around her waist. Lost in the pleasure of his mouth, she clung to his neck.

When they parted, she sighed happily, opening lazy eyelids. "We have plans later. We can't only paint and do laundry and make out in the kitchen."

"What plans?"

She trickled a fingertip down his neck and along the collar of his shirt, deciding to keep that surprise to herself. "You'll see. But first I'm going to have to do my hair and makeup—" he stole a kiss and hummed, a sound that thrilled her down to her toes "—and change out of these dirty clothes."

"Allow me to help." He yanked the paint-splattered, baggy T-shirt off her shoulder and kissed her skin. Sabrina's mind blanked of all other thought. Whenever Flynn put his lips on her, she wanted to climb him like a cat on a curtain.

"Oh, but it'd be much more fun if you let me do it," she purred, shaking off his hold. She backed out of the kitchen, lifting the edge of her T-shirt and revealing her stomach— teasing him and having a damn good time doing it. "I'll just throw these dirty clothes in the washer."

"You think this is going to work. You think I'll just follow you wherever you lead because you have no clothes on." But even as he spoke, he followed her every backward step toward the hallway.

She whipped the shirt over her head and tossed it to him. He caught it before it smacked him in the face and gave her the most delightful, reprimanding glare.

"Yup. I *do*." She rolled down the waistband of her sweatpants and turned, revealing the back of her black lace thong. She peeked over her shoulder to bat her lashes and found Flynn's gaze glued to her body. When that gaze ventured to her face, an inferno of heat bloomed in his eyes.

"You're right," he growled. He gave her a wicked grin, and then broke into a run. She yipped and giggled, dashing down the long hallway for the sanctuary of the laundry room. He caught her easily, before she was even halfway there, but she didn't put up even the weakest of fights.

Sixteen

At Chuck's comedy club, Sabrina pulled up to the valet. "We're here!"

"You're kidding."

"I'm completely serious. All of the kidding is done inside the building." She looked completely pleased with herself at his surprise. She should be. She'd surprised him, all right. Flynn climbed from the car, catching up to her as she handed the keys to the valet.

Chuck's was not a new establishment, but it was under new ownership. The club's facade was fresh and stylish rather than its former seedy dive-bar state.

"We came here, what, three or four times?" Flynn smiled at the memories. "I don't remember it ever looking this nice. When did they get a valet?"

"I know, right? I was flipping through one of my journals and there was an entry about us going to Chuck's one night when you were dating someone and I was dating someone else." She made a show of rolling her eyes. "Blah, blah, blah, details, details. Anyway, I checked to see if it was even open, and not only is Chuck's still open, but I found a coupon online for tickets tonight!"

There was an argument about her using coupons for comedy clubs on the tip of his tongue, but he'd digress. It was bad enough she insisted on surprising him and paying for this evening. He'd argued and argued and had finally given up. He'd buy her something to repay her—painting supplies maybe.

Since she'd had those brushes in hand, she'd been more focused on what brought her pleasure instead of trying to help him. She always did things for other people, but didn't do enough for herself. He was struck with the need to make her life easier, better.

He reached for her hand. Their fingers wove together as easily as if they'd been holding hands since the day they met. He'd touched Sabrina in the past, but never in an intentionally sexual or romantic way. Until the kiss happened.

The kiss that changed everything.

Earlier today they'd had feisty, playful, incredible sex against the wall in the laundry room, and then he'd added her discarded clothes to the washer. Through the clear glass lid he'd watched her shirt and pants mingle with his clothes, twist around each other in an almost…intimate way. Which was how holding her hand felt now. How had he never noticed that before?

Sabrina wore an A-line red dress that flared at the waist. Her knees were exposed, her high-heeled shoes tall and sexy as hell, and the simple gold chain at her throat was distracting to the nth degree. When she'd stepped out of the bedroom ready for their date he could think of nothing other than getting her out of the dress. If it was up to him, she'd keep on the shoes and the necklace. Something to look forward to tonight.

Their seats were at a table in the middle of the room rather than up front. He'd been heckled by comedians a time or two in the past when he'd had front row seats, so the middle was fine with him. The headliner was some-one he'd never heard of, and Sabrina admitted she hadn't either. He ordered a beer and she ordered a cosmopolitan, and they made it through the opening act. Barely.

As they pity-clapped, he leaned over to whisper, "If that was any sign of what we can expect from the headliner, we should cut our losses and leave."

"Nope. We're here for the duration," she whispered back. "That's half the fun."

It came as no surprise that she could enjoy even bad comedy. Sabrina enjoyed *everything*. He took a sip of his lukewarm beer and mused that she'd probably found a redeeming quality in her watered-down drink. Her su-perpower was that she found joy everywhere. Even in a formerly seedy club where the tickets were overpriced and the acts should've hung up their jokes years ago.

That same knot that had loosened in his chest before loosened a bit more. He pulled in a deep breath and took her hand again, shaking his head in wonderment at how lucky he was to touch her this freely.

The headliner was introduced and Flynn decided that no matter what crap joke the guy trotted out, Flynn would enjoy the show because he was here with Sabrina. She was contagious in the best possible way—infecting the world with her positivity. That, he'd known for years. That she enjoyed sex and he enjoyed it with her was a surprise.

This sort of ease with a woman shouldn't be simple. Nothing was.

He applauded the opener, shutting out the thought that had the potential to ruin his optimism. Halfway through the guy's set, which was much funnier than his predecessor's, Flynn's phone buzzed and buzzed again. A third insistent buzz had him reaching into his pocket to check the screen.

As if he'd tempted fate by wondering how things could

be this simple, there sat Veronica's name on his phone. *Simple*, she was not.

He read through the texts, wanting to ignore them and brush her fears aside as Veronica being Veronica—dramatic and attention seeking. Except he couldn't. Even though he was 90 percent positive there wasn't a decent bone left in her body, there was in his.

Under his breath he muttered an expletive before leaning close to Sabrina's ear. He whispered that he had to step outside for a moment. When he stood, the target landed squarely on him and the comedian on stage ribbed him for getting up in the middle of his show.

Flynn amiably waved a hand as he exited the room, taking the insults in stride. Go figure. Outside the darkened club, he walked past the ticket counter and bar, forgoing a return text to call Veronica instead.

"Flynn, oh my God. Thank God you called." Her voice was frantic, hushed. Part of him suspected that the text messages were merely to get his attention, but she sounded legitimately frightened.

"What's the problem?" Other than a few veiled words about how his mother's estate was big and Julian was gone and she was hearing things, Veronica hadn't come out and said what she wanted.

"Julian is away at an art show in California and I'm stuck here in this massive house by myself." Her voice shook. "I wasn't sure if the sound I heard was someone breaking in, or if the house was settling."

In that house a break-in was pretty damned unlikely. The neighborhood was gated, and the house itself armed with a security system.

"It's a big house, and it's old. Probably the latter. What do you hear?"

"Cracking. Popping. I don't know." What she described didn't sound like a burglar to him.

"Can you come over and look around? I hate to ask, but…"

He sighed from the depths. She didn't sound frightened but inquisitive and a touch desperate. She wasn't afraid. She wanted to see him. And given the nature of the texts from earlier this week, which had revolved around her being sorry and saying that she missed him, this entire situation was damn fishy.

"Veronica, if you believe that someone is in the house you need to lock the bedroom door, call the police and wait for them to arrive. If I left now, I wouldn't arrive for at least forty minutes."

Silence stretched between them before she spoke again.

"I checked the camera system. And the alarm. Neither of those have tripped." She admitted it sheepishly, like she knew if she'd started the conversation that way she'd be talking to dead air. He cared about her well-being; he did *not* care for being manipulated.

"If you're afraid," he reiterated, "call and have an officer come to the house to take a look around."

"I just… I thought if you were here…we could talk."

"We don't have anything to talk about. Especially when Julian isn't there." Her texts had been hinting at some sort of resolution between them, which he didn't see the point of. He didn't love her and he didn't trust her. He cared about her, though, which she must've known or else she wouldn't have baited him into this call.

"Look, I'm on a date, so I'm going to go."

"Who are you on a date with?" she asked, sounding wounded.

He took a breath, debated telling her, then decided to tell her anyway. "Sabrina."

"I knew it." There was venom in her voice, and the ugly, petty tone compounded with her next comment. "You two have always had a thing for each other."

"We never had a *thing* for each other. I *had* a thing for you." He walked to the exit in case this call required him to raise his voice. "You exclusively. There was a time when you had a *thing* for me, too. Before you had a *thing* for Julian."

Pain seeped in without his permission, so he covered it with anger.

"Since Julian's your guy now, I suggest you call him in a panic."

"I was worried someone was in the house," she snapped.

"Well, the someone who will *not* be in that house tonight is me."

He ended the call, glaring down at his cell phone's dark screen.

"Everything okay?" Sabrina's tender voice asked from behind him. He turned to find her holding her clutch in both hands. "You were gone awhile so I closed our tab. We probably shouldn't attempt to reenter that club given how much crap the comedian gave us both for leaving."

"You don't have to miss the show." He regretted his ex-wife snaring him in such an obvious way. "I shouldn't have taken the call, but her text sounded…" When he met Sabrina's gaze, he noted a dash of surprise.

"Her? You mean Veronica," she stated flatly.

"She's at Mom's estate and was afraid someone was breaking in. I told her to call the cops."

Concern bled into Sabrina's pretty features, magnified through the lenses of her black-framed glasses. "If you need to check on her…" She winced like she didn't want to continue, but then she did anyway. "It might not be a bad idea to make sure she's safe."

God. Sabrina. So damn sweet. She hadn't liked Veronica before, and liked her less now that she and Flynn had divorced for the ugliest of reasons.

"You'd let me end our date to go to her?"

"If it would ease your mind, I would. And hers, I guess."
She quirked her mouth. "I want her to be okay. I just don't
want her to hurt you anymore."

Ah, hell. That got him.

He tucked his phone into his back pocket and grabbed
Sabrina and kissed her, losing himself in the pliant feel
of her lips and the comforting weight of her in his arms.
When they parted, he shook his head. In the midst of the
unluckiest time of his life, he was lucky to have her at his
side. "I'm sure Veronica's fine."

Sabrina must've heard the doubt in his voice. She pulled
her coat on and flipped her hair over the collar. "There's
only one way to be sure. We'll go check."

"We?"

"We. I'm coming with you."

Thirty-five minutes later, thanks to light traffic and Sabrina's lead foot, they arrived at his mother's estate. On the
way, Flynn had texted Veronica to let her know that Sabrina suggested they come by. He expected Veronica to tell
him never mind, or that a visit wasn't necessary, but she
didn't. Either she was playing a long game when it came
to winning him back, or she really did need to see a familiar face tonight.

After they'd been buzzed in at the gate, Flynn studied
the house, sitting regally in the center of a manicured lawn.
It looked the same as when he'd grown up here, save for the
missing rosebushes lining the property—his mother's passion. He hadn't missed this house when he'd moved out just
three years after she'd passed away. His father hadn't stayed
there either, moving to his downtown penthouse instead.
Flynn would drive by his childhood home on the rare occasion, but only to remember his mother. It always made him
think of her. It occurred to him for the first time that there
had been no reason for his father to keep the house, except

for a sentimental one. Flynn hadn't thought of his father as a "sentimental" man, but why else would Emmons have kept the house clean and the grass mowed all these years?

Flynn wasn't sure if he was more disturbed over the idea of his father's hidden feelings, or the fact that Flynn was here for the sole purpose of checking on his ex-wife.

Veronica opened the ornate etched glass, cherry-red front door.

"Sabrina." The greeting was a jerk of her chin. "I'm sure this is the last thing you wanted to do tonight."

Sabrina smiled patiently. "Pour me a glass of wine and I'll consider the trip worth it."

Veronica gestured for them to come in and Flynn followed Sabrina into his mother's house. The place had the same vibe as when his mother was alive: an improbably homey feel for an unbearably large home. That was his mom's doing. Everything about her had been approachable and comfortable even in the stuffy multiroomed estate where she'd passed.

"I'm going to poke around and make sure no one's hiding in any closets."

"Here. Take this." Veronica opened a drawer and pulled out a flashlight. "Check the closets. And under the beds."

Much as he didn't want to look at the bed Veronica slept in, he gave her a tight nod before consulting his date.

"You two going to be okay alone? Did you want to come with me?" he asked Sabrina.

Veronica pulled a bottle of white wine out of the fridge. "I can be amicable, you know."

Sabrina gave him a sultry wink that made him wish they were anywhere but here. "I'll let you battle the bad guys while Veronica and I have some Chardonnay."

"Fair enough." Sabrina could handle herself. She didn't need him hovering over her. With a nod of affirmation, he started down the first hallway and flipped on the lights.

Seventeen

Sabrina accepted a wineglass from Veronica and sipped the golden liquid. It was good. Expensive, she'd guess. Seemed like Veronica to demand only the best.

The square breakfast bar where Sabrina sat was positioned at the center of a huge kitchen. The stainless steel gas stove had eight burners and a tall decorative hood. There were roughly two million cabinets painted a regal buttercream with carved gold handles.

"This is a beautiful kitchen." It was the safest thing to say in this situation.

"For the amount of cooking done in it, it might as well be a bar." Veronica's smile was tolerant.

Sabrina honestly didn't mind that they were here, but she wasn't about to suggest Flynn come alone. Not that she thought anything would happen between him and his ex-wife, but Sabrina felt much better keeping an eye on Veronica.

"I always knew you liked him," Veronica said.

Sabrina had been waiting for the gloves to come off. She

didn't have a snappy comeback prepared, but she was less interested in being witty than being honest.

"He's been my best friend for a long time." *Predating you*, she wanted to tack on, but didn't. "We weren't planning on dating. It just kind of...happened."

"Uh-huh."

"It's true," she continued as if Veronica wasn't growing increasingly peeved about this conversation. "We went out on Valentine's Day as friends. I was trying to extract him from the office since he's been so stressed." *No thanks to you.* "It was his idea to kiss me on the pier."

The look on Veronica's face was priceless. Sabrina was half tempted to pull out her cell phone and snap a picture for posterity.

"I was the one who asked him to kiss me again. We didn't expect it to turn into more. Or at least *I* didn't. I was testing a theory." A theory that had since been proved false. The idea that Sabrina and Flynn could go back to just friends was as dated an idea as Pluto being a planet.

"I'm not sure there's anything long-term there for you," Veronica spat, "but you're certainly welcome to look."

Ouch. Gloves off, claws out.

"Oh, I'm looking. I don't want to *overlook* it. Life is about trying. We never know if things will work out or not until we try. I didn't expect your approval, and that's not why we're here." Sabrina purposely referred to herself and Flynn as *we*. "I didn't want you to spend the evening in fear."

Veronica took a healthy gulp of her wine before tipping the bottle and refilling her glass. "How big of you."

Sabrina had attempted to be polite, but apparently Veronica wasn't going to reciprocate. Sabrina refused to sit here and take it.

"While I totally disagree with you for cheating on Flynn, I don't begrudge you for following your heart. I do think you should have ended your marriage before you started an affair with your husband's brother, though."

Veronica gaped at her for a full five seconds before she managed, "How is that any of your business?"

"I'm here tonight at Flynn's side. That's how it's my business."

A condescending, but musical laugh bubbled from Veronica's throat. "Oh, I see. You think this little rebound he's having with you is going to last."

Sabrina couldn't help flinching. She didn't like the word *rebound*. The word itself hinted that their affair was temporary and meaningless. What Sabrina and Flynn had was layered and complex.

"I disagree." Not her strongest argument, but there it was.

Veronica's brow bent in pity. "I'm sure you're building castles in the sky about how you two are going to be married, have babies and live a wonderful, long life together, but, Sabrina…" She sighed. "Woman to woman, I'll level with you. He's not cut out for it."

"I'm not building anything except for one day on top of the last. But I'm not going to waste time worrying and wondering about an expiration date."

"He's not working now, right? I called the office earlier this week to talk to him and Reid said that Flynn was on hiatus. Are you on hiatus with him?"

Thrown by the line of questioning, it took Sabrina a second to regroup. "I—I took my vacation at the same time as him, yes."

"And how long are you two *lovebirds* off work together?"

She ignored the sinister smile and answered Veronica straight. "We go back around Saint Patrick's Day."

"A bit of advice—think of this as your honeymoon stage. Right now, you're with Vacation Flynn. I remember him from Tahiti and that month we spent in Italy." Her gaze softened as if she was remembering the things they'd done together on those vacations.

Sabrina tried not to imagine the details, but her stomach tossed.

"Anyway." Veronica snapped out of her reverie. "Vacation Flynn is very different from Workaholic Flynn. When your fun, albeit temporary, traipse down romance lane comes to an end, don't be surprised if it coincides with the day he returns to the office. You'll see what I mean soon enough. He can't balance a relationship and a bottom line."

Anger bubbled up from the depths. Sabrina hated being talked down to, or having her future predicted for her. Especially by this woman.

Plus, a part of her begrudgingly admitted, what Veronica was saying felt too close to the truth. Hadn't Sabrina already witnessed Flynn's inability to balance their friendship with the demands of Monarch? But a larger part of her didn't want to believe Veronica was right, and that was the part of her that spoke next.

"Are you blaming your divorce on Flynn's work ethic? He had a massive company to run, and his father was terminally ill." And Veronica had been the one cracking the whip. She was more than happy to let him work his ass off so she could buy more, have more and look like she *was* more.

"The erosion of our marriage didn't start with my affair with Julian," Veronica said, surprising the hell out of Sabrina by using the word *affair*. "Our marriage has been falling apart for years."

"*Had*," Sabrina corrected. Veronica was getting to her. As much as she'd sworn to herself that she was Switzerland when she stepped through these doors, either the wine or Flynn's ex-wife's sour attitude was beginning to loosen her tongue.

"*Had* been falling apart," Veronica amended. "A marriage can't sustain cheating. But make no mistake, it was Flynn who cheated first. With Monarch."

"Oh, give me a break! You can't come at me with the 'his job is his mistress' argument."

"Half the company is threatening to leave, and Legal begged you to remove him from the building."

An exaggeration, but that wasn't the point. "How do you know that?"

"I have friends there, too, Sabrina. I also know that he's rapidly morphing into Emmons Parker. You knew that man. He was horrible. Death literally could not have come for a better candidate. And when Flynn is at work, mired in numbers and focused on success, he's exactly like him."

Sabrina paused, her brain stuck on how unflinchingly *true* that assessment was. And if Veronica was right about that, was she also right about Flynn being unable to maintain a relationship?

No.

Sabrina refused to believe it. She couldn't refute the relationship part, but she could argue Veronica's other point.

Sabrina pushed to standing. "Flynn is a caring, generous, amazing person. Whatever combination of Emmons and his mother he ended up being, he has the best of both of them."

"Honey, you are in for a rude awakening."

"No, *honey*—" the words dripped off Sabrina's tongue "—I'm already *awake*."

They stared each other down, Sabrina with her heart pounding so hard she was sure Veronica could hear it. Veronica's smile was evil, as if she began each morning polishing the skulls of her enemies.

"All clear." Flynn entered the kitchen, flipped the flashlight end over end and set it on the countertop. "How are things going in here?"

Sabrina tore her eyes off Flynn's ex-wife and speared him with a glare.

"Everything's peachy, dear," Veronica cooed. "I was just warning Sabrina about what she can expect if you two attempt to stand the test of time."

"So, that went well."

It was a lame attempt to lighten the stifling air in the car. Flynn had been debating what to say and when to say it since they'd walked out of his mother's home. He knew better than to let Sabrina drive, especially when he noticed her hands shaking as she pulled on her coat. He'd made the excuse that she'd had a glass of wine and shouldn't drive, but that wasn't the real reason he took her keys.

She'd been sitting in the passenger seat, her arms folded over her waist, watching out the window since he'd reversed out of the estate's driveway.

"Sab…"

"I was trying not to hate her. But I do. I hate her."

"You don't hate anybody." He leaned back in the seat, settling in for the easy drive home on a virtually traffic-free road. "Veronica is not worth hating. Trust me. I tried for months and my only reward was heartburn."

Sabrina said nothing.

"You wanna tell me what she said that frosted you?"

"She insinuated that I've been in the wings for years waiting for her to screw up so I could swoop in and steal you away!" The words burst from her like soda from a shaken can. Like she'd been wanting to say that for a while. It hurt him that she was hurting, especially because he knew it wasn't true. What had happened between them since the kiss on Valentine's Day had been as unexpected as it was incredible.

"We both know that's not true." He lifted her hand to kiss her fingers. When Sabrina spoke again, her voice wasn't as angry as before.

"She went on and on about what a horrible person you

were. Which is also *not* true, by the way." She apologized by squeezing his thigh, which didn't do much for him in the apology department, but gave him plenty of other ideas. "She wants you back, which I'm sure you figured out since you have the texts to prove it."

"I don't know what she's doing." He was suddenly tired. Too damn tired for this conversation. He'd rather have it sometime around, oh, never. Never would be good.

"Well, *I do*. Julian's probably behaving like a total flake and she realizes that he can't sustain her high-maintenance needs. She's regretting losing you, her sugar daddy." Another thigh pat accompanied an apology. "I'm sorry. I'm not trying to insult you. You're not a horrible person. And I don't think of you as a sugar daddy."

"I know you don't," he said on the end of a chuckle. Could she be any cuter trying to protect both his feelings and his ego? "Veronica was trying to ruffle your feathers. From where I sit, they look pretty ruffled." He took one hand off the steering wheel to run his fingers through her hair. "I like you ruffled. It's hot."

"You *cannot* be flirting with me right now."

"No? You don't think?" He shot her a lightning-quick smile, pleased when she smiled back. It was the first time he'd seen a real smile since they'd left the comedy club. That was his fault. It was his fault for running off to take care of Veronica when his focus should've been on Sabrina. "You planned a great night and I bailed. I should've ignored her texts."

"No," she admitted on a breezy sigh, "you shouldn't have. If you *weren't* the kind of guy to run to the aid of a woman in need, I wouldn't be friends with you. You did the right thing. It's my fault. I forgot how heinous a person she was when I suggested we go over there."

It felt good to laugh off the evening, so he allowed himself another chuckle at her comment. "I promise to make it up to you."

"Deal."

"Home okay with you?"

"Home sounds good."

Home did sound good. And her coming home with him sounded even better.

Eighteen

Sabrina insisted on baking M&M cookies when they returned to his penthouse. While she measured the flour and sugar, Flynn considered how the last week-plus had been a blur of domestic activity.

He'd checked on the status of her apartment's plumbing—progress, but no solution yet. She seemed content to stay here with him and he wasn't in a hurry for her to leave. She'd been painting almost every day in between trying out a few new recipes his stomach was enjoying.

She'd nibbled at the freshly baked cookies, and he'd wolfed down half a dozen while stretched out on the couch and watching the rain. He finally stopped itching to check his email so he'd kicked back to read a spy novel instead of a business book—something he hadn't done in ages.

His entire adult life had been about bettering himself and gaining knowledge of his father's company. Flynn had assumed Mac, or someone like him, would be put in charge of Monarch if and when the impervious Emmons Parker passed on. Though Flynn had always known it was a possibility the company could fall to him, it seemed unlikely. Now that he had what he'd always wanted, it'd come at a price he wouldn't have paid—his father's death. Reconciling grief over a man who was hard to love hadn't been easy, and unbelievably, inheriting ownership of a company he loved had been harder.

Being owner/president of Monarch was and wasn't what he'd expected. Flynn knew that taking over would be hard work, knew that stepping into his father's shoes would rankle Mac's back hair, but what Flynn hadn't counted on was to turn into his father in the process. Before this hiatus, he'd scarcely been able to tell the difference between them.

Thank God for Sabrina for tirelessly pointing out he was changing—even when he hadn't wanted to hear it. He'd felt that gratitude for her tenfold tonight, while she'd lain on the couch next to him, her feet propped on one of his thighs, her eyes fastened to a book. That same book now sat on the kitchen counter as she poured a few inches of Sambuca into two glasses. She'd insisted on a nightcap, and he'd agreed. It was rounding midnight, but he wasn't the least bit tired.

"Do you have coffee beans?"

"There." He pointed to a cabinet.

She dropped three into each snifter, saying for each one, "Health. Wealth. And happiness."

She turned around to present his glass of warmed licorice liqueur, but his hands were full at the moment. Of the book she'd been reading.

"What are you doing?" Her mouth dropped into a stunned O, her voice outlined with worry. "Close that book immediately and take your drink."

"Why?" He edged around the long end of the counter, putting them on opposite sides of it. "Something juicy in here?"

"No." But her pink cheeks begged to differ.

He opened to where she'd slotted her bookmark, skimmed a few sentences and hit gold. He grinned at her.

"Flynn." It was a plea he ignored.

"'His mouth was as intoxicating as any liquor, but a thousand times more potent,'" he read.

"That's out of context." She came around the counter but he walked backward as he continued reading from another section.

"'He replied to her complaint by sliding warm fingers over her bare back, and then snicking the zipper of her dress down over her backside.'"

"Flynn, please." Her giggle was a nervous one. "Please don't read that."

"Why not? It's a hell of a lot more interesting than what I was reading earlier." He let her catch up to him and snatch the book from his hand. She hugged it to her chest, hiding the cover from him. "Anything in there you want to try?"

He thought she would protest. Her cheeks were rosy as her teeth stabbed her bottom lip in what he assumed was indecision. Hooking a finger in the belt loop of her jeans, he tugged her to him, enjoying the plush softness of her breasts against his chest.

"Is my mouth intoxicating, Sabrina?" He nipped her bottom lip.

"You're making fun of me." She shoved his chest.

"I'm not. I promise I'll try anything in that book."

Her eyebrow rose even as her cheeks stained a darker shade of pink. "Promise?"

He trusted her not to find a section where the hero was kicked in the balls. He raised a hand and took the oath. "I swear."

"In that case." She flipped through the book, back and then forward, before relocating her bookmark and handing it over.

He scanned the page quickly and smiled over the cover

before tossing the book onto the couch. "I had no idea you liked that sort of thing."

She shrugged one shoulder, adorable and tempting. He couldn't refuse her.

Bending at the waist, he threw her over his shoulder and started up the stairs. Her laughter warmed every part of him and chased away the chill from the wet, rainy night. He set her on her feet at the door of his bedroom.

Then he kissed her, skimming one hand under her shirt and tracing his fingertips over her bare belly. Her breaths shortened as he kissed and tongued her neck. He moved his hand higher, higher still until he reached her nipple, thumbing the tender bud. When she gasped, he caught it with his mouth, their tongues battling as he drank in her flavor. He used his other hand to cradle the back of her head as he walked her toward the bed.

He took off her shirt and soaked in the sight of her gorgeous breasts before lowering his mouth to sample each one. And when her fingernails raked over his scalp, his jeans grew uncomfortably tight.

"I don't remember what came next in the book," he murmured in between kisses.

"You're doing great."

He smiled against her skin, and her belly contracted with her laughter. Rising to capture her lips with his, he stole a kiss before undressing her further and pushing her to her back.

He liked her like this, naked and sighing his name. With Sabrina he lived in the present rather than in the future—where work trials awaited—or in the past—where the people he loved the most had betrayed him.

There was only the feel of her heated mouth on his neck, and the way they moved together.

She was the perfect distraction, but a part of him insisted that she was much more than that. A part he ignored since he couldn't imagine a scenario where they could live happily ever after. No one did. Of that he was certain.

He cast aside the thoughts as he thrust into her, making love to her in the lazy rhythm he set, and doing his level best to match the fantasy that'd been brewing in her head.

"Hmm." Her limbs vibrated pleasantly from her last powerful orgasm, one that'd had her shouting Flynn's name as she clutched his shoulders and ran stripes down his back.

She smoothed her fingers over the raised skin on his back and winced. "Sorry for the scratches."

"No." He lifted his head from where it'd been resting on her chest—he'd worked hard—and speared her with an intense blue-flamed glare. "Never apologize for sex injuries. Those are bragging rights."

Her cheeks paled.

"Not that I'd brag." He gently slipped free of her body and climbed out of bed. "I don't kiss and tell, Douglas," he called over his shoulder as he padded to the bathroom.

When he stepped back into his bedroom she admired the full view of him naked. The rounded shoulders, muscled limbs, narrow waist and hips. He truly was a work of art.

"Are we going to tell?" she asked. "Eventually?"

His brow crimped.

"We'll be back to work soon. Reid and Gage already assume you and I have done more than kiss. Other people will probably notice that we act differently around each other." How could they not? She doubted she'd be able to keep a flirty smile under wraps or resist standing close to him, or touching him. "Come to think of it, HR might ask us to disclose our relationship."

She'd been enjoying herself and their break together, but reality was creeping closer. Their relationship had changed—drastically—and while her original goal was to help Flynn remember who he used to be, she had to wonder if there was more at stake.

Sabrina needed Flynn's friendship. He was a constant, made her day better. Made her *life* better. He made her feel valued. *Important.* She saw now how badly she'd needed his attention after being sidelined during his marriage.

If sex risked their friendship, well…that wasn't an option.

"Let me worry about HR." He kissed the space between her eyebrows and climbed into bed.

Veronica had warned Sabrina that this was a rebound. As much as Sabrina hated to admit it, there was a large part of her that wondered if Flynn's ex was right.

If there was one outcome Sabrina refused to accept after their brief affair, it was losing Flynn entirely. She'd not risk their friendship for the sake of sex—no matter how much she was enjoying herself.

Under the blankets, Sabrina snuggled with Flynn and squeezed her eyes closed. He wrapped his big body around hers, an arm over her middle. She pressed one of his hands beneath her cheek—her mind spinning.

She'd never imagined Flynn being hers. He'd always seemed meant for someone else. Now she wasn't sure if her hesitancy was a premonition or worry that'd she'd potentially ruined what they had.

She'd moved from the girl at his side to the girl he was *inside*, and the shift was significant. Veronica had been wrong about Sabrina envisioning her future with Flynn or imagining what their kids or wedding would look like. But Sabrina *was* planning some sort of future with him if she was wondering how they'd handle being around each other at work.

But why?

Because you love him, her mind accused.

Of course she loved him. He'd been her best friend since college.

You're in love *with him.*

No I'm not, she argued silently. A chill streaked down her spine despite Flynn, the human heater, blanketing her back. She wasn't *in love* with him. She cared about him. She loved him as a friend.

It's more than that. Think about it. You can't wait to open your eyes and find him next to you every morning. You go to bed next to him every night, dreading the end of this break. You've been silently hoping your apartment's plumbing is never fixed so you can live here for good.

Fear joined the chill in her body and she shivered. She'd never been in love before and certainly hadn't planned on falling in love with Flynn. And because she knew him as well—*better*—than herself she also knew the last thing Flynn wanted was for her to be in love with him. After Veronica he'd sworn off love permanently, and who could blame him?

Which was why he slept with you.

Sabrina wasn't clingy. She was familiar. She made him M&M cookies. Everything he wanted in a friend with all the benefits of a lover.

The word *rebound* danced around her head like a demented performer.

She was in love with Flynn Parker. Her best friend.

Your lover.

He was also the last man on earth she should give her heart to.

So she wouldn't.

They'd abandoned their snifters of Sambuca on the kitchen counter to indulge in a different sort of nightcap, but she could use that drink now.

She eased out from under Flynn's arm—his low snore signifying he wouldn't wake anytime soon. Feeling around in the dark, she found her thong and pulled it on before snagging the first T-shirt she found—his. It took more rooting around blindly before she found her own. It felt wrong to slip into his clothes after her personal revelation.

She walked down the stairs as silent as a soft-pawed cat and grabbed one of the snifters before curling into a ball on the couch. Blanket over her legs, she listened to the rain pound and watched as it streaked the windows and muddied the ambient city lights.

She'd fallen in love with him and she could fall back out. It was as simple as that. How hard could it be? She'd been his best friend for over a decade and his lover for only a few weeks. For the remainder of this hiatus, she'd find a way to separate her feelings of friend love and true love.

For both their sakes.

That would hurt, but she was a strong woman. She would get through this. They both would. Nothing would ruin their friendship together, especially a bout of great sex they could chalk up to timing and proximity.

She sipped her liquor and studied the three coffee beans in the pale light from the city lights outside.

Health, wealth and happiness.

Two out of three wasn't bad.

Nineteen

Sabrina and Flynn had been back at Monarch for a little over a week. There was plenty to do, so at first she barely had time to think about anything other than her burgeoning email inbox.

Last week the landlord had called her to let her know the plumbing had finally been fixed in her apartment. In addition to a hectic work pace, she'd been cleaning up the plumber's mess and unpacking.

She didn't enjoy having the space to herself as much as she'd anticipated.

She'd focused on laundry and preparing meals and definitely did *not* read any of the new romance novels Mrs. Abernathy had dropped off. Sabrina had also dodged a few questions from her well-meaning, prying neighbor about whether or not she and Flynn were in love. Mrs. Abernathy took Sabrina's silence as confirmation, rather than assuming the relationship had imploded.

Not that Flynn *knew* things had imploded. Sabrina hadn't exactly stated anything for the record.

Since they'd returned to work, the distance between them had come naturally. Flynn was doubly busy after his month off, staying at the office some nights until eight or nine.

She'd told herself that this was a good thing—that it was her chance to slot him back into the friend zone where he belonged. They could write off the last four weeks as a fling, and go back to normal.

Instead, she'd thought about how Veronica was right about Flynn's new love being Monarch Consulting. Why did that hurt so much when she'd done exactly what she'd set out to do? Flynn was no longer stomping around like an angry ogre and the senior execs at the company were more accepting of him. Everything was back to normal.

Except for her.

She'd tasked herself with reversing the mistake of falling for him, but her heart wasn't cooperating. Every night she lay in bed alone, her mind on Flynn and the way his mouth tasted. Missing the comfort of his body, big and warm and wrapped protectively around hers, or hearing his light snore in the middle of the night whenever her eyes snapped open and her mind was full...

"Hey." Flynn's low rumble brought her head up from her laptop. He stood in her doorway, dressed in an expensive suit with a silver-blue tie bisecting a crisp gray shirt. His jacket was buttoned, his shoes were shiny and he was the most delicious vision she'd seen all day.

There used to be a time she could look at him and think, "Hey, there's my friend, Flynn." Now she looked at him and thought about touching him and being close to him. Touching him and watching the raw heat flare in his eyes. Which made working directly across from him and keeping her hands to herself pure, unadulterated torture.

"What's up?" She was aiming for casual, but the greeting sounded forced.

"Finally managed to poke my head out of the water. I thought Reid and Gage were supposed to handle my email, but I came back to about a million of them. Lazy bastards."

That made her smile. "Yeah, nobody took care of mine while I was gone either."

A heated smolder lit his eyes that was 100 percent intriguing and 1,000 percent out of place at work. He ducked his chin and stepped deeper into her office. "I've missed you."

Her heart hammered against her ribs as she anticipated what he would say next. Would he ask her out? Invite her over? And how was she going to say no if he did?

How could she possibly say anything but yes when what she wanted was to be with him more than her next breath? Not only tonight, but the night after that and the one that followed...

Definitely, she was terrible at breaking up with him.

"How's the plumbing?" he asked. "I'm talking about your apartment, not your person."

"Har, har. I see that your sense of humor hasn't improved."

"Well, you can't expect a month off to work miracles."

"Thanks to you, my apartment is perfect." *Except that you're not in it with me.*

Those were the kinds of thoughts she shouldn't be having about him and yet they boomeranged back no matter how hard she threw them.

Last night she'd sat down to add a female partner to the chickadee painting, her mind on Flynn and their conversation about those philandering little birds that were together only for the sex.

What a metaphor for how things had ended up. She couldn't look at the chubby, charming, whimsical birds without thinking of what she'd lost.

Except Flynn wasn't looking at her like he'd lost anything. Or like he wanted to change anything. More proof came in what he said next.

"What do you say we carve out some time for each other?" His eyebrows lifted in the slightest way, his sculpted lips pursed temptingly. "Tonight?"

"Tonight?" Her brain jerked to life and provided a handy excuse that happened to be true. "Sorry. Can't. Luke is coming over. I've been ignoring him lately, so I promised to cook him dinner. You know my brother. He rarely indulges in any food outside of his gym rat diet, so when he's ready for a cheat day, he calls me."

"Later this week, then."

She didn't say anything to that since it wasn't a question.

He lingered at her desk, running his eyes down the royal blue dress she was wearing. "I'd like to get you out of that dress. Sure you can't reschedule with your brother?"

Never had an offer been so tempting and terrifying at the same time. She could say yes and blow off dinner with Luke. Then she and Flynn could have wine, and make love on the couch or the bed. He could carry her up the stairs or they could walk up hand in hand, side by side. An entire choose-your-own-adventure scenario unfurled itself like a red carpet leading to a night of absolute indulgence.

Out of her dress and into his arms sounded perfect, but that wouldn't help her fall out of love with him.

"Rain check," she muttered, but couldn't help adding, "I can always wear this dress again."

He leaned over her desk, coming closer, closer until his lips nearly brushed hers. Then he turned his head and pretended to study the screen of her laptop, his minty breath wafting over her cheek when he said, "I like the sound of that."

A thin breath came out in a puff when he straightened and walked out of her office. She'd made the wrong decision for her heart, but she'd made the right decision for their future. As much as she wanted to believe that they were meant to be, she had an uneasy feeling that they *weren't*. Their fun new pastime would soon grow old and wither on the vine.

She refused to let that happen—to risk losing him completely when having him forever as a friend was well within reach. There was time to put Jack back in the box. To corral the loose horse into the barn. To cork the genie's bottle...

Horrible metaphors aside, she was going to make this right.

Their friendship deserved no less.

"So let me get this straight. You're not dating Flynn, but you're trying to think of a way to break it off with him?"

Luke lounged on her sofa, scrolling through his cell phone. She'd spilled her guts at dinner and told him everything. Well, *almost* everything. He was still her brother and she would never be comfortable sharing sex stories with him.

"How can you say we're not dating?" she called from the kitchen as she rinsed the dishes and loaded the dishwasher. "I lived with him! We shared a bed. That's dating."

Luke winced when she said the word *bed*. He set his phone aside and shoved a pillow under his head, regarding her patiently.

Dish towel in hand, she stepped into the living room and collapsed into a chair. "What? Tell me."

"It sounds like you went on some dates. That's dating. The other stuff... I don't know what the hell that is. Not dating."

"Of course it's dating. What else could it be? It's more than a hookup."

"Have you at least admitted to yourself that you're in love with Flynn Parker?"

She let out a sigh of defeat. "Yes. I have."

"Any reason in particular you're not sharing this news with him?"

"If you had a girl as a best friend for nearly half your life, would you want her to profess her love for you when you knew it wouldn't last?"

"First off," he said, pushing himself into a seated position, "I would never have a girl who was a friend for that long without attempting to get into her pants."

She frowned. "That's unsettling."

"It's also true. Second." Luke held up two fingers. "How do you know he thinks it won't last?"

"Because of the pact. The bachelor pact. Or whatever they call it."

"That's stupid."

She used to agree, but now she wasn't so sure. "He didn't reinstate it lightly. Which makes me the biggest rebound of all rebounds."

"He'd better not think of you as a rebound or I'll kick his ass myself."

She didn't know if Flynn felt that way, but it was good to know Luke had her back.

"I don't want to see you hurt, Sab."

"I don't want to see myself hurt either." Back in the kitchen, she scrubbed the counter with a damp cloth and continued her thought from earlier. "Which is why I'm trying to wrap this up while I have a scrap of dignity left. Yes, the dates went well. Yes, we had a great time while I lived with him. Yes, it was the best sex of my life—"

Luke groaned.

"Sorry. But you see my point, right? I can't top that off with an *I-love-you*. I've made up my mind to go back to being friends with Flynn. Just friends. When I make up my mind about something, you know I do it."

"I know." Luke walked over to her, bending his head to look down at her. Funny, she remembered when he was shorter than her. He'd been a pain in her butt then, and not one of her closest confidants. "Are you sure this is how you want to play it?"

She wasn't, but there was no other graceful way out of it. "I'm afraid if I wait too long Flynn will have to give me a speech explaining how temporary we were."

"Okay." Luke sounded resigned as he went to the fridge and pulled out a bottle of beer. "Let's make a plan for you to pull the trigger before he can."

Hope filled her chest. "Thank you, Luke!"

Her excitement about making a plan mingled with pain in the region of her lovesick heart, but she ignored it.

This was the best solution—the only solution. Soon enough she'd be on the other side, Flynn back where he belonged, her heart having accepted that he wasn't theirs for keeps.

The sooner she let him know they were through, the sooner she would heal.

She hoped.

Twenty

It was like ripping off a Band-Aid. That was the comparison Luke made last night.

He'd suggested she text Flynn, but there was no way Sabrina could break the news via a text. She and Flynn were too good of friends to have an important conversation via text message. Besides, she knew him. He would've shown up at her apartment and demanded she explain herself.

She entered the executive conference room with her fresh cup of coffee to meet with Flynn, Reid and Gage. As much as she wanted to tell Flynn her decision sooner than later, now wasn't the time for a private conversation.

"Thanks for joining us," Reid said with a smile.

"I was stuck on a conference call the three of you insisted I make." She narrowed her eyes at them in reprimand, but when her gaze hit Flynn's, she rerouted. She couldn't look him in the eyes with a whopper of an announcement sitting on the tip of her tongue.

"Gage, you called this meeting. We're here." Flynn set aside his iPad, thereby giving Gage the floor.

"Now that Mac and company have retracted their threats to leave Monarch and take their friends with them," Gage started, "we need to massively increase sales. A huge boom in profits means bonuses all around, which makes Flynn look good, my sales department look good and Monarch look good. If we're growing and Mac threatens to leave again, chances are he won't have many followers. If any."

"I'm all for growth." Flynn's eyes narrowed. "I feel like there's more."

"There is. I'm bringing in an expert. Someone who can aid me with coaching my team. I don't love the idea of handing this to someone else, but I can't handle my workload and training and expect to do both efficiently. I found a guy who comes highly recommended. I read about him in Forbes and then stumbled across his website. He's incredibly selective about the jobs he takes, but several profitable Fortune 500 companies are on his client list."

"Who is this wizard?" Reid asked.

"His name's Andy Payne. He's made of smoke, and somewhat of a legend. He's also virtually unreachable. I couldn't get him on the phone so I settled for a discussion with his secretary."

"Sounds mysterious," Reid said. "If he'd be open to sharing that he's working for us, we could use the media curiosity. Flynn?"

To Sabrina's surprise, Flynn turned to her. "You've been quiet."

"I've heard of Andy Payne. His website isn't much more than a black screen with his name on it. If we share that we're working with him across our social media channels, it might not even matter how much we improve sales. His involvement alone would be enough to gain stockholders' support." She looked at Gage. "It's smart."

"Thanks." Gage smiled.

"Okay then." Flynn nodded. "How much is this guy going to cost us?"

Sabrina shut down her laptop for the day and glanced at the clock. The digital read was 5:05, which meant the lower floors had already packed up to enjoy a rare day of sunshine.

Flynn's assistant, Yasmine, had already left, Gage and Reid were at their desks, and who knew how long they'd be here. They usually didn't stick around as long as Flynn, but if she waited for them to leave she might be sitting here another hour-plus.

She was tempted to chicken out and leave without talking to him at all until he looked up from his computer as if he'd felt her eyes on him. Once his mouth slid into a wolfish smile, she knew she didn't have a choice.

"Now or never," she whispered to herself as she strode across the office. His door was open but she rapped on the door frame anyway.

"Sabrina." The way he said her name sent a warm thrill through her. One that harkened back to long kisses and their bodies pressed together as they explored and learned new things about each other. She had the willpower of a monk and the hardheadedness of a Douglas. She could do this.

She *had* to.

"Do you have a minute?" she asked, pleased when her voice came out steady. "I wanted to talk to you about something."

"Of course." He didn't look the slightest bit worried. Not even when she shut the door behind her and sat across from him in a chair on the opposite side of the desk.

"It's about the pact."

"The pact?"

"Yes. The pact you reinstated with Gage and Reid about never getting married."

"I know what the pact is, Sab." He didn't look worried but he definitely looked unhappy. Maybe she was on the right track here. Maybe Flynn *was* worrying about the future as much as she was and didn't want to ruin their friendship with more complications.

"In college I thought the pact was a stupid excuse for your horndog behavior."

His mouth eased into a half smile.

"When you met Veronica, you threw it out because you knew it was a stupid excuse. But I was unfair to call it stupid this time around, Flynn. You're only trying to protect yourself. And I respect that."

"Okay…" He was frowning again, probably waiting for her to arrive at a point.

"Even though I've never been in love before—" *a tiny lie* "—I expect to fall someday. I envision walking down the aisle in a big, white dress. I may not want it now, but I will."

He shifted in his seat, nervous like she was going to propose to him then and there. She wasn't, of course, but last night she'd intentionally tried to imagine a groom at the end of the aisle waiting for her, and guess who she pictured?

Flynn.

"I'm getting married someday, Flynn. And you're not."

She let the comment hang, watching his face as he understood that she wasn't asking him for more, but less.

"While being with you in a new way has been fun, it's time to move on. We arrived in good places—you're back to yourself and I'm painting again…" Kind of. She didn't feel much like painting now. "I don't know if you want a pair of chickadees over your mantel, but the painting's yours if you want it."

She didn't want it. She related too much to the female

who had been foolish enough to fall in love with an emotionally unavailable bachelor.

Flynn's brow dented in anger, but still he said nothing.

"So. That's it, I guess. We just go back to the way things were before…you know. We'll pretend this never happened." She stood in an attempt at a quick getaway.

"Where the hell are you going?" Flynn stood and pointed at her recently vacated chair. "Sit down."

She propped her hands on her hips in protest. "I will not. That's all I had to say."

"Well, I haven't said a damn thing."

"There's nothing for you to say!"

"Oh, trust me. There's plenty to say." He flattened his hands on the desk and gave her a dark glare.

She folded her arms over her chest to prevent her heart from lurching toward him.

"Are you breaking up with me?" he asked.

"Are we…dating?" Her voice shook.

"You bet your beautiful ass we're dating. What would you call what we've been doing for the last two or three weeks?"

"Having fun." She gave him a sheepish shrug. "Having a fling."

"A fling." He spat the words.

"A really fun fling," she concluded.

"Listen to me very carefully."

She glared, attempting to match his ferocity, and leaned over his desk, her fingers pressing into it. "I'm listening."

"Good. I don't want you to miss a single word."

Twenty-One

Flynn's thunderous mood only grew darker as the evening grew later. The moment last week in his office when Sabrina confronted him still banged in his head like a gong, vibrating from every limb and causing his fingertips to tingle.

Granted, he hadn't handled it well. He'd told her under no circumstances was she dumping him on his ass when they were just getting started.

That hadn't gone over well, and if he hadn't been simultaneously pissed off and hurt by her suggestion to stop seeing him, he could've predicted as much. It seemed they'd both succeeded during their break from the office. Sabrina stopped his metamorphosis into his father and he'd convinced her to put herself first.

She didn't want him. Not anymore, anyway.

He made himself respect her decision. Even when she left crying and told him she always cried when she was angry and not to read too much into it.

After the explosion in his office, Reid and Gage barged

in to offer their two cents, a.k.a., find out what the hell had happened.

Flynn hadn't told them everything, so they were probably still confused about why Sabrina left crying and never came back. They blamed him, and since he'd behaved like a horse's ass, he didn't blame them for blaming him. He'd digressed to pre-Valentine's Day Flynn, and felt every inch the corporate piranha he used to be. He wore a dark suit, a darker outlook, and palpable anger wafted off him like strong cologne.

How the hell else was he supposed to feel when Sabrina had come into his office, looking beautiful and sexy, and then broke up with him? He'd been yearning for her so badly, he could scarcely get her out of his head and she'd been ruminating on the best way to let him down easy.

She'd called what they had a fling.

What a load of crap.

She'd emailed him the morning after their argument telling him she was taking a "leave of absence," without an end date. He'd been sure she'd come to her senses in a day or two.

Unfortunately, the week had passed as slowly as the ice caps melting, and her office remained empty and dark. There was a lack of sunshine in Seattle, and he blamed that on her, as well. Even when Seattle wasn't sunny, which was almost always, Sabrina brought her own light with her.

It wasn't only that he missed her, or that he'd been forced to outsource some of their marketing for the time being, it was that she was…gone.

Gone from the office, gone from his bed. Gone from his *life*. Her absence was like a shadow stretched over his soul.

Waiting for her to come to her senses was taking a lot longer than he'd thought.

He rubbed grainy eyes and shut his laptop, considering what to do next. At that moment Gage darkened his office door.

"Did you call her yet or what?" Gage sat in the guest chair, looking tired from the long day. The workload that hadn't been outsourced had fallen to Gage and Reid.

"I have not."

"Reid and I tossed a coin to find out which one of us was going to come in here and ask the question we promised not to ask you."

Flynn pressed his lips together. Saying nothing was the safest response. As expected, Gage didn't let him get away with it.

"More than hanky-panky went on in your apartment, didn't it?" He lifted one eyebrow and paired it with a smug smile. "You guys rushed in, expected a little slap and tickle, and ended up falling flat on your faces."

Before Flynn could decide how loud to yell, Reid stepped into the room.

"What our fine cohort is trying to say is that you two kids accidentally fell in love with each other, and neither of you have admitted it."

Flynn blinked at his friend, unsure what to make of his assessment. It wasn't as if Reid went around accusing people of falling in love. He'd sooner die than bring up the topic of love at all.

"We're not blind." Gage tilted his head slightly and admitted, "Okay, we were blind for a while. But after that outburst between you and Sabrina in your office—"

"And the fact that she left crying and hasn't returned," Reid interjected.

"We caught on."

Reid sat in the chair next to Gage and they each pinned Flynn with questioning expressions. No, not questioning. *Expectant.* And what the hell was Flynn supposed to say?

He'd been accused of falling in love with his best friend.

The same best friend who'd come into his office on this day last week and told him she didn't want anything to do with him. What would either of them say if they knew that the month he'd spent with Sabrina had been the best one of his life? What would his buddies say if they knew the truth—that he'd never experienced sex the way he'd experienced it with Sabrina?

With her, sex was more than the physical act. She towed him in, heart and soul. Blood and bones. He'd been 100 percent present with her, and then she threw him away. Walked out!

He'd told her if she really believed that what they had was a "fling," she could march her ass out of his office for good. He knew damn well what they had wasn't just sex or convenience. The dream he'd had about her was a prediction. Some part of his mind had known that she belonged in his arms and in his bed.

He never counted on her cutting him off at the knees. He missed her. He wanted her back. And yet he cared for her too much to demand more than she was willing to give.

"She told me she was getting married someday," he told Gage and Reid. They both blanched at that confession. "That's right, boys. She made sure to tell me she was getting married and since I made a pact never to be married, she didn't want to lead me on."

"She wouldn't ask you to give up the pact," Reid said with a disbelieving laugh.

"Wouldn't she?" Flynn asked. He didn't know the answer to that. "We only had a month together. What the hell am I supposed to say when she tells me she's getting married someday and I have a pact not to so we may as well wrap up whatever fling we were having? She called it a fling, by the way. A fucking *fling*."

"Was it?" Gage asked, his face drawn.

"Hell no it wasn't a fling!" Flynn boomed. "And if she's

too hardheaded, or too dense or whatever other adjective you'd like to assign her, to realize that what we had was something special, then...then..."

"She doesn't deserve you?" Reid filled in with a smirk.

"Shut up." Flynn glowered.

"You know, we can sit here all day and wait, or you can admit how you feel about her now." Gage crossed one leg, resting his ankle on his knee. He propped his elbow on the arm of the chair and did a good job of appearing as if he *could* sit there all day.

"Yep, and after you admit it to us—" Reid made a show of stretching and lacing his fingers behind his head "—then you can go tell her."

"Tell her what?" Flynn asked, his blood pressure rising.

"You tell us." Gage lifted his eyebrows in challenge.

"We can order in," Reid said to Gage. "I haven't had Indian in a while."

"Great idea. Amar's has the best naan."

"Wrong. Gulzar's is much better."

"Hey," Flynn growled. "Remember me? What the hell do you two want me to say?" He stepped out from behind his desk to pace.

Hands in his hair, he continued complaining, mostly about how he should fire both of them if this was the support he could expect from his other two best friends.

"What am I supposed to do? Go to her and tell her I have no idea what we had, but it's not worth throwing out?"

"I think you're going to have to do better than that," Gage said and Reid nodded.

"What, then? Tell her she was special and I didn't want her to leave?"

"Warmer," Reid said.

"You want me to tell her..." Flynn sighed, his anger and frustration melting away. Could he say it aloud? Could he tell his two boneheaded friends the truth that he'd been avoiding since the first time he'd made love to Sabrina? "Tell her I'm in love with her and that she belongs with me?"

"By God, he said it." Reid grinned.

"Shit." Flynn sat on the corner of his desk, the weight of that admission stifling. Too stifling to remain standing.

"And then she'll admit she loves you, too," Gage said.

"Weren't you listening? She ended *us* in this very office."

"She's scared of losing you," Gage told him. "She cut things off before you could so that the two of you could remain friends."

"I wasn't going to cut things off! And if that's true, why isn't she here, huh?" Flynn gestured to her empty office. "Wouldn't my *friend* be here still?"

"Not if you told her to bugger off," Reid said.

"I ran your situation by Drew," Gage said. "She agreed you need to tell her."

"I highly doubt your sister has any insight into Sabrina." Reid snorted and Gage turned on him, glaring. "I only mean because she hasn't been around. I haven't seen Drew in an age."

"This isn't about Drew." Gage let his glare linger on Reid a moment before snapping his attention back to Flynn. "Tell Sabrina you love her. Kiss and make up."

"We hereby release you from the pact," Reid announced. "But Gage and I are still in it." He shot an elbow into Gage's arm. "Right?"

"I have no plans on matrimony. So, yes."

Flynn's head spun. "No one said anything about marriage."

That he was in love with Sabrina was a massive leap for his head and heart to make.

"Either let her go or allow yourself to be open to it. She walked in here to tell you that she's marrying someday. So

if it's not going to be you, you should let her off the hook."
Gage was clearly in lecture mode.

"You two should've married years ago." Reid stood as if
his business was concluded here. "You've always belonged
to Sabrina and vice versa. She won't look at me sideways
and I've been flirting with her for years. If she's managed
to keep from sleeping with me, there must be something
stopping her. In this case—" Reid leveled Flynn with a
look "—you."

Gage stood, too. "He's right. Go get her. Marry her. Either that or we quit. We never wanted to work for Emmons
Parker, and if you don't show some favor to your neglected
heart you're going to end up just like him."

"Filthy rich and hopelessly lonely," Reid summarized.

Then they walked out of his office, yammering about
eating naan at Gulzar's.

Without inviting Flynn to join them.

Twenty-Two

Sabrina had spent her third straight morning in a row at the gym with Luke. She was sad and upset and punishing herself. There was no other logical reason on this planet to do burpees.

Her body took the doled-out sets like a trooper, but that wasn't really why she was working out so much. She was paying penance for believing for a single second that she could fall out of love with Flynn.

As Luke had told her this morning, "I knew that wouldn't work."

She'd slugged him in the arm and asked him why he'd let her do it, but he'd only shook his head and said, "Like you'd listen to me anyway."

Unfortunately, he was right. Her stubborn nature had shown up at the wrong time—outshining her positive, Pollyanna attitude and leading her astray.

And when Flynn had demanded she keep seeing him, she'd dug in her heels and fought out of principle. He couldn't tell her what to do, not when she was trying to stop loving him. Turns out she didn't have to stop loving him, since Flynn probably hated her for leaving Monarch high and dry.

Okay, fine, he probably didn't *hate* her. But he'd let her leave and that felt like the same thing.

She'd ended what they had so that they could be friends, but she'd lost him altogether. Couldn't he see she was trying to help both of them?

"By keeping your feelings to yourself," she grumbled as she hooked her purse on her shoulder.

Gage had asked her to meet him at Brewdog's for a cup of coffee. The hip café was a block from her house. She'd told him no but then he'd begged, saying he had a work problem that only she could solve. "The outsourcing Flynn hired, Sab, they're a nightmare. Don't leave me hanging. This project is too important."

Outsourcing that was her fault because she'd walked out without notice. She'd felt too guilty to say no again. Besides, she would like to go back to work eventually. After however long a cooling period she and Flynn needed before they rekindled their friendship.

They *had to* rekindle their friendship. Living without him in her life was miserable. Monarch Consulting had given her a sense of meaning and purpose. She wasn't so stubborn that she didn't recognize that Flynn was a very big part of that. He was important to her, and she'd just have to woman up, convince her heart to accept that he wouldn't fall in love with her back, and move on.

She could do it. She just hadn't figured out how yet.

Outside, the spring rain fell in a light drizzle, but she didn't bother with an umbrella since she'd worn her contacts instead of her glasses. She was as grumpy about the weather as she was about agreeing to help Gage. On the steam of her own bad attitude, she stepped into Brewdog's and nearly plowed into a man picking up his coffees at the counter.

"Sorry." She moved aside, but then her gaze softened on the most handsome face she'd ever seen.

Flynn's.

His jaw clenched, a muscle ticking in one cheek.

"I'm…meeting Gage?" But even as she said it, she doubted Gage was here. This moment had setup written all over it.

"So am I." Flynn's eyes narrowed in suspicion. "He called two minutes ago, asking me to grab his coffee for him since he was running late. I'm supposed to meet him—"

"At the table by the plant," they said at the same time.

"Does one of those cups contain a salted caramel concoction?" she asked of her favorite indulgence.

"I knew that sounded off when he ordered it." Flynn handed her one of the cups and they walked to the corner table by the plant, which was currently occupied by a British guy in sunglasses pretending to read a newspaper.

"*Et tu*, Reid?" she asked.

He lowered the paper and feigned shock. "What are you two doing here? No matter. You can have my table. I was just leaving."

"Convenient," she muttered.

Reid stood and kissed her forehead. "Miss you, Sab."

That was sweet. The jerk.

She watched him leave and then she and Flynn sat across from each other, her stiffly, with her purse in her lap.

"You feel nothing for him when he pulls that charming shtick?" Flynn asked.

"For Reid? I feel… I don't know. I feel like that's just Reid."

"No butterflies?" Flynn asked. Weirdly.

"No." Reid Singleton was good-looking and all, but just…no.

They sipped their coffees and sat in silence for a few lingering seconds. The café was filled with the din of chatter and the sounds of steaming milk and the clattering of cups and spoons.

Someone had to end this standoff. That's why Gage and Reid had set them up. They wanted reconciliation, and had probably convinced Flynn to talk her into coming back to work. She never should've walked out on them. Plus, she really did want her job back...

Determined to eat her crow while it was still warm, she would be the first to apologize. "Flynn—"

"I'm in love with you."

Every word she was going to say next flew out of her head. His expression was desperate, pained. Because he regretted saying it, or because he wasn't sure if she loved him, too?

"It's inconvenient and the timing is completely wrong and I'm not sure if you feel the same way, but I'm in love with you and I miss you like crazy."

Her heart beat double time, the joy in it hardly able to be contained. Flynn was in love with her!

He lowered his voice. "I don't want the painting."

Well. That was an odd segue.

"The birds. The birds who only want each other for sex," he explained a little too loudly. "That's not what I want. That's not what I ever wanted. And when I was finally brave enough to take the leap, I did it with the wrong person."

"Me?"

"No," he practically shouted. "Veronica."

She wasn't going to deny the punch of relief she felt hearing his ex-wife's name.

"She screwed me over and I was sure the universe was trying to show me that my original plan never to marry was the right call all along. If we hadn't married so quickly, we would've ended years ago."

"You...would've?"

"She knew it. I knew it. Neither of us came out and admitted we were unhappy. It doesn't forgive what she did, but I understand why she left." His eyes dashed away before finding Sabrina's again. "I haven't thought about getting married again. Only about avoiding the pain of having my wife leave me. She was supposed to love me. She didn't do a very good job of it."

Sabrina opened her mouth to agree, but Flynn spoke first.

"You do." He reached over the table, palm up, and she slipped her hand into his. It felt inexplicably good to touch him. To have him here. To listen to the words tumbling out of his mouth like a rockslide he was powerless to stop. "You love me better than anyone ever has, Sabrina Douglas. You show it in every small gesture, and in every action. Even the one that led you to come and tell me that we were through. I'm sorry it took me this long to pull my head out of my ass."

"Me, too," she whispered, tears stinging her nose. She blinked her damp eyes, Flynn going momentarily blurry as she swallowed down her tears.

"You, too, meaning you're also sorry it took me so long to pull my head out of my ass, or..."

He waited, eyebrows raised, and then she realized that she hadn't told him the most important news of all.

"I'm in love with you, too. And you're right. I do a very good job of loving you. The only time I didn't do a good job was when I walked away. But I never stopped loving you, Flynn."

"God, am I glad to hear you say that."

His smile was the most welcoming sight she'd seen in over a week.

"I'm not saying you have to marry me now or...ever, honestly," he told her. "I'm saying that if you try this thing with me and you start imagining the guy at the end of the aisle and see my face—"

"I already do."

"Yeah?"

"Yeah. Which is nuts." She let out a nervous laugh. "That's nuts, right?"

"I don't know anymore." His sideways smile was filled with chagrin. She loved it. She loved him. "We don't have to decide that now, but you do have to decide something."

"Which is?" She couldn't wait to hear what he said next considering his every confession had been better than the last.

"You have to come back to Monarch," he said so seriously that a few banked tears squeezed from the corners of her eyes.

She sniffled and swiped them away. "Done."

"And you have to be mine. Not like the chickadees, Sabrina. Like...whatever species of bird mates for life. Paint that kind of bird—two of them—and I'll hang that painting over my mantel."

"The only species I know that mates for life is black vultures." She wrinkled her nose.

"How the hell do you know that?"

"I went through a macabre phase in my angsty teenage years."

"Yikes," he said, on the end of a deep chuckle.

"Oddly enough, a pair of black vultures is fitting for your apartment," she teased.

He squeezed her hand, but instead of teasing her back, he said, "So are you. You belong there with me. I used to think I was good by myself. That I liked my space and having things easy, simple. But since you walked into my black and white penthouse, you changed all that. You've been too far away during the years Veronica and I were married. Then you came back and brought color into my life, Sab.

And you brought love—real love. The patient, kind type of love they talk about in wedding vows. I've known for a while there's been something missing in my life. I used to think it was success or money. But all along, it was you. You're what's been missing in my life. I'm tired of missing you. I don't want to miss you again. Not ever."

As he gave the speech, an earnest expression on his face, his hand held hers tightly. The words were stacked on top of one another like he was trying to say them all at once.

She had to make sure she understood what he was saying. There'd been too many moments lately where she and Flynn had been vague. They'd paid the ultimate price— losing each other. She wouldn't risk him again.

"Just to be crystal clear," she said, "you want me to work with you. And…live with you? Maybe marry you in the future?"

"Yes, yes and hell yes. You're my vulture, Sabrina." He winked. "Plus, I was absolved from the bachelor pact."

"You were?"

"Yep. These two weird guys I know don't want me in it. They'd rather us be together."

Okay, she was giving Reid and Gage huge hugs the next time she saw them.

"They said I've always been yours. I thought about that a lot this past week. Over the years you and I have known each other, no matter who we were with at the time, we stuck together. You and I never strayed. I've always been yours, but you've also always been mine."

The truth of his words resonated deep in her soul. She, too, thought of the years they'd spent in each other's company. The easy way they could talk and pass the time together. Of course it'd always been Flynn. Who else would it have been?

"I've always known the right place for you was by my

side," she told him. "I never dreamed you'd be more than a friend."

"Then it's a good thing I kissed you on the pier on Valentine's Day."

A thrill ran through her as she remembered the first contact with his lips. How surprised she was to explore another side of him. Who knew it could get better, then worse, and then better than before?

"I'm taking the rest of the day off." He stood and pulled her to her feet.

She lifted a hand to his forehead, checking for a fever. "A half day? Are you sure you're not sick?"

"Lovesick." He lowered his lips for a soft, way-too-brief kiss and then handed over her coffee cup.

"Besides, we have a lot to do. Pack up your apartment, hire movers—"

"Redecorate your colorless apartment."

"You'll bring the color, Sab."

Yes, she would.

Outside of the café, Flynn paused under the awning as the rain went from a drizzle to a borderline downpour. Fat drops splattered the sidewalks as people ran for the shelter of the coffee shop and other surrounding stores.

"Do you think we've been in love with each other this entire time but we're only just now realizing it?" he asked.

"It doesn't matter."

"How could it not matter?"

"Because you were a different you before this exact moment. And I was a different me. It never would've worked out if we'd attempted it before we did."

He pulled her in with one arm, careful not to spill their coffees as he leaned down to nuzzle her nose. "I love you."

Her smile was unstoppable. "I love you, too. I don't know how to not be in love with you, so I may as well stick around."

"That's the spirit." He looked out at the pouring rain. "Nice day for a walk."

"The perfect day for a walk," she agreed.

His arm around her neck, they stepped out from under the awning, allowing the rain to drench them as they meandered down the sidewalk. "Plus, no one else makes me M&M cookies."

"The foundation of every strong relationship," she said.

"That and sex in the laundry room."

"Or on the couch."

"Or the balcony."

She blinked up at him, the rain soaking her cheeks. "We didn't have sex on the balcony."

"Not yet. I read a balcony sex scene in the romance novel you left at my penthouse. I think we should try it."

"You read a romance novel?"

"I have a lot to learn."

"Seems like you've learned a lot already." She gripped his shirt and tugged him close. "Now kiss me in the rain. It'll make the perfect ending."

Flynn dipped his mouth to hers and drank her in, the cool rainwater causing their lips to slip. He held her tightly, making good on his promise never to let her go. Rain or shine, apparently.

When they parted, his blue eyes locked on hers, his arms still holding her. Then a genuine, perfect grin lit his face. "Say it."

"Say what?"

"The ending."

"Oh, right." She cleared her throat and announced, "And they lived happily ever after."

* * * * *

THE SECRET
TWIN

CATHERINE MANN

To Vickie Ostrander Gerlach,
a dear friend and amazing beta reader!
Thank you for cheering me on during
the Alaskan Oil Barons journey.

One

Breanna Steele didn't have much time to search the CEO's office at Alaska Oil Barons, Inc. If she got caught, the consequences could be catastrophic.

But she was out of options.

Brea needed answers and she didn't know who to trust. What if she chose wrong?

There were things far worse than prison.

She'd made a quick search of paperwork, and now she dropped into the sleekly modern leather chair behind the massive desk. She tried not to think about the times she'd visited this space as a child, when the office had been her father's. Saturday mornings coming here with her dad and her twin sister after breakfast at Kit's Kodiak Café. Playing hide-and-seek under the huge desk, or watching cartoons on the big screen at the other end of the office space, sharing a blanket while they fell asleep on the leather sofa.

Now the space belonged to another man, someone outside of the family. The desk and the corner walls of windows overlooking the frozen bay and distant mountains were the same as she remembered. But the rest of the space was now filled with new furniture—sleeker, minimalist wood and leather pieces. Her father's office had been packed with family photos. Ward Benally had only one picture on his desk. Him with a little girl, elementary-school-aged, sledding.

She knew he wasn't married, but clearly this child meant something to him. And that made him more personable. More than just an arrogant leader of a company that now belonged just as much to her rivals as to her family. Her father's oil empire had merged with the Mikkelsons' after his recent marriage.

Of course, Brea hadn't really been a part of any of that, since they had believed she'd died as a young teen.

Brea's conscience pinched. But her sense of survival dictated that she continue looking for the damning information.

She pulled a flash drive from her purse and plugged it into the computer. She'd lived off-the-grid for years, and while some thought that meant no computers, no communication with the outside world, she'd actually learned to use the internet without leaving a trail, building on knowledge she'd learned from her dad.

Learning to hack and code were skills stitched and threaded through much of her young life, before the airplane crash that had taken her from her family. She had shared that with her father. Once her mind was made up, Brea could accomplish anything. Dogged, unrelenting persistence. Also like Jack Steele. Her daddy.

Her chest went tight.

She blinked back tears and clicked through the keys, her fingers slick from the thin latex gloves she wore to keep her prints out of the office. Paranoid? Maybe. Maybe not. Bottom line, she couldn't be too careful.

Someone connected to this company had played a role in the airplane crash that had killed her mother. The crash that had changed Brea's life forever, in ways she still struggled to understand.

She had to have answers before she could put the past behind her, before she could feel safe here. Yes, she wanted to believe her relatives had nothing to do with such horrible treachery. Yet everything she'd learned pointed to someone in the Mikkelson family having been a part of the crash.

And now her father was married to the Mikkelson matriarch, merging their rival oil companies into Alaska Oil Barons, Inc. How surreal after their years of bitter competition and even outright enmity.

Almost too surreal. Like there might be a setup.

Hopefully she could find a clue here. If she didn't? Well, she didn't plan on giving up. She needed closure. But she also needed safety.

She wanted to reunite with her siblings, but she couldn't be sure where their loyalties lay. The risk of showing her hand was too high. She would be persistent. And patient.

Glancing at her watch, she checked the time. Earlier, she'd ferreted information out of the assistant that Ward would be in a conference call for most of the afternoon. But she didn't want to press that time to the limit.

A file name caught her attention, one simply titled with the date of the plane crash. She stifled a shiver at memories of the aircraft's plummet from the sky. The terror. Her mother's tight grip on her hand.

The air sucked from her lungs now. The same as it had then. A pull back to that day. The fear was a blood rush dragging her down. She could hear the whine of dying engines and the rustle of rapidly approaching earth.

Brea relived this moment more often than she cared to admit. Her body time traveling to the day that drew a line in the sand of her life. An eternal before and after.

A distraction Brea couldn't afford right now.

She clicked to copy the file to her flash drive, the urge to read it now overwhelming. Her heart raced, her speeding pulse hammering in her ears.

"What are you doing in my office?"

Brea jolted upright, the masculine voice making her heart stop.

Not only had she been discovered in the act of spying. But she'd been caught by the man himself. Ward Bennally. The new CEO of Alaska Oil Barons, Inc. A sexy dark-haired man wearing an Armani suit, cowboy boots...

And a heavy scowl.

Ward Benally had expected the first months as CEO of Alaska Oil Barons, Inc., would be challenging. He welcomed that. He lived and breathed his job.

It was his whole life.

It was all he had left.

He'd just finished a brutal board meeting that had almost broken out into a fistfight over disagreements about modifications to the oil pipeline. He'd come to his office to get documents he hoped would satisfy both sides. He'd also looked forward to a few moments alone to quiet his frustration.

Instead he found his office invaded by the last person he would trust alone with sensitive company data.

Brea Steele, the long-lost daughter of Jack Steele. The same daughter who'd posed as an employee of Alaska Oil Barons, Inc., not that long ago, to gain access to heaven only knew what kind of encrypted information. She could not be trusted. That should be obvious to everyone. But Jack was so happy to have his presumed-dead daughter back, they all had to put up with her, even though, by all rights, she should be under prosecution.

Ward eyed her with suspicion as she kept her hands out of sight, her brown eyes guarded as she sat at *his* desk.

"Well?" he repeated. "What are you doing in my office?"

Slowly, she rose from the buttercream leather chair, her hands now tucked in the back pockets of her black jeans. Jeans that clung to her long legs like a second skin. "I was waiting for you."

Her voice was cool and composed. Her sleek ponytail swished as she made her way around the desk, the silky glide of dark hair drawing his gaze like a hypnotic pendulum.

She was a smoke-and-mirrors show.

And his body reacted to her every time, no matter how often his brain reminded him she was trouble. "Looks to me like you were snooping around."

"I'm nosy." She shrugged, watching him through long dark eyelashes. "What can I say?"

"You call it nosy?" He strode forward, risking coming close enough to catch a whiff of…mint. "I call it breaking and entering."

"Your assistant let me in," she said neatly.

That gave him pause. He made a mental note to check her story. Even if it was true, she still should have been seated on the sofa or one of the guest chairs. "Did my assistant give you permission to use my computer?"

Her shrug called attention to her gentle curves. He snapped his attention back to the facts he knew about her. The woman before him had lied. Pretended to be someone else. Her actions were downright criminal. Brea could not be trusted. No matter how drop-dead sexy she looked in a turtleneck sweater.

"I just chose the most comfortable place to wait." She picked up the silver picture frame from his desk, no doubt to distract him. "Who's the kid? Cute little girl."

"Put that back." His voice was low, brooking no argument. The way he should have spoken to her about sitting at his desk. When she didn't put the frame down, he took it from her hands.

Ward had lost everything when his ex-wife left him, taking his stepdaughter with her. Since he wasn't little Paisley's biological father, he'd lost all rights to her after the divorce from Melanie. He'd hoped his ex would be open to letting them visit—or at least talk—but that hadn't been the case. His former wife just wanted to move on with her new life with her new husband.

Ward had been, for all intents and purposes, Paisley's dad since he'd started dating Melanie, when her daughter was eight months old. He and Melanie had married a year later. The marriage had lasted for six more years…longer than it would have if there hadn't been a child involved.

Ward wasn't sure he ever would have given up, for Paisley's sake. But Melanie had cheated, filed for divorce and was married to a guy twenty-five years her senior, wealthy, retired and ready to shower her with his money and time.

The metal on the frame dug into Ward's palm.

"Sorry." Brea twisted her hands in front of her, nails short, chewed down. "It was right out there for display."

"Only if you were behind my desk, in my chair." He placed the frame facedown so the picture of his stepdaughter wouldn't distract him. He glanced back up to find Brea's face showing a rare moment of vulnerability.

Calculated or legit? Experience with women told him it was more likely the former.

Her elegant throat moved with a slow swallow. "So, I wanted to see what my father's office felt like, if it was the same as when I was a child, spinning in the CEO's chair."

He stuffed back images of his child doing the same.

And yes, he was surprised Brea had gone for the heartstrings. "That was well-played."

"What do you mean?"

"You are throwing out that childhood memory to try and garner sympathy...or distract me from where you were sitting."

He wasn't letting her get away with invading his space. Heads would roll over her getting in here. For now, though, he couldn't afford to let her escape until he had answers.

"Okay, I sat in my father's chair because once I thought I would have a right to be there, that I would lead the company." She nibbled her bottom lip, slick with gloss. "For a moment I wanted to pretend that life had played out the way I'd hoped."

Was that another ploy to tug at his emotions and distract him? He wasn't sure.

Regardless, his eyes were drawn to her mouth.

He tamped down a rush of attraction. "You were still in my chair. At my computer."

All vulnerability slid from her face. She crossed her arms over her chest defiantly. "Fine. You're right. I had no business parking myself there. What do you intend to do about it?"

"I could call security." Ward's mouth tightened into a thin line. He met her brown eyes with an unrelenting stare. The kind of stare he'd perfected in long games of poker, after his divorce. The poker table was where he'd regained command and control. Honed his skills for leadership. For impassive demands.

"You could. And when they find there's nothing on me and it's just your word against mine?" Her voice was rich and sultry. Those dark brows arched…playfully?

"If they find nothing on you." He watched her face for signs he'd struck a chord.

Was it his imagination or did her eyes widen with fear? As fast as the look was there, it left.

"And my father? What will he think?"

Jack Steele would do anything to keep her here—in town, at the company, in the family—and they both knew it. Still, Ward bluffed. He was good at it. His fast-track career attested to that. "He's on the board, but that doesn't mean he can fire me."

She ran her fingers along the edge of the desk, the movement slow and intentional as she looked up at him. Fire flashed in those eyes. "He'll be upset and his opinion still carries a lot of sway with the board and investors."

It was rare someone called his bluff. Instincts told him she was a worthy adversary.

Which made her all the more attractive.

Damn.

"You're right. So, why were you in here when you know it could make things tougher for the two of you to reconcile?"

"I guess that proves I wasn't doing anything wrong." She toyed with the end of her sleek ponytail.

He chuckled softly, not tricked at all by her little hair twirl. "Are you sure you're not a lawyer like your twin? Because you sure do have a way with words."

"Must be genetics." She flicked her hair back over her shoulder, drawing his attention to the curve of her breasts, outlined by the formfitting black sweater.

He cleared his throat and backed up a step, needing air that didn't carry a minty scent. "Enough flirting."

"Flirting?" She smiled slowly. "Were you hoping I was flirting with you?"

Yeah, actually, he was.

And that was dangerous.

But not as dangerous as having her wandering around unchecked, peeking into the everyday operations of Alaska Oil Barons, Inc. It was bad enough she'd gotten away with it once. That was when she was in disguise and no one had an emotional connection to her. Now that the Steele family was emotionally vulnerable over her return after being presumed dead, there was no telling what they would let her do.

He needed to come up with a plan to keep her in his sights, sooner rather than later.

* * *

Brea needed to get out of Ward's office sooner rather than later.

How could she have let herself get caught up in flirting with him? Every second she remained here increased the chances of him finding the flash drive in her purse. She'd barely had time to peel off the latex gloves and stuff them away. If he'd seen them, he would have realized she'd been up to something shady for sure.

Although, if her fingerprints had been found on the keyboard, in the file cabinets or in the desk, she would have been in even worse trouble.

"I need to go." Was that breathy voice hers? She cleared her throat and started toward the door.

Except, Ward's broad chest was in her way. She should have worn heels. But she'd been thinking about stealth and not whether she could meet Ward's eyes once she got caught. Vibrant blue eyes, the color of an Alaskan lake, lightly iced over and ready to thaw.

"Of course." He nodded, waving her through the door. "After you." When she hesitated, he said, "Really, after you."

Only then did she realize she'd been standing, rooted to the spot, looking into his gaze like a starstruck, sex-starved idiot.

She forced a vampish smile onto her face. "I promise, I'm not going to work my wiles on your assistant to get through the door."

"Again."

She blinked. "What?"

"Get through my door...*again*." His smile matched hers, making her realize he'd seen right through her.

Was he as affected by a simple grin as she was? Because if so, then they were both in trouble. Her body was tingling from head to toe. There'd been a combustible chemistry between them from the moment they'd met. And the timing couldn't be worse, given the mess with her family.

The mess she *still* had to settle.

She couldn't afford the distraction of this man. Too bad his job put him firmly in the way of her goal of finding closure for her past. She needed to know who was responsible for blowing apart her family. For ending her mother's life.

And until she knew whom she could trust, she had to maintain a laser focus. Keeping him off-balance would help. "Who was the child in the picture?"

She nodded toward the metal frame he'd placed face-down on the desk. The Ward Benally in that picture seemed so different from the one before her. Against the surreal backdrop of a snowcapped-mountain range, he and the young child—maybe a four-year-old—leaned forward in a wooden sled. Snow wicked off in a wave to the side of the sled. Ward's blue eyes, somehow visible, were soft. Filled with joy. His protective arm was around the child, who was dressed in a puffy pink jacket and snow pants. Laughter was present on her little face.

"That's my stepdaughter." His smile faded, his face somber.

Mission accomplished in knocking him off-balance. So why did she feel so bad? "But you're not married."

"Not any longer." Tight voice. Tight response.

Off-balance indeed. A moment of guilt passed through her. The glimmer of pain in his words stung.

That shouldn't have mattered to her, but given their undeniable chemistry, it did. "I'm sorry."

He nodded toward the door again, not budging from his position. He obviously wanted to ensure she walked out first. "I need to get to work. As soon as I escort you from the building, I can do that."

She really should make tracks and get out with whatever info she'd gained. She's was risking too much by staying here, drawn in by Ward Benally's allure.

Striding through the door, she tried to ignore the sensation of his eyes on her. One breath at a time. She forced her heart rate to slow in time with her steps. She kept her gaze forward, off the window view of Alaska—icy water, snow and mountains. All so familiar. She wondered how the memories of this place had become dulled during her years away in the isolated little Canadian village, where her "adoptive" parents lived, a close-knit community that had become her world after the plane crash.

"Benally," a deep voice rumbled down the corridor.

Her father's voice.

Brea froze.

Ice crackled through her veins at this next surprise. Nothing she'd planned from this data-gathering mission had gone as expected. But this next hiccup truly rattled her to the core.

She should have thought of the possibility of seeing her father when she came here. Should have been prepared. She was working on talking with her family, trying not to close doors until she figured out whom she could trust. But she usually had more time to prepare herself.

Was that Ward's hand on her back?

Her brain scrambled with too much to process at once. Her vision cleared, and she saw the conference room was half full—her father, his new wife and a slew of Mikkelson and Steele relatives, along with investor Birch Montoya and environmental scientist Royce Miller, husband to Brea's twin sister, Naomi.

Brea stumbled. Air sucked from her lungs again.

Even though she'd come back to Alaska last fall—albeit in disguise—it was still like a sucker punch coming face-to-face with Naomi. Seeing all her siblings was tough. But Naomi? They'd shared more than similar looks. They'd shared a bond.

Or so she'd thought.

When Brea had come to this office before, she'd half expected Naomi to recognize her even while she posed as Milla Jones. She'd chosen the fake identity to infiltrate the company and find out what had happened all those years ago. But when her initial snooping had been uncovered, things had gotten complicated. She'd just wanted to know who she could trust, to get answers about the past and gain vengeance for her mother.

And yes, maybe she'd had the tiniest hope that she could have her family back.

But Naomi hadn't even recognized her. There hadn't been a single spark of recognition. Even knowing it was irrational to expect Naomi to know her—even in disguise, even after all this time—that total loss of connection had still hurt.

Her father stepped from the doorway, into the corridor, the others still hanging back in the conference room, behind the glass window. "Good afternoon, Brea," her lumbering father said in that voice that sounded like he'd gargled rocks over the years. "I didn't know you were here."

Somehow he managed to look exactly like she remembered him from before the plane crash. Broad-chested. His eyes the unflinching blue of the Atlantic Ocean. Hair still dark and thick, although flecked with gray these days. As he looked at her now, she saw hope cross his angular jaw as his mouth relaxed into a small, nearly imperceptible smile.

That sure seemed to be the comment of the day. "I came by to speak with Ward."

Her father's eyebrows met, creasing his forehead. "What about?"

Her heart hammered again as she looked at Ward with panic. Was he going to rat her out? She wouldn't blame him. And she hated how easily she'd just lied. And lied poorly, for that matter. Could her inability to think quickly have had something to do with the distracting touch of Ward's hand on her back?

Just as she opened her mouth to spin out a better version of her fib, a breathless woman rushed up the hallway, toward them, pushing a stroller. It took Brea a moment to place her as Isabeau Mikkelson, wife of Trystan, mother of little Everett, and a media consultant.

The frazzled redhead thrust a binder toward Jack. "Here are the printouts of the guest list for the engage-ment party for Delaney and Birch, so you and Jeannie can work with them on the seating chart." She rushed to add, "And I locked down the vintage roulette wheel for the casino theme."

Smoothing her shoulder-length hair, Isabeau smiled gently. A calming soul. One of the people Brea instinc-tively felt to be genuine. Besides, Isabeau wasn't con-nected to the Mikkelsons by blood. And Brea had to admit, that lack of connection made Isabeau intriguing as a potential information source. There was that old saying that those on the margins could see the center best. And damn, did Brea need a better vantage point.

Jack nodded. "Seating chart. Casino theme. Got it."

His words blurred together as Brea studied her family through the hall window. They were scattered around the conference room, some speaking in pairs, others clustered behind Jack.

Brea's gaze skirted to her baby sister, Delaney, a slender woman with dark wavy hair, standing quietly. Dressed in a simple red sweater dress and knee-high cognac-colored boots, Delaney visibly brightened as she leaned forward to look at the paper Isabeau handed to Jack Steele.

Brea swallowed hard. Memories of playing dress up with her sisters, decades ago, scrolled through her mind. Days of making bridal veils from towels with her sisters. They'd dreamed of planning those real family events together.

Her life was such a jumble.

Brea remembered her family, her childhood. But in the years that had passed since the crash, it felt like those memories had become unreliable. Thanks to the lies and betrayal of her "adoptive" parents, she questioned what was real…and what she wanted to believe.

There was so little she knew for certain. Such as how her mother had a special seal hunting knife called an ulu that she'd used to cut their pizza. Her mother's impossibly strong and reassuring "I love you" as the plane had plummeted.

Everything else? Up for debate and analysis.

The caress of Ward's hand on the small of her back pulled Brea back to the present. She looked at him, startled, curious.

His smile gave her only a moment's warning before he announced, "I guess this is as good a time as any to let them know our little secret."

Panic sent her heart racing. Had he seen her take off the gloves after all? Maybe there were cameras in his office?

"Um, let's talk about this."

"You're such a tenderhearted woman." His hand slid up her spine in a body-melting stroke that ended with his arm around her shoulders. His expression showed a warmth she'd never seen from him before. "It's sweet of you to worry what your family will think. I know they've only just gotten you back, but I think they'll understand the need to share you."

"Share *me*?" She was struggling for air.

Talk about being knocked off-balance. Her efforts to pull one over on her family had been amateur compared to this move. And she was too damned speechless to come up with a rebuttal as he tucked her closer to his side.

"Yes. Share you. With your boyfriend." Ward's grin dug dimples in his wind-weathered face before he announced, "Brea and I are dating."

Two

Ward was a man of action and swift decisions.

And he saw that this was the perfect opportunity to keep Brea in his sights—as his "girlfriend." Now he just needed to get Brea away from her family ASAP to convince her that he was right before she denied they were dating and blew up the whole charade.

"I'll be right back, after I see Brea to her car so she's not late for her dental appointment." Ward filled the stunned silence so he could direct the conversation. "Go ahead and get started without me. I'll catch up."

With a quick nod, he hustled her toward the elevator, as fast as possible, before the stunned Steeles and Mikkelsons could start asking questions. As he walked quickly down the corridor, thank heaven, she stayed at his side, for whatever reason. Shock? Curiosity? Or... Who knew what went on inside that woman's mind.

The minute the elevator door closed them inside, Brea stomped her foot, leveling him with eyes as dark as fire-hot coals. "Have you lost your mind? What the hell was that all about back there?"

He tapped the stop button, halting the elevator mid-floor. "That was about keeping you close to my side. The snooping has to stop. At least while you're pretending to be my girlfriend, I can watch you."

Her eyes widened in shock. "You can't be serious. You actually expect me to pretend to be your girlfriend so you can keep tabs on me? And you think people will believe that we've been secretly dating?" She shook her head quickly, restlessly turning away, then back to him again. "You have got to be kidding."

"I'm dead serious." That much was true. His job was everything to him. He would not be made a laughing-stock by a snoop who should just talk to her family… unless she had some darker motive. In which case, she should be kept under close scrutiny. He would be the one to take on that task because he was in charge. And yes, because of attraction crackling between them like sparks showing from a blazing fire. "I'm single. There are events I need to attend with a plus-one. This also saves me time."

"That's an absurd excuse." Her voice went higher with frustration. "Be real. What could you have to gain from this charade? If you're that worried about little ole me, why not just install some security cameras?"

"You're right. I could up the security system to watch every inch of any space we control on the off chance I catch you getting up to something." He paused, and then pointed out logically, "And then, if I were successful, your dad and your siblings would forever see me as the person who revealed their princess to be an evil queen. This way, I can be more proactive."

"Princess? Evil queen? You're weird." Sighing, she furrowed her brow. "How is that different from catching me at something while I'm your pretend girlfriend?"

"I'm not weird. Just logical. If I'm watching you, you won't have a chance to be in that position. Besides, you'll get to stick close to me. And since you seem to be there every time I turn around, I have reason to believe that must hold some kind of appeal for you, too." He tugged her ponytail, testing the silky texture between his fingers, imagining it spread out over the pillow next to him. "And yes, there's more in it for me than just a plus-one for events. As a bonus, I gain acceptance by the board of directors. Being with you makes me a de facto member of the family."

Her eyebrows shot up in horror. "We are *not* getting married just to lock down your new job in the company."

"Of course not. I'm not that Machiavellian." He smoothed her silky ponytail back along her shoulder, her pupils widening with awareness at his touch. "But by the time that would be an issue, you and I can break up."

"I'm not dating you for that long." Then she rushed to add, "I'm not dating you at all. Start the elevator."

Ah, she'd mentioned dating. He was making progress. And that filled him with a surge of success. And desire. "We would only go out for a month, until the vote at the next general board meeting for all the shareholders."

She hesitated, worrying her bottom lip. "Then we just…what? We break up?"

He pulled his eyes off her moist lips.

"That's how it works, yes. You can even dump me." He winked, taking heart in her light chuckle. "And by all means, make it public and humiliating, in front of your entire family and all my friends—"

"You have friends?" Her deadpan words didn't match the hint of amusement in her eyes.

"I do." He nodded, leaning in such a way that he blocked the elevator buttons. Before long, someone would start it again, but he intended to make the most of their time alone for now. "I have to pay them to be my friends. But they stay loyal as long as I deliver the roll of quarters each week." Which wasn't totally true. He didn't have many friends, not even paid ones. He wasn't the sort to hang out with buddies. He was too busy working until midnight.

She scrunched her nose. "You really are weird."

"Maybe." He was certainly a workaholic. Although, so was most of her family. It was one of the reasons he now held this CEO position. "But the offer for you to dump me in a billboard fashion stands."

"How generous of you. Maybe I'll get one of my siblings to fly a seaplane with a banner." She lifted her chin, jaw jutting with signature Steele confidence that no amount of years away could erase.

"Trust me, my ego can take it."

She studied him for a moment, her exotic eyes narrowing. "Then what's in it for me?"

"Aside from getting to dump me? Isn't that entertainment and payment enough?" He thumped himself on the chest in faux shock.

She rolled her eyes. "While that is an enticing proposition, I'm going to need a little more before I sign on to this plan."

He straightened, ditching the humor and closing the deal. "You'll keep me from ratting you out about being in my office. And you'll get more access to your family with me as an excuse for you to be in and out of this office."

"I'm listening." She waved him on, leaning a slim shoulder against the mirrored elevator wall. "Continue…"

Her sweater pulled snug across her breasts as she folded her arms. His gaze followed the curve of her hip, which was cocked to one side. She drew him in, no doubt.

"I can be a buffer between you and your family." Which would give him the chance to gauge her motivations. No way was he going to let her tank this company. He'd always been a driven individual at work. But even more so now. His career was all he had left, and he refused to allow any threat to his professional reputation. "If you're feeling stressed or uncomfortable, cue me and we can leave."

"Or I could just walk out if they upset me."

He liked the confidence in her voice. But he also knew the situation with her family was far more complicated than that. "You could. But having a buffer so you could make a speedy, nonconfrontational exit would be easier."

"How so?" She looked skeptical.

"We come up with a safe word. If you say it in casual conversation, that lets me know you want to leave. I'll find an out so you don't have to make awkward excuses on the spot."

"Safe word?" Her eyebrows shot upward.

"Bear with me," he said. "I had this uncle who was a preacher. His wife used to get stuck at long functions and meals. So she came up with a conversational gimmick that let her husband know she needed to leave. Immediately."

"What was their word?"

"Words. Anchors aweigh. Which is technically two words, but you get the gist." Stifling a grin, he imagined his aunt working the safe word into their conversation.

A smile twitched at her lips, mesmerizing him. "That's a strange phrase."

"It worked." He enjoyed seeing her lighter hearted. He didn't want a real relationship, not after his bitter divorce, but he couldn't deny he was enjoying the banter. And she was smoking hot, to boot.

A part of him was hoping she'd say yes to this for more than just reasons related to her family. He couldn't deny he was drawn to her. And since he was going to be leading this company, he needed to work through the attraction to her sooner rather than later. Issues left unaddressed became distractions.

And she was already a major distraction.

"Okay then. What do you suggest?"

He thought for a moment, his eyes landing on a framed painting of a home with stone figureheads worked into the architecture. "Gargoyle."

"Gargoyle?" She burst out laughing.

Tension faded from her expression to be replaced by a smile that knocked the air from his lungs. Damn, she was a beautiful woman. Pulling his attention off her delicate features and back on the task at hand, he took heart in making progress with her.

He'd been in business long enough to know when he'd closed the deal. "Do we have an agreement?"

Her eyes narrowed, but her smile didn't fade. "Just until the next general board meeting."

"One month," he said, confident now that he could win her over to extending their time together if needed. For now he'd made major progress. He was going to be able to watch over her. And if she was up to something, he would find out what.

And he had to admit, spending time with her wouldn't be a hardship in the least. She drew him with everything from her sexy curves to the sweep of her eyelashes when she cast a glance his way… She was definitely a distraction he needed to work out of his system.

"So, this is just pretend?"

"As long as you say so. And if you're ever uncomfortable, just remember." He winked, tapping the start button on the elevator. "Gargoyle."

Even five hours later, in her new one-bedroom apartment, Breanna's brain was still reeling from Ward's surprise proposition. Sure, he was smart, sexy, and powerful, and while all of that drew her in, she'd been holding strong.

Until she'd been knocked off-balance by his surprise sense of humor.

She should have put up more of a fight. Or extracted additional tradeoffs. But she'd been unsettled by being caught in his office, and then unexpectedly seeing her family, all of which had lowered her defenses.

Checking her emails on her phone now, she leaned against the cool counter space. The granite pressed into her skin as she skimmed her inbox to see if any of her clients needed anything. As a virtual shopper for those who were homebound or in need of help, her hours were a little inconsistent. No new emails since she'd checked an hour ago, which meant she could turn her attention

back to the blueberry and raspberry muffins she was baking, needing to do something productive since she hadn't
managed to find anything useful on the flash drive yet.

Frustration filled her. She forced herself to focus on
the routine of baking. Grounding herself in the moment.
Muted light filtered in through the windows, dappling
the dark wood floors and small kitchen area.

She was so grateful to have found this space for her
time here in Alaska while she sifted through the rub-
ble of her past. Her uncle's new wife—Felicity Hunt
Steele—had offered this space to sublet. Other Steele relatives had suggested Brea stay with them, but the stress
of that was more than Brea could wrap her head around.

A chirp of the kitchen timer in the shape of a plump,
plucky hen snapped Brea to attention. She grabbed the
gold polka-dot oven mitt from the kitchen counter and
peeked into the oven. A wave of warmed-berry scent
rode the air, escaping through the open oven door. Such
a sweet scent. It made her stomach growl in anticipation.
A memory flashed through her mind of berry picking
with her siblings and parents, of her dad telling her to
avoid the white berries, which were poisonous.

She swallowed hard before the past could swamp her
with too many recollections at once. The faster they
came, the tougher it was to gauge which ones were real.

A dish towel in hand, she pulled the muffins from the
pan, one by one. Since she'd shed her disguise as Milla
Jones and returned to Alaska last month, she'd been
spending controlled amounts of time with her family.
Always with others present, including her uncle's new
wife, who was a social worker.

Felicity had even given Brea a list of therapists. Not
necessarily to facilitate a reunion. But to make sure she

kept a clear head and didn't get hurt. Brea had called
numbers on that list until she found a counselor she was
comfortable with, one who could help her.

She wasn't sure if she would reconcile with her family or not, but she needed some semblance of peace with
her past before she could move on with the future. She'd
known that on some level when she'd come to Alaska,
posing as Milla Jones.

And how did her attraction to Ward play into that? It
was a dangerous distraction. She would have to keep a
close guard on her hormones around this man.

A rapid knock caused her door to shudder, startling
her. Rattling awake other memories she did her best to
keep locked up in the corners of her mind.

Her gut clenched with tension. She'd spent so many
years in that minimalist, off-the-grid community, she
still wasn't used to having such a cluttered world. She
walked from her kitchen, through the living area to the
front door. She peered through the keyhole…and sighed
with relief.

Felicity stood with Tally Benson, Felicity's friend and
the woman who was dating Marshall Steele. These two
were easy company, since they weren't a part of her past.
Brea clicked through all three locks and opened the door.

"Hello," Felicity said, holding up a basket full of pampering bath items—salts, a loofa and towels. She had a
way of taking care of everyone, perhaps something to
do with her chosen career as a social worker. "We've
brought housewarming gifts."

Tally carried a wicker laundry hamper. "All natural
cleaning supplies, just for you."

While trust was difficult, these two women were the
only ones Brea had met since her return whom she felt at

least partially comfortable with. Although, her relationship with Tally was still complicated. Tally's father had
been the mechanic who worked on the airplane before
the crash. He'd committed suicide because of his guilt
over what had happened. No one yet knew the full extent
of the details of the crash, and Tally's father had taken
his secrets to the grave. But at least the man's name offered a place to start searching for answers.

"Thank you so much," Brea said, touched by their
kindness, and a little overwhelmed too, especially with
the berry-picking memory still so fresh in her mind.
"Um, please come inside."

Felicity hesitated. "Are you sure we're not imposing?"

Brea laughed softly. "Of course I'm sure, not that I
would turn you away. It is your condo and you've been
kind enough to sublease it to me for next to nothing."

"You've done me a favor," Felicity said without hesitation. "Now I'm able to live with Conrad without this
place hanging over my head unused."

Brea gestured for the duo to come into the apartment,
appreciating the down-to-earth nature of both of these
women. "The gifts are lovely. You two didn't have to
do this."

"Conrad sends his thanks as well for the help with
my lease," Felicity called over her shoulder as if they
all didn't already know Conrad Steele could have paid
the rent for her apartment multiple times over. Felicity
continued to work at the local hospital, where she'd been
today, and her hair was still swept back in a French twist.
"You can soak out the tension."

Tally strode past, her red ponytail swishing. Felicity
had taken her under her wing not too long ago. Tally
had been a housekeeper and now attended college on a

scholarship to become a social worker, as well. "If you need any help, just call me."

Felicity set the basket on the coffee table, cellophane wrapping crinkling. "Although, for the record," she said with a smile and an elegantly arched eyebrow, "I did leave the place spotless."

"You did," Brea agreed, chewing her bottom lip. It seemed so surreal to have the two women move so effortlessly into her life. Making friends was hard for her after all she'd been through. Even though the small Canadian community had been welcoming, her adoptive parents had been guarded with others. She'd been alone, not even sure she could trust her own instincts, for a long time. Being told that her biological family was deeply corrupt. She was safer away from them. "Thank you for coming over. Both of you. Could I offer you something to drink?"

"Well, actually—" Tally paused, unloading the cleaning supplies and stowing them under the kitchen sink "—we did have another reason for coming by."

Brea's stomach knotted with nerves. Closing the front door was tough, especially when she wanted to run. "What would that be?"

Felicity pinned her with a knowing gaze. "When did you start dating Ward Benally?"

Brea exhaled with relief that they weren't going to grill her about her past. Only to have her nerves return with a vengeance over the mention of her fake boyfriend.

Her very sexy, surprisingly charming fake boyfriend.

She really wasn't ready for fielding questions about Ward.

"The relationship started very recently." Very. Very. Recently.

"Well, I'm not surprised at all." Tally pulled out a barstool from behind the counter and sat, her boot heels resting on the lowest rung. "I noticed the chemistry between the two of you at the fund-raiser last month."

Had it been obvious even then? Brea had felt the sparks, but she'd liked to think she'd hidden her reaction. Apparently not.

Felicity leaned over to look at the baked goods. "Was that when it started, at the fund-raiser?"

Brea *hmmed*, taking a bite to fill her mouth and avoid talking. Too bad no one was around who could help if she shouted *gargoyle*. "Anyone want a muffin?"

Tally pulled napkins from a counter holder. "Yes, please. Although I do hear you trying to change the subject. I imagine you're wondering how much you can trust the two of us."

True, but not the sort of thing Brea expected to hear voiced aloud.

"Although—" Felicity broke a muffin in half, then pinched off a bite "—that's an unwinnable proposition, since no matter what we say, there's really no way to prove you can trust us at this point. Trust takes time."

How long? Brea wished she knew. "Spoken like a counselor."

"Because I am one." Felicity swept up a crumb into her hand and then into the sink. "For what it's worth, Tally and I are both new to the Steele family realm. As such, we weren't a part of the old days, the old problems and whatever happened then. But we're here for you now and want to be your friends, as well as family."

Brea wanted to believe that. "I'm still getting to know everyone again."

"Give it time." Felicity squeezed her hand.

Tally scrunched her freckled nose, grinning. "And while you're giving it time, tell us… Does Ward kiss as incredibly as it seems he would?"

Brea felt the heat steal up to her face. That particular topic was occupying far more of her thoughts than it should. Her cell phone dinged with an incoming text and Brea embraced the excuse to step away from the intense conversation. She wanted—needed—a chance to regain her footing. "Excuse me for a moment. I need to check that."

She raced to scoop her phone off the coffee table and turned her back on the two women, who seemed content to snack on their muffins. She thumbed the text open to find…

A message from Ward.

Butterflies launched inside her. She shouldn't feel this excited, but she did. And she couldn't afford to be distracted by hormones, not when she finally had a real chance at the answers she craved.

Then she read his message, and it was as if the floor fell away beneath her feet.

I'll be by at seven to pick you up for supper with the Steeles. Be ready to help me make nice with all your family members on the board.

So much for keeping a lock on her emotions. Her body was already on fire at just the thought of seeing him again.

Ward knew he was pushing it with the impromptu dinner out with the Steeles. But he'd wanted to see Brea, and this was the fastest, easiest way to lock that down.

He didn't want to think overlong about how damn much he looked forward to seeing her. Better to keep it simple. This was a short-term thing between them. He was married to his work.

So he could just enjoy the moment, and yes, this potential for a fling. By the time she figured out he had set up the get-together, it would be too late. She would already be sitting at the table.

Would she be mad?

Almost certainly.

Was she sexy when riled up?

Absolutely.

He'd been surprised by how much he wanted to see her again. How his intentions had shifted so quickly from wanting to keep an eye on her to wanting to follow through on their attraction. Now he saw that his dating idea had no doubt sprung from the heat that flared whenever they were near each other. But if that played out into a fling, he could handle it. His emotions were locked down tight after the number his ex had pulled on him.

He guided his SUV through the night, headlights striping bands of illumination into the snowy air ahead, Brea in the passenger seat, quiet since he'd picked her up. Likely there were other ways to keep watch over her, but this was far more…entertaining.

Snowflakes sprinkled down, glinting in the beams. Brea looked stunning sitting beside him in a royal-blue wool coat and black leather boots. Her hair was draped over one shoulder in an appealing onyx waterfall. She sat so still and regal, he would have thought her unaffected by this evening together if not for the way she picked at her short fingernails.

Low music played from the speakers, his playlist of classical guitar music.

Brea sighed heavily.

He stifled a grin. "You seem angry, my dear."

"My dear?" She turned in her seat toward him, the dash lights casting her face in seductive shadows. "Are you serious? No one's watching us."

"But you are my dear, new girlfriend." Flicking his eyes from the road, he met her eyes.

"*Fake* girlfriend. And since no one's around, let's make some ground rules."

"Such as?" He gripped the leather steering wheel as he accelerated. The sound of the exhaust mingled with the few other trucks on the road.

"You could start telling me about these plans of yours—the whole dating thing and going to the family dinner—earlier than a few minutes ahead of time."

He didn't bother noting that he'd given her a few hours to prepare. He got her point. "If I had given you too much advance notice, would you have come along?"

"You'll never know, will you? You didn't give me the chance to decide." She crossed her arms, head turning away from him to look out the window at the snow lightly falling from the sky.

"I do know," he retorted without hesitation. Then felt the need to own up to planning this. His gut served him well in business. He would think of this arrangement with her like business. "If I'd made the reservations for later in the week, you would have come up with excuses."

"That's my right."

"Yes, it is." SUV idling at a stoplight, he waited, knowing she would come to the obvious conclusion.

"All right, but if I decline, then I don't get the inside scoop on my family. Fine." She huffed in exasperation. "So how about from now on, you give me the opportunity to say yes or no and see what happens."

"Fair enough. I will take that under consideration."

Mouth twitching into a satisfied smile, he approached the one-story brown cottage, which had been turned into a restaurant, more eager for her approval than he wanted to admit.

The historic brown building with cream trim seemed bright against the gray backdrop of February skies. Guiding the SUV into the parking lot, he readied himself for this next encounter.

A favorite place of his. Simple from the outside, like a small home, but the restaurant boasted top-notch Alaskan seafood cuisine, the menu changing weekly. With only a dozen tables, it offered an intimate setting. He'd booked the place for the entire night to avoid prying eyes as they became comfortable with other.

He passed the keys to the valet and joined Brea under the covered walk leading to the front door. He clasped her elbow to make sure she didn't slip, even though the path had been shoveled and salted. The simple touch launched a wave of heat through him. Her quiet gasp told him she wasn't immune either. The pace of her breathing increased, puffing tiny clouds of air into the night.

He paused outside the door, turning to face her, her eyes locking with his. He lifted a curl of her hair and stroked the length of it, testing the silky texture between his fingers. Her eyes went wide with awareness. He understood the draw well.

More than this ruse, than her family, it was that draw that had brought them both here tonight.

The door swung wide, a host greeting them with a smile as the warmth gusted out. "Welcome to Chez Louis, Mr. Benally. Most of your party has arrived. They're enjoying drinks in the lounge. Ma'am, if I could take your coat?"

The small crowd of Steeles and Mikkelsons already filled the dining area, most of them standing beneath vintage antler chandeliers. Conversation wafted over in murmurs.

No sooner had Ward and Brea passed off their coats than his date bolted away, under the guise of talking to Felicity and Delaney. The duo stood by a crackling fire, sipping wine. Waitstaff walked from person to person, offering roasted-eggplant pâté on pita bread and gnocchi with cambozola and red crab. Another waiter flourished a tray with Alaskan oysters and Neapolitan seafood mousse.

But Ward's attention was still on Brea. His smile faded. He didn't want to frighten her. When he'd roped her into this pretend relationship, he'd been so focused on protecting the company, he hadn't thought much about what she'd been through, losing her family, for all intents and purposes kidnapped. He needed to weigh his next move carefully to protect the business. And yes, to protect this woman too, if she was somehow as vulnerable as she'd looked in that flash before she'd retreated.

A tap on the shoulder had him looking away to turn and find Broderick Steele, Brea's oldest brother. "We need to have a talk. Are you actually dating my sister?"

"Why is that a question? I already announced that we are, and we came here together." Had Brea said something to tip off her brother? Ward studied the man in front of him—the eldest Steele was a carbon copy of his father.

"You barely know her," Broderick said. "She's hardly speaking to our family. We don't know if we can trust her. Shall I keep listing the reasons why this seems like the strangest relationship ever?"

Broderick was sharp from years in the boardroom.

But so was Ward.

"She's an attractive woman." His gaze landed on her all over again, enjoying the way she looked in her red sheath dress with long sleeves and a low back. "Circumstances drew us together. We have chemistry. It's nothing serious at this point, but we're giving it a go. How's that for a list?"

"She's fragile." Broderick's shoulders braced protectively as he tightened his grip on his lowball glass.

"You clearly don't know Brea—the woman she is now—as well as you think." Even considering that moment of fear in her face, he knew how brave she must be to face all of them after what she'd been through.

But brave didn't necessarily equate with honest.

"That could be true," Broderick conceded, tipping his drink from one side to the other, making the ice cubes clink against cut crystal. "I'm not sure anyone does know who she is now, since she's playing things so close to the vest. What if your relationship explodes in your face?"

Ward glanced across the room to where Brea stood with the other women by the thick cream-colored curtains. Her dark features schooled into practiced neutrality. "Then that would be a damn shame, but I don't see what it has to do with my contract with the company."

Broderick's eyebrows raised as his face became tight, foreboding as a winter storm. "It could make things awkward for you with the family if you two are tangled up with each other."

"Could. But it won't. I'm a professional." And if Brea really was intent on harming the company in some way, he was the only one likely to push hard enough to figure it out. Her family seemed to just want her back, no matter what she'd done.

He understood that feeling well after losing his stepdaughter. But he couldn't let it jeopardize what he was building here at Alaska Oil Barons, Inc. He had big plans for the company, working with Royce Miller to implement his inventions for the safer transportation of fuel and alternative energy sources. Delaney Steele was also an advocate with strong connections. He had a chance to make a difference.

Broderick eyed him skeptically. "Do you actually think life is that simple?"

"Sometimes it is. Sometimes it isn't," he answered as honestly as possible, given the circumstance.

"Okay then, I'll make this clear and simple for you." Broderick's voice dropped an octave as he leaned closer. "Be careful with my sister. Because even if I don't know exactly who she has become, she is—and always will be—my sister. If you hurt her, there won't be a place in Alaska remote enough for you to hide."

"Message heard." Ward met Broderick's icy gaze with all the warmth of a tropical island. With a boardroom smile, he inclined his head. "Now I have a date. With your sister."

And despite all the warnings—from Broderick, and from his own wary nature—Ward very much looked forward to kissing her good-night on her doorstep.

Three

If someone had told her a year ago that she would have a subdued casual dinner out with her family, Brea would have called them crazy. But with Ward at her side, she'd faced the Steeles—and the questionable Mikkelsons—through a whole five-course meal.

She'd almost managed to quell her nerves. Almost.

And now that she stood outside her apartment door with the sexy new CEO of Alaska Oil Barons, Inc., her heart raced. He stared down at her with mesmerizingly blue eyes, seeming to see deep inside her. Was that an illusion? Or did Ward Benally somehow have insights into her that her own family—and even she herself—lacked?

The idea was crazy, of course. He was only going through with this dating scheme to keep tabs on her. But she couldn't deny that their connection felt personal.

And that, despite all the reasons she shouldn't trust him, she felt a level of ease in his presence.

Except for right now, when she also felt something dangerously close to…temptation.

"Dinner was nice. The food was delicious." She needed to bring the evening to a sensible close. Thank him and be done with it. "You were a gentleman. I appreciate that you respected my boundaries."

The location had been public enough to avoid confrontations, while also staying away from prying eyes. She was touched by his thoughtfulness, his intuitive understanding of what would be easiest for her. Touched, and surprised.

"You didn't use the safe word even once," he teased, his hand resting on the doorframe beside her, his shoulders broad and the stubble along his jaw an alluring shadow.

She swallowed to clear her suddenly dry mouth. "Because I couldn't remember what it was."

A lie, of course. To cover the fact that she'd actually felt sort of safe with him all evening long.

"Gargoyle." He winked, his blue eyes glimmering with mischief.

"Got it. I won't forget again."

Was there a safe word to protect her against the draw of this man?

Fiddling with the fringes of his wool scarf, Ward seemed to take his time before speaking. "Your family's trying hard to respect your space while welcoming you back into the fold."

She wanted that to be true. But trust was difficult to come by after all she'd been told by the couple who'd rescued her. Her recovery after the crash had been lengthy, and at the start they hadn't known who she was. Then they'd told her that her family had given up looking for her. Now she knew they'd kept her secluded, kidnapped and brainwashed. Her counselor said she suffered from Stockholm syndrome. And because they'd lied, that had crumbled her confidence when it came to believing other people, too. Not that she intended to share all of that with this man, who had questionable motives of his own.

So she stayed silent. Waiting. Wondering why she didn't just say good-night and slide into her apartment. Alone.

Ward's gaze held hers. "There are a lot of you Steeles."

She wished she could see into his thoughts as easily as he seemed to divine hers. "And your point is?"

"Just that they seem to care. They seem to think of you as one of their own." He shrugged his broad shoulders as he took a step toward her.

The distance between them was electric.

"Gargoyle." She swallowed, but didn't back away.

He stilled, head tipped to the side. "You want to leave?"

"Leave this conversation." And still she didn't go into her apartment.

"Okay then… The casino party is still a couple of days away. I think we should make arrangements for another date." He eased back a step, giving her space. "Just to be sure people don't question our devotion to each other. What would you suggest we do next?"

Now, that sounded like a loaded question. "You're in charge of the dates."

"I'm a modern guy, completely okay with you choosing what we do between now and your sister's engagement party."

She mulled over ideas, but she wasn't one for hobbies. Her adoptive family had been hardworking, their community insular and self-sustaining. She'd felt safe there, accepted, loved. Her adoptive parents had convinced her the outside world was dangerous—and she saw now that their fears were overblown. But in many ways, they had treated her well, like the child they'd always wanted and never had. In spite of their betrayal, she couldn't bring herself to hate them.

Damn, but her life was all so confusing.

Her mind wandered back to the time before the crash. Her mind filled with memories of ice fishing with her dad. Of horseback riding with her twin sister. Of climbing into the tree house with her brother Marshall to read—he always preferred quiet, his thick head of curls falling forward over his forehead.

All those memories, though, still felt too questionable, given how much she was working to piece everything together. She should devote time to digging through more data in the files she'd copied from Ward's computer.

Should.

But she wasn't.

There was also something compelling about spending time with her family, especially with Ward as a buffer. He led conversations, allowed her to be quiet when she wanted to observe and process.

The fake dating arrangement could actually benefit her more than she'd ever guessed.

Either that or she was justifying wanting to indulge this attraction just a little while longer.

"Let's get coffee and shop for books," she found herself saying. "Pick me up tomorrow, after seven."

"It's a date," he said, dipping his head to cover her mouth with his.

Surprise stilled her for a moment. The warmth and pressure of his lips on hers was a sudden, pleasant jolt to her senses, drawing all her focus to that place where they touched. The scent of his aftershave tantalized her as he gently deepened the kiss. His tongue touched hers, stroked, and she found herself swaying closer. Her body was ahead of her brain.

Before she could question herself further, though, sensation took over, nerve endings tingling to life, pleasure flowing through her veins. She swayed forward, her breasts lightly skimming against the hard wall of his chest. Her hands slid up to his shoulders. His low growl of approval rumbled between them, and he brought her closer. His tongue carried a lingering taste of dessert and a hint of something else. A breath mint maybe?

Her senses were awash in desire.

Her breath caught. Her fingers fisted against his jacket, gripping him tightly.

The heat and strength of him was apparent even through the wool, and it stunned her to realize how much she wanted to lean in closer. To part the fabric and feel more of him, test and learn the texture of his skin.

He angled back to look into her eyes, and she knew he was giving her control, letting her make the next move. Or not.

Breathing hard, she couldn't deny that she wanted him. She was all the more tempted by his restraint, a quality she appreciated. Admired.

Still, things were moving too fast. Her world was in turmoil.

And this wouldn't be her only chance to be with him.

Before she could succumb to the temptation to invite him inside, she spun away and slipped into her apartment, barely hanging on to the tattered shreds of her control.

She didn't want the night to end, but she would wait.

She *had* to wait. Be certain she wasn't making a mistake.

Because even as she tipped her head back against the door inside her apartment, she was already anticipating their next date.

Shopping for books had never sounded so appealing, when she'd be in the company of the sexiest man she'd ever met.

Ward had wined and dined women. A five-star dinner was a surefire way to get himself out of the doghouse when he'd been married to his ex.

So he'd been caught unaware by Brea's request last night for a simple coffee date, along with book shopping at a local two-story establishment. Although *shopping* wasn't quite the right word for his date's approach to the shelves. Her walk down each aisle was something more akin to worship. She read the spine of each title, touching some reverently.

She gave an elegance to skinny jeans that drew him like a magnet. Turning a corner, she headed for the used-book section, toward the ladder. She climbed up two rungs, her soft red-and-black plaid shirt hugging her curves. Loose hair swaying, she leaned toward the shelf, smiling. The curve of her lips sent his thoughts chasing back to last night. To that spark between them that had leapt into something so very intense during that kiss.

It had been all he could do to walk away from her door last night.

For a moment he could have sworn she had considered taking things to the next level by inviting him into her bed. Maybe the next time they kissed, she wouldn't want to stop.

He certainly hoped that was the case, because thoughts of her were turning him inside out. Considering a fling was one thing. Having her occupy his thoughts so fully was another matter altogether. Obsession was not an option.

She climbed down from the ladder and picked up another book, her fingers stroking over the leather binding. Brea appeared lost in her own world as her hair waterfalled down her back. She was a siren indeed, her curves and the silken glisten of her hair calling to him.

Her beauty almost helped him push back the painful memory of another bookstore outing. Two years ago, he'd taken his stepdaughter to lunch and then out to buy a stack of books for her summer reading.

His mind filled with heartbreaking images of her smile when she found the new superhero-canine story she'd been looking for, her excitement when the store clerk had given her a bookmark with a picture of the fictional dog on it. Ward had promised they would read the first chapter together later that week, but it was a moment that had never happened because Melanie had left him, taking Paisley with her. Losing his little girl had torn his heart out, and he didn't intend to put himself in that vulnerable position ever again.

Clearing away the lump in his throat, he stopped beside Brea, who was thumbing through a mythology collection. "Would you like a refill on the coffee?"

She turned to him with startled eyes, then blinked

back to a more neutral expression. "Yes, please. Extra milk. Extra sweetener."

"As ordered." He pulled his hand from behind his back, already holding what she'd ordered. He'd listened. He tuned in to everything she said.

Not just because he needed to search out any possible hidden agenda.

And to be honest with himself, even if she did have an agenda, he still wanted to sleep with her.

"You know what I like?"

He let the double entendre pass. For now. "I paid attention to your order."

"That, too. Thank you." Cradling the cup in her hands, she eyed him over the top. "What would you have done if I'd said no just now?"

"Then I guess the coffee would have gone into the garbage." He pulled his other hand from behind his back. "Along with mine." He took a swallow of his steaming java while the store music swapped to a light jazz tune.

Foot traffic around the shelves was quiet in this section, although a student with bright red hair and a leather backpack passed now and then, singing to whatever played through the earbuds.

Brea stood in a beam from the track lighting streaming down. After her sip of coffee, she sighed with bliss. "You don't have to romance me."

The hardwood floor squeaked as she shifted her feet.

"I'm attracted to you, and I consider myself a man of finesse." It didn't appear as if she wanted a long-term attachment, which made them a good match for an affair.

If only he could trust her, this would be an easy call, since he wanted her as much as air.

Although, the fact that he couldn't trust her would also protect him emotionally if they did indulge in a fling.

"I noticed." Her nose scrunched with her smile.

"Good. And the more we know about each other, the more authentic our dating ruse will seem to your family." He pulled the book from under her arm and set it on a table by a two-seat sofa tucked in the corner of the store. He motioned for her to sit.

Then he joined her, his thigh against hers, the intimacy of the quiet space wrapping around him. The floral scent of her shampoo teasing his every breath.

She set her coffee down, her brown eyes troubled. "You must realize I'm using you as a buffer with them. Those were the terms for our pretend relationship."

"Of course. And I don't have a problem at all with you using me as much as you like." Taking a sip, he appreciated the bitterness of his black coffee. The way even the scent of the beans kept him alert.

She laughed softly. "You are a strange man."

"A strange man who's piqued your interest." He could see it in her eyes. Feel the crackle in the air between them.

"How is it you manage to make a trip to the corner bookstore seem risqué?"

"You bring it out in me." His eyes lingered on her lips for a moment before he met her gaze, finding a heat that met and matched his own.

He dipped his head, angling his mouth along hers. Not for long. While it was private in this aisle for the moment, he couldn't count on that for long. The hum of voices around the store was muted through his passion-fogged senses, but he maintained enough cognizance to know he and Brea were too close to being discovered. And he wouldn't disrespect her with public displays. He grazed a quick, final kiss along her lips.

As he drew back, he found her eyes warm and dazed with desire. He understood the feeling well. Being this near her turned him inside out. So much so, he ached to get her alone, which was contrary to the whole fake-couple idea. But a quick trip… Hmm…that was simple to pull off with the corporate jet at his disposal. He wouldn't even have to be disconnected from work during a twenty-four-hour date.

"May I have my coffee?" she said, her voice husky.

"Of course." He passed it over, her fingers brushing his, his plan coming into crisp focus. "If you find a couple of books to read, it would help you pass the time on the plane."

"On the plane?" She paled.

"To get coffee—the best. You choose. Guatemala? Tanzania? Kenya? Hawaii? Say the word and you can wake up in the morning to java bliss."

He gestured toward the world map on the wall, a vintage print from the early twentieth century. The chart matched the rest of the travel motif of the bookstore. Old cameras, sextants and suitcases populated the store. A cozy atmosphere with this incredibly sexy woman.

"Taking me to another country for coffee is undoubtedly a romantic gesture, but I'm good with this." Her hands trembled, and she set the coffee down again before twisting her fingers together on her lap.

But he didn't miss the signs of her nerves. For a moment he thought it had to do with him, but then he thought back and realized she had first looked upset when he'd mentioned the plane.

Damn.

He should have remembered the crash she'd experienced. She seemed so fearless, though. He'd lost sight of what she'd been through, a trauma that would leave anyone with a boatload of apprehension.

"The offer stands," he said gently. "But we can adjust the plans. I'm open to whatever you want."

"I'll be fine with this." She picked up her cup again and took a long swallow.

"You're a cheap date."

"You haven't seen how many books I plan to buy." Smiling, she stood and walked back to the racks, her fingers grazing the book spines. "What do you like to read?"

His mind filled with the children's books he'd read to his stepdaughter. They'd had a set routine. Thirty minutes an evening of reading. Even when he was away on business, he made arrangements to Skype their story time. She often asked for more, and right now he would give anything to give her those extra minutes she'd requested.

"Business reading. Topics like financial research, corporate leadership—things like that," he answered gruffly, pushing aside thoughts of his stepdaughter asking for one more chapter. "What about you, Brea?"

Her eyes sparkled. Turned wistful as she patted the stack in her lap. "Anything. Everything."

He tapped the novels in her hands. "Do you not read digitally?"

"Now I do. At my other home, I read faster than they could restock books." She looked down at the growing stack of books in her arms, her gaze pensive. "This is a treat."

His conscience pinched. Part of this ruse meant placing her in her family's path more frequently than before. What if she wasn't guilty of anything more than curiosity? "Are you sure you're okay going to the casino party?"

"I went out to dinner with them. I think I can handle a big party, where there are plenty of distractions to keep me from speaking to people I wish to avoid."

He wondered if she meant anyone in particular. He hadn't noticed nuances like that last night at dinner, but he would try to be more cognizant of subtleties like that going forward. Especially if he was going to keep an eye on what she was up to. He had to stay alert and not be distracted by the attraction. If they pursued it, he could only indulge if he kept his focus where it belonged. On his new job at Alaska Oil Barons, Inc.

"But there will also be a lot of curious eyes on you."

And if she did have an alternative agenda, a party like that might reveal any and all accomplices. He didn't want to think like that. But he needed to remain vigilant. Aware.

"So, you planned the dinner yesterday to be just the family out of concern for my feelings?"

"Of course not." He nudged her knee with his. "That kind of sensitivity would do serious damage to my reputation as a boardroom shark."

"Well, we can't have that now, can we? It wouldn't be good for the company."

"Spoken like a true Steele." Something he would do well to remember.

They were a ruthless lot when it came to business. Like him. Which meant he was better off not feeling sorry for her. He needed to keep his sights firmly set on keeping the corporation safe.

And if he and Brea shared a bed along the way?

All the better.

Brea walked into her sister's engagement party with her head held high, her grip on Ward's arm tight. It was a double-edged decision to touch him this way. Yes, she needed bracing to face this event. But the handsome man beside her filled out his tuxedo so perfectly that she found herself thinking about the kisses they'd shared, and ended up feeling unsteady on her feet.

"Are you okay?" he asked, his blue eyes full of deep concern.

Pull it together, she told herself. The last thing she wanted was for him to know how deeply he affected her.

"I'm fine. I will be an attentive, adoring date." She rubbed a thumb and index finger together, attempting to quell her nerves.

He'd opted for them to arrive after the sit-down dinner and to make their appearance during dessert and dancing so she wouldn't have to make chitchat. Another thoughtful move from a man who worked so very hard to appear heartless. She'd told him that seeing her family at a crowded event would be easier. And she'd genuinely believed that to be the case when she'd said it.

She was wrong.

Her world had been so sparsely populated in the remote Canadian farm town, that off-the-grid community. She wasn't used to so many people crammed into one room. Even a massive ballroom like this. So it was more than just her family that was overwhelming. She was still acclimating to being surrounded by such a sheer number of people.

Sometimes, when she was in Canada, she'd thought she'd dreamed the opulence of her father's Alaskan world. Right now, she saw she hadn't dreamed up a single detail. The Steele family wealth was real. Not a penny had been spared for Delaney's casino-themed engagement party.

As she strolled farther into the party, her eyes were drawn to the intricate details of the Monte Carlo feel. The indicators of unrivaled wealth made this event seem like a scene from a movie. She had vague memories of such lush parties when she'd still lived in Alaska as a child. But her off-the-grid teenage time was a world away from anything of this scale.

Oversize cards with hearts were suspended from the ceiling. Centerpieces of long-stemmed red roses in shiny black vases sat on crisp white tablecloths, which held a collection of discarded drinkware the waitstaff cleared regularly.

Chatter mingled with the thrum of the grand piano, making Brea's heart beat faster. She glanced over her shoulder. Her pearl drop earrings teased along her neck as she eyed the photography station in the corner, with a table full of costume pieces, as well as larger-than-life king and queen of hearts cards with the faces cut out.

Men in tuxedos who were standing with their glittering dates waited in line to have their photos taken. Laughter billowed from the costume-fitting area, where women in designer gowns donned feathered masks and boas or tiaras and faux-fur shawls.

Ward's warm hand palmed her back as they moved

deeper into the soiree, past the active roulette table, where a skinny blonde woman excitedly clapped at her winnings. Past the blackjack tables, where important figures of the Alaskan community sat with neutral faces as the pot in the center grew. The blackjack tables captivated some of the Mikkelsons. A woman's voice crooned over the sound system, an A-list celebrity.

Brea stumbled as she caught a glimpse of her twin. Naomi. Her closest sibling hadn't been at the family dinner the other night, which had made things easier, and harder, too.

Suddenly Brea's legs and limbs felt heavy as she studied her sister, who was wearing a rhinestone gown, the skirt black tulle, in a Cinderella poof. But Naomi had always had a flare for the dramatic. Broderick's wife, Glenna, somehow managed to carry off a gold lace dress with a short train of tan feathers.

Brea smoothed her hands down her simple black sheath dress, cinched at the waist with a wide pearl-studded belt. True, she'd felt like an outsider before tonight. But even her level of dress seemed to mark her as different. As someone who didn't belong to this world.

Despite being born into it.

Her stomach dropped thirteen stories. Heat pulsated on her cheeks, and for a moment the world of the party felt distant. Muffled. Underwater.

Until Ward cut through, his hand gently touching her back again.

"Would you like to get something to eat?" He gestured toward the tables of sweets.

On the far wall, Brea spotted cube truffles that were decorated like dice, and a woman in a sequined silver ball gown scooped them onto her crystal plate.

But the real eye-catching feature of the dessert area was a yet-to-be-cut tiered cake that was decorated to resemble a roulette wheel.

"No, thank you. I ate plenty before you picked me up," she lied. Truth be told, the thought of food sent waves of nausea through her. No. Brea's nerves were too electric to keep food down at this point.

"Dance?"

She wanted to, anything to escape speaking with these people. She wasn't ready for this after all. "But aren't you here to work?"

"My presence is enough." He took her hand and pulled her to the dance floor, taking her into his arms.

A welcome haven right now.

"I don't recognize some of the guests." She felt less conspicuous watching other people from the safety of his embrace.

He nodded toward the front two tables near the mahogany-planked dance floor. "That's the future groom's family. But no one expects you to know everyone."

His fingers were light on her spine. Strangely reassuring and tantalizing at the same time. And a touch that made her more aware than she wanted to admit. "I should though, after my time working for the company, using a fake name."

"You're admitting what you did?" His brows shot up as he and Brea moved to the music. So close. So distracting to be caught up in his strong arms and sexy gaze.

Yet she couldn't deny that being close to him somehow settled her nerves.

She just needed to keep her head on straight and quit thinking with her hormones. She weighed her words carefully. "It's no secret."

"Your lawyer wouldn't be pleased you're talking about it."

"Good point. I guess I was feeling too comfortable around you," she said tightly. "I won't make that mistake again."

A slow smile creased dimples into his cheeks, his hand moving in slow circles along her back. "You're gutsy. Like your twin."

Lord knows she and Naomi had been close as kids, but competitive. She wasn't so sure she wanted that competition now. Even though her sister was married, with twins of her own, and Brea had no business feeling proprietary about Ward. "Is that a compliment?"

"It is. She's respected in the business world."

Business? That was their arrangement. Still… "What about personally?"

"She's tough. So are you," he said simply, his words carrying a weight of emotion. "You've both been through a lot."

Her eyes stung, and she was grateful for the dim lighting that hid the way she was battling back tears. "I barely recognize my own relatives."

She meant that literally and figuratively. She'd lost so much time with her siblings. They'd grown from gangly kids into beautiful and handsome adults. But what threw her the most was the interaction with the Mikkelsons, their once-sworn rivals, in business and in personal affairs.

"Your family has grown now that two families have managed to mesh their immense empires." He pulled her closer as the saxophone let out a wailing, soulful note. Her nostrils filled with the spiciness of his aftershave.

Her eyes slid closed for a second before her common sense kicked in and walls went up.

"Managed how? You're the boss. Seems to me that means they failed to mesh very well since an outsider is now at the helm." Nothing about coming home was as she had expected.

"I see it differently." His voice was gravelly as they swayed together, the warmth of him tempting.

A man in a tuxedo, with a gold bowtie, maneuvered past them. A woman in a shimmery turquoise gown with glitzy jewels followed close behind, dancing as she went by, empty champagne glass glinting in the soft light.

"How so?"

The pianist paused, reaching the end of a piece. A dramatic violin joined along with the singer's sultry voice.

"The siblings on both sides have found where they fit best rather than where they were expected to step in. They're now in the places I would have hired them to fill instead of nepotism appointments."

"Are you actually saying that having my brother—Broderick—run Alaska Oil Barons, Inc., would have been a bad choice?"

Ward shrugged his impossibly broad shoulders. "He could have run Steele Enterprises. But the combined Steele and Mikkelson corporations? I'm the stronger CEO to take the helm."

She laughed softly. "It's a shame you don't have any self-confidence."

"This isn't about confidence or arrogance. It's about our resumes and strengths."

Somehow his practicality managed to keep arrogance

out of the equation. "I'm glad you're happy with your new job. But what happens when a bigger fish comes along for you?"

"Right now, there isn't a larger company with this much autonomy. And with me at the helm, Alaska Oil Barons, Inc., *will* grow."

She pressed her head against his chest, his heartbeat echoing softly, steadily against her ear. "I hope that confidence proves to be true."

"For your family's sake."

"Can we talk about something other than business?"

"You aren't angling for your fake job back?"

His accusation stung. "I only pretended to be Milla to get the lay of the land before returning home as myself. That's all."

"Hmm… Maybe you should work for the business."

His touch and gaze had her wits addled. "Whatever for?"

"Your skills at bluffing could be of use to the company in negotiations."

She couldn't decide whether to be complimented or insulted by his words. Then a movement just over Ward's shoulders distracted her.

Naomi crossed the dance floor with Royce, her husband. Naomi's gaze moved past Brea, then back again and she stopped in the middle of dancing couples for a moment.

For a split second, Brea thought they could just pick up where they'd left off, that their twin-sister bond would make everything okay. Then Naomi's face twisted into something that looked an awful lot like suspicion. Her twin's furrowed brow sparked alarm in Brea. The last thing she needed was some residual twin bond giving away her charade.

Brea looped her arms around Ward's neck, and she arched up on her toes to do away with suspicions the best way possible.

She kissed him in full view of all the guests.

Four

Fire scorched through Ward at Brea's kiss.

His senses went on overload at the soft give of her mouth against his, her fingers on his neck, toying with his hairline. His mind flooded with all the ways he wanted to touch her, to explore her gentle curves without the barrier of clothes between them. Not that he could pursue those thoughts or even indulge the kiss to the fullest with so many people around them.

But someday they would share more.

He was determined.

When the time and place was right, he would kiss every inch of her beautiful body.

With a final skim of his lips over hers, he eased back, taking in the heat in her molten dark eyes. "Damn, lady, you take my breath away."

"You're a smooth talker," she said skeptically, but

he could see that her pulse still raced, throbbing along her neck.

"I'm actually better known for being a blunt speaker of truth." Which was important for her to know.

If she couldn't be trusted, she needed to know where he stood. And if she was being truthful and was a victim, then she needed to know he was a straight shooter.

"Since the pianist is taking a break," he said, "let's get something to drink and have a seat. We can talk."

She nodded, her pupils still wide with desire. With a tender hand trailing down her spine and resting on the small of her back, Ward guided her past the partiers. She seemed to sigh into his touch, the muscles melting with his caresses. A reaction that made his heart hammer with impatience. Anticipation.

As they rounded the roulette table, a bevy of applause erupted. The crowd moved around a blonde in her mid-fifties. Even from across the room, he would know that glittering silhouette anywhere. The gap in the crowd revealed Jeannie Mikkelson standing cross-armed in a jade-green sequined ball gown, talking to her youngest son. Brea's neck snapped to attention, and he felt the tension return to her. Could see the unease work upward from her low back to her shoulders. Knew her nerves must be fraying. Knew he had to take action.

Ward steered her toward the quieter corridor. On his way, he snagged two glasses of champagne. Echoes of music from the grand piano drifted with them down the hall. The casino theme continued—larger-than-life cards with hearts flanked the walls. And there, in front of them, was the quietest Steele of all the siblings and the woman of the hour, Delaney Steele.

Brea backed up a step.

Delaney's spiral-curled hair bounced as she took a step forward. Her smile was as bright as the crystals that edged the bodice of her fitted black dress.

"Hello, Breanna," Delaney said gently. "Thank you for coming to my engagement party. It means so much to me."

A slow swallow moved down Brea's throat. She nodded toward her sister's left hand, which sported a pear-shaped diamond ring. "That's lovely."

"Thank you. I'm just happy to be marrying the love of my life." She smiled. "Like Naomi, you and I dreamed of when we were kids, dressing up for weddings with a towel for a veil."

Ward inched aside, giving them space, but keeping his gaze on Brea's face, gauging her reactions. He hadn't considered until now that having her spend more time with her family was perhaps the best way to get to the bottom of her reasons for returning after she'd revealed herself as Milla Jones. Sure Shana Mikkelson's private-eye skills had uncovered Brea's locale, but with the skills she had from living off-the-grid, she could have disappeared. Instead she'd gotten a lawyer and come back to Alaska.

To what end?

"I want to trust you all." Brea's legs folded, and she sat on the velvet settee. "But it's so difficult to figure out what's real in my memories, good and bad."

"If you have any questions, I'm happy to help however I can. I *want* to help." Delaney sat beside her, resting a hand on Brea's arm, her engagement ring catching the chandelier lights. "You don't need to tell me any details of that memory. You could just ask something, like 'family vacation to the Gold Rush festival when we were in elementary school.' I'll tell you what I remember. You can decide if it matches up with what you recall."

Brea's eyes widened in surprise. "That's a good idea. Maybe we can try it sometime next week."

"Or you could ask me something now."

Brea hesitated, then shook her head. "This is your engagement party. I don't want to monopolize you when you should be celebrating your dreams coming true."

"You're family." Delaney waved a dismissive hand, her engagement ring glinting. "And having the chance to talk to you is a joy I never thought I would have again."

Ward leaned forward in the chair. No one had asked him to leave and he didn't plan to offer. He couldn't deny the protective urge to stay near Brea. And as much as he reminded himself of his uncertainty about trusting her, bottom line, he had to make sure she wasn't hurt by whatever her sister had to say about their childhood memories.

Brea nodded. "Okay then. Tell me about Saturday-morning breakfasts."

Delaney's smile spread wide and fast. "I remember all sorts of special times at Kit's Kodiak Café. But my favorite memory is the morning we shared a candy bracelet…"

Delaney Steele looked forward to going to Kit's Kodiak Café with her dad and her brothers and her sisters while their mom had a morning all to herself.

Today was special. She got to sit next to Brea. Brea liked to sit at the end, and Naomi usually sat beside her, since they were twins. But this morning, Delaney had run so fast into the restaurant that she almost slipped on the ice. But she made it.

She had Brea all to herself.

Well, sort of. Everyone was talking so much, Delaney couldn't get a word in edgewise. Well, everyone except for Marshall. He was quiet, reading a book about horses. If he didn't have his nose in a book, he was in the stables.

Delaney swung her legs back and forth, her feet not reaching the ground. She loved this place. It wasn't fancy. She felt comfortable. The diner looked like a big barn near the water. The windows showed a pretty view of a dock stretching out into the lake. Inside, long-planked tables were set up for big, noisy groups—like her family.

Menus crackled in front of the others, but she knew what she wanted off the Three Polar Bears menu. Pancakes and reindeer sausage.

Usually she was impatient to get her food. But today she was content to wait. Besides, their family was well known in this café and they'd be served quickly. But their dad always said not to ask for special treatment.

She and her siblings had been coming to Kit's for as long as Delaney could remember. Their father brought them most Saturday mornings and even sometimes before school so their mom could have a break. He would bundle them up. He wasn't good at remembering to match up everyone's gloves and hats. But they were all warm. Even if Marshall was mad over wearing a pink kitten hat.

Her mom told her once that their dad, who had more money than anyone, was trying to keep them grounded by taking them to regular sorts of places, the kinds that played country music and oldies over the radio. The air smelled of home cooking and a wood fire. The stuffed bear was a little scary, but she didn't want to admit to being afraid.

Delaney tapped Brea's leg with her foot. Her sister looked over, frowning. "What?"

"Shhh," Delaney said softly and held her hand out under the table.

She'd brought an extra candy bracelet, just in case she got to sit by Brea. Delaney had used her allowance to buy it. She kept her hand out of sight, though, so her dad couldn't see and say they were going to wreck their appetites.

But no amount of candy could make her too full for Kit's Kodiak food.

Brea smiled. "Thanks, kiddo."

Kiddo? She was only three years younger. But Delaney had a tough time standing up for herself. It was easier to stand up for others. Like how she'd done a report on saving the whales at school even though the mean girls made fun of her at lunch and called her whale girl. Not that she told her family. She didn't want to make things tougher for her parents.

Their dad always said their mom had the hardest job of all, dealing with the Steele hellions, and the least he could do was give her a break sometimes. He'd rolled out that speech at the start of every breakfast and reminded them to listen to their mom and their teachers. If there were no bad reports, then they could all go fishing with him. Fishing was so fun, they didn't even tattle on each other. They figured things out on their own when they argued.

She and her siblings had a tight bond. She couldn't imagine what life would be like without her family. Just

thinking about it made her stomach hurt so much she
passed the rest of her candy bracelet to her sister...

Back at her apartment, after the engagement party,
Brea wasn't sure if she felt better or worse hearing her
sister tell her story about that breakfast morning so long
ago, when Delaney had shared her candy bracelet.

Brea's emotions were all jumbled up. A dangerous
state as she stood in her apartment entryway with Ward.
He'd insisted on walking her to her door. With that kiss
on the dance floor still fresh in her mind—and tingling
along her senses—she wasn't sure it was wise to be
alone with him.

Not that she didn't trust him. He hadn't pushed faster
than she was ready.

But she didn't trust herself.

The draw to him had grown stronger than ever tonight. It was getting tougher and tougher to resist him
and the undeniable chemistry between them. But she
needed to remember he was loyal first and foremost to
her father, to the Steeles, to the company.

Still, her memory churned with thoughts of his hand
on her back at the party, steadying her when she'd
needed it. Helping her make a graceful exit when she'd
been tongue-tied after Delaney's story.

Her emotions were a jumble.

She needed an outlet, and the man in front of her was
one sexy, welcome distraction.

As he stepped from the apartment building hallway
into her entry, he tucked his gloves into the pockets of
his long black wool coat. She closed the door and he
unbuttoned the coat to reveal his tailored tux. Still, he
didn't move any deeper into her apartment.

Neither had she.

He took her hand in his, his thumb rubbing along the inside of her wrist. "Are you okay?"

"Of course. I only had two glasses of champagne," she answered, deliberately dodging the obvious reason he asked.

"I meant are you all right with what your sister said. You've been quiet."

Nerves threatened to return, and she forced something that felt like a smile to her lips. But her lips wavered as words formed. "I was shouting *gargoyle* in my head."

His forehead creased with concern. "I apologize. I should have been paying closer attention—"

"That was a joke." Brea squeezed his hand, his strength and calluses launching a fresh wash of tingles through her.

He shook his head. "What's happened to you and your family is indescribable and not at all material for humor."

"I'm working on my attitude." She kept her hand in his, the warmth of his touch grounding her and exciting her all at once. "Although, somehow I'm still telling lies about us being in a relationship."

Ward shifted his weight, and she caught a whiff of his spicy cologne and his own musk as the floorboard beneath him creaked. "Your life has been…confusing."

Understatement of the year.

Brea took a deep breath, her mind racing back to certain touchstones of her complicated existence.

"After my foster parents died, I had my own sort of off-the-grid lifestyle."

Ward's strong fingers offered her palms a massage. He looked at her with those deep blue eyes. "I'd like to hear more."

"I spent some time on my own in Canada, doing jobs for cash. Learning about how the world worked. Trying to figure out where my head was at, trying to figure out what I wanted to do about my…relatives."

Her blood relations, as well as her adoptive ones. She'd wrestled with reconciling her feelings for everyone. She'd grieved when her adoptive parents died, as had their small community. But then when she'd come across a box under her mom's bed, her world had tipped.

The box had contained the clothes she'd been wearing that day of the plane crash, along with a mermaid Beanie Baby that her grandmother had given her. The memory of that simple present had made her realize there was no more hiding from the truth.

She needed to go back to see her Steele relatives.

If only her brain didn't still push back every time she tried to analyze those walled-away years.

"So you snuck into the company."

She recoiled from his touch for a moment. Her hands to her temples, shaking her head and squeezing her eyes shut. "It doesn't make complete sense now. I didn't know who to trust for advice on what would be the best way to approach them." She shrugged. "I'm here now."

"And they hadn't come looking for you?"

"I would have come back in my own time, as myself. I came here in disguise, on my own, didn't I? I just feel this…reunion isn't something to rush." Her mind was a jumble of thoughts from those teenage years. There was so much, too much, to process. She wanted life to be simple for once. "You're not one to cast stones on role-play for a goal. You're pretending to be my boyfriend."

"I could be your for-real lover. Our chemistry is off the charts. Just say the word and we can pursue that."

His eyes danced with a dangerous anticipation she felt echoing in her blood. In the restless pounding of her heart. In the small step she took toward him.

The scent of the lavender potpourri in a dish in the foyer relaxed her even as the scent of his aftershave tempted her closer. Leaning toward him slightly, her voice dropped a notch, her words breathy, her pulse speeding twice as fast as the soft ticking of the clock. "And that word would be?"

"Let's have sex? Or let's go out to dinner? Or how about both?"

Awareness crackled between them, her skin tingling. The heat built to a desire that wiped away the confusion and grief she'd been battling since her sister shared that heart-tugging memory that matched Brea's recollection to the letter.

She needed, craved, a respite from the tension. She wanted to feel the love of this family again, but she was scared if she let her guard down enough to let that happen, she could be opening her heart to a hurt she wouldn't recover from. The tension of it—the wanting and wishing for an acceptance she wasn't ready to take—was draining. And it hurt. But with Ward touching her this way, she knew she could put her worries aside for a few hours in his arms. And with the heat simmering in his eyes, his touch stirring her inside, she really, really wanted to lose herself with him.

"And there's nothing to say we can't turn this into a real affair. Just say when." She walked her fingers up his chest to smooth his lapels.

"When," he growled, clasping her hands. "Absolutely when."

His mouth met hers again, the kiss deepening in the

way it couldn't in public at the party. And oh my, the man knew how to kiss, fully, his whole attention on her and turning her inside out with the stroke of his tongue and his hands over her clothes...then under. The rasp of his calluses along her tender flesh was a sweet temptation.

A sigh whispered between her lips.

Her restless fingers swept off his overcoat, and then his tuxedo jacket, before tugging at his tie. She couldn't get him undressed fast enough.

"So, Ward Benally," she said, her voice husky, "are you sure I'm not taking advantage of you? Because I wouldn't want you to do anything you don't want to do."

"If you are taking advantage of me, keep on going."

She angled back to see if he was teasing her. "Benally..."

"Trust me, I want you, Breanna Steele. Absolutely. Fully. Here and now. Soon, or I'm going to lose my mind." He growled his chuckle and appreciation.

And she was happy to keep up the pace until his shirt and T were gone, her hips pressed against his, the impressive length of his erection a promise she eagerly anticipated.

He turned her around to pull the zipper down her back, exposing her spine an inch at a time, kissing along the bared skin until she was a quivering mass of need. Her feet shaking, she faced him again, easing the dress down, slowly, savoring the passion and appreciation in his gaze as the dress pooled around her feet.

Emboldened, she stood before him, wearing nothing but a satin strapless bra and matching panties. And by the looks of his erection, which strained against his fly, this sexy man was every bit as turned on looking at her as she was by looking at him. Knowing he wanted her as much as she craved this time with him made her head swim.

Her fingers connected with his chest and static snapped. A tingle radiated up her arm. She reached out again, her touch connecting this time, and she trailed lower, lower still, until she slid her hand into his tuxedo pants.

His eyes slid closed and his head fell back as she stroked, learning the feel of him, anticipating what was to come. His chest expanded with a deep sigh. "We need to move this to the bedroom."

"Or the sofa is closer." She arched up on her toes to kiss him again.

"Hold that thought for one second." He knelt to reach into his jacket…and pulled out a condom. Thank goodness at least one of them was thinking clearly enough to take care of birth control.

Then he returned to her, and her thoughts scattered, instinct taking over.

Their legs tangled as they made their way from the hall to the sofa, leaving a trail of his shoes and her heels. She caressed his pants down his legs. His hands made fast work of her bra and panties.

Flesh to flesh, they tumbled back onto the sofa in a tangle. She nipped along his strong jaw, the leather cushion soft against her back, his touch gentle along her sides.

The thick pressure of him between her legs almost sent her over the edge then and there. Her breath hitched. He thrust deep and full, holding while she adjusted to the newness of him, of them linked.

She arched into the sensation, taking him deeper inside, savoring the connection she'd dreamt of since she had first met him. Being with him was everything she'd

hoped—even more. It was chemistry like none she'd experienced before.

And she wanted more.

He held his weight off her with one hand on the back
of the couch. She rolled her hips under his and he took
the cue, resuming the dance they'd started earlier. Her
fingernails dug half-moons into his shoulders, urgency
pulsing through her.

She buried her face against his neck, breathing in the
scent of his aftershave. He kissed, nipped and laved his
way to her breast, his five-o'clock shadow rasped against
her sensitive skin.

Passion ramping higher, hotter, she wrapped her legs
around his waist and writhed, nearly sliding from the
sofa. But he caught her, steadied her, secured her. His
eyes held hers as firmly as his hands. His expression
challenged her, encouraged her.

He seemed so in control, it gave her pause. Until she
looked closer and saw tendons straining in his neck with
restraint. His pleasure pleased her. His gravelly voice
filled the air with all the times he'd watched and wanted
her as he slid his hand between them. He circled his
thumb with just the right skill to take her to the edge,
and then he eased back again. Then…

Bliss.

Her release shimmered through her, pulling a cry of
pleasure from her with each ripple of her orgasm. He
braced his hand against the sofa back and thrust into her,
once, twice more. His completion echoed hers, sending
more shimmers through her until she was limp in the
aftermath.

Somehow he managed to stand. He scooped her up
and carried her to the bedroom. He eased her onto the

comforter and stretched out beside her, tugging a pink quilt up from the foot of the bed. He pulled her close and stroked her hair, his touch gentle.

She kept her gaze from his, not ready to let him see the vulnerability she knew he would find in her eyes. Instead she focused on the glass lamp.

He was too perceptive, and she feared he would see the truth of how much he'd affected her. How she'd never felt this level of intensity before, and she wasn't sure how to handle the feelings he stirred.

Inhaling the scent of lavender that wafted from her oil diffuser, she attempted to bring herself back down to something more grounded. Something less dangerous than the feel of her body pressed to his.

She was in way over her head.

She had gone into this to escape from her confusing feelings about her family, but now she had a whole fresh batch of tender feelings to deal with, and this time those emotions had Ward's name on them. She didn't know where to put all of the rawness she felt, but she already wanted to be with him again. And if she wasn't careful, she would throw caution to the wind, which would leave her defenseless. Something she vowed never to be again.

Sitting on a barstool in Brea's kitchen, wearing only his boxers, Ward felt like he'd time traveled back to his marriage.

Which was the last thought he wanted to be having right now with the scent of Brea still on him, with the rush of their incredible sex still humming through his veins.

He wanted this affair with her. He deserved it, damn it.

And except for their morning coziness, it was *nothing* like his marriage.

Through sheer force of will, he shoved back memories of his broken marriage and lost child. The here and now was all that counted for him. His job. This moment with an incredibly sexy woman.

A woman with whom he also needed to keep his wits about him.

Beside him, Brea fluffed her long, dark hair. Slicing through his thoughts with the way his tuxedo shirt rolled up along her thighs, hinting at the curves of her bottom. She'd made a sangria blend from wine and fruit, serving it with avocado slices, shrimp and chips. Working beside her to prepare the snack had been easy and intimate.

A bit too close to domesticity for his peace of mind. And from the looks of her, she was as uncomfortable as he was.

He rested a hand on her knee. "I don't regret what we did."

She gave a shaky breath. "I don't either. It was just more intense than I expected. Apparently, I'm no good at casual sex."

He hadn't expected such an honest response from her. "We are fake dating." Even though they were most definitely having real sex. He squeezed her knee, smiling. "That's a step beyond casual."

"Okay, I can see that." She gave him a wry smile. "Thank you for not taking my words as some kind of request that you get down on one knee and propose." Brea scooped up an avocado slice and a piece of shrimp onto a blue corn tortilla chip and popped it into her mouth absentmindedly.

Her words chilled him. "Not a chance. Been there. Done that. Bear the battle scars."

"Because of your daughter?"

Brea's knee brushed his. The touch brought a mixture of exciting newness and a past that haunted him.

"My stepdaughter," he reminded her. "I thought a person got married, and the rest fell into place over time. I was in love with my wife. I loved her kid—thought of Paisley as my own child. We were going to be a family."

"What happened to Paisley's biological father?" She brought the strawberry to her lips. Bit into it and watched him thoughtfully. Intensely.

He swallowed another swig of wine. "He died before she was born. Paisley thought of me as her dad." And that stabbed clean through him. "She thinks I abandoned her."

"Oh, Ward, that's so sad. Is that what her mom told her?"

Silence pressed on him for a moment. The weight nearly stifled his next words. The reality and truth they spoke.

"She told her she has a new dad, and that I wasn't her real father."

"I'm so very sorry—for you and for Paisley."

"People tell me kids are resilient." He drew in a shaky breath, his memory echoing with Paisley crying when he said goodbye. He reached for a blue corn tortilla chip. Pressed it into his palm until it broke into two. Then he scooped the avocado and shrimp onto one of the pieces and chewed thoughtfully.

Brea nodded, quiet for so long, he wasn't sure she'd speak again. He waited, letting her find her pace.

"That may be true. But it wasn't true for me." She

frowned down into her glass. "Maybe I should have told you otherwise."

Again, she'd offered more openness than he'd expected.

"I appreciate that you're honest. I hate being lied to."

"Me, too. The truth is confusing enough without having to sift through deceit."

He stroked her hair back, tucking it behind her ear. "Then let's agree that no matter what else is going on, we'll be honest with each other."

She bit her bottom lip, looking away for a moment before continuing, "You can't think we're going to tell each other everything?"

His Spider-Sense went off.

What was she hiding?

Even as he wondered, given how closed off she'd become so fast, he knew his chance of getting her to say it was next to nil. "I don't think any man wants to talk that much."

"Okay then." Brea took a delicate sip of sangria, smiling as the glass touched her lips. The dark red wine deliciously stained her mouth. Drawing him in again.

She gave him the laugh he'd hoped for, some of the tension easing from her shoulders.

But it didn't do much to quiet his questions; in particular, the need to know what Brea was hiding that made her so wary. And he couldn't escape the niggling sense that he was focusing on what she was hiding to keep from thinking, from feeling, all the things she made him think and feel.

He damn well wasn't going to put his heart on the line ever again.

Five

Brea couldn't sleep.

She didn't regret having sex with Ward. She did, however, regret that she couldn't just enjoy the aftermath of lazing next to him in a haze of post-sex bliss. Judging by the pounding of her heart, the window of such utter contentment had firmly closed.

She wanted to be with him again.

Too much. Desire pounded through her. So much, she needed to reestablish her equilibrium before facing him again.

Making love to Ward had set her senses ablaze, made everything more vibrant. Even her mind was firing on all cylinders, which made her think of the past. Or rather, both of her pasts. Her life seemed sliced into two parts—before and after the plane crash that took her mother's life.

Brea sat at the kitchen island, laptop open in front of

her. She'd been searching the internet for the past few hours. The quest gave her something to distract her from how much she wanted to crawl back under the sheets. Each breath she took drew in the scent of him lingering on his shirt, which she still wore.

Focus, she admonished herself. For so long she'd searched for clues about the accident—about what might have caused it, about who might have been involved—but it was like searching for a needle in a haystack.

Today's quest involved looking into aircraft-maintenance records. Her research quest wasn't exactly a sanctioned one. But she was afraid if the wrong person learned she was still prying, they would destroy any leads to what happened all those years ago.

She studied the aircraft reports in front of her, losing herself in the monotony of page after page that had been scanned into digital files. She knew Tally Benson—soon to be Steele—was related to the mechanic who'd worked on the aircraft. But there had been a number of others who'd worked on the aircraft or had been involved with the flight. Even though Tally had told everyone about her father's connection, it still seemed surreal for her to now be a part of the family in spite of that connection. Even though the crash wasn't the woman's fault, how could the Steeles look at Tally and not think of what her dad had done?

Brea wondered if she too was a reminder of what had happened, what the family had lost.

What someone had wanted to destroy but had failed.

And if someone harbored feelings of guilt or vengeance, wouldn't those feelings be magnified by Brea's presence?

Scanning her gaze along the photos lining the mantel, she felt something tug at her subconscious. Something she needed to pull into the forefront and examine. But her memories about that day were as clear as mist.

She'd never been able to bring into sharp focus the events of the twenty-four hours surrounding the crash, the terrifying images too laden with her emotions for her to sift down to the facts underneath. Afterward, when she'd gone to her adoptive family for answers, their accounts had swayed her strongly. They'd told her that her Alaskan family was no good, that they had given up on her. That they were corrupt. She was better off without them. And even knowing that the couple who had claimed to love her for her entire teenage life had been lying to her, she still couldn't bring herself to trust the Steeles.

It was ironic that while she'd been with her adoptive parents, she'd mistrusted her biological family. And now she was finding it tougher to believe in the people who'd taken her in, her perspective tilting completely. It was enough to drive a person mad.

The tingly sense of being watched had her sitting up straight and fast. So fast, she nearly toppled the barstool at the island. She turned to find Ward standing in the bedroom doorway, watching her.

His boxers hung low on his lean hips, drawing her eyes to his washboard abs, then lower. Her mind flooded with memories of the passionate way they'd tangled in the sheets and all the sensual things she still wanted to experience with him. They could find that bliss again, if she let herself.

He combed his fingers through his rumpled hair. "What're you working on?"

Ice chilled her heated blood. She swiveled on the

barstool, back to her computer, rapidly shutting down the screen. How could she have forgotten what she was doing? And why had she allowed herself to be so reckless as to research the Mikkelson and Steele families while Ward was under her roof?

She slammed the lid closed. "Just, um, checking emails and researching articles on relaxation and meditation to see if it can help me sift through the memories of my past. Hearing Delaney talk about childhood memories was really helpful."

The lies rolled off her tongue with an ease that made her uncomfortable, especially so soon after discussing being honest with each other. But she'd realized she would never find the answers she sought if she didn't circumvent the truth on occasion. She didn't enjoy lying, but it was a means to an end.

She also knew those fibs needed to have something with teeth, something with an element of truth. In this scenario, Delaney had been helpful in confirming her confusion and mistrust.

"That's a good idea." He strode closer to her, his steps silent, like a lean tiger's. "Any interesting emails?"

Very. Including one from a lady who'd worked at a local airport around the time of the crash. Not that Brea intended to tell him that. Instead she settled on sharing another email. "My family—the Steeles—want me to come to lunch tomorrow. Delaney told them how well our discussion about the childhood memories went."

"Are you sure it's wise to push that hard?" Blue eyes shone as he gave Brea's hand a squeeze. The touch passed fire between them even now.

There was no rule book for this sort of situation. She hadn't meant for her life to grow so enmeshed with

Ward's, but what had started as a fake relationship had surprised her by giving her an outlet for the intense stress she'd encountered while digging for answers. Now she could only move forward and try to make the best of her situation.

She was in too deep to turn back now.

"I don't think it's wise to bury my head in the sand and assume all will work out." Which she'd done in the months after her adoptive parents had died. She'd packed up a couple of trunks full of belongings—books they'd read together on long winter nights, crafts they'd made, a dress she'd worn to a high school dance and, of course, that fateful shoebox she'd opened later to find her few surviving belongings from the day of the crash. "The only way to know who to trust is to get to know my family better. So yes, I want to go to lunch."

To learn more.

Information was power.

"What would your counselor say?"

She appreciated his concern, but his coddling? Not so much. She needed her independence, to learn to trust her instincts again. "That I should trust my instincts more when it comes to taking charge of my life."

That was easier said than done. She wanted evidence. Tangible truths.

He rested a hand on top of her computer. "What do you think you should do right now?"

Find out if he'd seen anything. But if he had, then she might have to push him away. And she couldn't scrounge for the will to do that when she wanted more than anything to lean into all that sexy strength and warmth. She couldn't deny herself the pleasure of spending more time with a man who captivated her so thoroughly. He chased all her muddled memories and confusion away. She might well have to leave this town one day. Before that time came, she intended to make the most of every moment with him. The past would have to stay in the past for a few hours.

"My gut says we should go back into the bedroom, and you should give me a thorough massage before we go back to bed for a few hours." She stroked the toes of one foot along the side of his calf. "In the interest of relaxing, of course."

A slow smile spread across his face as he lifted her off the barstool and into his arms. "You should follow those instincts more often."

Ward had never given anyone a massage before. But he fully intended to do so again—if the person happened to be Brea.

Their hours of sex had been mind-bending. Even now, the next day and a shower later, his senses were still saturated with the sweet taste and floral scent of her. Not to mention the creamy feel of her skin under his hands.

Of course those were dangerous thoughts to have while standing in the stables with her father. But Ward was here to learn more about the man who'd founded such an impressive oil dynasty.

And of course there was Ward's affair with Brea. A long-lost daughter Jack might feel overprotective of, with good reason, after all she'd been through.

It was more important than ever that Ward keep his wits around this man. He didn't know Jack Steele all that well—something that needed to change.

It seemed quite clear that Jack loved his kids, though. But what about his dead wife? Could the man have had something to do with her death, and he'd never meant Brea to be in harm's way? The man had made a marriage to the business enemy. Some might see that as mighty Machiavellian. And while not so long ago, he would have taken pride in that, now he wasn't so sure.

Brea was getting to him in more ways than he could count, and although he needed to keep his eyes on her, that proximity also made objectivity tougher.

Ward definitely intended to keep a close eye on Jack Steele, for Brea's sake.

Leather cowboy boots punching through the hard, packed snow, Ward moved into the barn. Bits of hay were scattered on the ground surrounding an onyx-colored horse that Jack had clipped to the crossties.

Stetson tipped back on his dark head, and Jack crouched down, examining the horse's back left hoof. The Friesian's eyes were rimmed with white. Clearly nervous.

Looking over his shoulder, Jack cradled the hoof with his leg and hand. Motioned for Ward to approach. "Meet Flash—our newest rescue. She's a little skittish. Owners abandoned her in a stall when their ranch got foreclosed on. Bridlebrook Rescue got to her in time. Thankfully. Put some meat back on her bones. We took her in yesterday."

Ward reached out to touch the mare's flowing black mane. As he touched her neck, Flash lowered her head down. Eyes growing soft. A sigh escaped.

Jack smiled. "That's a good sign. She's a nervous thing, but we're going to work on rehabilitating her spirits. And—" Jack glanced down at the semi-swollen hoof "—healing this abscess."

Nodding absently, Ward was hit between the eyes with

a memory. For a moment, a life Ward never got to live flashed through his brain. Once he had imagined getting a horse for Paisley. Teaching her how to ride. How to care for a horse. How to notice the start of an abscess or colic. He could practically hear her crystalline laughter as he imagined her learning to canter and barrel race.

The almost-memory cut him deep and true before Jack's movement beside him brought him back to the barn.

Jack touched the frog of the horse's foot, assessing the abscess before bringing his deep blue eyes to meet Ward's. "What brings you here, Benally?"

With an effort, he breathed out the ache of losing his daughter. Focused instead on why he came.

"Your daughter's having lunch with the family. I came along with her." Not exactly a lie. Not exactly the truth. He found himself quickly returning to his night with Brea. He craved that again. A dangerous feeling. Damn it, he was getting too emotionally involved with her, wanting to help her family.

"Brea actually showed up?" Jack straightened, his face surprised and vulnerable in a way that Ward doubted many people had ever seen. "Thank you."

His hand rested on Flash's hindquarters. The mare kept weight off her injured hoof.

"She makes her own choices. She's strong-willed, like her father."

Jack relaxed into a nostalgic smile. "You should have met her mom."

He wished he had. What might Brea be like today if her mother hadn't died in a tragic accident that involved her, too? The crash, her mother's death and the loss of the rest of her family had all defined her in so many ways.

Ward stayed silent as Jack returned to Flash.

Jack felt the tendons along Flash's leg. "How're you liking the new office?"

"The job is an exciting challenge. We're going to make great things happen for the company, which will expand the reach of your family's new charitable organization, as well. There are good things on the horizon."

Damn, he sounded like a PR piece. He extended a hand for Flash to sniff. He kept his palm open as the horse's muzzle blew hot air into his hand. The horse relaxed even more.

Jack swept off his Stetson and wiped a wrist over his forehead wearily. "This isn't the way I saw things playing out when we decided to merge the companies."

"You wanted your son at the helm. I get that."

And Broderick Steele probably would have made a solid choice for the position, except he no longer had the killer instinct.

"Or Jeannie's son."

"Really?" Ward asked in surprise as Flash let out a nicker.

"Maybe…" Jack nodded, seeming earnest enough. "But…"

"But not some stranger like me," Ward finished the older man's sentence.

"You're a top-notch choice," Jack said diplomatically. "I understand we're lucky to have you."

Ward noticed Jack still hadn't admitted to being okay about the way things had turned out. But the guy had bigger concerns now, which could also account for his lack of ire. Clearly Ward wasn't going to find out anything about Jack's feelings for his dead wife. Could there be valid reasons for Brea's suspicions? "I guess I should head back in for lunch. Which is the reason I came out here. Jeannie says they're ready to serve."

Jack gripped his arm, stopping him. "Do you really care for my daughter?"

"Whoa, don't start looking at me as a future son-in-law." Ward tried to pass off the conversation as light-hearted but found no humor in the man's blue eyes. "No disrespect. We're just dating."

"I wasn't renting a church hall. Just curious." Jack turned over the hoof pick in his hands. Metal glinting in the barn light. "She's still so closed up when talking to me."

"I'm sorry, sir." And Ward was.

The older man's words struck a chord. Ward understood what it was like to lose a child. While his daughter hadn't died, he'd been cut out of her life, and that hurt like hell every day. It was an ever-present knot in his chest that, on most days, threatened to crack his rib cage.

Jack cleared his throat. "She's here. She's alive. I can be patient as long as I know she's okay and I can see her. That's so much more than I ever imagined."

Ward couldn't even wrap his brain around how Jack Steele must have felt, believing his daughter had died.

That kind of pain was inconceivable. Suddenly the whole fake relationship with Brea stung Ward's conscience…except in some ways, it wasn't fake anymore.

They were lovers, for however long that lasted.

He needed to tread warily with the family patriarch.

"Jack, your respect means a lot to me. I'm doing my best to earn your trust."

"As the head of the company or as my daughter's boyfriend?"

"Both," Ward said, because there really wasn't another answer to give.

Too fast, Brea was filling his thoughts, and that could be dangerous for a man who'd vowed to make business his life. He'd seen his personal life go up in smoke once before, and he had no intention of repeating that mistake.

Brea regretted not signing up for meditative-yoga classes back when she'd lived in Canada. She could have really used the training on how to be mindful when her life felt out of control. To understand how to use her breath to quiet down her galloping thoughts and racing heart.

She could add it to a list of things she needed to accomplish. Skills to acquire to make it through this fractured life that was still so full of shards and questions.

A life that felt strangely surreal as she sat in the great room of Marshall's home, formerly the Steele home, where she'd spent much of her life as a small child.

The towering ceiling and the railing around the upstairs hallway was so familiar—rustic luxury. Not that such a familiarity put her at ease or clarified a thing.

Fat leather chairs and sofas filled the expansive, light-filled room. She'd curled up in those chairs many times to read.

Rafters soared upward, dotted with skylights, as well as lantern-style lights for the long winter nights with her siblings, mother and grandmother.

One stone wall held a fireplace crackling with flames. Antlers hung above the mantel. The granite-slab wet bar overflowed with snacks and drinks. Voices hummed in the great room past the open French doors, leading into the main part of the house.

And outside the glass walls was the most familiar part of all.

She took a deep breath. Counted to three on the inhale. Pushed the exhale slowly out through her nose as memories surged forward.

How had breathing become so difficult?

Chunks of ice breaking loose in the water caused the family seaplane to bob. Her dad had taken her fishing in those waters. He'd insisted his girls bait their own hooks.

She could see tracks where others had ridden earlier today. And in the distance, she could swear she spotted a tree house just like the one she and her siblings had used as children. Her heart squeezed.

So many memories here, in this place.

She let memories roll over her, unprompted. Her uncle helping her onto a paint horse, teaching her where to place her weight in the saddle. Her twin sister's peal of laughter and whispered secrets. Brea knew better than to let her eyes linger on Naomi, the toughest one of all to forget.

Losing her family had been hard, but losing her twin had felt like a limb had gone missing. On so many nights, she'd gone to sleep, seeking that connection twins had, reaching out to Naomi in her mind, convinced that Naomi would know somehow that Brea lived. A childish thought, maybe. But it had persisted well into adulthood.

Had her sister felt that same crippling sense of loss?

Silence stretched as Brea sat alone for the moment, taking in the view, this pristine beauty that stole her breath as fast as the man walking out of the barn and back toward the house.

So much had stayed the same, but the most important things had changed. The people.

It was still surreal seeing her siblings grown-up when they'd stayed frozen as young in what memories she'd retained, those images superimposing over anything she'd managed to find on the computer when she could sneak a search during unsupervised time.

"Hello?" A deep voice carried over her, one she didn't recognize. She barely recognized the face of her youngest brother. He hadn't even been in preschool when she'd…left.

She remembered carrying him on her hip, walking around the house with him like a baby doll in her arms.

"Hello, Aiden. I thought you were off working in the oil fields."

"I got time off to see you." He strode into the room, looking more like a lumberjack than her baby brother. He must be pushing twenty years old now, his hair dark and thick like all of theirs.

"You probably don't remember me." The words tumbled out of her lips even as the statement cut through her.

"I do—a little anyway. And Dad had us watch videos of you and Mom so we wouldn't forget." Aiden offered a small smile.

It was so strange to see him older without having watched him grow up. But that smile…she would recognize it anywhere. It was their mother's smile. He carried that with him even after having lost her when he was so young.

"I should probably watch those videos." It would be painful, but could also be helpful to have visual confirmation of her memories.

"Dad would like that."

"Tell me something you remember on your own." She found herself making the request before she could second-guess herself. Hearing things from Delaney's point of view had been gut-wrenching but authentic.

Aiden dropped to sit in front of the fire, his shoulders broad in a green flannel shirt. "Well, I remember winter camping in one of those glass igloos. It wasn't cold, and the stars were awesome."

The vision of the past was so vibrant, the memories almost stung. She remembered doing that more than once, the tradition stretching back to before Aiden was born. Had things been as idyllic as they sounded? Or was it all a re creation of moments perfected for video?

She glanced outside again, at Ward, wondering if what she felt with him was as intense as it seemed or only heightened because of how upside down her life was. And was he with her because he was looking for some sense of family after losing his?

She stayed quiet, letting her youngest brother talk.

"At night, before bed, our mom sang some song about a bear cub chasing the Northern Lights across the sky. I thought I was that little cub."

Brea remembered the night-light that simulated the same scene, but the rest was tougher to pull free from the tangle in her head.

Aiden stood, dusting off his jeans. "I hope I didn't make you feel uncomfortable."

"We're okay. It's important to get to the bottom of this. Important for all of us."

"It would mean the world to Dad."

She bit her lip, the ache of what was in the past being almost too much to bear. She didn't want to break down and cry in front of him. "I don't want to monopolize you. I'm sure everyone is eager to visit with you, too."

"Well, I am sorta dating Alayna Mikkelson."

"Really?" This family just got more and more tangled up, with her dad marrying a Mikkelson. Then her older brother Broderick marrying one, too. And now Aiden?

"It's still pretty new, and we're figuring it out." He shrugged. "She's been having a rough time lately—something about thinking she saw her uncle stalking around. Apparently he's a real loser—a drinker and drug addict."

Alarms went off in her head. "Is the uncle a Mikkelson? I thought Charles Mikkelson Sr., was an only child."

"It's their mom's brother. Jeannie's brother."

Somehow that made it more chilling. But Brea didn't want to tell Aiden as much when all she had to go on was her hunches.

"Thank you for talking to me and sharing what you remember about our past. The memories from you and the others are helpful." Even if they made her sad.

Even if seeing her dad made her apprehensive, like she was betraying her adoptive parents. Or like she would be vulnerable if she opened up about the past to him. Maybe if her mother had still been alive, things would feel different. But even with the house looking the same, too much had changed, what with her father's remarriage. Even Broderick had defected to the Mikkelsons.

Because she remembered very clearly how deeply the Steeles had hated the Mikkelsons. Her dad had labeled them crooks more than once, a strong opinion that had made it easy to accept her adoptive parents' version of the past. That her wealthy and powerful family had corruptive forces all around them, and that someone obviously wanted the Steeles dead. In her mind, Brea had filled in Mikkelson culprits, knowing how fierce that rivalry had been.

But had any of that been true?

Maybe not. But just forgetting all of that enmity and accepting that their rivals were now some kind of family felt unsettling and even a little scary.

There weren't enough breathing exercises in the world to make her okay with any of this. She had to get out of this room for a moment. To regroup.

Brea found herself searching for Ward, needing him at her side.

Six

Stabbing her spoon through her chocolate mousse again and again, Brea was full, done, finished.

And it had more to do with the people than the food.

She was on overload from what should have been a simple meal with her relatives. Coming here had been difficult, but if she didn't step into the lair, she would never have the answers she sought.

Conversation hummed around the table, led mostly by Broderick and Glenna, the others following their lead in pretending this meal was just like any other. She'd hoped having Ward at her side would help, but the meal had still been tense as she sat at the long table the way they'd done in the past. But things never could be that way again. Finding a path to a new sense of family was easier said than done.

Aiden's story about the camping trips had left her even more jittery, with too many memories of those outings flooding her mind. Many of them focused on her father, who now sat at the other end of the table. He didn't pressure her, but she felt his unspoken need for more from her, for a return to the family fold, sooner rather than later.

Anxiety churned in her stomach, along with the king crab and the salad they'd eaten for lunch. She'd taken note of her childhood-favorite seafood showing up on the menu, and yes, she'd been touched. How could she forget those earlier memories of her dad cracking the shells to get the best chunks of meat for her?

This would be easier if it weren't for the Mikkelsons. Her gaze skipped to Jeannie. The blonde woman gushed all over Jack, seeming like a happy newlywed.

Could all of this be real? No hidden agendas? No culpability from the Mikkelson clan?

Brea's eyes went back to her father, who was currently holding a sleeping baby in the crook of his arm, one of Naomi's twin daughters. Brea swallowed hard. Seeing those two little girls was…tough. Seeing the way the clan adored them was even tougher, piling more layers of confusion on her already difficult past. Seeing all that love she'd missed out on hurt.

Her throat closed up and she abandoned her spoon in the chocolate mousse and angled toward Ward to whisper in his ear, "Gargoyle."

Ward pulled his attention from his conversation with Broderick and nodded quickly. Then looked at his Patek Philippe wristwatch. "This has been great, but I have a conference call I'll need to take at the office." He placed his linen napkin on the table. "Brea and I should be going. I have work to get through."

Broderick inched back his chair. "A meeting on a weekend?"

Standing, Ward shrugged while waiting for Brea. "Just making sure your stockholders are happy."

She couldn't help but see the disappointment in Jack's eyes as she left. Her father always seemed to have such unrealistically high expectations every time their paths crossed. She could understand. And she was trying. She just wished he understood her position, as well. Then maybe she wouldn't feel so smothered.

She'd tried to explain herself to the Steeles in a statement she'd labored over with her lawyer. Doing her best to fill in the gaps for them with a summary of what had happened with her other family after they rescued her from the crash site. Brea had hoped the Steeles would see how tangled the truth of her reality had become. But what had felt like an outpouring of emotion on her end had apparently come across as terse and aloof on the other.

Another curse from her years away.

She wasn't on the same emotional or mental footing as these people.

To his credit, Ward had made good on their safe word. He whisked her quickly and convincingly away toward the coatrack, which was flanked by family photographs on the wall.

Brea averted her eyes, feeling for her thick blue parka. Sliding into her coat, she smiled at Ward. The sound of her family's laughter and conversation hung in the air as he passed her a wool scarf.

Just like that, the walls of her childhood home seemed to close in on her. Ward spoke in hushed tones to a staff member about getting his SUV brought around. She pushed past him, stepping across the threshold into the crisp night air.

An involuntary shiver pulsed through her spine in the frigid air. And yet the physical sensation was welcomed. As was the smell of pine and cold. Familiar smells. Yes. But smells not completely tied to her past here.

The past she couldn't quite make sense of as hard as she tried.

Behind her, she heard the door clicking open to reveal Ward. Warm light from inside washed over his black wool jacket. He yanked on a hat, shading his blue eyes from the sun, which was already sinking at midday.

Royce shouldered through the door before it closed, flipping up the lapel of his long wool coat as he stopped beside them, his gaze locked on Brea. "Do you have a minute to talk?"

"Sure," she said, nervous and curious all at once about what her twin's husband had to say away from the others.

As anxious as she'd been to depart and leave behind the pressure of all the family together, Brea didn't have that same level of nervousness now. Speaking to Royce one-on-one—speaking to any of them one-on-one—was always easier for her. Fewer agendas to sift through. Less noise for her brain.

Royce bristled as a wave of wind tumbled through the Steele compound. His eyes were soft in the yellow-orange hues of the sky. "The Steeles are a great family. But I understand how overwhelming they can be in full force," he said with insight. "Naomi and I are heading to North Dakota to check out the pipeline construction." Royce was a research scientist, who was responsible for groundbreaking ecological innovations in the oil industry. "Chuck Mikkelson's in charge of that arm of the operation, but you and Ward could both join us. You can still call it work, but it would also give you two some time away from feeling obligated to come to these family meals."

For a quiet guy, he sure noticed a lot. Still, as much as she wanted to figure out what happened, she balked at the thought of going to stay on a Mikkelson's home turf.

Her stomach twisted at the idea of spending time with any of the Mikkelsons. With her vision turning fuzzy, she took a settling breath. Focused her eyes on the tree line, where a few elk weaved around low-hanging limbs.

"Chuck's wife has struggled with amnesia," Royce reminded them, his breath visible in the cold air. "She may also have some insights when it comes to reconciling all the mixed-up parts of your past."

Brea chewed her bottom lip. "She might." Her chest went tight with anxiety. Maybe Shana Mikkelson would understand this anxiety, too. "It's generous of you to mention this opportunity and invite us on your trip."

The scientist arched an eyebrow. "I'm not totally altruistic with this. My wife wants time with her twin. I want that for her—peace, reconciliation. I'm not good at romantic gestures, but this trip falling over Valentine's Day would make it a perfect gift for her."

Her heart hammered as Brea inhaled a deep breath of cold air. It stung in her lungs as night birds squawked in the towering pines.

Valentine's Day? She hadn't even given a thought to the impending "lover's holiday." Her skin prickled, and it had nothing to do with the cold and everything to do with her sexy lover as Ward placed a steadying hand on her back. "How long were you planning to stay?"

Brea shifted on her feet, sleet crunching beneath her

sheepskin-lined leather boots. Filled with the urgency to run, she imagined what it would be like to dash head-long for the elk loping in the tree line. To leave all of this behind.

"It'll be a three-day, two-night trip." Royce leveled a stare at Brea. "You need to understand. I'd do anything for her—and anything to protect her."

Maybe she should have taken that as the warning it was no doubt meant to be. But Brea couldn't deny a certain satisfaction that Naomi had found someone to stand beside her.

Ward might not have shared her feelings about Royce's warning, however. She felt tension in the arm he slung more tightly around her shoulders.

"I'm sure you understand, I feel the same." Ward held the other man's gaze for a moment to let that sink in. "It's time for us to leave."

As they strode toward the SUV, she thought about how easy it was to lean into the strength of Ward's pro-tective arm, to pretend their fake relationship was in fact becoming something more than a one-month agreement.

But she also recalled his grief over his broken mar-riage and losing his stepdaughter. The memory of the pain in his voice when he'd shared that still tore right through her, speaking to a part of her that understood what it was like to lose everything.

Sleeping together had been incredible, but it put them in a dangerous position on so many levels. Emotionally and practically. What would come of their affair if she found that the Mikkelsons—or the Steeles—had played a role in that crash? She wasn't sure, but she guessed where Ward's loyalties would lie. He'd worked too hard for this position to turn his back on the Steeles.

Beyond that, she wasn't even sure she could trust her memories, her past or her family. How could she pursue something real and long-term with him when she was still getting to know herself?

And where would that leave her? She wanted to think she could simply walk away. But the more time she spent with him, the more difficult she realized that would be. So before they celebrated any kind of Valentine's Day together—before she slid back into his bed again—she needed to figure out a plan B, for when things fell apart.

Because she wasn't sure she could handle her world falling apart again, especially when she still wasn't over everything that had happened to her.

Pressing his foot down on the accelerator, Ward maneuvered his SUV through the massive, elaborate gates that enclosed the Steele compound.

"What do you think about making that trip to North Dakota? We don't have to go if you prefer not to."

To block the sinking sun, he flicked the visor down, more eager for her answer than he should be—eager to spend time alone with her away from the larger contingent of her family. He'd been playing the role of buffer. Her family was one of the reasons they'd started.

He waited for her answer as he drove toward the setting sun. Short Alaskan winter days sent the sun's rays shrinking behind the mountains all the way back to Brea's apartment.

"It sounds like I could learn a lot about the newly merged family business."

He mulled over her words. Was she already thinking about ways to play sleuth on Mikkelson territory, as she'd likely done around Ward's office the day that had launched this dating charade? What would Brea's family think if they knew about the information he suspected she'd taken off Ward's computer? He was risking his job by not telling anyone. But once he'd figured out what records she'd accessed, he'd determined there was nothing proprietary involved and decided to keep the incident to himself.

Glancing to his right, he watched the way silence made her mouth grow taut. He hated seeing her uneasy.

Clearing his throat, he turned onto the main road. "And it really doesn't bother you that Naomi and Royce are the ones who invited us? That Marshall Steele is going to be our pilot?"

She twisted her hands in her lap, picking at her fingernails. "I can't avoid my siblings forever just because I'm afraid the world will open up under me if I gain total clarity about my past."

"Is that really how you feel?" He held her gaze for a moment. "We don't have to go."

"I'm not afraid." She tipped her chin, eyes full of that fiery determination he admired.

Once he had stopped at a red light, he reached over to stroke her jaw briefly before returning to the steering wheel. "It's going to be a quick trip, but it also sounds like a good idea. Like Royce said, you could get a breather from so many people here, while still getting to know the Steeles—and Mikkelsons—in smaller groups."

Brea toyed with her hair, rubbing it between her fingers. "What if I change my mind? You could go without me."

What was she hedging about? He understood the lunch had been stressful, but throughout the meal, she'd leaned on him, touched his knee under the table. Something had shifted when they were outside, and he wasn't sure what that might be.

He accelerated again into traffic, sludge crunching under the tires. "For the business, I should go. But if we're apart over Valentine's Day, it sounds like you're not holding up your end of our bargain. People will question why we're not together."

"Well, we can't have people gossiping." Brea's jaw tightened as she reached to hold her hands in front of the heater vents. The scent of her perfume drifted toward him on the gusts of warm air.

Ward drew in a deep breath, then looked at her, her face so beautiful, bathed in the warm glow of the dashboard lights. "I want to spend time with you."

Flicking the blinker on, he turned onto a road where a light dusting of snow had begun to accumulate.

Turning her head to face the window, she muttered, "Spend time in my bed, you mean."

He detected something dark in her voice. Careening his head to see her, he noticed the way she chewed her bottom lip.

"Is that a problem?"

The red light just ahead of them turned green. An ancient snowplow lurched forward in a sputter of black smoke. Ward steered the SUV around the choking vehicle.

The leather creaked as Brea shifted in the seat. "I just want to be sure we're on the same page about what's happening between us. This is an arrangement that allows me to be around my family with your protection. And I'm helping you blend into the family corporate culture."

"And the sex?"

The question hung in the air in between them. Electricity palpable before she answered. "The sex was amazing, truly amazing. But it can't be anything more."

He agreed, but hearing her say as much still stung. "I don't recall saying otherwise."

She looked down at her hands, her hair rippling in front of her eyes like a curtain. "The family vacation to North Dakota just seems…like something more."

"It's not a vacation. It's business."

"And our timeline to break up is still the same?"

Was that regret in her voice?

He pulled off the road, into a parking lot, and turned to face her. "If that's what you want. I thought I made it clear I'm not interested in a white picket fence. Been there. Done that. Have the battle scars to prove it." He stroked her hair back over her shoulder, lingering to caress her neck. "But that doesn't change how much I want you. And after what we experienced, I'm not backing off."

He sealed his vow with a kiss. He intended it to be a brief skim of his lips over hers. But she gripped his jacket and pulled him closer, sighing. The kiss quickly spun out of control. But then Ward had learned things were often that way with Brea. Never had he met a woman who turned him on as fully and as quickly as she did.

She was a feast for the senses. The hint of her floral shampoo, the taste of chocolate mousse she'd picked at. Best of all, the satin texture of her skin. He wanted to take her here, now—

A car door slammed near them, a few parking spots away, and they bolted apart. His heartbeat sped up, heat still flaring up the back of his shoulders from wanting her. Damn, he'd lost sight of where they were. She deserved better from him.

"Your place or mine?" he asked, hunger for her edging his words with stark need.

"I'm—" She hesitated. Licked her lips. "I'm not sure that's a good idea."

Surprise—and a hefty dose of disappointment—rushed through him. Especially since he could see her pulse jumping in the fast-ticking vein in her neck, where he'd just kissed her. "Why not?"

"I don't regret what we did." She stroked his face lightly, as if unable to trust herself to deepen the connection. "But things are moving too fast for me. I need space to think."

He saw the resolution in her deep brown eyes and knew enough about negotiations to realize he wasn't going to win this round. "You're right, of course. This afternoon had to be rough for you."

A hint of regret chased that resolution in her gaze. "I wonder what it would have been like if we'd met each other on totally neutral territory."

He wondered the same. But they would never know. He could only go with the hand they'd been dealt, and his resolve to keep her close was strong as ever. He needed to keep her in his sights. Yes, this was about helping him gain entry to the family, and being her buffer. But it was also about making sure she was on the up-and-up.

And if he wanted to return to those out-of-control kisses and the passion that swept them both away, he damned well intended to make sure she had an unforgettable Valentine's Day.

The past two days preparing for the trip to North Dakota, Brea found her mind full of Ward. Thoughts of what it would be like if she hadn't turned him away.

She was more apprehensive about seeing Chuck Mik-kelson than she'd expected. While he was too young to have had anything to do with the crash, if his family was involved, she feared his reaction when the truth came out.

If only she could trust Ward with all her concerns. She felt so alone.

Which was a feeling exacerbated as she sat white-knuckled in the small private airplane. Marshall, her brother, acted as pilot. Flying them over the impossibly blue lakes in Canada.

Inching toward the window, Brea made herself look out. Her stomach promptly plummeted as her gaze rested on a snowcapped mountain. Painful shards of her past rose to her consciousness, as intently as the peaks below her did.

This flight to North Dakota stirred memories in her. Not just from the crash, which she'd expected. But of that life before. The life after. Life with her adoptive parents and the things they'd done as a family and with their tight-knit community.

She'd spent so much time recovering from the crash and her mother's death, dazed and full of grief. By the time she'd healed in the home of Steven and Karen Jones, she'd stopped questioning why her father hadn't come for her. She'd believed Jack Steele had given up on her. That the Steeles and their circles were corrupt. And she'd been so empty inside, needing a family to fill the void. She'd gladly accepted the Joneses' invitation to stay, to be their daughter. Life was simpler in their home. Sparse. Orderly. Emotions were more predictable. Restrained. All of that had appealed to her when she'd been hurting so badly inside, she thought she might fly apart at any moment.

The twin engines of the private jet hummed. Became something like white noise as she released her grip from the leather seat below her. Looking at the shimmering lakes beneath the plane, she found herself thinking about her off-the-grid upbringing. Or should she say second upbringing?

Steven Jones had been the community's electrician, working with micro hydro and wind sources for energy to power the small group of homes. He'd taken her along when she was maybe fourteen years old, once she'd realized she wouldn't be leaving. No one was coming for her. She'd been eager to belong. Confused, but desperate to keep her place in the world she'd found herself in. She'd soaked up the way he assessed different weak points in the systems, gladly throwing herself into a completely new world.

Swallowing a lump in her throat, she cast a look to Marshall. Rather than sitting in the back, she'd opted to sit close to her brother, in the cockpit. Family bonding. Her brother wore the headset, his thick dark curls in need of a cut.

Though maybe next time she ought to choose a less-traumatic space as grounds for her healing with her estranged family. With as much time as she'd spent in counseling about her past, she ought to have known better than to throw herself headlong into difficult situations.

It was almost painful sitting there, with her anxiety about flights and her family keeping her on edge. But after their last conversation, she wasn't comfortable sitting by Ward.

In the back of the cabin, he clacked away on his laptop. Keystrokes muffled by the sound of the engine. But as she glanced over her shoulder, she noticed the way he threw himself into work. Brow furrowed. A pencil tucked behind his ear.

Her twin also busied herself with work. A flurry of papers surrounded her. Naomi's lips pursed as she made her way through a brief. Royce was sleeping. Life with twins had clearly drained him. The girls had stayed back with Jack and Jeannie, as well as Delaney, who was on hand to assist during the short trip away.

Swiveling in her seat, Brea forced her attention back to Marshall, whose steady gaze kept the plane even. For a moment she felt as though some of the air returned to her lungs. Impossibly, she felt a surge of trust in her brother's ability to deliver them safely. He'd always been a quiet kid in their noisy family, but whatever Marshall had tackled, he'd done well. He paid attention to detail, and it showed. They'd all seen that from him at a young age.

"Thank you for flying us today, Marshall."

"No problem," he said. "It's a good opportunity to log some flight hours. I'm also going to take in a rodeo while I'm there before resting up for our flight back."

She wasn't surprised he didn't plan to join them at the pipeline site. He'd always been more of a loner than the others in their family.

"I'm surprised you enjoy flying," she ventured. "You didn't like it when we were kids. And then with the crash…" She hesitated. "Or maybe I'm remembering wrong about when we were kids. Was it Broderick who was nervous about planes?"

He shook his head, an easy smile on his lips. "No, it was me. After you and Mom were in the crash, I decided I had to conquer the fear. Maybe it sounds strange. But I felt like if I conquered the sky somehow, it would be a way of paying tribute to you both."

Brea's throat closed with emotion. No matter what else she might believe about her Steele siblings, their love for their mother was without question. Would it have helped her get past her own fierce sense of loss if she could have grieved with them?

She swallowed hard and said, "Tell me something about our past."

He glanced at her. "Are you sure that's a good idea? I wouldn't want to do anything to mess with your therapy." He hesitated. "Especially when we're in the air. I can tell this isn't easy for you, Brea."

Touched, she felt the warmth of gratitude for his keen observation.

"Delaney and Aiden shared some things with me, and it helped." In fact, after listening, she found it easier to trust them. "Please, pick something…"

Her pleading eyes met his. He nodded, understanding drawing tension away from his jaw and brow before he returned his attention to the windscreen.

"Sure," he said somberly. "Remember that day we flew together, and Dad let me take the yoke…"

Marshall had always been closer to Brea than to Naomi, and sometimes he felt left out, since the two of them were thick as thieves. His grandma said it was the twin bond. That didn't make him feel any better.

Naomi was supposed to go on the flight today, but she'd canceled at the last minute to go fishing with their grandmother. So Marshall had jumped at the chance to spend time with Brea without having to compete with her twin. Even though he hated flying. The sensation of looking down at the ground. He nervously tightened his seat belt.

Brea sat next to him. Understood his unease. She tightened her high ponytail, her attention turning to her father, who smiled behind aviator glasses.

Pointing excitedly, Brea squealed. "Wow, that's our house. And the boathouse. And the horses are so tiny. This is so cool. Can I hold the steering wheel?"

"It's called a yoke," Jack Steele said patiently. Beaming at the interest his children were taking in the flight.

"The yoke." Brea squinted her eyes, inquisitive as ever. "Can I touch the one on this side?"

"As long as you let me know before you touch it."

"Okay," she said, her ponytail bobbing like crazy, she nodded so fast. "I'm letting you know."

Their dad laughed. "That's my fearless girl."

"That's Naomi."

"You too, kiddo."

Marshall felt like a coward. So he said, "Dad, I wanna fly."

With shaking hands, Marshall approached the yoke. He grasped on to it with all the gusto of a World-War-II-era fighter pilot.

Made himself look out to the horizon, the colors whooshing before him. His stomach as choppy as an uneasy sea. And that sea rose within him until he felt the burning sensation of vomit bubble in the back of his throat.

No. No. No. Not like this. He could tamp it down. Had to.

But then there was the expanse of land before him. The height. And try as he might, he could not stop the hiccup of vomit from exploding out of his mouth and down the caribou shirt his grandmother had given him.

Cheeks burning, he fled to the small on-plane bath-room to wipe his mouth.

Brea was there, waiting for him when he left the bath-room. She knelt beside him, passing him a washcloth like their mom would have done. "Marshall, you're good on horses. I'm scared of falling off."

He knew she meant well, but it didn't help him feel any better. Steeles didn't flinch. They didn't give up. Ever...

With her brother's words still echoing in her mind, Brea stared out the aircraft window, the North Dakota plains stretching out for miles and miles. Far away from Alaska, leaving even Canada behind.

Maybe this trip was a good idea after all. Time away from both parts of her childhood, and a chance to embrace tomorrow rather than the past.

Because thinking about any part of her childhood knocked her more and more off-balance at a time when she needed to keep her head straight. If any one of the Mikkelsons was involved in trying to harm her family, she couldn't afford to let her guard down.

This time with Chuck Mikkelson could offer a chance to ferret out clues about the day her world imploded, breaking her ties with everyone who'd once been so important to her.

Seven

Ward had been to forty-two states over the course of his career, but this was his first trip to North Dakota. And normally he would have been all about the job, about the new insights on the pipeline. Not today. He just wanted to finish the meeting and get Brea alone, to see if he could persuade her to reclaim the explosive chemistry they'd shared too briefly.

He forced his attention back on work for the moment, since the faster he finished here, the sooner he could return with her to their hotel suite. At least maybe he could get more hints about what made her tick. He stomped his boots to get the circulation flowing again in his feet as they stood in the frigid weather. Snow whipped all around this section of the pipeline. He was used to cold, having lived in Alaska, but the wind sweeping across the Dakota plains had a bite that stole his breath.

But despite the bone-cold scrape of the wind, Shana and Chuck Mikkelson seemed to love their new home state.

Ward stayed back a step, listening as Chuck gave them all a tour of the modifications on the pipeline. He covered everything from innovations made, thanks to Royce's work on efficiency, to the safety upgrades.

Lord, this was a stark wasteland. They'd traveled for two hours in a luxury RV. Chuck said he'd bought the vehicle because of how often they traveled out to remote sites. If they were caught in a storm, he and Shana could park the RV and ride out the weather in their own little home away from home. There was even a storage compartment underneath for a car if they needed to park at a work site and wanted the freedom of a smaller vehicle.

Wind whistling past his ears, Ward wondered what Brea was making of all of this. Was she glad she'd come? Or was she feeling stressed? She had stayed glued to his side, and he wasn't sure if that was to play along with their fake relationship or because she genuinely needed him. She'd made a point of wanting to be here, but had stayed unusually quiet since they'd arrived, especially once Marshall had headed off to catch a rodeo on his own.

It seemed to him she was avoiding Naomi. Which was hard to do in these luxurious, yet close, quarters. But he couldn't determine why.

Snow came down faster, the wind blowing it sideways. Hard. Pellets stung his cheeks.

Chuck angled a look at Ward while tugging his overcoat collar up more securely over his ears. "Should we put this tour on hold due to weather?"

Ward cocked an eyebrow. "I doubt it's going to get

much better for a couple of months. So I'd just as soon we finish today. Royce? Your thoughts?"

"Press on," the man of few words replied.

Her blond hair peeking free from her hood, Shana Mikkelson waved a gloved hand toward Naomi and Brea. "Let's get some coffee in the RV."

Indecision chased across Brea's wind-reddened features. She bit her chapped lip and then said, "Sure, I could use something warm."

So much for getting clues about her by watching Brea with her sister. He studied Brea's retreating figure as she left his side, her thick braid specked with ice and snow.

Chuck adjusted his Stetson, pulling it further down his head, covering more of his golden-brown hair. "I'm glad you could both make it here. There's a lot of work left to be done, but it's an exciting new venture for the company."

Ward forced his thoughts back to the job at hand, focusing on Chuck and the work he was doing here. Networking was an underrated portion of the CEO job, but something that always paid off. "How's your move coming with starting the new job?"

Shrugging against the wind, Chuck angled his body toward Ward and Royce. Snow began to accumulate on his wool coat. "We're building a place on a ten-acre piece of land that already had a converted barn on the property. It's great to be on-site and watch every stage of the process. We figure the barn will make a great guesthouse, too."

Royce stuffed his hands into his coat pockets. "Looking forward to seeing it."

"You're staying with us, of course," Chuck said, his voice rising to combat the wind.

Sharing an afternoon together was one thing. Staying under the same roof was another, and an arrangement Ward didn't think Brea would want. "I made reservations downtown."

"We have plenty of space at the house," Chuck offered. "Guest rooms and a loft."

Ward whistled. "That must be a mighty big barn. I'll see what Brea thinks."

Chuck nodded. "Family is important to us. Leaving Alaska was a big transition, one we felt we needed to make for our marriage. But we want to maintain the close relationships we have, especially once we have kids. Hopefully the house will be done before the baby needs a nursery."

"You're expecting?" Ward extended his hand, trying not to think of the stepdaughter he couldn't see. "Congratulations."

"We're adopting." Chuck shook his hand, a smile of pure happiness spreading across his face. "The timing could be tomorrow, or months, or years from now. We have to wait until they match us to a child. We're just glad to be together after a rough patch not too long ago."

"Good to hear it."

Chuck's eyes narrowed as he squinted against the pelting snowfall. "If you don't mind my asking, how did you and Brea become an item?"

"We met through the business. Alaska Oil Barons, Inc., sure does host more than its fair share of charity events, and Brea and I ended up in the same corners of the room a few times. She's a beautiful woman," Ward said simply, honestly. Best to keep it straightforward. Private.

"I'm just surprised she'll have anything to do with the

company after all her reservations about coming back
into the family fold."

Ward didn't intend to tell him that she wasn't fully
embracing the family—not yet. "She was gone for a
long time."

Kicking the snow beneath his boot, Ward noticed
the way stress lines creased the corners of Chuck's
mouth. "She seems to resent us, the Mikkelsons. How
she could blame my mom—or even Jack—is beyond
me. I've found no proof that anyone in the business had
anything to do with that crash. I've searched my father's
records at length."

"And Brea knows this?" Ward couldn't keep the surprise out of his voice.

"I've told my mother. A lot of rumors floated around
at the time of the accident, especially because of the
deep rivalry between the families." Chuck shook his
head. "But there's just no proof my family had anything
to do with it."

Royce, who had been content to observe the conversation, cleared his throat. His quiet sensibility was something Ward appreciated. The man didn't waste words. He
had a scientist's way of synthesizing important elements.

"It can be very difficult to accept that sometimes ac-
cidents just happen."

Chuck thumped a piece of equipment. "I'm obviously
relieved Brea's alive. But it's tough watching this family
feel all torn up again, between the merger and the riding accident Jack had last year..."

"And your mother's marriage..." Ward reminded
him.

The family had gone through a lot in a short period of
time. He felt for them, but Brea was his priority.

"Yeah," Chuck agreed, sighing out a white cloud into the cold air, "that was a shocker."

It didn't appear Chuck Mikkelson had any new insights to offer, as much as Ward would have wished otherwise, for Brea's sake. "Let's finish up out here before we freeze our asses off."

Both men agreed, and Chuck launched back into details on the gauges and valves, waving for them to follow him to a garage-sized workshop full of control panels.

Anticipation charged through Ward. He was that much closer to ending the workday. That only left an obligatory supper out, and then he could move forward with plans to get Brea alone at the hotel.

He only wished he had better news to share with her about her search for answers. Because, truth be told, he guessed that her personal quest was the main reason she'd taken this trip.

And her being here didn't really have a damned thing to do with him.

He shouldn't be bothered by her reaction. He wasn't in the market for a serious relationship after being burned by his ex. Paisley had paid the biggest price, and that hurt him most.

After such a massive mistake, he was better off focusing on what he did best, running the Alaska Oil Barons, Inc.

Brea looked around the RV that was as large as some of the off-the-grid houses in her former community. And definitely far more luxurious with a buttery-soft leather wrap-around sofa and a recliner. Decorated in warm browns, tans and copper, the space made for a lovely home away from home.

Shana stood at the counter, making coffee, while Naomi sat crossed-legged on the couch. It was so surreal being in the same space with her twin after so many years apart. They'd been so close once. Would they ever be so again?

The other two women's conversation hummed around Brea, and she turned her attention to stare out the window at Ward, his shoulders broad, taller than the other men who wore Stetsons.

"Don't you agree, Brea?"

She looked back quickly at her twin. "I'm sorry. What did you say?"

Naomi tapped the window pane, gesturing toward the men outside, whom Brea had been staring at. "Royce has made brilliant innovations for a cleaner transfer of oil."

"Oh, yes, it's fascinating on a number of levels." Brea couldn't help but be intrigued personally, too. "In my community, getting those sorts of cutting-edge inventions was often difficult, due to being so separate from the rest of the world."

Maybe if the village had been more accessible, she would have been found? That shift in her thinking gave her pause.

Shana's hand moved with smooth efficiency as she pulled mugs from the cabinet. "I'm glad we had a quiet day to look over things. Chuck's brother got caught in the middle of quite a scene with the media last summer."

Brea had read up on the Mikkelsons and the younger son, Trystan, who had been in scrapes with the press. "He's the one who married his media consultant."

"They have a baby boy," Shana said wistfully, then smiled as the coffee maker gurgled. "We're planning to adopt. It's going to happen for us, I just get impatient."

Brea hadn't given much thought to having children. Since her teenage years, her life had been so consumed with figuring out the past and how to weave whatever she found into her present so she could move forward with the future. But right now, she found her thoughts captivated by the notion of holding an infant in her arms.

What an unsettling notion, though, the idea of permanence, family, longevity—especially when she could barely wrap her brain around the notion of an affair.

The aroma of hazelnut and coffee beans filled the luxury RV.

Brea's gaze slid to the window overlooking the trio of men striding across the icy lot, toward a large garage-like area. Ward was so tall and imposing, his long-legged steps confident and sure-footed. Could she really hold strong to her decision not to sleep with him again? She wanted to give in to temptation, but the strength of that draw made her all the more cautious. She needed to tread warily for just that reason. Their simple affair wasn't turning out to be so simple after all.

Shana set a bamboo tray of stoneware coffee mugs down on the small table in front of Brea. Steam rolled from the mugs, and both twins blew over their steaming cup of java at the same time.

Brea looked up self-consciously. An echo of her grandmother's words whispered through her.

It's the twin bond.

Shana had already made her way back to the coffeepot and was filling a silver thermos. "I'm going to take some coffee out to the guys." She waved them back to their seats. "Don't get up. I can carry it all."

Thermos under her arm, she carried stacked cups and opened the door. A blast of frigid air filled with snow rolled inside. The door closed after her, slamming from the force of the wind.

Naomi looked at her sister. "I know this whole situation is awkward, but I don't want you to feel uncomfortable around me as we figure out how to be a family again."

"Thank you." Brea poured creamer into her coffee. "And I'm trying to push past the awkwardness. It's just scary to me that there are still a lot of unanswered questions about what happened. You should be worried too, for your girls."

She glanced up at the array of Mikkelson family photographs on the built-in bookcase. Her eyes focused on one of the older photographs of the Mikkelson clan as she remembered them from her limited exposure in the past—this was the family who had been their bitter business rivals.

Her stomach catapulted at the image.

Naomi shivered, her arms wrapping protectively around herself. "You can't really believe someone is still out to get us."

Her twin's eyes were concerned, but not suspicious. Not accusing. Whatever Naomi might believe, she was at least inclined to listen with an open mind, and Brea appreciated that. So often since she'd returned, she felt like she had to weigh every word.

"I think someone could have a reason to hide what they did. You're a lawyer. You should know that."

Naomi bit her bottom lip. "Okay, I can see your point. Whatever you need me to do help you investigate, I want you to know, I'm on board. I'm sure Shana would offer her professional assistance, too. She's a top-notch investigator."

"I know. She found me." Brea's skin prickled. "If it's okay, I'd rather refrain from involving the Mikkelsons any more than we have to."

"So, you really think they…" Naomi's words hung in the air between them as the aggressive wind rocked the RV slightly.

"I think their loyalty to each other could make them close their eyes to possibilities and make it tougher for me to find the truth. What if it were Charles Mikkelson Sr.? How far would they go to protect his memory?"

Brea looked away from her twin's horrified expression, the pinch of guilt over inflicting pain on the family making Brea uncomfortable. She peered outside, watching Shana pass the thermos and cups to the men inside the shelter of the open garage that was big as a hangar.

"But if it was him, he's dead now and not a threat," Naomi pointed out logically.

Naomi leaned forward, putting her mug of coffee down on the side table.

Brea considered her twin's words, her attention wandering around the luxury RV. Little touches of photographs and Alaska memorabilia—knickknacks, such as elk and bear figurines, on the shelves—showed the blended life of Shana and Chuck. Normally, personal touches would be comforting.

But in this situation?

She couldn't shake the feeling that there was more to the Mikkelsons—something she was missing. Some sign of foul play in relation to the plane crash. And while she didn't want to believe it could be these people she now had to call family…

"Or there could have been others involved, along with him." Her eyes went out of focus for a second, lingering back on the pictures on the bookshelf. "Once I know the truth, I hope the path forward will be simple for us all."

"As do I." Naomi uncrossed her legs, leather creaking with the movement.

Brea tried to put together the right thing to say, and found there were no perfect words for something like this. She drew in a deep inhale of coffee and leather. She squeezed her eyes shut, resolved to talk, knowing the time frame would never be right. "How will Dad feel if Jeannie's family is involved? Will he even believe the truth? Or will he subconsciously block me from finding out a truth he can't bear to know? I honestly don't want to see him hurt."

Slowly, Naomi nodded. "I can understand that."

A keening bark of North Dakota wind added its lonely wail to their dark conversation.

"Really?" Brea hadn't expected that concession. "Thank you. It makes it easier to talk to you if there aren't expectations in place that I can't meet."

Pushing her lips into a sad kind of smile, Naomi gathered her dark hair into a ponytail, changing the waterfall effect it had while cascading onto her cashmere sweater. "In the interest of honesty, the counselor the family and I have been talking with made it clear that expectation management is important."

"The family counselor," Brea repeated, making sure she understood that correctly. "You're *all* seeing a therapist?" She blinked, surprise circulating through her.

"Felicity suggested it, and we all agreed it was a good idea. We want what's best for you. And…" Naomi paused to swallow heavily, the mug of coffee untouched in her hand. "Dad's been struggling with renewed grief over Mom. We all want to be there for him."

Her sister's shoulders slumped. It might have been a long time since they'd lived together as sisters, but Brea could still read the hurt and pain in Naomi's eyes. Brea stood up on shaky legs. Willed them to move across the small distance to her sister. Settling onto the leather couch next to Naomi, Brea gulped down air.

"She's been gone so long." Brea twisted her hands in her lap.

"But you still miss her too, right?"

Brea looked up sharply, hoping the answer was already plain in her eyes. "Of course." Their mother had died in fear for Brea, holding her in her arms until Brea blacked out, surrounding her with a mother's love. That loss had been the toughest of all those Brea had sustained. "It couldn't have been easy for you, losing Mom, then you getting cancer."

It really hit her then that her sister could have died. That she could have missed the opportunity to see Naomi again. Her throat clogged. Why hadn't the twin connection worked to alert her? Brea pressed two fingers to a headache that was suddenly blooming.

"It was a difficult time after you were gone. I missed Mom. I missed you. I missed my hair," Naomi said with a wry grin that slowly faded. "And I was terrified of what it would do to Dad if he lost me, too."

A sharp pain pierced Brea's chest. Her twin's pain.

"I wish I could have been there for you." Brea touched her sister's hand lightly.

"Thank you." Naomi clasped Brea's hand tightly. "I have my husband and my twins. And now I have my sister back… At least I hope I do."

"I'm trying," Brea admitted, although she felt twitchy and wanted to pull her hand back. Instead she carefully eased it away. The quick flash of disappointment on Naomi's face made Brea feel petty and small.

"Well," Naomi said in a lowered voice, "remember when we sisters all wanted to be mermaids, and I made us stay at the pool, working on our synchronized mermaid dives until our fingers wrinkled from being in the water so long?"

Brea laughed, her smile lighting up her face. "I do. And after our swims, Mom would braid our hair while it was still wet so we would have waves the next day."

A memory chased through Brea's mind, one of those that she couldn't quite tell if it was real or something she'd just dreamed in those first months at the Joneses' house. "Did she braid our hair for—" she searched for a way to ask the question while still leaving part of it unsaid, to see if Naomi's story matched Brea's recollection "—special events?"

"Yes," Naomi said excitedly. "Mom loved going to *The Nutcracker* at Christmas. She would always braid our hair prior, and then put matching red plaid bows in yours and mine."

Her words matched what was in Brea's mind so perfectly, down to the bows. "Could you tell me more?"

"I would like that," Naomi answered without hesitation. "The Christmas before your accident, we'd both decided we were too old for braids, but Delaney wanted them, and Dad told us to make her and Mom happy..."

Naomi huffed with an angry sigh, crossing her arms over her chest stubbornly. She wasn't giving in without a fight. "I don't want go to a play. I want to go sledding."

Their mother nodded, though Mary pointed for Brea

to sit, a vintage brush in her hands. "We'll do that, too. Tomorrow."

Sledding sounded more fun than a play they'd already seen every year of their lives. She was getting too old for kid stuff. She just had to convince her mom, although it would be nice if her sisters would chime in and help.

"We should skip the ballet and go to bed early so we won't be tired."

Mom didn't miss a beat brushing through Brea's hair, working out the tangles before starting the French braid. "We could skip sledding altogether if it's too tiring for you."

"Fine," Naomi sighed, wishing Brea would have helped her fight the battle. "I'll get ready for the ballet."

"This is about making memories," Mom said, crossing clusters of hair, one over the other. "Someday you'll all be grown-up, and you'll do this with your kids."

Delaney looked up from her book in the corner of the room. Her braids were already completed and tied with a bow. These braids were special, Mom had told them. She'd been taught by her Native Alaskan grandmother. Part of keeping the tribal traditions alive, even as Alaska modernized.

Closing her book, Delaney asked, "But there are so many of us. When we grow up, how will you and Dad be able to pick which one of our houses to go to?"

Brea looked at her reflection in a handheld mirror. "Mom could come to one. Dad could go to another. And Delaney will get Uncle Conrad."

Delaney's bottom lip trembled, and a tear rolled down her cheek.

Mom gently cooed, still brushing Brea's hair. "We'll fly everyone home, and we'll all go to the ballet together."

But Naomi's brows furrowed. All together? Something seemed off in that statement.

She imagined traveling faraway sometimes, where no one could find her while she wrote a book and became a famous author. You had to be a hermit to be an author. That's what her favorite television character had said, and she seemed glamorous enough for anything she said to be true.

Mom's fingers moved quickly, expertly. "How about I tell the story you always ask your grandmother to tell at bedtime? You always say it gets better each time. Maybe The Nutcracker *could be like that."*

Naomi knew when she was beaten. And truth be told, she liked the story. "Okay, since we've got time to kill while you finish our hair. Tell us 'The Legend of...'"

Brea soaked in her sister's words, finding that each one opened a doorway to her memories that matched perfectly. So poignant. And sad.

They'd been so unaware of the pain ahead of them.

She wished she'd paid more attention to the moment, enjoyed the feel of her mother brushing her hair. Or the oral tradition her mother instilled in them. The stories of her mother's tribe. The way she'd wake them with songs.

Brea hadn't thought about that time in years. How much else had she lost of her childhood? She wanted to remember. She tried...but she couldn't quite grab it; the memories too elusive.

Something that chilled her until she realized the men had returned and the door was open.

Her gaze collided with Ward's.

Ice flecked his hair and brows, making him look like some elemental prince of winter come home at last. His wind-chapped, chiseled face was somehow made more handsome from the environment. It brought out the deep blue of his eyes. Awareness tingled over her in the way she was beginning to learn was standard around this man.

"Everything okay?" His question was clearly only directed at her.

But rather than making Brea feel weak or pressured, she felt…protected. And not in a smothering way. He looked like he cared, but he hadn't swept her out of the room.

"I'm fine, thank you." She smiled at him. "We're sharing childhood stories. I'm remembering things. It's okay."

The truth of that simple statement warmed her inside, while his hand on her shoulder stirred a different kind of heat.

Remembering a sweetness in her past that she'd forgotten made her want to celebrate this momentary pocket of joy and peace in the most elemental way. She knew too well the pain of loss, how quickly life could change for the worse. Spurred by her memories and the loss of her mother, all her reasons for not sleeping with him seemed to evaporate.

Wise or not, she knew when they got back to their hotel room, she and Ward would be sharing a bed.

Shaking the ice off his coat, Ward's hand went to the back of his neck as he took in the surprise of seeing Brea and Naomi sitting close to each other.

"Sorry to have interrupted," he said.

Brea's eyes danced. "Naomi was going to tell me 'The Legend of Qalupalik.' It was a favorite for most of us when we were kids, but it's been so long since I heard it..." She bit her bottom lip for a moment before continuing, "I'm not sure I remember it correctly."

Ward waved toward the door. "We can go if you want to be alone."

Brea's laugh electrified the room. "You have icicles on you. I wouldn't send you back out there. You should have some more coffee."

She scooted over, allowing Royce to take a seat next to his wife. Brea patted the spot next to her on the leather couch. Ward shrugged out of his coat and took a seat next to her. The light scent of pine and cold wind still clung to her. Awakened his senses. As did the heat in their locked gazes.

Shana brought out a tray of Danish pastries and small dessert plates, setting them on the coffee table. Chuck shoveled one of the cheese-and-berry Danish pastries onto his plate, and then sat across from Shana at the small table.

Naomi took a sip of coffee before clearing her throat. "Our mom's parents made sure we heard local legends directly from them, not from a book. To keep our heritage alive."

Ward was surprised for a moment. While he recalled reading that the Steele kids had Native Alaskan relatives on their mother's side, he hadn't given it any thought. Hearing this now, from Naomi, showed him more facets of Brea's childhood. "What was your favorite story?"

"'The Legend of the Qalupalik,'" Brea said softly, then glanced at Naomi for her to confirm.

"Yes," Naomi answered. "Qalupalik was green and slimy and lived in the water. She hummed and would draw bad children to the waves. If you wandered away from your parents, she would slip you in a pouch on her back and take you to her watery home to live with her other kids. You would never see your family again. Our grandmother used to tell us that one, and I think it was to get us to behave."

Had Brea thought something like that had happened to her? In a way, it had—except she wasn't bad. No one should endure what she had.

Naomi looked at everyone over the top of her cup. "The story scared us when we were younger, and then once Brea taught us how to be mermaids, we girls embraced the story. We also liked the werewolf legend about the Adlet. They had the lower body of a wolf and the upper body of a human, like a centaur. After Brea was…gone… Broderick and Marshall tried to hunt one once. They had to turn back, though, because I tagged along, and Aiden followed me…"

Ward was only half listening as he registered the warm press of Brea's leg against his own. He could feel her nerves calming as they touched. How was it that he'd developed that ability to read her so clearly? The knowledge knocked him off-balance a bit, though he was only too glad for the excuse to drape his arm around her shoulders.

Shana leaned forward. "What happened?"

Naomi tore off a piece of the pastry. "I took the little twerp home. I was worried about Marshall being so sad and didn't want him to lose out on something fun, so I had to be the grown-up and take Aiden back."

Brea stood, glancing through her thick hair at him. Gave him a wink. An ease rested on her lips. He smiled up at her, enjoying the lightness in the air in this RV. "Can I get refills for anyone?"

No one took her up on the offer.

Brea opened the refrigerator for the creamer since she'd used all the rest set out. Ward's eyes followed her curves. The real, genuine smile that reached her eyes.

She closed the door, then frowned. She stared at a framed photo tucked into a shelf near the refrigerator, her expression frozen, other than furrowing her brow. Then her hand lifted and she touched one picture, her face paling.

Worried, Ward stood and walked the two steps to her, protectiveness surging. "Is something wrong?"

Brea's hand shook and she set the creamer on the counter. "Chuck, I recognize you four Mikkelson kids in this photo. That's you, Glenna, Trystan and Alayna. That's your mom and that must be your father. But who are the other two?"

Chuck rose to join them. "Actually, that's not my mom. That's Trystan's mom—who gave him up to Jeannie to adopt not too long after that." He pointed to the other blonde woman, whose face had been in the shadows. "That's Mom. And this—" he pointed to the other man "—that's Uncle Lyle."

Brea's face paled, and she wavered on her feet. "He was there at the airport that day, and so was…" Her finger wavered over the photo, back and forth between the two women. "One of them."

Eight

Brea felt dizzy, her brain awash with fragmented memories that she couldn't seem to blend into a whole image because of the jagged edges. She recalled seeing the couple at the airport, the man and a woman.

Tension mounted, making her grind her teeth down so hard, her jaw ached. But she couldn't unlock the pressure. Couldn't stop the submerged, underwater sounds in her ears as panic and anxiety took root. All the research she'd done on the Mikkelsons had involved their finances. Their business. She hadn't looked at pictures.

It was the visuals that unlocked the memory.

"Which woman?" Shana asked Brea while resting a comforting hand on Chuck's shoulder.

The spacious luxury RV suddenly seemed to crumple in around her. Air tasted heavy as the hint of knowledge danced in her memory.

Silence wouldn't help her, though. Willing her jaw open and fighting past the panic in her chest, Brea stared at the photo. "I'm pretty sure it's the other one and not your mom, but I can't be certain."

Brea tried to bring the image from the day of the crash into better focus in her mind's eye.

Chuck strode closer to the shelves to look at the photograph, his face somber. "What reason would my uncle and aunt have to harm your family?"

Royce leaned forward, elbows on his knees as he addressed Chuck. "To make your dad's company have less competition so he could make more money?"

Ward put a protective arm around Brea's shoulders. "That's farfetched. What kind of people were they?"

Chuck let out a sigh. He crossed his arms, crumpling his plaid shirt. "We didn't know them well. And when my aunt gave up Trystan for adoption to Mom, our connections with my aunt and uncle faded away."

Shana touched his arm. "Alayna said she thought she overheard something suspicious about your uncle, but was too young to understand. And she thought she saw him at the rodeo a couple of month ago."

Brea sagged to sit. She'd been searching for answers, and now that it seemed she might have them, it overwhelmed her as she realized how much pain could ripple out from this discovery. "Chuck, I'm so sorry. I know this can't be easy for you."

Her heartbeat hammered in her ears. For years she'd thought about this kind of clue. Fantasized about finding a lead to what had caused the event that was the dividing line in her life—the point of turmoil that had sent her spinning for years afterward. Yet in all of her imaginings, this had been a triumphant moment.

In the abstract, the idea of foul play from anyone on the Mikkelsons' side had seemed like an easy answer. But now? Sitting in Chuck's RV, watching his face turn from shock to something like rage and pain…now it was real.

And she wasn't sure of anything.

Not that she had much to stand on in terms of things she was sure of, or solid evidence to pursue. She took a deep breath, catching the aroma of leather, coffee and Ward's aftershave. She anchored herself with Ward's comforting touch.

Chuck cleared his throat. "Whatever the truth is about my mother's family, I want to know the full extent."

"And if that hurts the rest of the family? Your mom? My dad? The business?" She took another breath. "I thought learning the truth would make me happy, but now that I know you all better, it's so much more confusing than it felt when I came back the first time…" Heat rushed to her face, embarrassment over how she'd snuck into their lives with a fake identity. "I'm sorry for the whole Milla Jones deceit."

Shana looked at Brea with concerned eyes and genuine compassion. "I've had amnesia. I understand how difficult it is to put the pieces together when you don't even know who you can trust." She reached to squeeze her hand. "The best thing to do—truly, the only thing to do—is live in the moment."

Could it be that simple? In a life so very complicated, she desperately wanted something that simple. To be able to grasp joy with both hands. With Ward sitting next to her, his aftershave in her every breath and the memory of his touch so tempting in her memory, she found herself grateful for Shana's advice. For her understanding.

Because right now, Brea couldn't imagine recovering from this day anywhere else but in Ward's arms. So she planned to seize the moment and act on her impulse to be with Ward, whatever that meant for the future, as she learned who was responsible for her mother's death.

In the hotel bar two hours later, Ward leaned forward, palms pressing into the rose-quartz bar countertop. He ordered two drinks—a winter ice-cap ale for him and a glass of sparkling rosé wine for Brea. The bartender smiled as he handed the beverages over to him.

Passing the wineglass to Brea, Ward settled back into the leather-backed barstool. The Petru, the most exclusive hotel in town, had been decorated with attention to sophistication. Rustic lights hung, illuminating the pecan-wood shelves and succulents. A live jazz quartet was awash in soft lights on the small stage.

Brea's hair swept upward, a deep side part letting her bangs fall into her face. The proximity of her dark hair seemed to make her blue eyes brighter in this dimmed light. She raised her glass to his beer stein. The clink affirmed the electricity between them in spite of the hellish revelation back at Chuck's RV.

Ward had told her the suite still needed to be cleaned and had suggested they snag drinks at the hotel bar. That had been the first and only lie he had ever uttered to Brea.

Instead the hotel staff was busy finishing the romantic surprise he'd planned for her.

He hoped she would enjoy the gifts he'd ordered. He sensed a shift in her. Something about her body language hinted that she was backing off her no-sex-for-now rule.

At least he hoped so. He wanted to tread warily after the emotional afternoon she'd had. Shana had agreed to do more research into Chuck's aunt and uncle, but no one knew where they lived.

There were reasons people hid from their family. And usually those reasons were not good.

Brea grinned. "That RV of Chuck and Shana's was pretty impressive."

Just when he thought he understood her, she found new ways to intrigue him. "I'm surprised."

"By what?"

He reached out to tuck her silken hair behind her right ear. Savored the touch of skin. "That you like that sort of thing."

"It was bigger than most of the places in the community where I lived during my teenage years." Her face took on a faraway look for a moment. No doubt calling ghosts to mind.

The saxophone crooned, spinning Ward into the past. He pictured his father clutching a jazz cassette tape. Driving music, he'd always claimed.

The day hadn't been without memories for Ward either. "My parents had an RV, although it wasn't anything like the one we rode in today."

"What was your favorite trip with them?"

He turned thoughtful, swirling his drink as the bartender passed by with his hands full of limes and oranges.

Leaning closer, Ward reached for her palm and then traced the outline of her fingers. "I think it was when we drove to Denali National Park when I was twelve. We piled into the RV." Ward could picture the deep purple flowers and snow-crested mountaintops. "We didn't take trips where we couldn't camp. My parents wanted to keep vacations cheap and cheerful. Besides—" he took a sip of his beer "—if we hadn't traveled that way, I would never have experienced bears rummaging through our campsite."

"You didn't come from a wealthy background?"

"I did not," he said. "I come from down-to-earth, working-class folks."

People began to swarm the bar. He squeezed her hand, gesturing toward the plush white sofa in the far left of the jazz lounge. She smiled, nodding her agreement. He'd learned that about her. She liked the quiet corners.

He folded his fingers around hers as he picked their way past the tables, where couples spoke in hushed tones. Settling into the sofa, she stroked his hair. For a moment he leaned into her touch. Leaned into this moment with this sexy woman.

"They must be proud of your success."

His good mood faded. "My divorce was a disappointment to them."

"As I understand it, your ex-wife left you." She reached for his hand, linking fingers and squeezing. "Surely your parents realize that."

Taking a swig of beer, he looked down, feeling the storm grow in his chest. "Well, I'm damn sure not going to let down them or a child ever again."

She touched his arm lightly. "You had no control over what happened with Paisley."

"That doesn't make me feel any better." The words were gravel in his throat. "I just don't want her to think I abandoned her, that she can't trust people. I'm sorry you have to worry about who to trust."

She sketched along his jaw with a gentle hand, a determined fire in her eyes. "What's really unfair is that I've lost my mother. I lost the two people I thought had adopted me. And yes, it sucks that I don't know who's to blame for this chaos. But I also know I'm alive, I'm here and I'm determined to take charge of my future."

"God, you're incredible." He kissed her palm, lingering along the creamy-soft skin and taking pleasure in the pulse speeding in her wrist.

"I'm not." She blushed, but didn't pull her hand away. "Not really. I'm just a survivor."

"In my book, that makes you incredible."

"Let's stop with the depressing talk." Her pupils widened with desire. "I believe the room should be ready now."

He hoped his effort would pay off. He definitely needed to lose himself in the bliss of tangling in the sheets with Brea. To indulge a connection more intense than any he'd ever experienced.

Definitely, the last thing he wanted was to discuss darker subjects. He had his own painful past to contend with, and while he wasn't interested in the future, he refused to let that past steal from what he shared with Brea in the present.

Brea tapped the key card in her hand as she shifted in her heeled boots. Calf muscles tense as she scanned the key across the card reader. Green lights and a ding sounded, indicating the door was unlocked.

Normally, even high-end hotels had a sterile smell to her. But as she crossed the threshold, she felt like she had stepped into a spring meadow. Scents of flowers clung to the air, immediately upgrading her expectations for this swanky hotel. Had they burned candles to make it smell this great?

Turning the corner into the heart of the modern-looking suite, her pulse skipped a beat. Candles weren't the source of the meadow-like scent.

Instead multiple floral arrangements—tulips, roses, lilies—spiked from large vases on the end tables flanking a crisp beige couch with soft gold throw pillows.

On the coffee table, a huge sunflower arrangement waited in welcome. Her favorite flowers. Next to the clear glass vase sat a silver ice bucket with a bottle of champagne and two glasses. Chocolate-covered strawberries drizzled with what looked like caramel sauce were arranged in a heart shape on a silver platter. But the most surprising feature of all?

A gift wrapped in soft pink paper with an elaborate bow on top.

She was thoroughly stunned—and enchanted.

"Happy Valentine's Day," he said, helping her out of her coat.

"But it's not the fourteenth yet." She was touched by his thoughtfulness, at the way he listened to her passing mention of her favorite flower.

"It will be by midnight, and I wanted to make sure your celebration started spot-on the minute."

"I wouldn't have thought you were a romantic." She walked toward the rose arrangement, breathing deeply of the perfume.

"Well, it's not my forte," he admitted. "But I'm trying. We may not know what the future holds for us, but I'm sure as hell not ready for things to end."

She arched up to kiss him. "Thank you. It's all perfect."

He looped his arms around her waist, drawing her

closer. "When we get back to Alaska, what would be your dream date?"

She blinked fast, her shoulders rising. "Honestly, I'm not sure."

His hands rested just over her bottom, caressing lightly, anticipating more. Much more. "Then pick a type of memory you've been eager to replay since you got back but haven't wanted to visit alone—or with your family members."

"That's what you want to do with your romantic date?"

He kissed her neck, just below her ear, a spot where he'd learned a kiss could turn her knees week. But he still had his arms around her. He had no intention of letting go anytime soon.

"We'll be together and that'll help people believe we're really going out—in the interest of cementing my place at the company, of course. Trust me, since we don't want anyone to be suspicious that I'm not a real boyfriend."

"Well, we can't risk that." She laughed softly, the lilt caressing along his senses and stirring a flame deep in his gut. "What do you say we take some of these flowers and sprinkle petals all over the bed?"

His hands roved lower to cup the sweet curves of her bottom. "I think that is a great idea."

She appreciated that he didn't question her turnaround in wanting him back in her bed. Right now, she just wanted to lose herself in sensation. Kissing him. Savoring the hard, muscled wall of his chest against her while their mouths fused, tongues tangling on their way into the bedroom.

As they passed a vase of roses, he plucked out a couple of stems to carry with them, never breaking his connection to her. His hands roaming all over her body made her blood sizzle in her veins. His lips wandered down her neck and back up again, stirring desire to a fever pitch. Once in the bedroom, he tossed the roses onto the comforter. Longing made her impatient, eager. She peeled off her clothes, watching his every move as he did the same until they were standing—naked and wanting—in front of each other.

When he didn't close the distance between them right away, she retrieved one of the roses from the bed and trailed it over her face. Down her neck. Dipping it between her breasts in a seductive move that made his pupils widen with desire.

He picked up the other roses and began plucking the petals off, tossing them onto the comforter until nothing was left but the stems. He tossed them aside and strode toward her, his gaze intent. Heated. He wrapped his arms around her and lowered her to the bed. The scent of him mingled with the perfume of the crushed petals.

Her body was so in tune with his; no words were needed. They met in a blend of taste and touches that set her senses on fire. The crackle of the condom package registered dimly a moment before he nudged apart her thighs. She wrapped her legs around his waist and welcomed him into her body.

Their hips synched up, the rolling of hers in time with his powerful thrusts that sent shimmers of sensation tingling all over. The petals were satin against her back, and Ward's bristly chest a sweet abrasion against her breasts.

She knew from their other lovemaking that they

would take their time with the next coupling. For now, it was about a frenzied need charging through both of them.

All too soon her release crashed through her, without warning. There was no staving off the wave of bliss. It consumed her and she let it, wanting the all-encompassing sensation to drown out everything but this powerful connection. His thrusts quickened, and she could feel his muscles tighten in anticipation of his own orgasm as he joined her in completion.

His elbows gave way and he blanketed her body with his, her legs still locked around him. His face buried in her neck, his breath fanned over her shoulder. She held tightly to him, unwilling to let go of this moment.

Because as much as she'd worked to convince herself this was just a passing fling, that sex with Ward was a release for all the other emotional turmoil in her life, she couldn't ignore the deepening bond between them.

A fake relationship turning real.

Which might not be an issue if it hadn't been for his ties to her family. If she found the answers to her past that would allow her to fully reunite with the Steeles, she and Ward would be circulating in close proximity. When their relationship crashed, there would be no escaping the painful fallout of him staying in her life.

She would have found the truth, and her family, only to lose the man she was coming to care about.

Ward fluffed a plush pillow and set it behind Brea's still-damp hair. The scent of rose petals permeated the air. Scattered petals on the floor and on the bed. From the spa tub, where they'd made love later. Framing this moment in the kind of romantic hue he'd hoped to execute but wasn't sure someone like him could pull off.

He'd carried the small present into the bedroom with him earlier. Now he pulled it off the nightstand, knocking the glass of water ever so slightly. He sat across from her on the bed. They were at ease with each other in a way that tempted him all the more.

Placing the box into her hands, he smiled. She squinted at him, pulling the ribbon until the bow collapsed. Brea tossed the ribbon at him as she tore the pink wrapping paper. It drifted to the ground in her eagerness.

Her face lit with surprise as she touched the leather-bound journal and pens. "I'm not sure it's a romantic gift. Felicity mentioned you'd been journaling and I thought this would...well..."

She leaned forward to kiss him, briefly but so sweetly. "It's perfect. I'm touched that you went to so much trouble to find something personal." Her fingers skimmed along the gold embossing on the journal cover. "But I don't have anything for you."

"You're not supposed to. Valentine's Day is about the woman." Seeing her happy was gift enough for him.

"You are a charmer, aren't you?" She held the journal and custom-pen set to her chest.

"I wasn't sure you would accept jewelry." If she wanted jewels, he would gladly shower her with them. But something told him those years in the secluded community had given her grassroots kind of values. For that matter, Jack Steele was one of the most down-to-earth billionaires Ward had ever met. Maybe she'd had those kinds of values all her life.

"I may have started out my life in a wealthy family, but I spent my teenage years learning about frugality."

"Living off-the-grid."

"Yes, believe it or not, I can make my own soap," she said with an impish pride.

In his mind's eye, an image of a teenage Brea came to mind. Slaving away at creating lavender-infused soap with a rugged determination.

"I do believe it. You're a resourceful survivor."

She blushed, then looked away with embarrassment under the guise of thumbing through the journal. "What about your childhood?"

"I'm an only child. My parents owned a small business in Fairbanks. They ran a barber shop outside the base that catered to military personnel. They worked hard to put me through college." He stroked her thigh with a gentle touch.

"Are they still living there?"

He chuckled. "They retired to a condo on the beach in Florida."

Leaning over her, he grappled for his phone to show her photographs of his parents' newly renovated Venice Beach condo.

But as he swiped his phone to life, his heart hammered heavily.

A missed call.

From Paisley.

Brea set aside her journal. "Is something wrong? You look worried."

He was. Very.

He thumbed Redial while telling Brea, "It's my stepdaughter. She called—which her mother hasn't let her do before…"

The call went to voice mail. Two more tries later, the same. His worry amplified. The one time his child had reached out to him over this last year, and he'd missed the chance to be there for her.

Nine

The next evening, Brea went through the motions of enjoying Valentine's Day for everyone else's sake. Shana and Chuck had gone to so much effort to throw a dinner party for their visitors at their temporary home in the converted barn.

A long, rough-hewn farmer's table was set with heavy stoneware. Shana declared their meal to be completely composed of foods signature to North Dakota, from the creamy *knoephla* soup to the grilled walleye. They were just finishing the kuchen—rhubarb cake.

It should have been a lovely evening, but the strain of the renewed investigation into the Mikkelson relatives definitely circled around Brea's mind. And Ward's tension from yesterday's missed call from Paisley still hummed just below the surface, too.

Brea wished she could ease Ward's ache over the loss

of his stepdaughter. He'd finally reached his ex-wife, who'd informed him that she and her new husband had gone on a family vacation and Paisley had gotten homesick. Brea heard the woman insist again that she had nothing against Ward, but Paisley had a new "daddy" now. That it would be easier for all if Ward just faded away.

Those words still made Brea's chest go tight. She knew firsthand how much it hurt to have a father fade away inexplicably. But telling Ward as much would serve no purpose.

Luckily, the others at the table hadn't seemed to pick up on that tension during the day, when they'd toured the office buildings, or this evening, at dinner. Shana had proudly shared her husband's gift to her in honor of Valentine's Day—a donation to the foster-care system. In addition to buying her a "stakeout kit" of chocolates. Apparently the two of them sat on stakeouts together when Shana had to follow an investigative lead.

Royce had bought his wife a spa day and a pair of stunning diamond earrings. Naomi beamed as she touched them throughout the meal. This gesture elicited a matching, happy grin from the normally poker-faced Royce.

And as Brea sat listening to everyone, voices drifting up to the high barn ceiling, her mind was filled with a memory of her older brother being dared to hang from the rafters of the boathouse like a bat. She couldn't remember if she'd dared him or if Naomi had. In those days their actions were so tied to each other.

Ward repeated his line that Valentine's Day meant a day of pampering for the women. As such, the men cleared away the stoneware dishes and delicious food.

While they worked, Brea watched her twin pace in the living room of the converted barn. While Chuck and Shana's home was being built, they lived in the rustic beauty that had been reborn as a home. The exposed beams kept the smell of wood heavy in the air. She could hear Naomi coo into the phone, wishing her twins a good-night.

Shana moved down to take a seat next to Brea. She stacked a plate and handed it to Chuck, who'd come back in for the remaining dinner dishes. After sharing a sweet glance with her husband, Shana turned back to Brea. "Brea, you're quiet this evening. In fact, you've been quiet all day. Is something wrong?"

Brea nodded, looking at the remaining wine in her glass. As if all of the answers to her life could be read in the drip patterns. It worked for tea leaves, or so her adoptive parents said.

"I just have a lot to think about. But it's been a lovely working vacation. Thank you."

Shana nodded knowingly. "I'll keep you posted daily on what I learn about Jeannie's brother and sister. I've already got a line on the two of them, up near Fairbanks."

Brea shivered with anxiety. "That's a little too close to home for my peace of mind."

"Stick close to the family." Shana squeezed her hand, but her eyes were also dead serious. Clearly she wasn't taking this lightly, and that meant the world to Brea after feeling so alone. "You'll be well protected."

"Thank you. I'll let you know what I discover, as well." At least Brea hoped she could find the trust to make that leap. She'd been keeping things to herself for so long. "I have to confess, I'm worried about what will

happen to the family if it turns out Jeannie knew something about that plane crash all those year ago."

"Would it help if I'm sure she didn't?"

Again, Brea's jaw tightened. Certainty of that kind
seemed impossible.

"I wish it could." Brea had no reason to suspect
Jeannie. Certainly nothing had turned up on that useless flash drive. Something she still hadn't confessed
to Ward. "I've imposed on your Valentine's Day long
enough. We should go. Marshall's flying us back tonight,
since Naomi and Royce are missing the twins more than
they expected."

"That's sweet. They're wonderful parents." Shana's
face carried a longing that was impossible to miss. She
blinked fast and plastered a smile on her face. "Luckily
Marshall has slept the day through, so he's rested and
cleared to fly you back tonight. There's a bed on the
plane if you want to sleep."

"That's wonderful that he can be so flexible," Brea
said. "I just realized we've kept Marshall from Tally on
their first Valentine's Day."

Marshall hadn't joined them for any of the events,
which was no surprise. He wasn't particularly interested
in the family business, and his significant other was
back in Alaska. He spent most of his time on the family ranch, in the original Steele homestead.

Shana said, "Marshall told me that Tally had a study
session to attend for college. She's begun pursuing a degree in social work. He assured me that they have a day
picked out to celebrate and he has an incredible gift for
her. But yes, I see your point."

"She seems to understand he isn't the most romantic man on the planet. But he's a man of character, of strength. Like our dad."

Ward's familiar boot-falls called Brea's attention, and she couldn't help but think of how he too was a man of character and strength. Her breath hitched at the thought, bringing to mind the possibility that this was the kind of man a woman could fall for. Ending their affair was going to be more difficult than she'd imagined.

He moved back into the dining, and she was hit at once by his magnetism. Ward was a towering, charismatic man who drew her attention by the sheer force of his eyes.

She could see the strain still lingering on his face from worry about Paisley. She could only hope she was able to offer him some of the comfort he'd given her the night before. Except she knew it would be more than physical comfort. Every time they were together, every revelation they shared, chipped away at the protective walls she'd built around her heart.

For a woman well versed in hiding, she was finding it impossible to dodge the fact that he was an impossible man to resist on so many levels.

The flight home had been uneventful. Ward was relieved to see Brea gaining confidence with air travel. There were so many places he would like to go with her. His job took him around the world, and having her at his side would be incredible. Images filled his mind of making love to her in Paris, in a room with a view of the Eiffel tower, and in Australia, on an outback excursion.

The possibilities were endless.

For now though, even thinking of being with her in his penthouse apartment stirred him to a near-painful need. Luckily, once the plane landed, she didn't even question him driving them both to his place. Her overnight bag was already packed from their trip, so she had everything she needed.

The private elevator rose with them inside. He'd been given use of the penthouse apartment in the Alaska Oil Barons, Inc., building while he house hunted. The penthouse had previously been inhabited by the Steeles and Mikkelsons, if someone had to work late or weather was particularly treacherous.

The space offered a beautiful view of the mountains. He liked to start his day at the wooden kitchen table with a cup of coffee in a stoneware mug, just looking at the view. But coffee and mountain views were pretty far from his thoughts as the elevator door opened, revealing the space that was more than generous.

Exposed beams made the penthouse feel a bit like a country cottage. Elegant lantern light fixtures hung suspended from the ceiling. Their reflected glow gleamed on the polished wood floors and dark leather furniture. A good place to be. But certainly not a forever home.

Ward had been delaying his own home search, perhaps out of some foolish hope that he'd figure out a way for his stepdaughter to spend time with him. If that happened, he would need to pick a place to accommodate her. If she didn't come? He would just buy a condo much like this. That turmoil over Paisley reminded him all the more of the risk of an emotional connection with Brea, a connection that was growing in spite of his intentions otherwise.

He shoved the painful, futile thought aside and focused on the gorgeous woman beside him. He was in this for sex and yes, to comfort her through this transition back into the family.

But no more than that.

Still, he couldn't take his eyes off her. No one would have guessed she'd spent the night sleeping on an airplane. Her cable-knit sweater hugged her curves, and something told him the sweater had been hand knitted. Perhaps from her days in the small community? Her sleek black hair was swept back in a high ponytail.

Already his fingers itched to pull her hair free and run his fingers through the silken length.

"Brea…" His voice was hoarse with longing.

She flew into his arms, their kiss one of deep longing, the mating of tongues and need. Was she just seeking comfort?

"Brea," he said again. "Are you sure?"

"There are a million reasons why we shouldn't do this, but all I can think of is the reason we should. I want this, want you, so very much."

He agreed, the same need burning inside him. The feel of her body against his had him throbbing, aching to be inside her. And to hear she wanted him too stoked the fire hotter.

All day, every day, she filled his thoughts. He couldn't get her out of his mind. She was damn near driving him wild. He found himself imagining her naked when he should be focused on work.

He halted the thought because work was the last thing he wanted to think about right now.

Their legs tangled as they walked deeper into the penthouse. He yanked off his coat. Her coat followed, slipping off the sofa to the floor. His hands eagerly touched her side. Helped her out of her sweater. As they passed the control panel on the wall, he flicked the switch to start a blaze in the fireplace, the flames casting golden light.

Three steps later, they were naked and kneeling on a bear rug in front of the hearth. The crackle echoed the need inside of him. He started to angle her down and she stopped him with both hands pressed to his chest. With a siren's smile, she gently pushed him onto his back, the bear rug silky soft underneath him.

And he was more than happy to oblige.

Brea straddled his hips, over him in a beautiful display of creamy flesh. He cradled her breasts in his hands while she released her ponytail, her hair gliding free over the shoulders, along his hands. Raw need pumped through him.

Thankfully he'd snagged a condom from his wallet and had it ready to use. She plucked the packet from his hand and sheathed him with slow…oh so slow…precision. He bit his bottom lip in restraint.

Her hair swinging forward, she eased herself over him, taking him inside her. The sweet clamp of her warmth had him gripping her hips, slowing her to make this last for them.

He wanted to lose himself in her, in the mind-numbing bliss he experienced when she was in his arms. The soft curves of her body filled his every thought, shutting out the rest of the world.

Exactly what he wanted, what he needed—her.

She rolled her hips, meeting his thrusts, her hands flat on his chest, caressing. His fingers glided down from her shoulders. The sweet curves of her breasts filled his hands. He relished the way her nipples pebbled at his touch. Giving her pleasure pleasured him. He wanted to taste every inch of her.

One night, one week or even four wasn't enough to be with her.

The thought blindsided him, stealing his breath. She shouldn't be this important to him this fast.

"Tell me what you want," he whispered in her ear.

"You," she whispered, her voice husky, "I just want you."

The raw need in her tone sent a rush of pleasure through him. He reached between her legs to touch and tease the sweet bundle of nerves.

Kittenish moans rolled up her throat and became cries of release that sent him over the edge with her. Wave after wave of ecstasy washed over him. Brea bowed forward, her chest flush against his. His heart hammered in the aftermath, their sweat-slicked bodies sated.

He lost track of how long they had lain together, the heat of the fireplace keeping them warm as their perspiration cooled. Soon he realized she'd drifted off to sleep. Smiling, he stroked her hair gently. Then he eased her from him and onto the rug. She gave a sleepy sigh of protest.

Quietly, he pulled a throw pillow from the sofa, along with a cashmere blanket to spread over them. He pulled her closer to his side and she rested her head on his chest.

He couldn't deny the truth.

She was becoming important to him emotionally, in a way that surpassed even attraction and that was dangerous for him in ways that had nothing to do with the company. He needed to keep this simple, about the attraction. It couldn't be more. Although he couldn't deny that he wanted them to keep exploring the chemistry.

If he could just figure out how to do that without risking his already battered heart.

* * *

Morning sun gleamed through the windows as Brea stretched in bed. But not her bed. She'd slept over at Ward's, sleeping in because they'd arrived home so late and then made love. She reached to find the space beside her empty and cool. The indentation on his pillow tugged at her heart. She leaned forward to breathe in the scent of him.

It was becoming easy to fall into a routine with him, and she didn't want to think about what that meant for when the time came for them to end their relationship.

A shirtless, muscular Ward entered the room with a breakfast tray with two plates of breakfast burritos—made with corn tortillas, fried eggs with avocado slices, cheese and cilantro. Her mouth watered. He'd also brought coffee and juice.

"Ward, you're going to spoil me." The words escaped in a sigh.

He set the tray on the bed and slid in beside her. "I'm making up for all the travel we had to do on Valentine's Day. I know we're not a real couple, but I feel I owe you more." She felt her smile turn cold at the reality of his words. He seemed to notice the waver of expression, adding, "Damn, and I'm not even sure if that came out right."

"You only spoke the truth. We're not a real couple."

Although it certainly felt real enough to Brea right now as they sat together, naked on the bed, enjoying breakfast.

"We're sleeping together, and I want us to keep on sleeping together." His now-familiar gravelly tone ceased to reassure her.

Brea avoided meeting his eyes by reaching for coffee. "We have a couple of weeks before the board meeting and the vote."

"You could really just hit our deadline and then walk away even after we've shared a bed, calling it over, cold turkey?"

Was that a request for more? And if so, was she even ready for that?

Neither option felt viable. Or made sense. All the same, his request hit her hard. She still didn't know who she was—whether she belonged with the Steeles or if her adoptive family had been right. Whatever that truth was, could she reconcile with her blood relatives?

She wasn't sure what to do.

"That's what we agreed to," she said, sipping her coffee, not in the mood to savor anything delicious while talking of their uncertain future. She could barely deal with the present.

"And if we decide to change the rules and take things one day at a time?" He looked so hot with the blanket draped over his waist, his broad chest on display.

"Like a real relationship?" Her chest went tight with anxiety as she thought of how their "dating" had started and what she'd done in his office. "You don't even know me, not the real me. I'm the person who's hidden from her family because I was too scared to risk their rejection. I'm not honest—"

"Brea, you went through—"

"Stop. Let me finish." She needed to tell him the truth, because even if she dared to think about something more with him, that couldn't happen without honesty. Even if that revelation cost her any chance at even two more weeks. This was a big chance she was taking, but she didn't have any other option. If people had been honest with her, her life wouldn't be so complicated now. She'd come in search of truth.

Which meant she needed to start dealing in truth, too. She had to hold herself to the same standards she was holding for others. Whatever the cost. "I'm an adult and I know right from wrong. The day you found me in your office, I was stealing files from your computer."

Breath catching in her throat, she waited for his response.

"I already know." His voice dropped an octave.

Shock slashed through her. "You already know? For how long?"

"I suspected when I found you," he explained without even a hint of anger in his voice. "I had my IT guy run a test to check which files you accessed. They're fairly benign. I'm not happy you did it, but it's a nonissue, security wise."

Nothing significant. That lined up with her estimation of the files. She exhaled a hard sigh of relief. Then she realized what his words meant. "Yet you never said anything to me."

"Since there was nothing in that batch of data that could be harmful to the business by betraying trade secrets, I didn't see the need to make an issue of it."

She'd pushed the envelope of honorability too far when she'd pretended to be another person to get a sense of the Steeles without the pressure of a reunion. She deserved for them to be angry with her, and yet they weren't.

She'd pushed the boundaries again by stealing files from Ward. Again she deserved anger, and again that wasn't the reaction she received. Her eyes burned, and she blinked back tears. "But I'm a liar."

He bit into a piece of toast. "And I'm a CEO. We all have our flaws."

"You're letting me off the hook too easily." Guilt piled up inside her. She didn't deserve to be let off the hook.

"Maybe that's because I feel like I know you better now and I'm starting to care for you."

His words hung in the air between, drawing the oxygen from her lungs. She wasn't ready for this kind of talk. Theirs was a fake relationship, a fling. If he pushed the point, what would happen?

Was she scared? Hell, yes. An affair had been risky enough to her heart. But this? And what if he pushed the point? When she'd thought about the cost, she hadn't really considered this could be an all-or-nothing moment.

She stirred a spoon through her coffee to avoid looking into his eyes—or letting him see hers. "Are you sure you're in the right frame of mind to be having this discussion now, given how upset you are about Paisley? Can't we just...be in the moment? Or if you want to be upset, because you have every right to be, then let me comfort you. That's what I would do if something more was really happening between us."

Giving felt more comfortable than taking.

Looking up through her lashes, she blew on her coffee, half hoping he would run if pushed, because considering anything more scared her to her toes.

"There's nothing you can do to help with this," he said tightly, a hint of anger lacing his words.

"Why do you want to continue this relationship, even one day at a time, if we can't discuss the things that are important in our lives?" She held up a hand. "Or rather,

you want me to talk and share, but you're not willing
to do the same."

Anger bubbled in his bright blue eyes. They narrowed, and she felt a bitter victory in knowing she was
pushing him away and he was taking the bait.

Then his eyes narrowed even further. "Nuh-uh.
What's really going on here?"

Panic welled inside her.

"Ward, this is getting too real, too big for me to handle when there's so much unsettled in my life. I can
barely remember my own past clearly without people
helping me." And she'd been abandoned more times than
any one woman should ever have to be... She couldn't
take the risk that he seemed to want her to take.

But telling him that part was more vulnerability than
she wanted to show. He was already pushing so much
faster than she was ready to go.

If only she didn't have to look at the hurt in his eyes.
"Brea, we're already in a relationship. Why are we argu-
ing about the label? Call it fake if you want, but I think
we both know the feelings are getting pretty damned
real." He touched her knee, and heat spiked inside. "The
attraction we feel is pretty damned real."

Her shoulders tensed. He was asking for too much.
She wasn't ready. "Are you sure it's me you want and not
just a replacement family for the one you lost?"

His hand jerked away and his head snapped back as
if he'd been slapped. "That's a low blow."

"Not if it's the truth." She wanted him to deny it.

"Sure we started things with some calculated agendas. Have you considered I wasn't just a buffer? That
you only want me as an excuse to stay close to your
family without actually committing to facing your past?"

Speaking of low blows. His words knocked around inside of her, painful, and maybe even partially true. And if it was even the least bit valid, she'd been horribly unfair to him.

She needed to run, fast. She needed her own space, the quiet of her apartment; she couldn't handle his expectations. Her eyes stung. She was dangerously close to bursting into tears over losing what they'd shared. But she couldn't give him what he wanted, and she did care too much to hurt him, especially after all he'd been through.

Determined to save her pride, if not her heart, she wrapped herself in the blanket to shield herself for a bolt to the bathroom, where she could get dressed.

And hide her tears.

She looked up at him and whispered, "Gargoyle..."

Then she walked out.

Because there was no safe word for the kind of situation she was in now.

Ten

Ward had thought his world had exploded when he'd divorced. He'd also thought he would be insulated from that kind of pain again.

But losing Brea had opened up that old wound all over again.

Ward couldn't deny the truth. He missed Brea, wanted her in his life, but seeing those tears in her eyes made him realize just how high the stakes were. She'd already been hurt too much by people claiming to care for her. Even though he was in this emotionally, he wasn't sure he could manage a forever commitment. He refused to let her be hurt again. So he had to let her go.

Every accidental meeting at the office over the past two weeks was like alcohol poured on the pain, and he didn't have any idea how to keep from making the same mistakes. He didn't have a clue who to turn to for advice, which told him all the more how badly he'd screwed up his life.

Isolated. Again.

Right in the moment when he'd realized he had started building something with her. Offering her a relationship had been a big move for him.

And now she really wouldn't need him anymore.

He looked down at his notes on his desk. Shana had called, giving reports on the missing aunt and uncle. Police were expecting to pick them up within the week for questioning. They were already wanted in Canada for running a scam on tourists by selling bogus travel packages to tour the North Pole. Now there was a trail connecting them to the plane crash. Crime seemed to cling to their footprints, infiltrating every action.

But as far as Shana could determine, the criminal activity seemed to pertain only to the pair. Bottom line, it didn't appear that Jeannie had anything to do with what her brother and sister had done.

Brea would have a clean slate to reintegrate with her family.

His heart swelled. He was happy for her. Of course. He cared about her a helluva lot. If only there was a way to be sure he wouldn't eventually hurt her if they resumed their affair. If only he wasn't smack-dab in the middle of her family's business. There was no way to avoid seeing each other if the relationship ended.

Could he handle that? Was he willing to leave the business for her sake?

A knock on his office door drew his attention away from his computer. "Yes?"

The door opened to reveal Felicity Steele, the social

worker married to Jack Steele's brother, Conrad. "I'm just dropping off the reports from the meeting."

"The meeting?" His mind reeled as he went through his mental schedule. Realization dawned on him. "Oh, hell, the meeting."

He hit himself on the forehead. How could he have forgotten he was supposed to have met with the Alaska Oil Barons, Inc.'s, charity foundation for the revealing of the new therapy-dog program?

"Please accept my apologies. I have no good excuse for not being there, other than I lost track of time. Name the penance and I'll do it." He pulled out his checkbook.

Felicity stepped inside, a folder tucked under her arm. "While we wouldn't turn down money, we can always use extra volunteers for story hour."

His heart ached at the thoughts of all the stories he'd read to Paisley. All the stories he hadn't been able to read after the divorce. And then something shifted inside of him.

He might not be able to show his stepdaughter how much he loved her, but he could channel that and share it with others. "Send me a calendar of available slots, and I'll be there. No forgetting this time."

"Thank you. The kids will love you." She set the file on his desk. "We also still need someone to dress up as the Easter Bunny for the spring party."

Ward laughed, the sound raspy along his raw throat, and even more raw emotions. "Not a chance." Then he tapped the folder. "What's in here?"

"Handouts from the meeting, photos of the dogs and their handlers."

"You could have emailed those to me." He searched her face for her real agenda.

"I could have. But since I was already so close, I decided to pop by." The look in her brown eyes intensified as she touched the manila folder again. "And quite frankly, I'm worried about Brea."

He sat up straight, concern burning his gut. "Is something wrong with her? Is she hurt?"

Horrible scenarios pumped through his mind. Each one put her in a hospital room. Had she leveraged the information Shana had collected and decided to confront the people responsible for the tragic accident that had ripped her family apart? Sure, she'd been impulsive in the past. But something like that...

Felicity shook her head gently, her counselor training apparent. "Not in the way you mean. She's quiet and in retreat, just like you are."

His heartbeat calmed down, but his mouth grew taut over the intrusiveness of her statement.

"Obviously we broke up." Not that it was anyone's business. And yes, he was in one helluva bad mood.

"Must have been over something horrible."

"What do you mean?" He adjusted his tie. Attempted to put himself together. To gain control of the situation. Of everything.

Including his emotions.

"You've both been through so much in the past and yet you're still standing. So to send you both into such a sad state, I can only surmise something bad happened."

He searched for the right words to explain what had wreaked such devastation in his life.

"We had a fight." It sounded lame, even to his own ears as he vocalized it.

"Hmm..." Felicity mulled silently.

Maybe this wasn't intrusiveness on her part, but caring about Brea. And if so, that meant a lot. Ward wondered if he'd found the person to turn to for help after all. "I know you're not my counselor, and I wouldn't want to take professional advantage…"

She sat down in the leather seat across from him. Smoothing her simple purple dress, she gave him a reassuring, genuine smile. "You would like some advice."

"Yes. Brea thinks I only want her in order to replace the family I lost with her family. I accused her of using me to stay close to her family without facing her past." Words came out of his mouth with the intensity of a waterfall crashing down. "Truth is, I think maybe she was right about me. Divorce was hell for me. Losing my wife…but also losing my stepdaughter."

"Divorce is never easy," she said wisely, "and it's even tougher when children are involved."

He nodded, his throat too tight to speak.

"Sounds as if you and Brea had quite an argument." She steepled her hands. Raising a knowing brow, she added in a gentler tone, "It also sounds like when you're finding a person to love, things like common wants and families are important."

Ward's brows knitted together. He stayed silent for a moment longer. Processing. "So, you're saying it's okay if we were right in what we accused each other of?"

"If you love each other, then yes." She held up a hand. "But I don't need the answer. It's something only you need to know for yourself." She stood and backed away from his desk. "And I'll leave you with that since I need to get back to the hospital. Please feel free to reach out if you need someone to talk to."

Her generous offer hung in the air after she left. He

sifted through what she'd said and stumbled on a part he'd missed at first.

She'd said something about loving each other.

Love.

He hadn't even given a thought to that. He'd closed off his mind to letting that emotion back into his life. That was the one thing he hadn't offered when he'd asked Brea to keep their relationship going day by day. She deserved so much better. And he found that he wanted to give her that. He was determined to do so. He'd learned from the past and wanted to commit fully, no holds barred, to a future. With Brea.

He was beginning to realize it wasn't a matter of "allowing" the feeling. Love climbed walls, breached defenses.

Love had claimed him again.

He'd fallen for Brea, and there was no turning back.

Brea had spent two weeks in a daze, most of which she'd spent in her apartment, with ice cream, trying to figure out what to do with her life now that she had a clear path to reuniting with her family.

Now that she'd alienated a man who would be tied to that family far into the foreseeable future.

Sitting cross-legged on the sofa, she spooned up another taste of Moose Tracks ice cream. The television droned on with another romantic film that just made her feel worse about her life. But she couldn't seem to stop.

Family had called to check up on her and she'd made a slew of excuses as to why she was too busy to take them up on their invitations. Every excuse except the real one. She'd cried herself into dehydration. She'd hit the wall.

This was one blow too many.

The only thing that had stirred any interest in her was Shana's call about finding proof of a phone call between Lyle's cell and the airplane mechanic. Shana had turned it over to the cops.

Finally Brea might have the answers she sought.

A knock on the door pulled her from her self-pity. She placed her ice cream down, muted the television and padded to the door. She peered through the peephole and found the last person she expected…

Her father.

Jack Steele stood on her doorstop with a crockery pot in his hands. And a part of her that remembered her father from long ago realized he had his quietly determined look on his face. He wasn't going anywhere.

She opened the door, leaning against the frame. "Hello, Dad. What brings you here?"

He extended his hands. "Caribou stew. It's been cooking all day and I thought you would like some. We've all been worried you've caught a flu bug."

Her eyes burned with tears and she fought hard to blink them back. "Thank you. That's very thoughtful. Come in."

She waved him through and gestured for him to follow her into the kitchen.

His heavy footfalls thudded along her hall rug. "I'm glad to hear you're all right. No offense but you look like you may have a sinus infection."

She wasn't surprised. Her red eyes and nose probably gave that impression. She'd certainly rather everyone believe that than the truth that she'd hurt one of the most honorable men she'd ever met.

She didn't feel up to admitting she'd been crying nonstop.

"I've just been hibernating for a while, thinking things over." Aspects of the truth were slipping out involuntarily. She blew her nose into a tissue, attempting to recover. "How are you doing with everything?"

"What do you mean?" he asked, setting the red crockery container on the counter.

She dropped down onto one of the barstools. "I heard there's a warrant out for Jeannie's brother and sister's arrest. I know that must be hard for Jeannie."

Shana hadn't seen any signs of involvement from Jeannie, and nothing Brea had found indicated otherwise.

"My heart hurts like hell for Jeannie. Lyle's been picked up. We just heard from the police a little while ago. Her sister hasn't been located yet." He lifted the lid off the pot, stirring. "Her family's brought enough grief to her with the way her sister abandoned Trystan. But Jeannie just says Trystan's better off and that he's her son. That she has what matters...her kids...our marriage."

The scent of the stew wafted in the air, stirring childhood memories. This was a family staple, a recipe handed down from her grandmother to her mom.

Jack stirred slowly. "I never have been able to make this as well as your grandma. Naomi seems to have the knack, but she isn't sharing the secret ingredient with me. But it's not bad. I like to cook it. Makes me remember..."

Jack stirred the stew, overwhelmed at having all the kids to himself while Mary slept. Of course, the fact that he'd been up half the night with a colicky Aiden could have something to do with that.

He had the kids helping him cook, and mostly their feedback had been, "But that's not how Mom does it."

Broderick was chopping the tomatoes, while Naomi and Brea were cutting bunches of thyme into smaller pieces, carefully. Delaney was reading the directions from the recipe card while Marshall made trips back and forth to the pantry.

They had this locked and loaded. He hoped.

"Why can't Mom just make this?" Broderick sighed, huffing in exasperation.

Naomi rolled her eyes at her teenage brother and mimicked him. "Broderick needs his mommy to cook for him."

"Your mother has been taking care of baby Aiden. She needs a break," Jack said with a patience he was far from feeling. He wanted a nap. Some said he should have hired a sitter, and they did have one on hand, in addition to his wife's mom for emergencies. But he also wanted time with his kids, and he knew they needed him right now, with a new brother in the house. His mother-in-law was with Mary and the baby. They were a family.

Him, his wife and their six beautiful children.

"I don't see why that means she can't make the stew. Hers is the best," Brea said, smelling the thyme.

Jack smiled. "It is. But I think we all make a good team. And you know how your mother is always surprising you with things?"

Brea and Naomi exchanged grins, thinking back to their mother's most recent surprise: a playroom she had painted to mimic the Alaskan wilderness when it was too cold to go outside.

"Mmm-hmm." Broderick nodded.

"Well, it would be cool to give your mother a surprise, too."

He loved his wife and kids more than air. He would do anything for them...

The memory curled through Brea as surely as the aroma from the stew. Except this was steaming through from her brain to her heart.

Her father was Jack Steele. And she wanted her family back.

"It was hell for me when I realized you'd been home as Milla Jones and didn't trust us enough to let us know you were alive. I thought I'd lost you all over again. That you didn't care about me."

His words brought those painful months back in startling clarity.

Pain swelled in her chest. A tightness needing release, needing air and light instead of isolated darkness.

"I want you to know, Dad, I was sick for a long time after the crash—very sick. It wasn't like I climbed on that plane one morning and the next morning just decided my family didn't want me." Her inward gaze sorted through those initial months. The bevy of tears that would not stop. "The confusion was more of a gradual thing. I was grieving and alone, and very weak."

He listened with somber eyes. "I'm glad the Joneses kept you safe."

"How can you feel that way about them after they took me from you? Surely they had to know who I was..." A memory filled her head, of those early days after she recovered, of her sitting crumpled on the couch. Clutching her knees to her chest, her voice hoarse from crying and declaring her identity to her adoptive parents. "I told them who I was."

Jack looked down into the soup for a long moment, and she thought she saw his jaw flex for a moment before he looked at her again, with his face returned to calm. "The officer who called us about Lyle... He said the man apparently confessed to a couple of things... He was there at the crash site. He's the one who found you alive. Apparently he wasn't as adept at killing face-to-face as he was at making it happen by proxy. He knew the Jones couple and paid them to keep you until he could figure out what to do. I think they must have decided to protect you from our family because they perceived us as a threat to you."

Her lips trembled. Emotions rolled through her in a chain reaction—relief, grief, rage, all tangling together and making it tough to draw in air.

She gripped the counter for a moment, biting her lip to hold back a cry that would only upset her father when he'd been through enough. Finally she was able to draw a steady breath. "That's bighearted of you."

"Did they love you?" Jack Steele looked up from the stew again. His steady gaze resting on her.

At first Brea ground down her teeth. Thought back to her life with her adoptive parents. The way her adoptive mother would put a cool cloth on her head when she was sick, or would read the same books she did so they could discuss them. The way her adoptive father would take her with him to work on wiring projects to provide electricity to their small community. "They treated me as if they did."

Jack nodded. "Then I think we have to let it rest with

the courts alone if we want a clean slate to reunite as a family."

She knew that couldn't have been easy for her father to say. Because he had just as much—if not more—cause than her to be furious over what had happened, to want vengeance.

She reached out to hug him. "Daddy…"

He hauled her in for a bear hug that was so familiar, she couldn't imagine how she'd ever forgotten it.

"Brea, do you want to tell me what's really been wrong these past two weeks? Because I'm a father of daughters. I recognize the red-eyes-and-ice-cream combo."

He tilted his head toward the open Moose Tracks container on the coffee table in her living room.

With a watery sniffle, she angled back, swiping at her eyes. "I've made a mess of things with Ward."

The past two weeks had been so lonely without him. She'd missed the scent of him, the way he started the day off with a smile, by having a simple breakfast together, how he discussed business with her and genuinely valued her opinion. And right now she wished she could share this news with him.

"You and he are really a couple?" her father asked in undisguised shock. "I thought you two were working some mutually beneficial deal."

"You knew?" she gasped.

He winked. "I'm a damn good businessman."

"Well, it started out as something, um, logical, then became more. And now I've pushed him away."

"Then go get him," her father said simply. "Understand, I love Jeannie every bit as much as I loved your mom. But while your mother was alive, nothing would have kept me from her if I thought there was a chance to reconcile."

And hearing the determination in his voice, she realized, fully, that he really had thought she was dead, along with her mother.

She hadn't been abandoned, or merely forgotten after a short search.

She was loved.

She was a Steele.

And as long as there was hope, a Steele didn't give up.

Ward cracked his knuckles. A habit he'd picked up when he'd been a teenager. For the most part, he'd been able to kick it. But in moments of stress—before a big meeting or closing a deal—the habit resurfaced.

Of all the times he cracked his knuckles as an adult, none seemed as intense as this time.

He had a lot to lose.

Everything to lose, in fact.

But the lights were on him and he had to tamp down the habit. Play the part of CEO. And if he was lucky, a more important victory awaited him.

As he continued his speech, his mind was hoping he could pull off the win of a lifetime with Brea. No company stockholders' meeting could ever be as important as winning Brea back. He was nearing the end of his speech, which would close out the meeting, and he was coming to the most important part of his presentation.

The general Board of Directors meeting was going as well as he had anticipated. As well as he had hoped for, really. Pleased stockholders in expensive business suits nodded along at Ward's figures and charts.

The meeting was being held on the top floor of the

Steele building. It was set up as a dinner gathering, and the clink of silverware on plates around the boardroom table was subtle as he moved through his presentation. He shifted his weight from foot to foot, restless. A trickle of sweat gathered at the nape of his neck. Luckily his collar and suit jacket hid his unease.

Looking out on the audience around the fully set dinner table, his gaze landed on Brea. Ward's gaze took in every alluring detail of her, down to the way her silky black dress and cashmere sweater-jacket accented her curves in simple elegance. Even in the dimmed lighting of the boardroom, he couldn't help but notice her beauty.

But his feelings for her were about so much more than that. The depth of emotion, of love, he felt for her floored him.

She caught him staring as she chewed her steak delicately. The Alaska Oil Barons, Inc., held the philosophy that business was made sweeter by food. A philosophy he agreed with. Breaking bread together had a way of putting people at ease. He quickly searched her face, trying to determine if the food had indeed eased something in Brea.

He didn't want to, but he tore his gaze from hers to look at the stockholders as he finished his speech. The meeting would be over, and his time to win Brea would begin.

He clicked through the slides to a blank screen. "That concludes the business part of my presentation. I want to share some words that are more personal. I feel that's important since we'll all be working together for a long time to come." He grinned. "At least I hope we will."

His remark brought the expected chuckle that helped him transition to the more personal note. "I have had the honor of spending time with Breanna Steele. Some of you may have heard we've been seeing each other. As I've come to know her these past weeks, I've discovered she's an incredible woman of strength and brilliance. Like all the Steeles—and Mikkelsons. I have big shoes to fill around this place, and I look forward to the challenge.

"Should you trust me?" he continued. "I've learned that trust is a cagey thing. It comes with time." He held Brea's gaze. She didn't look away. Instead that electricity danced between them. For a moment he could pretend they were the only people in the room. "And I'm willing to put in the time, the hours, weeks—years, if need be—to make sure I'm your top choice, worthy of the faith you've put in me."

He took a breath before continuing, "Luckily I've got some top-notch role models around here in Jack and Jeannie." He grinned. "And I'm not just saying that to suck up. They're an admirable couple who've welcomed me into the Alaska Oil Barons, Inc., family."

With luck, he prayed they would welcome him into their real family, as well.

He smiled as he stepped off the podium. Board members and shareholders alike clapped. Some clapped him on his back as he walked by. Others shook his hand, offering praise. With the confident gait he was known for, he strode right toward Brea.

He leaned in and whispered into her ear, "Gargoyle."

She looked at him with wide eyes, before smiling. "You want to leave? Now? This is your party. Your welcome to the company. This is your everything."

She looked around the table at the chatter. Toward her father, who raised a glass of whiskey in their direction.

"*You* are my everything," he said. "Now let's find somewhere private to talk."

She nodded, discarding her cloth napkin onto her chair. She took his hand, squeezing lightly, her eyes shiny with emotion and even a hint of tears. Her hand shook in his but she didn't let go. A good sign as he led her toward the elevator to his penthouse apartment.

The ride up was silent but filled with fire and magic. Just as it had been the first day they'd met. He led her across the wood floors to the bearskin rug by the already crackling fire.

He planned to pull out all the stops for this, needing every ounce of charm to prove to her he was ready to risk his heart again, ready to be a part of a family again, not as a replacement, but as what came next, as where he belonged.

He loved Brea. Truly. Deeply.

They knelt together by the fire. Brea's knee-length black dress showing her shapely calves. After a moment she tilted her head, curls framing her beautiful face. "Was it my imagination or were you sending me some incredible messages through your speech, in your eyes?"

Clasping her hands, he rubbed his thumbs along the insides of her wrists. "These past two weeks thinking I'd lost you have been hell."

She bit her lip. Swallowing. He saw the pain reflect in her eyes. "For me, too."

"You've worked your way into my heart."

She stared at him, speechless.

"Why are you so surprised? I can't imagine I've hidden how much you mean to me."

"I know we have chemistry…"

He shook his head. Held her hands tighter, inching

closer to her. "It's much more than that for me. Brea, I'm in love with you."

Her mouth opened in an O-shape of surprise. Then her eyes welled with tears. "I'm so very glad to hear that. You mesmerized me the first time I saw you, and truly every time after that, with your brains as much as your body. Ward, I'm head over heels in love with you, too."

He spiked his fingers through her hair and guided her head closer for a kiss, one that sealed this moment, this first time they expressed their love for each other.

"I'm so glad you broke into my office."

She laughed lightly before her face turned serious again. She clasped both of his hands, squeezing. "I shouldn't have said those hurtful things to you. I understand how painful it was for you to lose your daughter. It was wrong of me to use that against you in an argument."

Ward swallowed. Needing to make sure Brea knew it was her that he wanted. Not her family. Not anyone else.

She, by herself, was valuable to him. He'd been hurt before, but she was worth taking the risk again.

"Do you really believe I'm using you and your family as a substitute for what I've lost with my stepdaughter?"

She shook her head. The tears still welling in her eyes. "I see now that you're drawn to me—and to them—because this is the kind of family life you want. And that's not a bad thing. I also understand it must be scary for you to risk being a part of that again."

"It's tough…very tough." His chest tightened. But looking into Brea's eyes, he knew this was right.

"It's not easy for men to admit to being afraid."

"True enough." He gave her a wry smile and then stroked her face gently. "I'm sorry for what I said about you using me. There's no way I—or anyone—can fathom all that you've been through."

"I do want my family back. But I also want you. Those two 'wants' are not tied to each other."

"I'm glad to hear it." So damn glad to have this second chance with her, he kissed her deeply, their breath mingling, their tongues mating.

Brea whispered against his mouth. "I've been thinking about my future."

"Oh, really. I'd like to hear." He kissed her neck softly, launching tingles throughout her.

She ran her hands through his hair. "Royce and I talked in North Dakota about his research and my experiences living off-the-grid. We would like to explore ways we can make resources more accessible to those in far-flung regions."

"That sounds like a great idea, professionally and personally." Ward rested his forehead against hers, breathing in the floral scent of her shampoo. Looking forward to being a part of her life for the rest of their days.

"We have forever together," she said, as if reading his thoughts. "I don't want to keep you from your board meeting."

"I've met my obligations to them. Your family—"

"Our family," she corrected him.

"You truly are an amazing woman. I hope you know that."

"You can feel free to tell me anytime you like." She looped her arms around his neck.

He angled her back onto the bearskin rug, already looking forward to making love to her thoroughly throughout the night. "I hope that means you intend to keep me around."

Her smile lit her eyes and his heart. "I can't think of anything I'd like more than for our relationship to be real. Maybe I'll even break into your office every day."

Epilogue

Two years later

Brea stirred the steaming pot in her kitchen, the scent of caribou stew taking her back to her childhood, in her grandmother's kitchen, with a clear, happy memory.

No panic. No fog. Just a joyful, simple connection to a happy part of her past that she held tight.

The scents of bay leaf and garlic drifted in the light-filled kitchen of her own design, the skylight perfectly positioned to let her look up and see the stars as often as she wanted. It had been Ward's idea when they had built the house just outside of Anchorage. This spot under the skylight was her place to breathe deep and take strength from the natural world, even as she was surrounded by the deep love of her big family.

The Steeles.

The Mikkelsons.

And Ward.

Brea met his gaze across the island as he entered the kitchen. He passed off Broderick and Glenna's daughter, Fleur, to Alayna Mikkelson, who was home from college for winter break. The whole family had gathered in Brea and Ward's home for a combination housewarming party and a viewing of the new episode of *Alaska Uncharted*, featuring Alaska Oil Barons, Inc.

Their family.

"That smells amazing." Ward stepped behind her while she put the cover on the stew.

"I have been tasting as I go, and I can promise you, it will be delicious." She leaned into him while his arms wrapped around her, his hands resting on her stomach.

"How are you feeling?" He kissed a spot beneath her ear, sending a thrill through her even now that they'd been married for a year. "I can take over and you can put your feet up."

"I'm feeling fantastic. And I can't wait for dinner. I've been craving this dish all week."

He nuzzled her neck. "The twins must be hungry."

This week's appointment with the obstetrician had shown a surprise—two babies. They hadn't even told the family she was pregnant yet, so the news would be another cause for celebration tonight. They'd had fun planning their big reveal, finally deciding on a cake for dessert that had a gold topper with two porcelain infants.

"It's a good thing we're telling the family tonight. I can't wait to quiz Naomi about everything twin related that happened with her pregnancy."

She had recovered her own twin bond with her sister, a bond that would only strengthen as they raised their own twins.

Brea was three months along. They'd waited until now to tell because they'd wanted to include Paisley in the celebration. With help from Felicity on how best to approach his ex-wife, Paisley's mother had finally consented for Ward and Brea to have contact, from phone conversations to an occasional vacation. Paisley was here now for her school's winter break, and Brea guessed she was having fun with all of her cousins.

The last time Brea had looked into the great room, she'd seen Paisley in a corner, reading books, side by side with Conrad and Felicity's daughter, Kylie, a teen they'd adopted last year. Seeing the two of them that way—happily reading while warm family chaos unfolded all around them—reminded Brea so much of Marshall.

Another joyful memory.

"Naomi is going to be thrilled. But so is everyone else," Ward assured her as he drew her toward the family room, where the *Alaska Uncharted* episode was playing in the background.

Jack and Jeannie held hands on the couch while Naomi's girls entertained them with the new moves they'd learned in their baby-ballet class. Marshall and Tally came in the back door, stomping snow off their boots from a horseback ride with Conrad and Felicity.

"Did we miss it?" Tally rushed into the living room. "I told them to hurry."

Tally was on winter break too, her college program in social work almost finished. She and Marshall were waiting to have children until she had her degree. The semester before, Tally, Aiden and Alayna had all ended up in the same online history class—a popular local offering since the professor was an expert on native Alaskan tribes.

Apparently Alayna and Aiden's short-lived romance had ended without drama. Aiden seemed happy working in the oil fields while he took classes online, and Alayna was dating one of the company's interns.

Glenna was seated at the desk in the far corner of the room with her toddler son, watching the screen, where Shana's and Chuck's faces were visible. Their three children, siblings ranging from ages two to six, adopted at the same time, took turns pressing their noses close to the camera, waving excitedly as they caught sight of their cousins.

Their blended family kept on blending and adding, but that seemed just right when they had so much love to give.

All was right in Brea's world.

She exchanged looks with Ward, the man who had helped her find her family again, while keeping her sense of self. She liked to think she'd helped him find his family, too. He held her hand in his, his thumb stroking over her knuckles.

"Happy?" she asked him while they surveyed the room of people coming and going.

Before he could reply, Tally hurried over to draw Brea deeper into the room.

"This is your part, Brea. Come see."

Brea let herself be pulled closer to the family even though she and Ward had already seen the *Alaska Uncharted* episode in a preview screening.

Thomas Branch's distinctive voice was narrating about the new Alaska Oil Barons, Inc., Energy Outreach initiative, the effort to bring energy innovations to off-the-grid communities. Brea worked on it with Royce and Delaney, but the online network for dispensing the information had been her brainchild. A path to connect her both lines of her past in a positive way. An overture toward the kinds of communities that helped nurture her when she'd been broken. They were still a part of her.

"I'm so proud of you," Ward whispered in her ear, reeling her closer to rub her shoulders.

His touch warmed her all over and she felt the tingle of tears behind her eyes. The good kind, though. She'd fought so long and hard simply to find peace, that to discover this well of deep-seated happiness was an incredible bonus.

On the huge flat-screen television, an image of Alaska General Hospital appeared as the host continued his narration. "The Steeles and Mikkelsons have made quite a name for themselves with their charity innovations, as well. The Steele wing of the Alaska General Hospital now has a new children's library, as well as a therapy dog program to comfort the patients."

Isabeau Mikkelson appeared on the screen as the hospital's PR director, commenting on the library that Conrad had personally overseen and the therapy-dog program that Felicity had put in place with Tally's help.

"The pipeline in North Dakota is fully functional now, increasing the reach of the Alaska Oil Barons, Inc. Chuck Mikkelson carries on his father's legacy with the help of scientist Royce Miller, with input from Delaney Steele Montoya and Breanna Steele Benally."

The last bit was drowned out underneath the shouts of "Daddy!" from Chuck's kids as they heard their father's name mentioned. Brea was so happy for him and

Shana, forging their own strong family with the love that had inspired her so much two years ago.

"The day-care addition to the corporate offices is state of the art—and put to use by much of the family. And the public has taken note of their trust in the company when they could have afforded full-time nannies."

The video image panned around the Alaska Oil Barons, Inc., day-care facility, where plenty of the children in this room spent time on a regular basis. While Naomi's girls and Fleur squealed to see themselves on the screen, Isabeau's son and Fleur's brother were both unimpressed, pushing their wooden trains in circles around the girls' feet.

"The stew smells so good!" Tally burst out as the television show came to an end. "I can't wait for dinner, Brea. Can I help?"

Not waiting for an answer, Tally was already halfway into the kitchen, a place she and Felicity had spent plenty of evenings over the last year, since Tally and Marshall lived close by.

Ward kissed Brea's cheek. "I hope that cake is well hidden," he whispered. "Or the cat's out of the bag."

"Ward Bennally, I think I know how to keep a secret. Don't you?" She turned in his arms, surrounded by his strength.

Their love.

Their family.

"Just not from me." He tipped his forehead to hers. "I get to share all your secrets from now on, Mrs. Bennally."

"You already do." She loved this man with a fierceness she couldn't describe. Having him by her side made her feel safe. Whole. And incredibly happy. "I love you, Ward."

"I love you too, Brea." He cradled her face in his hands and stroked his thumbs down her cheeks before he let her go.

Her heart melted a little at his touch. Even two years after she'd fallen in love with him, she knew they had the kind of love that was never going to fade. It was too hard-won. Too precious to them both.

Hand in hand, they joined their family for the real celebration that was only just beginning.

* * * * *